Lily wasn't ... ing about her simply because they cared.

Be careful, a voice whispered to her. *No one is to be trusted – not even Jon.*

Confused and frustrated, she became aware of a shadow falling over her eyes. It was slight, but clear: something was covering her eye the instant before her lid came down.

"Jon, what's going on? What's happening?" She started to shake.

Then she felt it, rising along her spine, from tail-that-wasn't to whiskers-that-weren't. A sense of connection, of power, of strength that was alien and yet entirely hers...

"Lily!"

"Oh." She gasped, her world reeling. "Oh goddess..."

Lily felt her knees give way and she collapsed in Jon's arms.

First published in Great Britain 2010
Harlequin Mills & Boon Limited,
Eton House, 18-24 Paradise Road, Richmond, Surrey TW9 1SR

His Best Friend's Baby © Rickey R.Mallory 2009
The Night Serpent © Laura Anne Gilman 2008

ISBN: 978 0 263 88191 2

46-0110

Harlequin Mills & Boon policy is to use papers that are natural, renewable
and recyclable products and made from wood grown in sustainable
forests. The logging and manufacturing processes conform to the legal
environmental regulations of the country of origin.

Printed and bound in Spain
by Litografia Rosés S.A., Barcelona

FRIE...

BY
MALLORY KANE

THE NIGHT
SERPENT

BY
ANNA LEONARD

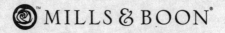

MILLS & BOON

HIS BEST
FRIEND'S BABY

BY
MALLORY KANE

Mallory Kane credits her love of books to her mother, a librarian, who taught her that books are a precious resource and should be treated with loving respect. Her father and grandfather were steeped in the Southern tradition of oral history, and could hold an audience spellbound for hours with their storytelling skills. Mallory aspires to be as good a storyteller as her father.

Mallory lives in Mississippi with her computer-genius husband, their two fascinating cats and, at current count, seven computers. She loves to hear from readers. You can write to her at mallory@mallorykane.com.

For Michael, for the usual reasons.

Prologue

The cold rain beat down on the white roses that blanketed Bill Vick's coffin, turning them yellow and soggy. The canopy flapped and creaked in the wind.

A dozen or so people had braved the weather to attend the graveside service, but Matthew Parker saw only one—Aimee Vick, his best friend's widow.

From his vantage point, several dozen feet away and partially hidden by trees, Matt could barely see the strands of brown hair that had escaped from beneath her hat to blow across her pale face.

Aimee didn't notice. She stood stiffly, her arms folded protectively across her tummy, nodding and smiling sadly as people filed by, offering their condolences one more time before they headed home.

Matt pushed his fists deeper into his pockets and hunched his shoulders against the bone-deep chill that shuddered through him. A chill that had nothing to do with the cold April wind or the freezing rain that poured off the brim of his Stetson.

Three days before, he'd done the two most difficult things he'd ever done in his life. He'd brought Bill's body home to Sundance, Wyoming, and he'd faced Bill's wife and tried to explain how a weekend adventure had turned into tragedy.

How, in the blink of an eye, she was widowed, and her unborn baby would never know his father.

Her utter shock and disbelief had been agonizing to watch, but he'd stood there, needing to see it. Just as he did now. He needed to share her grief, her pain.

Aimee wiped her cheek with a gloved finger, and bowed her head for an instant.

Matt's eyes stung. He blinked and looked at his watch. He needed to leave now. His flight back to the tiny border province of Mahjidastan was scheduled to leave in an hour.

For a few seconds, he debated whether he should speak to her. But he quelled the notion as soon as it surfaced. Seeing him would only hurt her more.

He'd known Aimee nearly as long as he'd known Bill, which was most of his life. He'd kidded Bill about not deserving her. She was generous and kind, and forgiving to a fault. She gave everyone the benefit of the doubt, until they proved they didn't deserve it.

Three days ago, Matt had proven he didn't deserve her forgiveness. She hadn't said it, but the look in her eyes had spoken louder than words.

If not for him, Bill would still be alive. He'd be safe at home with his wife, awaiting the birth of their son.

Bill's death was his fault.

Chapter One

A year later
THURSDAY 0900 HOURS

Matt Parker stepped outside Irina Castle's ranch house, the headquarters for Black Hills Search and Rescue in Sundance, Wyoming, and headed for the helipad a few hundred yards to the east. He lifted his head and took a deep breath of crisp, fresh Wyoming air.

The day before, for the first time in a year, he'd set foot on American soil, on Wyoming soil. He was back home, where he belonged. He loved the Black Hills. Even though they'd tried to kill him and his three best friends twenty years ago, he loved them. They sustained him.

He'd done his best to track down any rumors of Americans in the remote mountain province of Mahjidastan, which was located in a disputed border area shared by Afghanistan, Pakistan and China. His objective had been to find Rook Castle, Irina's husband. But ultimately, he'd failed, as had BHSAR specialist Aaron Gold before him. And now Irina had called off the search.

As he circled the Bell 429 helicopter that was BHSAR Specialist Deke Cunningham's baby, another fellow specialist, Brock O'Neill, appeared in the doorway of the hangar.

"Parker," he said as Matt approached. The terse greeting was typical of the ex-Navy SEAL. He held out his hand and cocked his head—the only indication Matt had ever seen that the patch over his left eye bothered him.

Matt shook his hand. "Brock. How're you doing?"

"Hmph. Watch out. Your buddy's in a mood." Brock broke the handshake and headed toward the ranch house.

Matt suppressed a smile as he continued toward the hangar. For Brock, that was a warm greeting.

When he stepped through the open door, Deke was leaning back in his desk chair with his feet propped up, tossing a steel bearing from hand to hand. A small TV was tuned to a morning news show, its sound muted.

"Hey, Deke," Matt said. "Playing catch with yourself?"

Deke's feet hit the floor and he set the silver ball on his desk. "That goober I just hired overtightened a bolt and ruined this ball bearing. Brock offered to take him out for me."

Matt laughed.

"How're you doing?"

Matt took Deke's hand. "Been a while. Can't say I'm glad to see you."

"I know."

"Man, I hate this," Matt said, nodding back toward the ranch house. "The place feels like a funeral home. I didn't see Irina. How's she holding up?"

Deke shook his head. "She's trying to act like she's fine, but she's not. She's in bad shape." Deke wiped a hand over his face and then pushed his shaggy hair back. "She's in town this morning, talking to her accountant again."

"So it's true?" Matt asked. "All her funds are wiped out?"

Deke nodded. "All her personal funds. Damn Rook for not signing everything over to her when they got married. I'd like to kill him—" Deke stopped and clamped his jaw.

Matt snorted. "Too late. But it's not like he knew he was going to die."

"No?" Deke's brows lowered and his blue eyes turned black. "He spent his whole life stepping in front of bullets for other people. He had to figure one would hit him sooner or later."

"I don't get it. She's his wife—widow. Why doesn't she get his money?"

"It's all about the suspicious nature of his death. Just because they don't have a body—greedy bastards."

"Hang on a minute," Matt said as he glanced at the TV. "Turn that up."

Deke scooped up the remote control and tossed it to him. "What is it?"

"Check out the pink dress. It's Margo Vick."

"Bill's mother? Opening another Vick Resort Hotel?"

"Not this time. That's FBI Special Agent Aaron Schiff standing next to her." Matt hit the volume control.

"—I am personally offering a reward for any information leading to the kidnapper."

Kidnapper. Alarm pierced Matt's chest as Margo

yielded the microphone to the FBI special agent. Among the dark suits, her brightly colored dress drew all eyes to her.

"We plan to hold press conferences on a regular basis, and we'll update the media as we have more information," Special Agent Schiff said. "Meanwhile, please let us do our job. Our primary concern is getting Mrs. Vick's grandson back home safe and sound."

"It's Aimee's baby. He's been kidnapped." Matt sat on the edge of a folding chair and propped his elbows on his knees, listening as Schiff answered questions from reporters. The cameras pulled back to reveal the front of the Vick mansion, located just outside Casper, Wyoming. Besides Schiff and Margo, several uniformed police officers stood on the marble steps, along with a couple of men in suits.

Matt's gaze zeroed in on a pale face behind Bill's mother. It was Aimee, dressed in something dark that blended with the suits and uniforms. Her eyes were huge and strands of hair blew across her face.

"There's Aimee." He didn't take his eyes off her until the camera switched back to Schiff. Then he shot up off the chair and paced, rubbing his thumb across his lower lip.

"There's something more going on here," he said as dread pressed on his chest like a weight.

"What—with the kidnapping?"

"About a month ago, my journal disappeared from my room."

Deke frowned and picked up the ball bearing again. He tossed it back and forth. "You mean on your laptop?"

Matt shook his head. With every passing second,

pressure in his chest grew. "I keep notes in a small leather journal just for my use. I write my reports to Irina from my notes. You know, rumors of Americans in the area, anything I can glean about what Novus Ordo or his terrorist friends are up to, lists of expenses."

"You think it was stolen?"

He nodded.

"Okay. How does this have anything to do with the grandbaby of one of the wealthiest women in Wyoming being kidnapped?"

Matt glanced back at the TV, but there was a commercial on. "Work stuff wasn't all that was in the journal."

He turned toward the window, letting his gaze roam over the jagged peaks in the distance. "It's been a year since Bill died, and I haven't talked to her."

Deke didn't comment.

Matt rubbed his lip. "I just couldn't face her. So I was trying to compose a letter. A way to—tell her how sorry I am."

"I don't follow."

"Novus knows we've been searching for any clue that Rook survived his sniper attack. I've been followed ever since I got over there. I'm sure whoever stole my journal was sent by Novus, so now—"

"Now he knows how you feel about Aimee," Deke supplied. He set the ball bearing down and sat up straight.

"How I feel—?" Matt frowned. "Well, yeah. He knows about her baby and about me being William's godfather. And now Irina's stopped looking for Rook. What if Novus thinks she stopped because I found him?"

"And what? You think Novus had Aimee's baby kidnapped—"

"To get to me."

Deke blew out a long breath. "Kind of a stretch. Why wouldn't he have grabbed you before now if he thought you knew something?"

"Think about it. I've been in Mahjidastan for the past year, searching for information about the only man on the earth who could identify Novus Ordo. And before me Aaron was there for a year. There hasn't been a day since Rook disappeared off that boat that a BHSAR specialist hasn't been looking for him. Suddenly, Irina pulls me out and doesn't replace me. Novus didn't have a chance to get his hands on me. I left within four hours of Irina's phone call."

Deke gave a short, sharp laugh. "That's quite a conspiracy theory. But it makes sense—sort of. What now?"

Matt met Deke's gaze and set his jaw. "If Novus Ordo has taken Aimee Vick's baby to try and get his hands on me to interrogate me about Rook, I'm going to make it easy for him."

So FAR EVERYTHING was working well. Not bad for a plan that had been put together in less than twenty-four hours.

The Vick baby was already in safe hands. The FBI was on the case. And, most important, Parker was acting exactly as predicted. He was inserting himself right into the middle of the kidnapping investigation.

A warm sense of satisfaction spread through him. It was immaterial whether Rook Castle was alive or dead. He had a larger goal. And finally, it was in sight.

He looked at his watch. Almost time. He had a telephone call to make.

THURSDAY 1430 HOURS

AIMEE VICK PACED back and forth across the living room of her mother-in-law's house. The room was crawling with FBI special agents, uniformed police officers, and technicians trailing spools of wire everywhere.

She looked at the grandfather clock for the hundredth time—or the thousandth. Two-thirty p.m. It had been eight hours. Eight miserable, terrifying hours without her baby.

When she'd woken up this morning and discovered that William was gone, she'd have sworn she couldn't survive eight hours without her baby. But she was still alive, and still rational—barely.

William Matthew was only seven months old, and she'd never spent a night without him. Hardly even an hour. He was her anchor, her life since her husband's death.

She didn't notice that someone else had come in the front door until she heard her name called.

She turned and found herself face-to-face with Matt Parker, her husband's best friend, her baby's godfather, and the last man on earth she expected to see.

"Matt," she croaked. Her voice was hoarse and sounded harsh to her ears.

The last time she'd seen him was a year ago, when he'd brought her husband's body home. He looked just as stricken as he had that day.

Her first impulse was to run to him and hug him. But she didn't. Her emotions were already in turmoil, and seeing Matt made things even more confusing.

She should be furious at him. After all, he hadn't shown up for Bill's funeral, nor for William Matthew's christening, even though she'd honored Bill's request to name him as William's godfather.

She'd spent a good portion of the past year filled with anger. At Matt for taking Bill skydiving. At Bill for going off and dying. At herself for not putting her foot down and refusing to let him go.

Matt looked down and rubbed the back of his neck. After a few seconds, he raised his head enough to meet her gaze. "Aimee, I'm so sorry about your baby. I've talked with Special Agent Schiff. He's agreed to let me help with the investigation—if you'll agree."

Aimee clutched at her abdomen, where the hollow nausea that had been her constant companion ever since Bill died was growing, threatening to cut off her breath.

"How did you get here?" She shook her head. "I mean, it just happened this morning—"

"It doesn't matter. I'm here. Will you let me help?"

Aimee looked at Special Agent Schiff, who nodded at her reassuringly. "I can't believe—I haven't seen you since—"

Matt's gaze faltered. "I know. I'm sorry, Aimee."

Aimee started when Margo laid a hand on her shoulder—a heavy hand. "Aimee, dear, why don't you get a glass of water?"

"Thank you, Margo, but I'm not thirsty." She tried to step away from her mother-in-law's grasp, but Margo held on.

"I'd like to speak to Matthew alone for a moment."

Aimee rubbed her temple, where a headache was gathering. She knew what Margo planned to do. She was going to tell Matt to leave. She could practically see the wheels turning in her mother-in-law's head. A lot of people in Casper knew that Matt had been with Bill when he died, and Margo didn't like the Vicks being the subject of gossip.

Appearances. They'd always been her main concern. The magenta suit she wore attested to that. Only Aimee and the owner of Margo's favorite dress shop knew that her first act upon hearing of her grandson's kidnapping was to have the suit rushed over in time for the press conference.

"Anything you have to say, you can say in front of me, Margo." Aimee stiffened her back and met her mother-in-law's gaze.

"If you're sure, dear." Margo turned to Matt. "Aimee is terribly distraught. I'd rather she not be upset further. Perhaps you should leave."

Matt raised his brows and gazed at Margo steadily. "I have every right to be here. William Matthew is my godson."

A godson he'd never seen, Aimee thought. To make matters worse, Margo had spent the year since Bill's death trying to coax Aimee to relinquish control of William's future to her.

I have the resources and the connections, dear. You don't.

Grief and fear and anger balled up inside Aimee, until she felt as if she were going to explode. She had to bite her tongue to keep from lashing out at both of them.

Aimee had loved Bill, but the six years of their marriage had been a tug-of-war between him and his mother. Now she was in the same position, standing between Margo and Matt.

"William is my child," she blurted out. "This is my decision."

Every eye in the room turned their way.

"Aimee," Margo said warningly as her fingers tightened on Aimee's shoulder. "Don't make a scene."

Aimee wasn't sure how she felt about Matt showing up after a year—almost to the day—since Bill's death, but she didn't doubt his ability. As a weather expert and survival specialist, rescuing the innocent was his specialty.

If anyone could save her child, Matt could.

"If Special Agent Schiff agrees, I want Matt here. It makes sense for him to be involved. He's trained in rescue and recov—" Aimee's throat closed on the word *recovery*.

"Rescue," she said as firmly as she could. *No crying.* She hadn't cried yet, and she didn't plan to start now. Crying never helped anything. She was afraid that if she started she wouldn't be able to stop.

Margo's dark eyes snapped with irritation as she drew in a sharp breath. Then, with a quick glance around the room, she consciously relaxed her face and nodded.

"Of course," she said stiffly. "I didn't mean to imply otherwise." Her grip on Aimee's shoulder loosened and turned into an awkward pat.

The shrill ring of a cell phone split the air. Aimee jumped.

It was him. The kidnapper.

She whirled, looking for her purse, and then remembered that the FBI had forwarded her cell to Margo's house phone. At that instant, the landline rang.

Special Agent Schiff motioned her over to the table, where wires and headphones and computers appeared to be piled haphazardly.

"Mrs. Vick—" Schiff said in a cautionary tone. "Remember what we discussed?"

She was going to have to talk to the man who'd taken her baby. Her stomach turned upside down. As she approached, a computer technician handed two sets of headphones to Schiff. Schiff, in turn, reached past her to hand a set to Matt. Then he donned the remaining set himself.

"Wait to see what he says," Schiff cautioned her. "Once he starts talking ransom, you insist it be delivered by a family friend—Parker. Don't let him bully you. Don't give in to any demands. *You* are in control, not him. Got it?"

Aimee had never felt less in control in her life. Her baby was in the hands of the monster on the other end of the phone, and she was being forced to bargain for his life. The phone rang again, the piercing noise sending terror slicing through her.

"On my count," Schiff whispered. "Pick up on three."

She nodded jerkily. Her throat was too dry to swallow. Her hands were shaking so much she wasn't sure she could hold on to the phone.

Schiff nodded at the computer tech, glanced at Matt, then held up a finger. "One," he mouthed to her.

A second finger went up. "Two."

Aimee bit her lip and reached for the phone. Matt stepped closer.

Schiff held up three fingers. "Three." He nodded.

She picked up the phone, her other hand pressed to her chest. "Hello?" she croaked.

"Hello, Aimee. Hello, Special Agent Schiff, and whoever else is listening."

Aimee stiffened at the kidnapper's menacing tone. At the same time, Matt's shoulder brushed hers. Coiled tension radiated from his body like heat. He rested a hand lightly on the small of her back. Somehow, his touch gave her courage.

"What have you done with my baby?" she cried. "I have to know if he's okay."

"Your baby is perfectly safe for now," the harsh voice said. "It's up to you to keep him safe. Let's talk business."

"What do you want?" she asked tightly.

"Money, of course," the man replied. "Are you listening, Schiff? Because I will only say this once. I want a million dollars in hundreds. Don't give me any problem about the money. I am aware of who your mother-in-law is." The man's voice was cold and hard. "I don't want to hear excuses about needing time to get the cash together. Just do it."

Aimee felt helpless and lost. She could hardly make sense of what he was saying. She took a deep breath. "Let me talk to my baby," she begged. "He must be so scared. He needs to hear my voice."

"Shut up. You're not giving the orders. I am. Now here's where the exchange will take place."

He rattled off some numbers that meant nothing to Aimee. Out of the corner of her eye, she saw Matt nod at Schiff.

"Got it?" the man snapped.

Schiff sent her a nod.

"Y-yes," she said.

"Tomorrow at 1500 hours. Aimee, if you want to see your baby again, *you* will deliver the money."

Matt jerked. He shook his head fiercely at Schiff.

"I—I don't know," she stammered, her heart stuck in her throat.

"Family friend," Schiff mouthed.

"Wait. I can't come alone," she said as strongly as she could. "I—I'll need to care for William Matthew. I need to bring a—a family friend—"

"Schiff?" the kidnapper said. "What did I tell you? I will not say it again. Make it happen."

The line went dead.

"Dammit," Matt spat.

Aimee's throat closed and her eyes stung with tears. She swallowed them as the phone dropped from her numb fingers. "What is it? What's wrong?" she asked.

Schiff didn't answer her. "Give me those coordinates," he told the computer tech, who repeated the numbers.

"You said you're an expert in weather and survival," Schiff said to Matt. "Know where that is?"

"That latitude and longitude puts it north of Sundance," Matt muttered. He pulled a small device out of his pocket and pressed buttons. "It's about halfway up Ragged Top Mountain. Rough terrain. Plus we've got a late-winter storm building. Could dump a foot or more of snow before it's done."

He turned toward Margo. "Isn't Ragged Top where your husband's hunting cabin was? I think Bill and I went up there a few times."

Margo nodded stiffly. "That's right. No one's been

there in years. I don't understand. What did the kid-napper say?"

"He's demanding that we bring the money to a loca-tion on the south side of Ragged Top."

"South—? That's—" Margo stopped, frowning. "Oh, dear." Her face drained of color.

It was only the second time Aimee had ever seen Margo shaken. The first was when she was told her son had died. Maybe her mother-in-law wasn't as cold and insensitive as she'd always appeared.

"What?" Matt demanded. "It's what?"

The woman blinked. "Nothing. It's just—it's so hard to get up there. Especially this time of year. I'd have thought—I mean how's he going to keep William safe up there?"

"I'll tell you how," Matt said. "He knows the area. I'd bet money on it, judging by the way he rattled off those coordinates. He knows Aimee can't go by herself."

Schiff raised his eyebrows. "What about you? Can you do it?"

Matt's jaw clenched in determination. "Yeah. I can do it. I've pulled innocents out of more remote locations than that. But this storm's coming in fast. By 1500 hours tomorrow, it'll be right on top of that peak."

Schiff frowned. "The weather service said it would be moving into this area late tomorrow night."

"Yeah, that's what they're saying." Matt set his jaw. "I'm going in alone."

Aimee stiffened. She knew he could do it. That wasn't the problem. He was a search-and-rescue spe-cialist, trained in the Air Force. There was no one better suited to the job.

But the kidnapper had been very specific.

"Don't even think about leaving me behind, Matt," she said. "William Matthew is my baby. He needs me. When you hand over the money, *I* will be there to take him in my arms."

Chapter Two

After coordinating times and plans with Special Agent Schiff, Matt drove straight back to Castle Ranch. He needed to talk to Deke.

At thirty, Deke Cunningham was one of the most decorated Air Force combat rescue officers alive. His skill with a rifle was legendary. The only thing he did better than shoot was fly a helicopter.

Which was exactly why Matt wanted him on alert for the ransom exchange.

When he got to the hangar, Deke wasn't there. But at the door to his office, Matt saw something he hadn't noticed before.

The plaque hanging beside Deke's office door. It had hung in Rook Castle's office since the day he'd created Black Hills Search and Rescue, Incorporated. It was small and plain, with a simple message.

IN MEMORIAM
Vietnam Veteran and Combat Rescue Officer

Arlis Hanks, 1944–1990. Our pledge—to honor
your bravery by rescuing the innocent.

Matt touched the four signatures that were embla-
zoned into the bronze. Robert Kenneth Castle, Deke
Cunningham, Matthew Parker and William Barker Vick.

Irina must have given it to Deke. Matt nodded to
himself. It was fitting.

He found Deke in Irina's office, sitting with her,
Specialist Rafiq Jackson and Aaron Gold near a bank
of windows that framed a view of the desolate, magnifi-
cent Black Hills. He nodded at Rafe and Aaron, and acknowledged Deke with a brief glance.

Irina smiled and stood to give him a hug. Rook
Castle's widow was as vibrant and lovely as ever. Her
blond hair glowed in the sunlight that streamed in the
window. But behind her smile and the sparkle in her
blue eyes, Matt saw a shadow of grief.

He couldn't imagine how difficult it had been for her
to give up searching for her husband. She'd seen him
shot, and watched him fall into the Mediterranean Sea.
Even so, she'd clung to the hope that because his body
had never been recovered, he might be alive.

Now, she'd given up. For everyone who knew her,
and who'd supported her efforts to find him, that made
it official. Rook Castle was dead.

"Irina," Matt said. "When you called me the other
day, I didn't get a chance to say—"

She held up a hand. "I know. Thank you, Matt." A
small, sad smile lit her face. "It's been more than two
years. It's time I stopped living in a fantasy world.

What's important now is rescuing Aimee's baby. All my resources are available to you."

He studied her face, wondering if Deke had told her about his theory that Novus was behind the kidnapping. He decided not to mention it. "I wanted to see if Deke could help me out."

"Of course. You two talk here. I need to check with Pam about my schedule. Rafe, Aaron, walk out with me."

After Irina left, Matt sat and propped his elbows on the table. He intertwined his fingers. "What's up with Rafiq? Did you talk to him about Novus?"

"He's listening in on activity around the Afghan/Pakistan/China borders. Chatter's way up in the region since Irina stopped searching." Deke rubbed his face. "Nothing concrete, mostly speculation."

"I'm glad we've got Rafe. It's good to have someone who speaks the language. Has he heard anything about what Novus is up to?"

"Well, you made big news when you left. Sounds like you're right. The chatter supports the theory that you left because you found Rook."

"Hmph. So much for my fifteen minutes of fame. I wish the chatter were right."

Deke didn't respond.

"What about you?" Matt asked him. "Are you on a case right now?" he asked.

"Nope. No case. Just hanging. I'd love to be out kicking butt somewhere, but I feel like I need to be here. You know?"

"Irina looks pretty good. How's she holding up?"

Deke shook his head. "It took a lot out of her to

make the decision to stop looking for Rook. All this time she's lived with the image of him being shot, then disappearing into the Mediterranean. It was awful—" Deke's voice cracked. "I mean, it had to have been."

Matt didn't have to imagine. He had his own nightmares. His dreams were haunted by the sight of Bill Vick spinning helplessly as he plummeted to earth, trailed by the parachute that failed to open.

"What about Aimee?" Deke continued.

"Not good. And I'm afraid I made it worse, showing up like that." Matt stared at his clasped hands. "With her about to break, and the kidnapper's demands, I've got a real situation brewing. Can you be on alert for the ransom drop?"

"Yeah, sure. When is it? Soon, I hope. There's a doozie of a winter storm heading this way, and my bird's not fond of snow."

"I know. I've been tracking the front. I think it's going to blow in earlier than they're predicting."

"You should know. I still say you should hire yourself out to the local TV station as a weatherman." It was an old joke.

"Hair gel and a blue screen? I'll do that the day you become a rodeo sharpshooter." Matt couldn't help but smile. Then he got back to business. "The ransom drop is scheduled for 1500 hours tomorrow. Here are the co-ordinates the kidnapper gave us." Matt handed Deke a scrap of paper.

Deke snagged it and stepped over to an area map hanging on the wall. He tapped the point with his finger. "It's pretty high up, and isolated."

"Yeah. I'm going to take one of our Hummers.

There's a maintenance road up the south side. It'll take at least two hours to get up there."

"I see it. But if you're right about the storm… Why don't I fly you up in the bird? It'd be a lot quicker."

"Because there's a complication. The kidnapper demanded that Aimee make the drop herself."

"The Hummer holds two passengers and it's heated. Coming back, we may have a baby."

Deke's brows shot up. "May? You don't think your kidnapper is going to turn over the kid?"

"That location gives me a bad feeling. How's he going to handle a seven-month-old, and make sure nobody gets the drop on him?"

"He'd have to have an accomplice."

"Right. That plus the storm—I don't like the odds. That's why I need you to be available. I want primary and secondary rendezvous points in case something happens and we can't use the Hummer to get out. Maybe even a tertiary." Matt paused and rubbed his neck. "The location he's picked is going to receive the brunt of that storm. He's got to know that. I have a feeling he's banking on it to cover his tracks."

"I'll have the bird ready to go."

"If you don't hear from me, head for the first rendezvous point. Be there by 0800. Here are the times and places I've got mapped out."

"Friday 0800 hours? That's sixteen hours. You're planning to ride out the storm up there? You could be blown right off that mountain."

"Thanks for that image. No. I *plan* to be back down the mountain in the Hummer with Aimee and the baby, safe and sound. The 0800 rendezvous is if we get caught by the storm or something goes wrong. If everything goes as planned, I'll call you. It'll probably be after dark."

"Just make sure you've got plenty of flares."

"Don't worry. We'll have flares. Do these times work for you?"

"Times are fine. And I see you're planning to move up toward the peak, rather than down."

"Right. I figure if we can't ride back down in the Hummer, we need to be heading to higher ground. The storm's coming in from the west. I'd like to try to stay either ahead of it or above it. Plus, your bird's not going to like dodging trees, so the fewer the better."

Deke nodded.

They quickly agreed on two alternate times and places, the second twenty-four hours after the first. Plus a third, twenty-four hours after that, in case the storm stalled.

"One last thing," Matt said. "Take these coordinates. This is a last-resort location. It's an hour's walk south from the Vicks' cabin."

"The hunting cabin. I forgot about that place. You think you might end up there?"

Matt shrugged. "It's good shelter. We might need it, if we have to travel that far."

Deke stuck the piece of paper in his pocket. "No problem. I'll hang on to these."

"Thanks, man. I knew I could count on you." Matt stood.

"You know there's another way to handle this."

"Not really."

"Sure there is. Leave Aimee out of it. You and I go

up in the Hummer, get the drop on the kidnapper and get the baby back safe and sound."

Matt sighed. "That would work—if one of us could pass for a medium-height, slender female. But there's another consideration. The baby. If everything goes well, which one of us is prepared to bring back a seven-month-old who needs his mother?"

He opened the door. "Have you ever been between a mother and her child? I'm not telling Aimee she has to stay behind."

Now CUNNINGHAM was involved.

He knew them all so well. Of course Cunningham would drop everything to help Parker. They were "brothers," after all.

It tended to get annoying, listening to the stories of their childhood friendship, and their oath to save innocents just as that broken-down Vietnam veteran had saved theirs.

He hadn't had time to sabotage Parker's equipment or vehicle. He'd had to trust Kinnard to handle that part of the plan.

His job was to make sure that when Parker needed help, it wasn't available. There were two ways he could handle that, but only one was a sure thing.

All he needed were some tools and a little private time.

FRIDAY 1430 HOURS

AIMEE BURIED HER NOSE more deeply into the high collar of her down parka. She'd rolled her balaclava up like a watch cap, ready to pull down over her face if she needed it. The vehicle was heated, but she was still cold.

The chill didn't come from the dropping temperatures outside, though. It came from her heart. As often as she told herself that William was safe, that the kidnapper couldn't afford to hurt him if he wanted his money, her heart remained unconvinced.

Matt's grim expression didn't help. He looked worried as he maneuvered the Hummer's steel snow tracks over the rough terrain. He glanced at her. "You okay?"

"Okay?" she croaked, then pressed her lips together. *Control,* she reminded herself. *It's all about control.* She had to hold herself together, for her baby's sake.

"If you're cold, there's a blanket under your seat."

She gave a harsh little laugh. "You think I'm worried about being *cold?*"

"Aimee, I know you're afraid something's going to happen to William. But I don't want you to neglect your own health. You're highly stressed and exhausted. You could become hypothermic without even realizing it. I need to make sure you're warm and comfortable."

"Well, don't. I don't need to be comfortable—I don't want to be. I just want to get up there, get my baby back and get home."

"That's what I want, too," Matt said.

She closed her burning eyes. *Control. Control.* She repeated it like a mantra.

"Dammit!"

She jumped and her eyes flew open.

"Sorry." His fingers tightened around the steering wheel. "I can't believe I let the kidnapper run the show. I should have jumped in and forced him to do it my way. It's dangerous for you up here."

"Where should I be? Back at home, all safe and warm? Waiting? No, thank you."

"Yes. Back at home, all safe and warm. I don't like putting you in danger. Plus, with you here, I can't do everything I'd be able to do if I were alone."

"Sorry I'm cramping your style."

"That's not—" he stopped and his jaw muscle worked. He kept his attention on the barely discernable path before them as the incline grew steeper, and the sky turned increasingly dark and gray.

Where they'd started out, near Sundance, spring was in the air, with new shoots of grass and fresh coverings of moss. As they'd climbed higher, the greenery turned brown, and patches of old snow dotted the ground.

Aimee hunched her shoulders in an effort not to shiver. Matt's hands were white-knuckled on the steering wheel. His face was expressionless, but his jaw was clamped tight. He looked the way he had the last time she'd seen him. The day he'd brought her husband's body home.

That memory spawned others. Like the argument she and Bill had a few days before that fateful day.

"It's just a weekend, Aimee. A guy trip. You're starting to sound a lot like my mother."

Aimee had yelled back at him. "Well, for once I agree with Margo. You have responsibilities here. Have you forgotten that I'm pregnant? That you're fighting cancer? Why would you want to waste even a weekend? You need to use your energy to get well. I need you to stay with me."

At that point Bill had gathered her into his arms and kissed her. "I'll be with Matt. He's safe as houses. Safer. He never takes unnecessary chances."

Then he'd looked down at her and a tender solemnity had come over his face. "Don't ever forget, Aimee. I trust Matt as much as I trust myself. More, maybe. No matter what happens, you can count on him. Ask him anything. He'll do it."

Those last words had been prophetic. Bill had asked Matt for something. Matt had obliged. And Bill had died.

The doctors had said it could have been months before the lymphoma took Bill. Long enough for him to know his child. But he'd stolen those last months from her and his son. And Matt had helped.

Then, when Aimee could have used a friend, Matt had disappeared for a year.

Bill had been wrong. She couldn't count on Matt.

"Aimee, tell me how it happened."

She started. "What? How it—?"

"The kidnapping."

"Didn't Special Agent Schiff tell you?"

He nodded. "But I'd like to hear what you remember."

Aimee closed her eyes and folded her arms. "I've been over it in my head a hundred times. I should have heard him. I should have woken up." She shook her head. "How could I have slept while someone came into my house and stole my baby?"

"William wasn't in your room, was he?"

"No. My doctor said that wasn't a good idea, for either of us. I shouldn't have listened to her. I should have kept him right beside me."

"Aimee." He put a hand on her knee. "Stop beating yourself up. You didn't do anything wrong."

His hand was warm. She could feel it even through her wool slacks and silk long underwear. She looked down.

He jerked away and gripped the steering wheel. "When did you realize he was gone?"

She was still looking at his hand. It was big and solid, with long, blunt-tipped fingers. "The sun was in my eyes, and I knew I'd overslept. William always wakes me up around five-thirty or so. He's such a sweet baby." She smiled. "He wakes up happy. I'll hear him through the monitor, cooing and laughing—" Her voice broke and her throat closed up.

He shot her a glance. "The sun woke you?" he asked gently.

"It was almost six-thirty. When I realized I hadn't heard him, I panicked. So many things can happen—"

"What did you do?"

"As soon as I realized I'd slept late, I grabbed the monitor. The camera points right at the head of the baby bed. But I couldn't see him. His bed looked empty." She took a shaky breath. "I ran across the hall. His bedroom door was open and I knew I'd left it closed. He wasn't there. He wasn't anywhere."

She felt the panic rising in her chest, heard it in her voice. Just like then. Had it only been yesterday morning?

"So I called 9-1-1."

"Schiff said there was no sign of forced entry. You're sure it was a stranger?"

Aimee frowned at Matt. "What do you mean?"

He spread his hands in a shrug without taking them off the wheel. "I just mean, is there anything specific you're thinking of when you say it was a stranger?"

She shook her head. "I just can't—it can't be anyone I know."

"Are you usually a sound sleeper?"

"No. Actually, I've been having trouble." Aimee thought about the past seven months since William Matthew's birth. All the nights she'd lain awake, worrying that something would happen to him if she went to sleep.

Dear heavens, something had.

"What about the evening before?" Matt drove steadily, watching the road and glancing occasionally into the rearview mirror. "Did you drink anything? Take anything to help you sleep?"

"No," she answered indignantly. "I would never take a chance like that with William. I gave him his bath and played with him a while, and then made myself some herbal tea and went to sleep."

Matt nodded and drove in silence for a few minutes.

Thoughts and images chased each other helter-skelter through her brain. What had she done? What had been different about that night?

"I didn't do anything differently," she said finally. "My life revolves around his, and his routine is pretty well set. I locked up the house and turned out the lights around nine, just the way I always do. I bathed him at the same time as I do every night. We played the same games we always play, then I put him to bed and went downstairs to the kitchen."

"So anyone who'd been watching the house could know almost to the minute what time you go to bed?"

Aimee nodded miserably. "Yes. My life is that ordinary. I make the same tea, use the same cup. Probably

even the same spoon. I can't think of anything un-
usual—" She stopped. There had been one thing different.

"What is it?"

"It's—it's nothing. It *has* to be nothing." She was
really twisted—or really desperate—to even be thinking
what she was thinking.

"Tell me."

"This is awful. I can't believe I'm even saying it." She
took a deep breath, preparing herself for Matt's ridicule.
"The tea? It's a new blend. Margo bought it for me at the
health food store. They told her it was good for insomnia."

Matt glanced at her, frowning.

"But Matt, I've been drinking it every night for
almost a week now."

"Is it helping you sleep?"

"Yes," she said. She hadn't really thought about it,
but she *had* slept better this past week than she had in a
long time. "It is. You don't think—?" Her breath hitched.
"No. That's ridiculous. Margo wouldn't— Not her
own—her only grandchild—" She stopped, horrified at
her thoughts. During the first moments after she'd
realized William was missing, she'd briefly considered
that Margo might have planned it, but she'd dismissed
it as impossible. She was his *grandmother.*

Matt glanced at her.

"No. She couldn't do that—could she?"

"You tell me."

"But it's outrageous. Not even Margo— I mean, yes,
she's been complaining about how hard it is for her to
get anything done through the Vick Corporation board
since Bill died."

"What's that got to do with anything?"

"Bill left everything to William, just like his dad left everything to him. Remember when Boss Vick died?"

"Sure, that summer after we graduated from high school."

"Right. Bill was all set to go to MIT. He wanted to get his degree in aerospace engineering, then go into the Air Force, like you and Deke and Rook."

"Yeah. After his dad died, he changed his mind, and decided to go to the University of Wyoming."

"Right. To stay close to home. Margo convinced him that he had to run the business. Because when he turned twenty-one, the entire Vick Hotel fortune—and responsibility—fell into his lap."

"Bill controlled everything—"

Aimee nodded. "And Margo controlled Bill," she said bitterly.

"And now?"

"Now that Bill's dead, William stands to inherit all of it."

Matt looked at her questioningly. "What about until he's twenty-one? Who did Bill name as William's trustee?"

"Me," Aimee breathed.

"So you're the one who votes the controlling interest. That must rankle Mrs. Vick."

"I go to the board meetings, but I've never opposed a single decision. Why would I?"

"But you could."

Aimee shrugged. "I suppose. You think she did it, don't you?"

Matt glanced in the rearview mirror. "Think about it.

What does she want? What does kidnapping her own grandson right from under his mother's nose accomplish?"

"Frightening me?" Aimee cast about for any possible explanation. "Making it look like I can't—"

"Like you can't take care of your own child. What would she gain if she had custody of William? She'd retain controlling interest in the corporation. But it's damn hard to get custody away from the mother. She'd have to prove that you're unfit. That you couldn't protect your own child in your own home."

She moaned under her breath. Hearing those words in Matt's carefully neutral voice made them sound true.

"Sorry," he muttered. "But it would explain a lot."

Aimee's face felt numb. Her *mind* felt numb. Intellectually, she understood Matt's reasoning. If he were right, her mother-in-law was setting her up to take William away from her.

His words echoed in her brain, taunting her with their truth.

You couldn't protect your own child in your own home.

Chapter Three

Aimee was still reeling, still trying to process the idea that Margo could have kidnapped her baby, when she realized that Matt's demeanor had changed.

Nothing outwardly was different. His hands still held the steering wheel in a tight grip at ten and two. His expression was carefully neutral, if a bit tight.

But tension suddenly crackled in the air, and it definitely came from him.

He'd gone on alert.

"Matt, what's wrong?" she asked.

"Wrong?" He glanced in the rearview mirror.

"Don't act like you don't know what I'm talking about. Something's wrong. I can tell. Did you see something?"

He didn't reply.

His sudden transformation fascinated and frightened her. Yesterday, he'd been the consummate soldier on a mission. This morning he'd acted more like a protector. She was his charge, his responsibility.

But now in the blink of an eye, he'd morphed from protector back to predator. He was a hunter, and he'd scented his prey.

She opened her mouth to ask him again when, without warning, he veered off the stark mountain road and stopped.

"What are you doing?" Fear raced through her.

"I'll be right back," he said. "If you hear or see anything while I'm gone, lie flat across the seat. The metal should protect you."

"Protect me? Matt—?"

"Do you understand?" He glared at her, his tone and the grim set of his face brooking no argument.

"Yes," she retorted.

He walked over to the edge of the graded area and stopped at the line of trees. For a couple of seconds, he surveyed the mountain road in both directions, then reached for his fly.

Aimee gaped. Was he—? He was! On the way to exchange a million dollars for her baby, he'd stopped to take a leak! She didn't know whether to scream or laugh. Was he so confident? Or so arrogant?

She reached for the door handle, prepared to jump out and yell at him for wasting time while her child was in the hands of kidnappers. At that instant he turned his head imperceptibly to his right, back the way they'd come. And she got it—his sudden transformation. His razor-sharp alertness. Her impression that she was watching a predator.

He'd detected a threat.

Her heart jumped into her throat and she twisted in her seat, looking behind them. But she didn't see anything. Of course, she wouldn't. Matt was ex-Air Force Special Forces. His skills and senses were sharper than an ordinary person's.

She watched as he took a step closer to the trees. The sight was awesome and frightening. The curve of his back and the set of his shoulders made her think of a leopard about to spring. Standing still, he might look like a regular guy, but when he moved—*oh my*.

Absently, it occurred to her that, although she'd known Matt as long as she'd known her husband, Bill, she had almost no knowledge of his personal life or his background. He might as well be a stranger.

She hunched her shoulders, feeling fragile and human and exposed.

All at once the very air around her went still. Only the occasional snap of a twig or the rustle of bare branches in the wind broke the silence.

The nape of her neck prickled. Her pulse pounded in her ears. She didn't move, not even turning her head to glance at the spot where Matt had disappeared into the trees.

She wasn't sure how long she'd sat there, not daring to move, like a rabbit sensing a threat, when she heard it. *The crunch of twigs and rocks.*

Someone was coming toward the Hummer from the opposite direction.

Without hesitation, she threw herself down across the seats, avoiding the stick shift.

It was Matt—it had to be. *Didn't it?*

She squeezed her eyes shut as the footsteps came closer. Her fingers twitched. If only she had something she could use as a weapon.

Then the driver's-side door opened.

Panic exploded in her chest and she curled her fingers into claws. Fingernails were better than nothing.

"Aimee." Matt touched her shoulder. "Good job."

Relief washed over her. Her scalp tingled. She sat up and tried to hide her trembling nerves. "You sneaked up on me," she accused.

He slid into the driver's seat. "Sorry I scared you. I wanted to circle around, make sure we weren't being watched."

"I knew you saw someone. Why couldn't you have just told me? I'd have been a lot less scared." She blew out a breath between pursed lips. "Who was it? The kidnapper?"

He shook his head and started the engine. "Can't be sure," he said shortly.

He was lying. But she'd already figured out that he would tell her just what she needed to know, and then only when she needed to know it—in *his* opinion.

Once she had William in her arms and they were safe back at home, she'd let him know what she thought about his gestapo tactics. For now, as much as she hated to admit it, his air of command, his complete confidence, and even his predatory edge, made her feel safe.

And feeling safe was dangerous.

Safety was what she longed for. But she'd learned as a child that trusting someone else to keep her safe was a fantasy. As the only child of older parents, she'd grown up with the weight of their health and safety on her shoulders.

When she'd married Bill, he'd promised to keep her safe, but he'd never been able to stand up to his mother. Then he'd promised her she could count on Matt, but he'd trusted Matt with his life, and Matt had let him die.

No. There was only one person she could count on.

Herself. She had to stay strong, stay in control. In the year since Bill's death, maintaining control was the only thing that had kept her going.

Now, at the very time when it was more important than ever to hold on to that control for her baby's sake, she was tempted to relinquish it to someone else—to Matt—and the urge scared her to death.

She lifted her chin. She was *not* going to depend on Matt. Her baby trusted her to save him.

She would.

After another fifteen minutes or so of navigating the winding mountain road, Matt pulled over again.

"What is it?" Aimee looked in the passenger-side mirror. "Did you see something again?"

He shook his head. "We're five miles from the meeting point." He pointed to the GPS locator on the dashboard. "And twenty minutes from the meeting time. So this is where I get out. I'll circle around, while you drive the rest of the way alone. You've got the case of money. You've got the baby seat, formula, diapers and blankets. The GPS locator is programmed for the exact coordinates. It's a straight shot. Just stay on this road."

He pulled a folded sheet of paper from a pocket. "Here's a printout of the route in case something happens to the GPS. You just stay on this road. Now, let's go over everything one more time."

Aimee nodded shakily. "Please. I feel like I'm in some weird dream—like all of this is a nightmare and I'm going to wake up tomorrow morning holding William."

"With any luck, that's exactly what'll happen."

His words were kind, his voice gentle. Aimee had to

clench her jaw to keep from crying. Time stretched out before her like an endless road. It would be hours before she'd be back home with William, safe and sound. Many hours and many opportunities for something to go wrong.

"Hey, Aimee," Matt said. He lifted a hand toward her cheek, then checked the movement. "It's going to be okay."

She lifted her chin. "Don't do that. Don't spout meaningless promises to me. I need to know what I'm up against. What if the kidnapper doesn't bring William? What if my baby's cold, or hungry—?" She bit her cheek. *Control,* she reminded herself.

"Whoa. You can't worry about any of that. And remember, being scared is normal. You're very brave."

"Oh, yeah. I'm the bravest woman on the planet, driving up this remote mountain to rescue my baby from a kidnapper." Tears stung her eyes and a lump lodged in her throat.

She was so *not* brave.

"Matt. I'm so scared." She touched his sleeve, and then squeezed the material in her fist.

A tender look softened his sculpted features. "Listen to me. You *are* the bravest woman on the planet. And—" He paused for a second. "Bill was the luckiest man in the universe. Aimee, I—"

"Don't—" She stiffened and held up her hands. "Please. Don't start. I have to think about William. I can't afford to get all emotional about what happened to Bill."

Matt's expression closed down. He nodded. "Yeah. Best to hate me for one thing at a time," he said flatly.

She caught what appeared to be sadness in his dark

eyes before he averted his gaze. His words and the look surprised her. It wasn't like Matt to feel sorry for himself.

He shrugged it off and climbed out of the Hummer, pulling a daypack out with him. Then he leaned his forearms on the driver's-side door. "I put on the emergency brake. Don't forget to release it before you head out."

"I've ridden ATVs in these hills all my life. I can handle this Hummer."

He nodded matter-of-factly. "I've got my route planned out. Going straight up, it'll take me about fifteen to twenty minutes to reach the rendezvous point. If you drive no faster than fifteen miles per hour, we should arrive at about the same time, since this maintenance road snakes back and forth, and the terrain is getting rougher. Just stay on it. Don't get lost."

"I'll be fine."

"Aimee, I can't stress too strongly how dangerous this man could be. If anything—*anything*—goes wrong, you have to turn the Hummer around and head down the mountain as fast as you can. With or without William. Understand?"

"No. I don't understand. There's no way I'm going anywhere without my baby."

"Listen to me. I *have* to know that you'll do as I say. I promise you, you won't have to deal with him. I'm going to ambush him. I don't expect anything to go wrong, but if something does, I have to know you'll follow my orders. Do what I say. I can't do my job—I can't rescue William—if I have to worry about you. Your baby will be safe. I swear."

Aimee frowned, studying his face. There was something else—something he wasn't telling her. He wouldn't meet her gaze. Instead, he stared down at his clasped hands.

Suddenly she understood. "You don't think he's bringing William, do you?"

His head ducked lower for an instant. Then he straightened.

"Do you?" Aimee grabbed his hand before he could remove it from the car door. She held on until he bent down again. His dark eyes finally met hers—solemn, guarded.

"Oh—" Her heart cracked wide open and all her careful efforts at control spilled out. She shook her head slowly, back and forth, back and forth. "No, please, Matt. Tell me my baby's okay."

He reached out and brushed a strand of hair from her cheek. "Aimee, I swear to God, if I have to die to make it happen, William will be back in your arms today, safe and sound."

THE MAN WAS LIGHTER on his feet than Matt had expected, given his size and the bulky daypack strapped to his back. His clothes and pack were a winter camouflage pattern that blended perfectly into the patchy snow and barren trees as he moved.

And he moved well, silently as a woodland animal, alert to everything around him. An assault rifle—military grade—was hooked over one shoulder.

Matt could tell he was ex-military. Maybe even ex-Special Forces. That explained this location, the timing and the man's obvious comfort in his surroundings. Not many people knew how to glide silently through rough terrain, leaving almost no trail.

Matt would bet money that he was also a survivalist. He had to have trekked every inch of this mountain, or he wouldn't have chosen it.

But was he here alone?

Matt had no doubt that he'd seen sunlight glinting off metal in the Hummer's rearview mirror as the vehicle had snaked back and forth up the maintenance road. That was why he'd stopped, to try and catch a glimpse of whoever was tailing them. But he hadn't spotted anything.

Whoever was back there was good. Probably as good as the man in front of him. Impressively close to having Matt's own skills.

The question in Matt's mind was—were there two guys following him? This man could have followed them up the road and then cut through just as Matt had and beaten him to the ransom drop point.

But it was also possible that he had an accomplice, and the accomplice had followed them while this guy waited up here.

Matt couldn't afford to let down his guard, so until he knew otherwise, he assumed the kidnapper had an accomplice.

Matt had to watch his back.

He'd planned out as much of his strategy as he could. He, too, was dressed in winter camo and carried a small daypack. Besides binoculars, he was equipped with a compact MAC-10 machine pistol he didn't plan on using, a mini-tranquilizer gun and a few flexicuffs.

His intent was to surprise the kidnapper and immobilize him with the tranq gun. Once he had him restrained, he could definitely make it worth his while to reveal the baby's location.

He crouched, hidden by scrubby bushes, and observed the kidnapper through his high-powered binoculars. The man was positioning himself for greatest cover and widest angle of sight.

For a couple of seconds, Matt held his breath, listening for the Hummer's engine, but he didn't hear anything. It was nerve-racking, waiting up here, knowing Aimee was about to drive straight into the lion's den. All this would be so much easier if he didn't have to worry about her being hurt.

Matt shifted, examining the area around the kidnapper. He searched for signs of another person—someone whose job it was to take care of the baby. He used a careful mental grid layout he'd developed in the Air Force.

The controlled search made it impossible to miss a person, much less a vehicle, but all Matt saw was a set of tracks made by a one-man snowmobile. He saw no trace of the vehicle itself. The kidnapper had done a damn good job of hiding his vehicle and covering his tracks.

Matt's respect for him went up a notch, and his fear for Aimee's baby went up three. The suspicion that had planted itself in his brain from the first moment he'd seen the TV news, rooted itself more deeply, undermining his confidence.

If this man were simply a kidnapper, out to make a quick million, and if he'd come to make a good-faith exchange, then why didn't he have the baby?

Matt continued his grid search until he'd covered every square inch of visible land surface. He saw nothing that indicated anyone but the kidnapper had been—or was—in the area. He pocketed the binoculars.

Damn. He would hate to be right about this one.

Although the kidnapper seemed to be all about money, and Aimee's revelations about Margo's need to control the Vick Corporation made Margo a prime suspect, Matt didn't believe it.

A silent vibration started near his left knee. His cell phone. Grimacing, he shifted enough to pull it out of the cargo pocket of his camo pants. Keeping one eye on the kidnapper, he glanced at the screen.

It was a text message from Deke. He focused on the letters.

GOT PSNGR LIST OF YR FLIGHT. HAFIZ AL HAMAR, AFGH NATL, ON IT. SEE PHOTO. DC.

It only took a couple of seconds for the photo to come through. Matt cursed silently when he saw it. He'd seen that man before. He'd run into him several times in Mahjidastan.

Still watching the kidnapper, Matt keyed in a quick message back to Deke and, making sure the sound was off on his phone, hit SEND.

RECOG AL HAMAR FR MAHJID. TRACE HIM? MP

A sick certainty burned in the pit of his gut. Novus Ordo had engineered William's kidnapping to get his hands on Matt, to interrogate him about whether Rook was alive. And that meant he wanted Matt alive. But Matt was sure Novus wouldn't blink at killing anyone who got in his way.

Matt had made a huge mistake by bringing Aimee up here. He should have come alone, or brought Deke or another BHSAR specialist.

If he was right about Novus, and he was becoming more and more sure about that by the hour, she and her baby were disposable pawns in an international terrorist's effort to protect his identity.

The kidnapper was on the move again. Matt pocketed his phone and cleared his mind. He needed focus and hair-trigger response. If he failed to return William Matthew to his mother's arms, he'd have plenty of time for regrets and unbearable sorrow later. His mission was to get the drop on the kidnapper and rescue Aimee's baby. He didn't allow the thought that William wasn't here to enter his head. He had to operate as if he were.

He crouched in a position from which he could spring in a fraction of a second, and let his senses feed him information. They were as clear as the mountain air. The smell of evergreen and the coming snow teased his nostrils. The tingling in his hands and face signaled the dropping temperature.

And the quickly darkening sky telegraphed the approach of the winter storm—early, just as he'd predicted.

The only sound Matt heard was the rustling of bare tree branches and evergreen needles in the rising wind.

The kidnapper raised his head, as if sniffing a scent on the breeze. He appeared calm and relaxed, and yet poised to react with swift reflexes.

Damn, the man was good.

A discordant hum rose in the distance. The Hummer. Aimee was almost here. The kidnapper swung the rifle from his shoulder and settled into a comfortable, balanced stance—observant and attentive—ready for anything.

Matt shifted, feeling the weight of the MAC-10 in its holster. He could get to it if necessary, but he didn't plan on using it. He held the tranq gun and the flexicuffs were looped through his belt.

The Hummer's engine grew louder, its steady roar filling the air around them. The engine's noise blocked Matt's keen hearing, but it also covered any noise he might make when he sneaked up on the kidnapper.

After an automatic glance around, Matt crept forward, until he was less than twenty feet behind the man. With his tactical-grade, compression-fit long underwear, he had far greater agility than the bulkily dressed kidnapper. He could rush him, sink a tranq dart in his neck and cuff him within seconds.

The Hummer crested the rise, and Matt's pulse kicked into high gear. He could barely make out Aimee's silhouette through the vehicle's tinted windows. As he watched, she slowed down, then rolled to a stop.

Stay in the vehicle. Make him come to you. He silently recited the instructions he'd given her.

He'd retrofitted a loudspeaker for her to use for any necessary communications. He'd warned her not to exit the vehicle until the kidnapper produced the baby. And, as he'd reminded her not twenty minutes before, at the first sign of trouble, she was to turn the Hummer around and get out of there.

Those were *her* instructions. But Matt had other plans. He had no intention of letting the kidnapper within twenty yards of her.

She inched the Hummer closer. The kidnapper shifted to the balls of his feet, holding the rifle loosely yet competently, like a pro. Another point in his favor and more cause for concern on Matt's part.

Matt made his move. He rose from his crouch and crept around the edge of the clearing, keeping the scrub bushes between him and the other man. Once he got into position, it would take him less than thirty seconds to get behind him, slip out from the trees at the last second, then grab and tranquilize him. In a situation like this, thirty seconds was a hell of a long time.

He'd choreographed every step ahead of time. He'd had plenty of experience with stealth from rescue missions he'd conducted in the Air Force and afterwards while working for Black Hills Search and Rescue. He knew how to approach an enemy and extract an innocent without detection. Given this guy's obvious expertise, he was glad to have the noise of the Hummer's engine as added cover.

He positioned himself directly behind the kidnapper. Staying low, he inched silently forward.

Then without warning, something hit him from behind.

With no more than a fifth of a second wasted on startle response, Matt whirled. He rammed his fist and shoulder into the attacker's body. As his knuckles encountered flesh and bone, he followed through, putting his whole weight behind the blow. But it wasn't enough. His attacker was quicker.

Matt went down—hard.

The man grabbed a handful of his hair and slammed his face into the frozen ground.

The blow dazed him. But the cold pressure of a gun barrel pressed to the side of his neck brought him back instantaneously. Adrenaline sheared his breath and cleared his brain. He jerked just as a quiet pop echoed in his ear. Something sharp scratched his neck.

A pop. Not a bullet. A tranquilizer dart.

Damn! Even as the thoughts rushed through his brain, he torpedoed his elbow backward. With a breathy grunt, the man fell away and his tranq gun went flying.

Before he hit the ground, Matt whirled and grabbed his collar. With a renewed burst of energy, and using muscles he hadn't used in months, Matt heaved the man's bulk around, between himself and the kidnapper.

Pocketing his own tranquilizer gun, Mat slid the MAC-10 from its holster and buried its barrel into the flesh of his attacker's neck. He was tempted to rip off the man's ski mask, but to do that, he'd have to let go of the man or the gun.

"You nearly got me with your tranq dart, but believe me, this is not a tranq gun," he growled, scanning the area in front of him in case the kidnapper had heard them. "It's the real thing. And it will take your head clean off if you don't tell me who you are."

His answer was a blood-chilling string of curses, some English, some Arabic. Dammit, the kidnapper had to have heard him.

"Are you *Al Hamar?*"

The man's head jerked in surprise.

"So—you are. Did Novus Ordo send you?" Matt whispered, digging the muzzle of the MAC-10 deeper into his flesh.

His prisoner shook his head, but Matt saw the truth in the man's black eyes. "Tell me what you know about the kidnapping—"

The crack of exploding gunpowder hit his ears a fraction of a second before the bullet whistled past his head.

Matt ducked.

Al Hamar used Matt's own elbow trick to knock the wind out of him, then leapfrogged across three or four feet of ground, diving for his own weapon. The kidnapper shot again.

Matt aimed the machine pistol at Al Hamar. But something was wrong. He couldn't clear his vision. He bent his head and squeezed his eyes shut for an instant. Just as he did, a second bullet grazed his ear.

He swallowed a pained cry and his hand flew to his ear. It came away bloody. His bloodstained fingers trembled as he stared at the proof of how close the bullet had come. If he hadn't paused to clear his vision, it would have split his skull.

A high-pitched scream, barely distinguishable above the roar of the Hummer's engine, sent his heart slamming into his chest. It was Aimee. She gunned the engine and the vehicle shot forward, toward the kidnapper.

Aimee, no! What was she doing? *Turn around. Get out of here.*

The kidnapper aimed at the Hummer's windshield.

At the same time, Matt saw Al Hamar whirl around, brandishing a semiautomatic pistol.

Matt ducked down and rubbed his eyes. The scratch on his neck had absorbed some of the tranquilizer. Enough to blur his vision. He cursed silently and gave his head a quick shake.

The kidnapper yelled something that Matt didn't catch, then several bullets thunked into a tree to Matt's left. He was shooting at Al Hamar again.

So, they weren't working together.

Al Hamar yelped and toppled forward.

When Matt looked back at the kidnapper, the high-powered gun was aimed at his head. From that distance, the man couldn't miss. But before Matt could react and dive, he swung back toward the Hummer.

Why hadn't he shot him? He might not get as good a chance again.

Rising to a crouch, Matt took a precious split second to make sure his head was as clear as possible, then sprinted toward the Hummer, spraying bullets on the ground in front of the kidnapper. He couldn't kill the man. He needed him alive—at least long enough to find out where William was being held.

As he crouched behind a stand of bushes, he heard the hitch in the engine noise that signaled shifting gears.

Good, Aimee! Now turn around and get out of here!

But a Hummer didn't turn on a dime, or even a quarter. Still, she was trying.

Careful to stay hidden, he lifted his head just in time to see the kidnapper raise his weapon and aim at the Hummer's windshield.

Alarm ripped through him. The kidnapper was about to shoot Aimee. The high-powered blast would be enough to penetrate the tempered glass.

Matt raised his weapon, his breath catching as his finger sought the hair-trigger of the MAC-10.

Aimee would hate him if he shot the man who could lead them to her baby. But if he had to kill the kidnapper to save Aimee, then so be it. He'd find her baby some other way.

Chapter Four

FRIDAY 1600 HOURS

Just as Matt's finger started to squeeze the trigger, the kidnapper lowered the barrel of his gun to the tires.

Matt's scalp tingled with relief. At least he was no longer aiming at Aimee. Still, he had to stop him from disabling their only means of getting down the mountain. He vaulted to his feet, brandishing the MAC.

"Hey!" he shouted. "You want your money? Then stop now! Or you'll never see it."

He swayed, but immediately caught himself. Blinking away the haze that threatened to obscure his vision, he yelled, "In fact, you'll never see tomorrow!"

He strafed the ground in front of the kidnapper. But the other man didn't take the bait. His rifle barrel didn't even waver. He fired.

A tire exploded with a loud crack.

A second shot. A second crack.

The Hummer rocked dizzily, then tilted to the passenger side. It was going over.

Aimee!

Matt loosed another volley of bullets, closer this time. He still hadn't ruled out killing the man.

The shooter dove for the ground. But in one smooth motion, he righted himself and fired again—this time at the Hummer's gas tank. Metallic thunks peppered the vehicle's frame.

Wincing each time the kidnapper shot, Matt tried to draw a bead on him, but the kidnapper's duck and roll had positioned the Hummer between them.

Matt sprinted toward the vehicle. He had to stop him. It was only a matter of seconds before a bullet hit the gas tank.

Suddenly, the man stopped shooting, slung his rifle over his shoulder and ran toward the disabled vehicle.

He was going after the money.

Matt had to stop him before he got to Aimee. He broke into a run. His legs pumped, his heart raced. The earth and the sky went topsy-turvy and he stumbled, but he recovered his footing and kept going.

The tranquilizer was doing more than turn Matt's world upside down, though. His legs were as heavy as lead weights. It was like a bad dream. As hard as he pushed, he couldn't beat the other man.

The kidnapper vaulted up the vehicle's undercarriage like a free climber and ripped open the driver's-side door.

Reaching in, he grabbed Aimee's parka and yanked her up and out through the door. She struggled, but she was no match for the big man. He shoved her over the side. Then he dove back down and popped out immediately with the briefcase.

By the time Matt rounded the rear of the Hummer, the kidnapper was back on the ground.

Finally, Matt had a clean shot. He stopped and took aim, blinking rapidly. He wanted to disable him without killing him.

But Aimee's crumpled form filled his wavering vision. She was lying near the Hummer. Too near. Her feet were mere inches from the widening puddle of gasoline.

The kidnapper seemed preoccupied with the briefcase, but Matt couldn't count on that. In one stride he'd be close enough to grab her. He could use her as a shield.

Or kill her.

Swallowing against dizziness brought on by the tranq, Matt carefully tightened his finger on the trigger.

Aimee stirred and moaned, distracting him for a split second. When he turned his full attention back to the kidnapper, the man had produced an old-fashioned silver cigarette lighter in his hand. He flipped open the lid.

Matt aimed at his right shoulder, concentrating on keeping the sights of the machine pistol steady.

Aimee sat up. The kidnapper's sharp gaze met Matt's as he stepped backward and sideways, putting her between himself and Matt. He crouched down, making himself too small a target to hit without endangering Aimee.

As Matt watched helplessly, he nodded at him, then struck the lighter and tossed it over Aimee's head and into the middle of the pool of gasoline.

The small flame looped through the air as if in slow motion. When it was a couple of inches above the puddle, the fumes caught and flared. By the time the lighter splashed into the liquid gasoline, the flames were two feet high and spreading.

The kidnapper turned and sprinted away to the east.

Matt couldn't worry about him. The fire was growing, and flames were rising only inches from Aimee's legs.

"Aimee, get back!" he yelled.

She scrambled backward, her eyes wide and bright with terror.

Pocketing his gun, Matt rushed toward her. A shot rang out—but not from the direction in which the kidnapper had run.

It came from the south. *Al Hamar*. Matt dove the last few feet. He landed next to Aimee as red flames licked at her hiking boots.

Scooping his hands under her arms, he lifted her and heaved her as far as he could and then dove on top of her, covering her body with his, shielding her head with his hands.

Behind them, the flames roared and spit like a massive beast. The ground trembled beneath them and a whistling sound filled the air.

The flares! He'd packed a dozen of them into the rear of the Hummer.

"What's that?" Aimee whispered.

"It's okay," he whispered. "You're okay. Just stay still." Matt hunched his shoulders and pressed his cheek against hers, doing his best to shield every inch of her body with his. He could feel her panicked breaths against his cheek, hear them sawing in and out through her throat. He could smell the lemon sweetness of her hair.

She stopped wriggling and turned her head a little more, which put her lips about an inch away from his. He closed his eyes and pretended they weren't there.

He couldn't tell how many of the flares fired because suddenly, with a deafening roar, the gasoline exploded.

For an instant, the air grew totally still and quiet, as the conflagration sucked in oxygen. Then a blast of heat strafed them, like the breath of a fire-breathing dragon. Matt felt the sting of heat across the backs of his hands and the nape of his neck.

After several seconds, he lifted his head slightly and peeked at the Hummer. It was still engulfed in flames, but they were weakening.

Their supplies and equipment. He stiffened, and felt Aimee move beneath him.

"Matt?"

"Stay still," he commanded. He rose to a crouch with his weapon drawn and rapidly scanned the clearing, but they were alone. The kidnapper and Al Hamar gone.

He turned back to Aimee. "Why didn't you turn the Hummer around and get out of here like I told you to?"

"He shot you!" she hissed. "I saw you go down. I thought you were dead. I had to save my baby."

He held her gaze for a moment, wanting to berate her for endangering her life by not obeying him, but she lifted her chin and stared at him with defiance in her eyes.

It occurred to him that there was probably no emotion in humans stronger than the one radiating from her. The fierceness of the love of a woman for her child.

There was no way he could counter that.

Setting the machine pistol down, he shrugged his daypack off his shoulders.

"What are you doing?" she asked.

Ignoring her, he quickly assessed his clothing. Had

he landed in gasoline when he dove for Aimee? He didn't see any stains, and didn't smell gas.

"Don't move," he said, pointing at the ground where she sat. "I'm going to see if I can salvage anything out of the Hummer."

"You can't go near that," Aimee said. "Wait until the fire dies down."

He shook his head. By the time the flames died down there would be nothing left. Hell, there was probably nothing left anyhow.

He approached the burning vehicle cautiously.

Everything inside was black and smoldering, or still burning. By the red-and-yellow flickering light, he saw what was left of the baby seat, melted down to a nearly unrecognizable lump of plastic. Behind it, in the back of the vehicle, he could see the damage caused by the flares that he'd packed to help Deke set his helicopter down in the dark.

Then he spotted his backpack. There was nothing left of his supplies and equipment. The nylon webbing that crisscrossed its lightweight frame had burned and melted.

Matt cursed silently. Everything he'd packed so carefully—planning for any contingency—was burned and useless. His double sleeping bag, the concentrated nutrient packs, rain gear, snowshoes, spare batteries for the GPS locator and phone, first aid kit, even the water canteens, were gone.

He sucked in a deep breath, and coughed as smoke scalded his throat. It was getting thicker and blacker as the flames died.

There was still plenty of heat, which would have come in handy if it weren't almost certainly toxic, judging by the smell. Between the upholstery, the gasoline, oil and other fluids, and the various plastics and dyes, there was no telling how contaminated the air was.

They couldn't stay near that fire.

He headed back to where Aimee was waiting.

She took a breath to speak, and coughed when she got a lungful of smoke. She took his hand and let him help her stand.

She looked over her shoulder. "I need to get my bag. William's baby food and diapers and—"

"They're gone. Burned up. My supplies are, too. We'll have to make do."

"But—"

"Come on. We need to get away from here. That smoke is toxic."

Aimee coughed again, proving his point. She looked up at him and gasped. "Oh! Matt, you're bleeding. It's all over your face and neck."

He touched his ear and winced, then looked at his hand. A fresh smear of blood stained his finger. "Don't worry. I'm okay," he said shortly, as a wave of dizziness reminded him just how handicapped he still was by the tranquilizer.

"Hell, another quarter inch and the bullet would have missed me completely."

Aimee pushed his hand away and stood on tiptoe, looking at the wound. "That's not funny," she snapped.

She touched the curve of his ear, near the raw scrape. "It looks like the bleeding has almost stopped."

He shrugged away her touch. It took concentration to ignore the gentle brush of her fingers.

"Stand behind me." He held the pistol waist high and swept the clearing with it and his gaze.

She grasped his sleeve and pointed toward the east. "He ran into the woods in that direction. We've got to go after him."

Matt twisted away from her grip and put a hand on her shoulder. "He's long gone. The fire gave him a big head start."

"No! We've got to go. We have to catch up—"

"Aimee. He's twenty minutes ahead of us. It's getting dark. We'll never catch up to him tonight."

She turned and stared at him, the brightness of her green eyes fading as understanding dawned. Her hands covered her mouth. A stray flake of snow caught on her lashes.

"But—he got the money," she cried. "And he's still got William. He doesn't need my baby any longer. What if—"

A giant fist squeezed his heart at the utter desolation on her face—in her voice. He opened his mouth to lie, to feed her false hope. "We'll find him, Aimee. Don't worry—"

"Don't worry? Don't—?" She gulped in a desperate breath. "He's my *baby*. He's so little. He's only seven months old. He will *die* without me."

She doubled her hands into fists. "Don't tell me not to worry!" she screamed.

He steeled himself for her attack, figuring she had a perfect right. He hadn't kept his word. He'd let both men get the best of him. One had sneaked up on him because he'd let his guard down. The other had turned his own equipment into a weapon against him.

But she didn't. She pressed her fists to her eyes. "What do we do now?" she whispered.

Matt gently pulled her hands away from her face. Then he touched her chin. "Aimee. Look at me."

She raised her gaze to his, and he winced at the unbearable sorrow in her eyes.

"The kidnapper doesn't have the money," he said.

Aimee's eyes went round. "What?"

"We put a few thousand dollars in the briefcase, on top. But as soon as he digs down a few layers, all he'll find is scrap paper."

"He doesn't have—?" Aimee's pale cheeks flared with pink. She sent Matt an incredulous smile.

Matt shook his head. "I've got it here, in the daypack. If he'd given William to you, I'd have given him the pack."

"He doesn't have the money," she said in awe.

Matt nodded. "That's right."

"So he *has* to take care of my baby until he gets it."

If the money is what he's after.

For an instant he allowed himself to bask in the joy on her face. Then a flake of snow drifted past her cheek, followed by another, and another.

He looked toward the west. The sky was dark with thick, gray clouds. He grimaced and shivered as a fat snowflake slipped down the back of his neck.

Where was his parka? There, on the ground near the woods.

"We'd better get going," he said as he went over to get it. "The storm's heading this way. As soon as it's over I'll call Deke and we'll—" He bent over to pick up the parka, and suddenly the world turned upside down—several times. His knee hit the hard ground with a painful thud.

"Matt?"

He jerked his head up. Her blurry, wavering face filled his vision.

"Matt! What's wrong?"

He held up a hand. With more than a little effort he closed his fist around the down-filled jacket and pushed himself to his feet. "I'm okay. I got a little dose of a tranquilizer dart when the second guy grabbed me. It's almost worn off."

"Tranquilizer dart?" Aimee's smile faded. "I don't understand. Why did the kidnappers need a tranquilizer dart?"

He rubbed his eyes and shook his head.

But she wouldn't let it go. "I don't understand. These men, these kidnappers—why bring all those weapons—" She stopped, her eyes narrowing.

"Why did *you* need a machine gun?"

When he met her gaze, his throat spasmed, and that punishing fist tightened and twisted until his heart wanted to burst. But before he could answer, she lifted her chin.

"Okay. Let me make it easier on you. Just answer this one question for me. The question you never answered yesterday. How did you happen to show up back in Wyoming just in time to be available when William was kidnapped?" she asked.

"What?" Matt answered automatically.

"You. Heard. Me." A muscle ticked in her jaw and her nostrils flared. She took a step toward him, holding his gaze. "I woke up at six-thirty yesterday morning to find that my baby had been abducted from right under my nose. And then before noon you showed up." She pressed her fingertips to her mouth for a second. "You must have been here for days, or—or weeks for all I know."

Matt swallowed. "I flew in Tuesday night."

She nodded shakily. "Not even two days." She looked away, as if composing herself, and then looked at him again. "Why?"

"Why what?"

"Matt, stop it. Why did you fly back here on Tuesday, and my baby was kidnapped on Wednesday? Am I supposed to believe that was a *coincidence?*"

"Aimee, I don't know what you're thinking—" He was lying again. He knew exactly what she was thinking.

What was the connection?

"Answer me."

More snowflakes fell. The storm was almost upon them. By sheer force of will, he stopped himself from examining the sky. Aimee needed as much assurance as he could give her right now—which admittedly wasn't much.

"I came back to Wyoming because Irina called me back. She had to stop looking for Rook."

Aimee's mouth fell open. "Had to stop? Oh, no. I didn't think she would ever give up. She must be devastated."

He nodded. "She is. But she can't do it anymore. She's out of money."

A little frown appeared between her brows. "She called you last week?"

He nodded, wondering what she was thinking. She didn't have the information he and Deke had. She knew nothing about Rook's relationship with Novus Ordo, or the threat he'd posed to the mysterious terrorist as long as he was alive.

"These men—"

"Aimee, I don't know either of them."

She shook her head slowly. "They don't have William, do they? This isn't about my baby at all." Her hands pressed against her chest, as if trying to stop the pain.

"Oh, dear heavens," she gasped. "That other man— he wasn't speaking English."

"I don't know them—" he repeated, but she cut him off with a gesture.

"But you know who they are, don't you?" she snapped. "They have something to do with whatever you've been doing overseas. They followed you back here to Wyoming. Somehow, they knew they could get to you by kidnapping my baby."

"Aimee, don't—"

"They don't care about William. They want you," she whispered. "For all you know, my baby is dead."

Chapter Five

Matt caught Aimee's shoulders as she swayed. "Listen to me," he said firmly.

She steadied herself by closing her fingers around the sleeves of his sweater.

"William is still alive. I know he is." Dear God, he hoped she believed him. The reticence in his voice was painfully obvious to him.

She looked at him, her eyes filled with doubt and despair. Slowly, a little of the anguish faded from her expression. "Do you really think so?"

He forced his stiff lips to smile. "I know so. I swear, Aimee, I have no idea who these men are, but you saw the way the kidnapper grabbed the briefcase and ran. He couldn't wait to get to the money."

Dear God, he hoped his desperate explanation sounded plausible.

He took a deep breath. "But he's going to find out that we outsmarted him. And now we've seen him. We can identify him. He can't afford to let anything happen to William now."

He did his best not to wince. He wasn't sure if it was

the tranquilizer circulating in his blood, or the desperation clouding his brain, but his reasoning had holes so big he could have driven the Hummer through them if it hadn't burned up.

He prayed that Aimee wasn't thinking rationally enough to dispute him. Right now what she needed was reassurance, not raw truth.

And she certainly didn't need to know that he echoed her suspicions. He wasn't sure who either of the men were, but he knew there was more going on than just the kidnapping of a baby for money.

He shook his head, trying to shake off the tranquilizer's effect, and another snowflake slid inside the neck of his sweater.

He looked up at the sky. The clouds were dark, feeding the dropping temperature. Within an hour, the sun would go down, and then the mercury would plummet. They were running out of time.

He had to make a decision. Several, if he could remember what they were. A lungful of icy air helped to clear his head.

He glanced at his watch and then stared at the tangle of briar bushes where he'd last seen the terrorist who'd followed him from Mahjidastan. He had to check on him.

He knew the man was wounded. He'd heard him shriek when the kidnapper's bullet had hit him. But after that the terrorist had fired a shot. Had that been the last brave effort of a dying man? Or a parting shot before he escaped to lick his wound? He had to find out.

Good. He rubbed his temples. At least he finally had come to a decision.

"Aimee, get over here and stay behind me. I need to

check the area, in case Al Hamar is wounded or dead, and I don't want to let you out of my sight."

"Al Hamar?" Her eyes widened, then immediately narrowed. "You know his name? I thought you said you didn't know either of them."

He sighed and spread his hands. "I don't. I got a text message from Deke, telling me—" He stopped. "It's complicated, Aimee. I just need you to trust me."

She shook her head slowly. "Do I have any choice?"

"No," he said grimly. "Have you ever shot a pistol before?"

"No. Rifles, shotguns, bows and arrows. But not a pistol." She sounded like she was about to cry.

"It's okay. This is a Glock." He pulled the small handgun out of his daypack and handed it to her. "It's loaded, and it doesn't have a safety, so it's ready to shoot. You pull the trigger the same way you do a rifle. And you hold it in both hands, like the cops on TV. Okay?"

"I think so."

"Trust me, you probably won't have to use it. But I need to know—can you shoot a man if you have to?"

She lifted her chin. "Will it help me get William back? Then, yes, I can."

"Okay. Stay directly behind me. By now the guy's either dead or long gone. But there's no way I'm leaving the area until I verify that he's not waiting to ambush us."

Aimee met his gaze. "I'm ready."

The determination in her expression told him she meant it. To his surprise, something welled up in his chest until it almost cut off his breath. Her bravery and trust awed and scared him.

"Good," he said roughly. "Let's go."

He held the MAC-10 at waist level, ready to shoot if necessary, as he moved cautiously toward the bushes. A couple of feet away, he held up his hand.

"Wait here. Remember what I told you in the car? Same goes here. If you hear anything—anything at all—hit the dirt. Copy?"

"Yes."

He crouched and crept forward to the edge of the patch. Peering through the tangle of bare briar-studded vines didn't work. They were too thick. He straightened, weapon at the ready, and moved close enough to see over the tops.

The briar bushes covered about four feet of ground. Beyond that he saw new scrapes and crushed twigs and leaves.

Glancing back at Aimee, he drew a circle in the air with his left hand. "I'm circling around," he mouthed, then held up his palm. "You stay there."

She nodded carefully.

He circled the bushes and bent to study the scrapes on the ground. In among the dried leaves and twigs, Matt saw a saucer-sized pool of blood. Beyond it, dark red drops drew a path toward the trees, like bread crumbs left by Hansel and Gretel.

"He's wounded, but not fatally. He got away." He followed the trail of blood toward the trees, dividing his attention between the ground and the wooded area ahead of him.

At the edge of the clearing, he stopped. For a few seconds, he stood still, listening for the sound of a motor, but all he heard was the wind rustling the bare branches. Carefully, he followed the blood trail for a few more steps, until the underbrush was too thick to penetrate, and the tree's roots met and intertwined on the ground.

He backed away, staying in his own footsteps until he reached the stand of bushes. When he turned, he nearly ran into Aimee.

"When I tell you to stay put, you've got to stay put," he said sternly, wishing he felt like smiling at her determined stance.

She stood, legs apart, holding the Glock like every cop on *Law & Order,* although her expression more closely resembled that of a terrified witness.

"The kidnapper definitely wounded him. He's losing a good bit of blood. I don't think he'll try anything else. If he's got any sense, and if he's got a vehicle—which I'm sure he does—he's probably headed down the mountain by now."

"What do we do now?" she asked.

He frowned. "If I had the Hummer, I'd send you down to it. But without it we're not going anywhere, except to find a way to get you out of this storm."

Aimee shivered and hunched her shoulders against the wind. She was already feeling the cold, even in her down parka and balaclava.

His insulated underwear was keeping him warm. If he thought it would help her, he'd strip it off and give it to her. But the suit had been custom-fitted to his body for maximum insulation. It would be much too large for her, and therefore useless. Besides, if he were going to keep her safe, he had to keep himself warm and mobile.

Aimee still held the Glock. He put on his parka and

lifted the daypack onto his shoulders. Then he took the Glock and stowed it in a side pocket.

After glancing up at the sky one more time, he pulled the satellite phone out of his pocket and looked at it. No signal.

Why was he not surprised?

He wasn't sure if the problem was the cloud cover or the cold, but it didn't matter. There would be no nighttime rescue tonight. He couldn't contact Deke or anyone else until the storm passed.

He put the phone away and pulled out the GPS locator. *Again, no satellite reception.* He'd have to rely on old-fashioned methods of finding his way. He'd memorized the maps, so he knew where they were going. He just hoped they could make it before the storm caught up to them in full force.

It was almost 1900 hours. Seven o'clock. They had, at best, thirty minutes of daylight left. A stab of apprehension pierced his chest. He'd mapped out three shelters within reasonable distance of the ransom drop point. The one closest to his primary rendezvous point was 4.8 miles, heading 41 degrees, almost directly east. The next closest to rendezvous was 4.5 miles at 18 degrees.

The third shelter would be the easiest walk. It was two miles away, but the direction was 30 degrees, which put it farthest from the primary rendezvous point.

He could picture the grid in his head. If he were alone, he'd head directly for the primary shelter. A hike of 4.8 miles would be less than an hour at his usual pace, even in snow.

But he figured Aimee could cover about three miles per hour at best, and that didn't take the snowstorm into consideration. It would take her almost two hours. Which wouldn't be so much of a problem if they'd gotten started an hour earlier.

But they hadn't. And as he'd feared, the storm was moving in at least three hours ahead of predictions, just as he'd told Special Agent Schiff. So he had no choice but to head for the nearest shelter, even if it was farthest from the primary rendezvous point.

"How far do we have to go?" Aimee asked, as if she were reading his mind.

"With any luck we can make it in an hour or a little more," he said, knowing he was being optimistic. The longer it took, the harder it would be. He could smell the snow in the air and he figured the wind was already up to twelve miles per hour. His prediction was that it would reach fifty miles per hour or more before the storm played out. And Matt didn't want to be caught outside in it.

He sure as hell didn't want Aimee exposed. Once they made it to the shelter, they could get a good night's sleep and get an early start.

Plus, as soon as the storm moved out, he could contact Deke and arrange a new, closer rendezvous point. He could tell Deke to bring replacement gear and supplies, and pick up Aimee.

He shook his head. Getting Aimee to leave without her baby was going to be a trick. Surely two ex-Special Forces operatives could convince one small civilian female to get into a helicopter.

Matt's brain fed him a life-sized picture of that.

"We'd better get going," he said.

She looked up at him and a couple of snowflakes

caught in her lashes. They looked like stars sparkling in her eyes. She blinked and scrunched up her nose, and desire lanced through his groin, surprising the hell out of him.

Damn. At least it chased the drowsy haze from his head.

AIMEE FLEXED her right shoulder and suppressed a groan. It was already sore, and she had a feeling it would be black-and-blue by morning. She'd landed on it when the kidnapper tossed her out of the Hummer.

Matt glanced up as if he'd heard her. When she met his gaze, he gave her a little nod and then quickly looked back down at the small, handheld electronic device he held.

His effort to be reassuring wasn't very successful, though, mostly because he wasn't the kind of guy who could hide his feelings.

Throughout high school, college and the six years of Bill and Aimee's marriage, Bill and his three friends had been inseparable. They'd called themselves the Black Hills Brotherhood because of the near-death experience they'd shared as kids.

She knew all of them—Matt the best, because he'd been Bill's best friend.

It was interesting how alike the four were—and how different. Deke Cunningham and Rook Castle would have had no trouble winning at poker. Even Bill had always had a pretty good poker face.

Matt, on the other hand, was as easy to read as a first-grade storybook. Like right now. His brows drew down in a V across his forehead as he looked at the tiny screen of his device and then up at the cloudy sky.

He was worried about them reaching shelter before the storm hit. She was, too. It was getting dark, and the wind was picking up.

She wasn't sure why she'd asked about going back down the mountain. Maybe because it would have been nice to have a choice, even though she'd never leave without her child. Or maybe so she could understand exactly how bad things were, now that the Hummer had been destroyed.

They were on their own, with no transportation, a snowstorm on its way, and not one but two men who wanted to harm them. And her baby was still missing.

She figured she had a pretty good handle on how bad things were.

Per Matt's instructions, she'd dressed for the trip as if they were going to picnic at the North Pole. Layers, layers and more layers, he'd told her.

Of course, she'd lived in Wyoming all her life, so she knew how quickly the weather could change in the mountains, especially this time of year. And she knew that the most important thing to remember was to keep one's body core warm. So she had put on a tank top, silk long underwear, a cotton pullover, a wool sweater and her down jacket. She was set for any temperature.

Aimee's fingers were beginning to tingle with cold. She pulled off a mitten and stuffed her hand inside the elastic sleeve that covered her other arm. The skin-to-skin contact warmed her fingers almost instantly. The chill seeped into the skin of her other wrist, but it would warm back up within seconds.

She pulled her mitten back on and then did the same thing with her other hand.

Meanwhile, Matt was still studying the weather.

"Is everything okay?" she asked.

He stuck the handheld device into a pocket of the small daypack he carried on his back, and then smiled at her. "Sure. We need to get a move on, though. As I told you, it's going to take us an hour or so to get to the nearest shelter. And that storm is catching up to us."

She clenched her fists inside the mittens, and bit her cheek in an effort to stop the tears that stung her eyelids.

She'd been congratulating herself for already figuring all that out. Hearing Matt say it, however, seemed to make their situation more dire, and less simple. It was one thing for her to wonder if she were overstating their predicament. It was quite another to hear Matt verify that things really were that bad.

"Remind me again how everything is going to be all right?" she begged.

Matt tugged off his glove with his teeth and took it in his other hand. He stepped closer to her and touched her cheek, then her chin, with his warm fingers.

"Hey," he said, coaxing her chin upward so he could look into her eyes. "Pull your cap down. You look like you're getting cold."

"I'm a little chilly," she admitted. "Matt? How sure are you that William is okay?"

A shadow of doubt flickered across his face as he curled his lips in a smile. "Very sure. I promise you, we'll find him and he'll be fine."

As he spoke, the weight of worry that was squeezing her chest let up a little. It occurred to her that whatever he told her, she believed without reservation.

It was strange that his thoughtful answer coupled

with the uncertainty that had briefly touched his features, made him more believable than Bill, who had often stared at her expressionlessly, rather than giving her a straight answer.

She watched him closely. Was he more trustworthy than her husband had been? Or was Matt, too, trying to protect her from the truth?

His teeth scraped lightly across his lower lip as he checked his pack and got ready to go.

Aimee arched her shoulder again.

He'd said it would take about an hour to get to the shelter. She hoped he was being realistic, although she was afraid he was overestimating how fast she could move.

FOR THE NEXT HALF HOUR or so, Aimee kept up with Matt better than he would have expected. Not so much better that he revised his estimate of how long it would take them to get to the shelter, but fast enough to keep his body producing heat. From the sound of Aimee's breathing, she was keeping her heart rate up, too.

That was the good news. The bad news was that the storm was about to catch up to them. The wind was easterly, so it helped propel them forward, but the sun had gone down, the sky was cloudy and dark, and the air was heavy with moisture, making the wind bitingly cold.

They didn't talk much, just trudged along doggedly. Most of their conversation consisted of Matt asking if she was all right and Aimee replying that she was.

Then it started to snow, and Aimee started slowing down—way down.

He figured they were at least another half hour from the shelter. The temperature had dropped by at least ten degrees, he was sure, and the wind was probably up to thirty miles per hour, enough to make Aimee stumble when it gusted.

He wrapped an arm around her waist and half supported her, pushing her to walk a little faster. "Come on, Aimee. We're getting close. You've got to keep moving or you're going to get sick."

"I am a little chilly," she said, just as she had every time he'd asked.

Only this time, her words were slurred.

He reached back to a pocket of his daypack and retrieved a windup flashlight. He gave it about a minute's worth of winding. Then he shone it in her face.

"Wha—?" she said, her hand coming up to block the light.

"Stop for a second," he said. "I just want to take a look at your face."

"No. I'm fine." She kept going, one foot in front of the other, shuffling along. "I wanna get there."

"Aimee," he said more loudly. "Stop." He gripped her arm.

She tried to pull it out of his grasp, but it was a half-hearted effort. "No. Keep going," she muttered.

He shone the flashlight in her face, and saw how pale she was, and how translucent and gray her lips looked. He aimed the light at her eyes. How did the prettiest, plumpest snowflakes always manage to get caught in her lashes? They drifted away as she blinked against the flashlight's bright beam.

Her pupils were dilated, and barely reacted to the light.

It was what he'd been afraid would happen.

Aimee was hypothermic. If they didn't get to the shelter soon, she could die.

Chapter Six

Matt knew hypothermia didn't require freezing temperatures to affect someone. But he also knew they were being pummeled by winds that made the temperature that was already below freezing seem at least five degrees colder.

Plus the snow was wet, and dampness was seeping into their clothing.

He pulled off his down jacket, wrapped it around Aimee and snapped it closed. That gave her two layers of down, the best light insulation there was.

Then he dug the hood out of its pocket and tugged it down over her balaclava. He should have done that a long time ago, but he'd overestimated her endurance.

"Not a good idea," she muttered.

"What?"

"Now you'll be cold. We'll both be cold." She giggled faintly.

He was worried about her. "Come on, Aimee. We're not far from the shelter. Let's race."

"No," she drawled. "Don't wanna race. Tired."

"I know," he said, putting his arm around her again to support her and urge her on ahead.

"Sleepy, too. I need to get home. William's waiting for me."

"Aimee, do you know where we're going?"

For a moment, she didn't answer. Then, quietly, almost too quietly for him to hear, she spoke. "Home?"

He tightened his arm around her waist. "Listen, Aimee. We're up on Ragged Top Mountain. We're having an adventure. It's kind of like a treasure hunt." The wet snow was beginning to penetrate his wool sweater and underwear. He shivered, wishing he had the waterproof poncho that had burned up in his backpack.

"It's really important that we get to the shelter within the next twenty minutes. Can you walk really fast?"

She nodded. "I'm not sure. My feet aren't there." She laughed, a sound like ice cubes tinkling in a glass. "I mean, I know they're there. I just can't feel 'em."

"That's okay. They're there. I can see them." Matt smiled at her and looked up at the dark, cloud-filled sky. *God, help me get her to the shelter in time. Don't let me lose her. William needs her—I need her.*

MATT LIFTED THE BLANKETS that hung over the door to the shelter and pushed Aimee inside.

He'd already made her wait while he reconnoitered to be sure no one else was there. He figured both the kidnapper and Al Hamar already had a destination. The kidnapper was headed for wherever he was keeping the baby. And if Al Hamar had any sense he'd get off the mountain and get his wound attended to.

The shelter was primitive, with a wide opening on the east side and blankets as the only coverings for the two windows that faced north and south. The inside was ice-cold, but this version of ice-cold was at least ten degrees warmer than the outside. He shuddered as his body took note of the small increase in warmth.

After shrugging off the daypack, he shone the flashlight's beam around. Two cots, a fireplace, a couple of chairs. He examined every inch of the space.

Firewood? Where was firewood? Then he saw it. A small pile of limbs and branches against the far wall.

Under a window. Coated with a sheen of snow. What idiot had stored the firewood there? He grimaced. The wood was wet.

"Matt?" Aimee's voice quivered.

He pulled her toward one of the cots. "I've got to get you out of those wet clothes," he said firmly. "And get you under the covers. Hurry."

She looked at him without moving.

He pushed his jacket off her shoulders and jerked the insulated hood and watch cap off her head. Her hair was wet and she was shivering so much her teeth chattered.

"Okay, Aimee. We're going to get you warm. Trust me?"

"I'm a little chilly," she whispered.

"I know, sweetie, I know." He unzipped her down parka and pushed it down her arms. "I'm just going to get these wet things off you, okay?"

She nodded shakily. "I'm sleepy."

"That's good," he lied. His second lie to her.

Drowsiness was a symptom of hypothermia, a severe one. It meant her body temperature was dropping to dangerous levels. He had to work fast.

By the time he got the parka and her hiking boots off,

she'd almost quit shivering. That wasn't a good sign, either.

He talked to her while he undressed her. Nonsense things. Little reassurances, endearments, the kind of things one might use to soothe a frightened child.

Finally, she was down to a little tank top and her underpants. They weren't wet, but there wasn't enough to them to provide any warmth. All they were good for was preserving a little of her modesty and titillating him a lot.

Her skin was cool to the touch, and her fingers and toes were cold. He examined them closely, but they didn't appear to be frostbitten—yet.

He was tempted to rub them, but he knew better. Too much rubbing could damage freezing skin and nerves permanently.

He checked out the cots, which, thank God, weren't near the windows. The blanket he unfolded was slightly damp, but it was made of wool. Even wet, wool would still keep her warm—once he *got* her warm.

He lay her down on the cot and put the blanket over her.

"Stay there, okay? I need to get a fire going." He grabbed two blankets from the other cot and piled them over her, too.

Then he turned to the fireplace. The wood stacked inside it was wet, like all the other firewood. He brushed the snow away from the wood piled under the window and dug through it.

Toward the bottom, he found some sticks that weren't wet through. Grabbing an armful, he stacked them in the fireplace and took a couple of wet-weather fire-starter sticks out of his pack. He placed them under the branches and lit them with all-weather matches.

The starter sticks flared immediately. Now if the wood would just catch before they burned out. He adjusted a limb here, a branch there, until he was sure it was arranged for the best draft, and that was it. That was all he could do.

He watched for a few seconds, encouraged by the crackling and spitting as the hot flames generated by the starter sticks burned off the dampness.

He stripped down quickly, until he was covered in nothing but his boxers and goose bumps. All his clothes were wet, even his insulated underwear.

He was shivering, and he knew his body temp was down, but he wasn't hypothermic, thank God. His core was still warm.

Working as quickly as he could, and keeping one eye on the struggling fire and one on Aimee, he spread their clothes on chairs that he sat in front of the fireplace. If he could get the fire going, maybe they'd dry by morning.

He found some hurricane candles on a shelf and lit them, then carefully poked at the fire, checking the draft. To his relief, a few of the small branches caught.

"Hey, Aimee, I think we're going to have a fire before too long." He rose and picked up one of the hurricane candles. Crossing the room to the cot, he held it so the light shone on her face.

"Aimee, are you awake?" Her eyes were closed and she was lying too still. He touched her cheek, then reached under the blanket and found her hand. Icy. Dammit. He looked at her fingers. They were still white and pinched.

"Okay," he said, hoping his voice sounded calmer than he felt. "I'll tell you what we're going to do. I'm going to move the other cot next to the fire and lay you there. I've got a mummy bag—that's a head-to-toe sleeping bag, made for subzero conditions. It's a single, but if I unzip it, we can both get under it, like a blanket. How does that sound?"

He didn't like that she was nonresponsive. He knew how to treat hypothermia, but most recommended treatments assumed that dry clothes and a heat source were available.

Until the fire caught enough to actually generate heat, Matt only had one source of warmth available— his own body.

He checked the other cot. At least it was no wetter than the one Aimee was on. He pulled it over in front of the hearth, grabbed two of the blankets from on top of Aimee, and spread them over the mattress. The wool would hold the heat in.

Then he bent over Aimee. "Aimee, sweetie, can you wake up? I need you to wake up for me."

She stirred and opened her eyes. They were glassy and not quite focused. "Is it William?" she whispered.

His heart twisted. She was dreaming, maybe even hallucinating. "Aimee, listen to me. Sit up for me. Can you tell me how you feel?"

"I'm tired," she said. "Sleepy."

"I know. And you can go to sleep, just as soon as we get you over closer to the fire and get you warm. Come on. Let's move over to the fireplace."

She pushed at the blankets covering her.

"That's good. Here. I'm going to pull the covers down so you can get up."

Her eyes met his briefly. "Matt," she said. "What a nice surprise. Bill will be so glad you're here."

He'd thought he couldn't carry any more guilt, but her slurred words cut him to his soul. She *was* hallucinating. She thought Bill was still alive, thought they were all still friends.

Don't worry, he told himself. *Tomorrow she'll remember, and hate you again.*

If she lived until tomorrow. Unless he got her warm, she wouldn't last that long.

"Let's go," he said and lifted her to her feet. She almost collapsed against him. He wrapped his arm around her waist and half carried her to the cot.

Her skin felt cool, pressed against his. He had to get her body temp up—and fast. "Here we are," he said softly. "Just lie down there, and I'll get the sleeping bag."

She obeyed him without protest. She lay down and closed her eyes. "Cold," she murmured.

"I know, Aimee, but I'm going to fix that." He grabbed his daypack and retrieved the small bundle that was the compressed down sleeping bag. He pulled it out of its stuff-sack, unzipped it and shook it out to fluff the down.

"I'm just going to lay the sleeping bag over you, and then I'll put a couple of blankets on top."

He looked down at her. She lay on her side, facing the hearth, with her arms wrapped around her middle. The warm light from the fire made her pale skin look like the color of a ripe peach. Her bare legs and arms were silky and delicately muscled. The little top and panties emphasized her slender curves. Her dark hair was still damp and beginning to wave around her face.

She looked the way she had in high school. Fresh, beautiful, vibrant. No wonder Bill had fallen in love with her.

Matt swallowed against the lump that rose in his throat from just looking at her.

"All right, scumbag," he muttered to himself as he spread the down bag over her like a blanket. "Stop ogling and get started warming her up."

He fetched two more blankets. The down inside the sleeping bag was the ideal insulator. It was lightweight, held in heat and wicked out moisture. But Matt wanted some weight on top to seal in the heat his body produced, because he couldn't afford to lose even a couple of calories to the chilly room.

He carefully placed the blankets over the spread-out sleeping bag. Then, after a check of the fire to be sure it was lit and growing, he slid under the covers. Aimee's back was to him, so he cautiously moved closer. The scent of lemon assaulted his nostrils. How, after everything she'd been through, did she still smell so fresh and clean?

Her skin was cold, but apparently his body didn't care. When his groin came in contact with her backside, he swallowed a groan and grimaced. The feel of her supple body affected him—a *lot*.

He felt himself growing hard, felt his heart rate rise. Clenching his teeth and cursing himself for his weakness, he pulled away.

Aimee whimpered and scooted backward slightly.

Since her skin felt cool to him, his must feel hot to hers. "Okay, Aimee. I'm going to get as close to you as I can—" *and keep my sanity.* "It's just to warm you up. I promise I won't make you uncomfortable." Too bad he couldn't promise himself the same thing.

He scooted closer, wrapping his arm across her shoulders and pulling her close to his chest. He knew he had to concentrate on her core, rather than her chilled arms and legs. What made hypothermia deadly was that the body got chilled straight through. The most important thing was to warm up the vital organs. Once her core temperature rose, her arms and legs would start warming up.

He gritted his teeth and pressed his thighs against the backs of her legs.

Keep it professional, Parker.

After a while, Aimee's breathing grew more even, and she relaxed.

Matt lay there, listening to the wind and silently thanking whoever had built the shelter for taking the weather patterns up here into consideration. The shelter's solid back wall was turned against the predominant wind direction, which was easterly.

Aimee sighed in her sleep, and half turned, so that her cheek was no more than an inch from his nose. In the firelight he could see the faint dusting of freckles on her smooth skin. The scent of lemon and the delicate curve of her cheek made his mouth water.

He slid his hand down her arm, doing his best to avoid touching any other part of her. When he reached her wrist, he pressed his fingertips against the silky skin and counted her pulse. It was faint but steady. Then he took her hand in his.

At least her fingers weren't icy cold anymore. He sighed in relief. She was warming up. He was pretty sure she was out of danger. But he knew that if it had taken them any longer to get here, and if he hadn't been able to get a fire started, she could have died.

He breathed deeply and tried to relax. For the

moment, they were safe. He needed to get as much rest as he could while he had the chance.

Because tomorrow wasn't going to be easy. Tomorrow, he was going to have to explain to her why they were pressed up against each other and practically naked, why it made sense that he'd brought her up the mountain instead of down, and why he hadn't kept his promise to her—his promise to place William Matthew safely into her arms before the day was out.

Chapter Seven

Aimee came awake slowly. She was hot. And thirsty. She stirred, trying to push the covers back, but they wouldn't move. Someone was lying very close to her—too close. Someone with a very large, very warm body.

Her eyes flew open, and she saw the crackling fire. *Fire?*

Where was she? Her pulse thrummed in her throat and she suddenly felt claustrophobic. She pushed herself up to a sitting position, kicking at the covers and gasping for breath.

"Aimee?"

"Who—?" She dug her heels in and propelled her body backward, away from whoever was pressing so close against her. She sucked in a huge breath, preparing to scream.

"Aimee, it's Matt."

A hand touched her shoulder.

She gasped and coughed.

"Shh. You're okay."

"Matt?" She blinked and looked at the figure that sat up next to her. "Matt? What are you doing—?"

She pushed at him.

"Aimee, whoa! You're going to fall off the cot."

He reached out toward her, but she recoiled instinctively. She was in bed—in bed! What kind of crazy dream was she having about Matt, of all people?

"I was just trying to warm you up. You were cold—too cold. I had to get your body temperature up. Do you remember?"

She stared at him, trying to process what he was saying. She couldn't, any more than she could figure out why she was here in this strange room next to him.

He was bare-chested, his skin glowing like gold in the firelight. His dark hair was tousled and wavy, as if he'd just toweled it dry.

She lifted the edge of the covers and looked down at herself. All she had on was a little tank top and panties.

"What's going on? Why—?" Had Matt undressed her? She raised her shocked gaze to his and absently registered a look of apology in his expression.

"I had to," he said. "You were freezing."

She stared at him as bits of memories flashed across her brain.

Matt wrapping an arm around her and telling her she was going to be okay.

Snow blowing in her face, her eyes and lips stinging with cold—the smell of gasoline—the sounds of gunfire—

And the awful, menacing words crackling down the phone wire. "If you want to see your baby again, *you* will deliver the money."

If you want to see your baby again—

"William!" she cried, his name ripping from her throat. Suddenly they were all there. All the memories. All the terror. All the anguish. "My baby! Where is he?"

"Aimee, shh. Try to stay calm."

She heard the words, but hardly registered where they came from. All she knew was that they cut like a razor through her heart.

"Calm? My baby is gone. They stole him, out of his bed." Her hands flew to her mouth. "I was asleep. I was asleep and they took him."

Her eyes burned, and her mouth was dry. So dry. She licked her lips.

"You're thirsty. I'll get you some water."

It was Matt, she realized. Bill's best friend.

Safe as houses.

But he wasn't. He'd taken Bill away from her and let him die. He'd shown up like a knight in shining armor at the very moment when she needed a hero, but he'd let William's kidnapper get away, and he didn't save her baby. Pain lanced through her and she clutched at her middle.

When Matt rose, she saw that his lower body was almost as bare as his upper. He was dressed in nothing but snug-fitting boxers.

They *both* were nearly naked. She rubbed her temple, wishing she could put all this information together and come up with a reasonable understanding of what was happening.

She knew who he was now. And she knew they hadn't rescued William. But where were they? And how had they gotten there?

"I melted some snow, once the fire got going," he said conversationally. He picked up a metal cup and filled it from a pan that sat near the fireplace.

"Here." He held out the cup.

She couldn't move. She still clutched the covers to her chest like a shield.

"Come on, Aimee. Take the cup. You need to drink some water." Slowly, carefully, he reached out a hand and took hers, gently prying her fingers loose from the blanket, and pressed the cup into her palm. It was cool.

He turned and went back to the fire, where he picked up pieces of clothing. For the first time she noticed two straight-backed chairs by the hearth.

He piled the clothes on the hearth and spread other pieces over the backs of the chairs.

She watched him as she lifted the cup to her lips. The flat, tepid water tasted wonderful. She drank the whole cupful.

"Our clothes will probably be dry by morning."

"Could I have some more?" she asked, and at once felt guilty because she was warm and safe and enjoying water while her baby was out there somewhere— alone. Maybe thirsty. Maybe cold. The pain hit her again, swift and sharp.

"Oh—" she gasped.

Matt took the cup from her hands. "What's wrong? Are you hurting?"

"I want—I need my baby." Tears stung her eyes, but she lifted her chin and swallowed them. "Do you—" She paused, terribly afraid she knew the answer to the question she was about to ask. "Do you know where he is?"

He filled the cup and handed it back to her, then filled another one and drank it himself. He went back to checking and rearranging the clothing. "No. I don't know where he is right now. But the storm is almost over and I'm hoping that by morning the clouds will have cleared away. We'll meet Deke at the rendezvous point and he can take you back with him. As soon as I find William, I'll—"

"What?" She was still having trouble sorting everything out, but her brain finally put his words together in the proper order.

He can take you back with him.

"No!" She slammed the cup down on the wooden floor with a clang. "I am not going back without my baby."

"Aimee, you have to. You can't stay up here. I don't have the supplies or shelter to take care of you."

"Why can't Deke bring supplies?"

"Because he's going to get you to get you to safety while I rescue William." He picked up a pair of dark leggings, pulled them up and tugged a matching long-sleeved shirt over his head.

"But—"

"Listen to me, Aimee. I can't concentrate on rescuing William if I'm worried about you." He sorted through the clothes until he found her silk turtleneck and handed it to her.

"You need to put this on and get back under the covers. It's still a couple of hours until morning. After the snowstorm started, you got hypothermic. So from now on you're going to be susceptible to the cold. You need all the strength you can muster."

She took the shirt and pulled it on. "Don't ignore me,

Matt. And don't treat me like I'm going to break. I was confused when I first woke up, but I'm not now." *Not completely.*

She smoothed the shirt down over her abdomen. "I can't sleep anymore. William is out there. I have to get ready. We have to go find him."

Matt sat on his haunches, tossed back the rest of his water and sat the cup on the hearth. He picked up a stick and poked the fire.

"You need to rest," he said again, not looking at her.

She wanted to be angry at him, needed to be. But his quiet, deliberate actions didn't invite attacks. In fact, his composure was calming.

For a moment she was mesmerized by the silhouette of his profile, outlined by the orange glow from the coals. It was classic and grim. She could believe he was an ancient warrior, staring into the flames as he prepared his mind for battle.

Suddenly, a memory from the night before flashed across her mind. He'd been lying next to her on the cot, his legs and chest pressed against her from behind. She remembered the thick warmth of his skin against hers, the rapid rise and fall of his chest and belly. The feel of his erection, hard and hot against her. He'd groaned, then whispered something.

I promise.

That was all she remembered. But she knew that, whatever that promise had been, he'd keep it.

It occurred to her that he was in his element here. Weather and survival had been his specialties in the Air Force. There were probably only a handful of people in the world as well trained as Matt to rescue her baby.

He hadn't been exaggerating when he said he couldn't take care of her and do his job. She was definitely a handicap. She knew that. He couldn't move as fast or as stealthily with her along. He couldn't focus all his concentration and energy on overpowering the kidnapper and rescuing William if he had to be concerned about her safety. But she was right, too. When he found William, she had to be there.

Matt might be the only person she could trust to find her child, but she was the only one who could protect him.

BY THE TIME they got away from the shelter, it was after 0700 hours. Matt had figured out hours earlier that they were going to miss the 0800 rendezvous point he'd arranged with Deke. To have any chance of making it, they'd have had to leave before daylight, while the wet snow was still falling. And he wasn't about to expose Aimee to the possibility of hypothermia again.

He'd ventured out of the shelter several times during the night to check the weather. The storm had done exactly what he'd figured it would do. It had moved in ahead of predictions. But what he hadn't expected was the second front that had moved in right behind it. He'd seen the low pressure system that had been building behind the first. It hadn't looked significant, and it had been hours behind the first, larger storm.

But then the first storm had stalled, hovering over the mountain for hours after its predicted movement eastward. The extra time gave the second storm plenty of time to catch up and gain strength.

Yesterday's weather forecast had the second storm not moving in for another twelve hours. However, by the time the first storm passed through, the second one was already rolling in.

The good news was that it was a weaker front, and hadn't dropped nearly as much snow. By 0630 the snow had stopped and the storm was beginning to dissipate.

Matt figured that within another hour the skies might be clear enough for him to use his satellite phone.

He'd found a pair of snowshoes in the shelter. He gave them to Aimee, despite her protests. He could survive, even if his feet got wet. She couldn't.

In the place of the snowshoes, the firewood, a liter-sized plastic bottle filled with melted snow, and two of the wool blankets, Matt had left four of his eight remaining fire-starter sticks and extra all-weather matches for the next traveler who sought refuge there.

He'd fashioned one of the blankets into a makeshift pack, tying the corners into knots and using duct tape from his daypack. So this morning he carried the makeshift pack containing his electronic devices, the water, the other blanket, several high-calorie protein bars, and the money, and Aimee carried the daypack with the sleeping bag and the lighter items. He had the heavy machine pistol and she had the Glock.

"Let's go, Aimee," he called. He'd told her to stay in the shelter until he was sure they were ready to go.

She appeared at the opening, stuffing strands of hair inside the balaclava she'd folded up and donned like a ski cap. Her face was rosy and fresh-looking. Thank God her pallor from the night before was gone.

"You walk in front."

"Are you sure?" she asked. "Wouldn't it be better if you set the pace?"

He looked at her in surprise. "That's a good question."

"You don't have to act like you're about to faint. I told you, I've done a little hiking in my time."

"Letting me set the pace would be a good idea, if we were evenly matched. But you wouldn't be able to keep up with me. If I lead, I'll be tempted to walk too fast, and then I'll have to slow down to let you catch up. That'll be extremely tiring for me. At the same time, you'll be trying to keep pace when I speed up, which will make *you* very tired. If you set the pace, you can adjust it to your level of conditioning, and I can find your rhythm. That way we'll both conserve our energy."

Aimee sent him a little smile. "All that *and* good-looking."

His brows rose. She'd surprised him again.

"Yeah," he replied. It was good to see her smile. He suspected it was unlikely that she was genuinely amused. She was probably just putting on a front, hoping he wouldn't figure out how scared she was.

As if he could miss it.

She moved in front of him, a little uncertain balancing on the snowshoes.

After the third time she almost stumbled, he called out, "I thought you'd done some hiking."

"I didn't say it was in snow."

He smiled again, and a warmth that had nothing to do with the temperature spread through him. "Now you tell me."

He looked at his watch. By his best calculations, they were about six miles away from where Deke would be circling, looking for them.

Judging by the time they'd made last night, allowing for the fact that they weren't battling a snowstorm and Aimee wasn't handicapped by hypothermia this morning, it would still take them at least two hours, maybe more, to get there, trudging through the wet, packed snow. He figured the temperature was about thirty degrees.

And it would rise as the sun rose. While that meant they'd spend the day peeling off layers of clothing so they wouldn't sweat, at least the heat would burn off the rest of the clouds.

Aimee said something that the wind picked up and blew away.

"What?" he called out.

She turned her head. "Do the clouds look like they're thinning? Can you get a signal on your phone?"

He looked up at the clouds that hung heavily above them. They were dissipating behind them, to the west. Pulling out the satellite phone, he checked the signal.

Nothing.

"Not yet."

He kept checking over the next hour. Finally, the phone responded with a weak signal. He dialed Irina.

"Matt!" she cried as soon as she picked up the phone. "What happened? Where are you? Do you have the baby?"

"No. But the kidnapper doesn't have the money, either. We're headed toward the first rendezvous point, but we're not going to make it in time. Tell Deke we can be there by 1000 hours for sure—"

"Matt, listen. The helicopter's been sabotaged."

Had he heard right? "Sabotaged? There at the ranch with all your security? That's impossible!"

"It happened. We don't know how. Someone drained all the oil. When Deke tried to take off, the motor burned up. It's going to take all day to put in a new motor."

"Deke would never take off without checking everything."

"Right. The oil gauge registered full. It had been tampered with."

"What can he do? I need to get Aimee out of here. She's not trained for this weather or this terrain, and most of my supplies burned up in the Hummer."

"Repeat. I missed that."

"My supplies burned up in the Hummer."

"The Hummer burned? You're on foot?"

"Yeah."

"—get Deke right on it. But listen. There's something—at least two more—"

"You're breaking up."

"More storms—this way."

"Okay. I'll check it out."

"There's one blowing in now. It'll probably reach—area—Ragged Top within the next two hours."

"Damn," Matt breathed. "Okay. I can deal with the weather. What else?"

"It's big, Matt. Schiff got an anonymous call early this morning. The caller said—Aimee's ba—the Vick cabin—get that?"

"Baby? Cabin?" Matt looked at Aimee. She'd been listening to his side of the conversation the whole time. She met his gaze. He knew shock and relief were plastered all over his face.

Her face lit up, tempered with hesitancy, as if she

weren't quite sure she should actually dare to be excited yet.

He nodded at her and smiled. "Got it."

"—gave him the kidna—"

"Gave him what?"

"Name. It's Kinnard."

"Kinnard?"

"The police are familiar with him. He's a small-time hood—muscle for some local loan sharks, that sort of thing. And years ago—arently did work for Boss—"

"For who?"

"Boss Vick."

That shocked Matt. He turned away from Aimee's curious gaze. For the moment, it might be wise to keep that last tidbit of information to himself.

"Can you verify that?"

"Margo denies ever hearing—less knowing him— warrant for—papers. But—to take—"

"Irina, I can barely understand you. Can Deke make the Sunday rendezvous?"

"—get in—pick up—Sunday 0900."

"Got it, 0900. Out."

Matt disconnected, and then tried to access the weather reports via satellite. But the cloud cover was getting thicker, and reception was spotty.

He'd have to continue to rely on old-fashioned methods of reading the weather and predicting what would happen next.

"Matt?" Aimee had waited patiently while he talked to Irina, but he could see that she was bursting with curiosity. "Did she say *baby?* At the cabin?" she asked hesitantly.

"Someone called in an anonymous tip this morning, letting the FBI know that your baby, your William, is there."

"He's there? At the cabin? Oh—" Aimee capped a hand over her mouth. Her eyes glittered with unshed tears. "Oh, Matt. Do you think the caller was telling the truth? Do you really think he's all right?"

Matt nodded. "From what Irina said, it sounds like he's fine."

She pressed her fingertips to her lips for a few seconds, then ran toward him.

Before he realized what she was doing, she slammed into him, wrapping her arms around his neck and hugging him tighter than he'd ever been hugged in his life.

He stood there for a second, not knowing how to react. But her joy, her relief, her sheer happiness at knowing her child was safe, began to seep in past his reserve. He wrapped his arms around her and hugged her back.

She buried her face in the hollow between his neck and shoulder and hung on. After a few seconds, he realized that he felt tears against his neck.

"Hey," he said, gently pushing her away and peering at her. "Are you okay?"

She nodded as tears flowed down her cheeks and ran over the corner of her mouth. She sniffed. "I'm so—so relieved. I was so scared."

His heart was twisting again. He'd never known an internal organ could warp in so many different directions. "I know you were. I don't think I've ever seen you cry."

She swiped her fingers across her cheeks. "I don't. Ever."

"I guess this is a pretty special occasion then."

Her smile broadened and she laughed. "I guess it is." She blew air out between her lips, wiped her cheeks again, and then straightened and looked him in the eye.

"So how far are we from the cabin? How fast can we get there? Who's there with him?"

"Whoa," Matt said, holding up his hands. "I can't tell you who's there with him, but I can tell you that we're about ten miles from the cabin and we can get there in four or five hours. But only if you turn around and walk."

She grinned at him. "Which direction?"

The maps he'd memorized suddenly went completely out of his head, knocked out by the dazzle of her grin. He'd seen it before, of course, but not in a long time. And never directed solely at him.

"Hang on a minute," he croaked, holding up a hand. He pulled his glove off with his teeth and retrieved the printed maps from his pocket. After a little shuffling, he came up with the right one.

"Okay. Bear 18 degrees north of east."

"Bear what?"

He laughed ruefully, held up the compass and took the reading, then pointed. "Go thataway."

She turned and looked. "Thataway?"

He shook his head. "Walk!"

With a swish of her hips, the impact of which was mostly lost under the down parka, Aimee turned and started walking.

Matt stuffed his maps back into his pocket and tugged on his glove, all the while lecturing himself about how uncool it was to be lusting after his best friend's widow.

Especially here. Especially now. They were in a dangerous situation. His job was to take care of her, to protect her. Getting emotional led to screwups. He knew that from personal experience.

Twenty years ago, he, Deke, Rook and Bill had found themselves trapped on a mountain ledge when a storm blew in. He'd been the youngest of the four, and the most scared. Rook and Deke, and even Bill, only two months older than him, had stayed calm. But he'd sobbed as the reclusive Vietnam vet Arlis Hanks had pulled him up using a rope and a block and tackle. That was the last time he'd cried.

Shaking his head at the memory, Matt looked up.

Aimee was nowhere in sight.

Chapter Eight

"Aimee!" Matt shouted. "Aimee!" His heart slammed against his chest wall, ripping the breath from his lungs.

He broke into a run. The terrain here was fairly even, and the trees were sparse. He could see for several yards. How could she have disappeared?

God, please don't let her have fallen over a ledge.

That thought stopped him in his tracks as alarm sheared his breath.

Stay calm. Cool. Rational.

The words echoed in his head with each cautious step he took. Combined with deep, even breaths, they helped to slow his pounding heart. He placed his feet into her snowshoe prints.

Within about ten paces he saw the indented ribbon of snow that marked a creek bed. She must have fallen in.

"Aimee!" he shouted.

"Matt! Here!" Her voice was shrill with fear.

"Stay still. I'll be right there." Within a few steps, he could see the hole in the snow. He approached carefully.

Several feet from the place where Aimee had fallen, he lowered himself to his hands and knees and crawled until he could peer over the edge.

Aimee was sitting in a pile of snow.

"Aimee? Don't move. Are you all right?"

She looked up. "Yes," she said disgustedly. "My butt hurts, but not as much as my pride." She moved to stand.

"Wait. Are you sure you're okay? Nothing's sprained? Wrists? Ankles?"

She shook her head. "I've checked everything. I didn't move because I didn't know how I was going to get back up there."

Matt laughed. "That's easy," he said, and proceeded to show her just how easy it was.

Back on high ground and standing beside Matt, Aimee brushed snow off her pants as she surveyed the place where she'd fallen. "What did I fall into?"

"A creek bed, and not even a very deep one." He pointed behind them and then in front, tracing the creek's meandering path to where it disappeared among the evergreen trees. "See that narrow ribbon of snow that's kind of sunken?"

"Oh. I should have seen that." It would have saved her a sore butt and sore pride. "So all that extra snow blew into the creek? It sort of collects it, I guess."

"That's exactly right. Spend much time hiking in the snow and you learn to notice things you might not otherwise. Little signs like that dip in the snow or a shadow that might indicate a rock. Things that can hurt you or even kill you if you don't pay attention."

"Okay, so tell me again why I'm leading, if you're the expert?" She grinned at him. Not even her fall could spoil her good mood. She felt like laughing and running and dancing.

In a little while, she would have her baby back in her arms, safe and sound. That was worth every minute of the past day. Every second.

Matt's brows drew down. "Good point," he said. "Okay. I'll take the lead, but you've got to keep up. Tell me if I go too fast."

"Okay, sir," she said. "You go in front, sir, and I'll follow. But please, keep showing me the secrets the snow is covering up. Never know when that kind of thing might come in handy."

Before they headed out again, Matt shed his parka and stuffed it inside his makeshift pack.

The snug-fitting wool sweater he wore over his insulated underwear glistened in the sunlight. Wool was too fuzzy to clearly outline the muscles in his arms and torso, but Aimee hadn't forgotten how he looked with the firelight glinting off the planes and angles of his naked torso last night. Nor had she forgotten how his warm, strong body felt pressed against her.

Bill had been good-looking, with his light brown hair, his hazel eyes and the dimples all the girls in high school had gone crazy over. He was always voted most handsome and most likely to succeed. He'd been big and tall, and captain of the football team.

Matt, on the other hand, had once been voted most shy. His dark hair, brown eyes and strong features weren't as classically handsome as Bill's had been. His nose was a little too long, and he'd never played football. He'd been on the swim team. His muscles had always been long and lean. In fact, some had considered him downright scrawny.

But after last night, Aimee had decided that Matt was a dangerously attractive and sexy man.

"Okay, let's go," he said, sending her a puzzled look. "You sure you're okay?"

She nodded and shrugged her shoulders to rearrange the daypack into a comfortable position. As she moved into step behind him, she considered her thoughts.

She was sure she'd seen him in a bathing suit. She was positive she had. She and Bill and Matt had all gone down to Florida on spring break one year, and they'd all stayed in the same room. But she hardly remembered Matt at all. What she remembered about that trip was that she and Bill had had sex for the first time. In the hotel room—with Matt asleep on the other bed.

Her cheeks burned. Dear heavens, what had she been thinking? Granted, it was years ago, probably long forgotten by Matt, if he'd even woken up, but still—how embarrassing.

And now, after having spent the night pressed against his lean, hard body, thinking about that long-ago experience kind of turned her on. Guilt brought heat to her cold cheeks.

Stop it, she warned herself.

Matt held up a hand. "Shh."

She froze.

He sent her a quick look over his shoulder, and then cocked his head, listening.

Before she realized that he'd moved, Matt had grabbed her arm and pulled her toward him. He propelled her over to a stand of trees and followed her several feet in, until they were surrounded by trees on all sides.

Then he crouched down, and pulled her back between his knees.

"Stay quiet," he whispered in her ear.

"What is—"

He put his fingers across her mouth. She nodded against them and after a couple of seconds, he removed them.

For a long time, they crouched there, spooned awkwardly. Even through layers of clothes, the sense of intimacy was as strong as it had been the night before.

Her insides stirred, tingling with sensations that she hadn't felt in a long time. She yearned to lean back, to press herself against Matt the way he'd pressed his body against hers last night. Her eyes drifted closed as the tingling centered itself in her core.

He put his hands on her shoulders. She wanted to cover them with hers, to take them and pull them around her, so she could feel the way she'd felt last night. As much as it scared her to admit that she wanted him, that was how much she longed for him to touch her, to kiss her and, yes, to make love with her.

She told herself it was because he made her feel safe.

His fingers squeezed her shoulders, massaging them. He leaned forward, his breath warming her cheek. Was he feeling the same thing she was?

Then she heard it. A buzzing sound. Very faint. She turned her head but she couldn't tell where it was coming from. What was it? An engine?

Her pulse sped up. An engine. A helicopter! Maybe it was Deke, coming to rescue them. He could take them to the Vicks' cabin and help them rescue William. Her breath caught in an excited sob.

But if it were Deke's helicopter, why were they hiding?

"Is that an engine?" she whispered.

Matt put his ear next to hers and nodded his head.

"Helicopter?" she asked hopefully.

He shook his head no. "Snowmobile."

Snowmobile? But that could be anybody.

Anybody.

"Oh."

He pressed his fingertips against her lips again, warning her to stay quiet.

Slowly, over what seemed to be an endless stretch of time, the noise of the engine grew louder. It kept growing louder, until it sounded like it was close enough to run them down.

Matt put his hand on the back of her head. "Put your head down. And don't move."

As she lowered her head, Matt pressed his forehead against her back. She could imagine what the two of them looked like. Two small, fragile humans dwarfed by the tall trees, crouched together, hoping and praying that they couldn't be seen by someone whizzing by on a snowmobile. Or someone searching for them—

Her heart pounded so loud she was afraid it could be heard over the motor's noise.

As the engine noise grew deafening, she felt Matt straighten. He left his hand resting gently on the back of her neck, so she didn't budge. He grew so still that if it weren't for the slow, steady rise and fall of his chest, she might have been able to forget he was there, pressed against her.

Okay, no. She wouldn't forget the feeling of his body molded to hers—not for a very long time.

Finally, the noise of the engine faded into the distance. Aimee waited until Matt took his hand away from the nape of her neck before she sat up.

"Ah," she moaned as her muscles relaxed from their cramped position. She looked at Matt. "Who was it? Could you see anything?"

He nodded grimly.

"Was it the kidnapper?"

"Nope. It was Al Hamar. There was a lot of blood on his pants. The kidnapper must have hit him in the side. He didn't look happy, but he didn't look like he was too handicapped by the wound, either."

"He didn't see us." She phrased it as a statement, but she watched Matt's face for confirmation. "Where do you think he's going?"

He rubbed his thumb across his lower lip, and averted his gaze. "I'm afraid he's probably headed for the cabin, just as we are."

And as quickly as that, all sense of safety, all confidence, all joy at the knowledge that William was only a few miles away and safe, dissolved, and Aimee was back in that awful place where she'd existed since six-thirty Wednesday morning.

"Why?" she moaned. "I thought you didn't think he was connected with the kidnapping. How would he know about the cabin?"

Matt's jaw clenched. After an instant of wavering, his gaze met hers. "All I can figure out is that both he and Kinnard are—"

"Kinnard?" Aimee didn't like how Matt was acting. He obviously didn't want to tell her something.

"That's the kidnapper's name."

"The man who took William? Who is he?"

"According to the FBI, he's a small-time hood who has operated around the Crook County area for the past twenty years or so."

"You said *apparently.*"

Matt straightened. "We should get going."

"No. *You* should tell me what's going on. Who do you think Kinnard is, and what are you trying not to tell me?"

"I think both men are working for Novus Ordo."

"Novus Ordo? The terrorist?" She felt the blood drain from her face. She'd thought nothing could be as bad as having her baby kidnapped. But by *terrorists?*

"You're talking about Novus Ordo?" she asked. "The man whose face nobody has ever seen? The one they say is more dangerous than Bin Laden?"

Matt swallowed and reluctantly met her gaze. "We believe he had Rook Castle assassinated, because Rook saw him—he may be the only person outside Novus's inner circle who has ever seen the man's face."

"I don't—understand." What did Rook Castle and an infamous terrorist have to do with her? With her baby?

"I know. It's complicated. But the theory is that since Rook's body was never recovered, and since Irina has been searching for him all this time, Novus has been watching her, just in case."

"In case Rook is still alive." Aimee couldn't believe she was hearing—much less beginning to understand—what Matt was saying.

Matt nodded. "So since security is so tight around Castle Ranch that Irina and Deke are virtually untouchable, Novus is trying to capture me, to interrogate me about Rook."

"So a *terrorist* kidnapped *my baby* to get to you?"

"I'm not positive, but if Kinnard is working for Novus, and if the anonymous caller was telling the truth—"

"Then the cabin is a trap." Aimee's heart felt ripped to shreds. She put her gloved hands to her mouth and breathed into them, trying to stop the panic from rising in her throat. She spoke, her words muffled by the thick gloves.

"We can't go to the cabin." She swallowed panic and fear and breathed in courage. "They'll capture you."

Matt took her hands away from her mouth and held them. "I made you a promise. Nothing—*nothing*—is going to stop me from keeping it."

Her breath hitched.

"Everything we know points to William being at the cabin. We're going."

SATURDAY 1400 HOURS

"REMEMBER WHAT I TOLD YOU," Matt said.

Aimee barely heard him. It had taken four hours, but they were finally looking down at the cabin from their vantage point on a rise to the west.

She stared at the primitive log structure. She knew a little about it from Bill. His father, Boss Vick, had spent an obscene amount of money to equip the simple dwelling.

He'd brought a crew up one summer who'd cleared trees, installed a generator and carted appliances and furniture up. He'd made it into a comfortable winter retreat, if one didn't mind skiing in or living with the prospect of being snowed in.

Aimee had always thought the idea of spending so

much on a hunting shack was wasteful, but right now, the amenities sounded wonderful to her—the generator, the appliances, the comfortable furnishings—because they meant that her baby was warm and comfortable and well-fed.

And in the hands of terrorists.

"Aimee? Did you hear me?"

She nodded. "I don't make a move until you've gone down there and verified that nobody is waiting to shoot us when we step out into the open." She couldn't take her eyes off the house. She squinted, but couldn't see through any of the windows. But that was okay. Whether she could see him or not, her baby was in there. Her fingers itched—her arms ached—to hold him.

But Matt was right. They had to take precautions. There were at least two people on this mountain who meant them harm.

"You'll wave *all clear,* and motion me to come down. Or you'll hold up your hands, palms out, and press them down, meaning stay where I am." She demonstrated what he'd shown her earlier.

"Good. And if something happens to me?"

She pressed her lips together and squeezed her eyes shut. "I run for the cabin. Matt, maybe this is not a good idea. Maybe we ought to wait until Deke gets here. Spend the night up here, or—"

It nearly killed her to suggest waiting. She thought she was going to die if she had to wait one second longer to hold her baby, but the prospect of Matt being captured by terrorists—captured and interrogated—was nearly as horrible to contemplate as the possibility that she might never see William again.

"No." He shook his head, dislodging snowflakes from his hair. He held out his gloved hand and several more fell onto it. "See that? It's starting to snow again. The storms from last night are only the beginning. There are more stacked up, waiting for their shot at us. And we have no shelter." He craned his neck and examined the sky.

"There's a very good chance that we wouldn't survive the night. With just the mummy bag for the two of us, it's too risky. Getting to the cabin is our best chance."

"What if we both go down at the same time? We can watch each other's backs. You'll have that machine gun thing and I have the Glock. We can hold them off."

His face softened into an almost-smile. "Or…we could wait until nightfall. We could probably sit out a storm during the day without freezing to death. Even behind the clouds, the sun still provides a lot of heat. But after sundown is a different story."

"I like that idea—waiting until dark."

Matt kept his gaze on the cabin and the surrounding area. "We need to get to work if we're going to spend the rest of the day here. I want to build a snow shelter. It'll hide us and keep us warm after the clouds roll in. Plus it'll protect us from the snow and the wind." He peered through the trees at the cabin, then scanned the tree line above and below the clearing. He didn't see anyone.

That didn't surprise him. Kinnard was definitely right at home on the mountain, and Al Hamar was almost certainly from a mountainous country—Afghanistan or Pakistan—and trained in guerrilla tactics. Either one of them could be anywhere—in the cabin or hiding out, ready to ambush Matt and Aimee as they approached it.

"We don't want to be seen, so we have to work quickly and at the same time stay hidden. So be prepared to crawl around."

"What do you need me to do?"

"Right now, keep an eye on the cabin while I scout around for the best place to locate our shelter. I like that overhanging rock over there. We need to hurry, though. From the looks of the sky, by the time we get the shelter built, we're going to be very glad to have it."

SURE ENOUGH, by the time the shelter was ready, the new storm had rolled in, bringing another sky full of heavy, snow-laden clouds and a nasty mix of freezing rain and snow.

Aimee sat inside the cramped space, waiting for Matt to come inside. He'd spread a space blanket on the ground and folded one of the blankets on top of it. He'd covered the downhill side of the lean-to with the other blanket, and that made a huge difference in the inside temperature.

Matt pushed aside the blanket and climbed inside, bringing freezing air and icy spray with him. He'd taken off his parka, which he draped over the make-shift backpack. "Not bad, if I do say so myself. What do you think?"

She tried to smile, but she knew she wasn't pulling it off. "Better than the Ritz."

"Hey," he said, his voice closer than she'd expected. It was nearly pitch-black with the blanket closed. And granted, the entire space of the shelter was about six feet by three feet. Still, she'd figured he'd hover near one side and she'd cling to the other.

"How're you doing? It'll be dark within about three hours. Then we can sneak down to the cabin and check things out. Meanwhile…" He paused and took a breath. "Meanwhile, you should take off your parka. Believe it or not, it'll be easier to adjust to the temperature without it on. Plus, when we get ready to go, you'll be glad you have another layer to put on."

Aimee carefully shrugged out of the down jacket. She held on to it and used it to cover her hands. She'd taken off her gloves, which were wet from piling and packing snow.

"Matt, can I ask you a question?"

"Sure. Anything."

"You said Irina and Deke were untouchable because of the security around the ranch."

"Right. Rook installed the best equipment money could buy. And all the employees are screened carefully."

"But when you were talking to Irina, you mentioned sabotage. At the ranch."

He stared at her for a moment. "I did. Somebody tampered with Deke's helicopter. Irina said it was definitely sabotage." He cursed. "I heard it but it didn't sink in. Irina could be in danger." He shook his head.

"You're awfully hard on yourself."

"What?"

Aimee sent him a small smile. "You're out here, protecting me, and doing your best to rescue my baby, but at the same time you're beating yourself up for not thinking about Irina's possible danger."

He shrugged. "I feel responsible."

"I know you do. It's the kind of man you are." She settled against the rock that formed the back of their lean-to. "From everything I know about Deke Cunning-ham, I'm guessing he can protect Irina."

"Yeah. He can."

For several minutes, they sat silently. Aimee could feel Matt's tension. Was he still kicking himself? She figured it was time to change the subject.

She looked around at the shelter he'd built. "I guess this is how the first Americans lived for hundreds of years."

"Thousands. Yeah. We're soft these days."

"Not you," she said, poking his bicep with her finger.

He laughed, a soft rumbling sound. "Yeah, me."

She lay her hand on his arm. "Not you," she murmured.

His gaze snapped to hers. Even in the near blackness, his dark eyes picked up a reflection from somewhere. And in that reflection was the thing that had been born of their necessary closeness in the shelter the night before. The awareness that they were not just two people bound by their love for his friend and her husband.

Aimee cringed at what she'd done. One poke might have been just an innocent gesture. One teasing touch could be ascribed to friendship. But she'd touched him twice. She'd *lingered.*

That was no innocent gesture.

After the awkward silence had swelled to uncomfortable proportions, he uttered a small chuckle. "Oh? Well, what about you? You aren't looking so bad." He slid his hand along the line of her shoulder and upper arm. "A little on this side of skinny."

That was all. Yet her body burned as if he'd trailed hot fingers over its entire length.

"My guess is you've got some fair-sized biceps yourself."

Aimee moistened her lips.

Innocent teasing, she told herself. That's all it was. How long had it been since she'd felt like laughing, even a little bit? Other than when she played with William. Besides, she'd known Matt for most of her life. He was a friend.

There might be a smidgen of sexual tension between them, the natural attraction between a man and a woman forced together by circumstance. That's all this was.

Natural. Understandable. Easily ignored.

What could a little teasing hurt? It was better than sitting here in gloomy silence for hours. A little humor would help pass the time.

She squeezed her fist and flexed her arm muscles. "Fair-sized biceps? I beg your pardon. Check this out."

His fingers closed around her biceps—it felt like they completely circled her upper arm.

"Yeah," he said softly. "You're a regular American Gladiator."

His breath fanned her cheek. He was that close.

Aimee had no idea what to do next. However, apparently he did. He let go of her arm and slid his hand around her shoulders.

"Here." His voice rumbled through her like the purr of a lion. "We can keep each other warm."

His arm was firm and big and comforting, and his body radiated heat. Aimee was tempted to tuck herself into the warm, safe nook created by his torso and arm.

He pulled her closer.

She sighed and gave in to temptation, relaxing against him.

His breaths ruffled her hair. She raised her head,

wanting to feel him breathing on her skin. When she did, her nose brushed his chin, and she breathed in his scent. He smelled of snow and evergreen, with a hint of smokiness. It plummeted her back to the night before and his warm embrace.

Her breath caught.

He uttered a small moan, deep in his throat, and then pressed his forehead against hers and slid his fingers up her shoulder to cradle the back of her head.

"Aimee—"

Her heart fluttered—with fear or desire, she wasn't sure. She had no idea what he was going to do or say. She had no idea what she *wanted* him to do or say. As far as she was concerned, they could sit like this for the next three hours.

She was pretty sure that three hours of Matt's full attention would bolster not only her courage, but her energy and her resolve, as well.

"Aimee, I need to tell you something."

She rolled her forehead from side to side against his. "No, you don't." *Don't ruin this moment with reality. Don't make it anything more than it is. A stolen instant out of time.*

"I do. I need to expl—"

She kissed him. Just grabbed his face between her hands and—smack. No hesitation, no nips or teases or nibbles. Just a full-on, openmouthed kiss.

And she did it because sitting here in this dangerous, tense situation, pursued by men who could be working for the most ruthless terrorist on the planet, waiting for nightfall so they could rescue her seven-month-old baby, she still felt safer than she had in years.

She didn't want him to jerk her back to reality with guilt-ridden explanations about why he didn't go to Bill's funeral, or come back for William's christening.

She *knew* how guilty and responsible he felt. She knew because he was that kind of guy. He took the heat, the hits, the blame. Not in some arrogant, look-how-responsible-I-am way, either. When he succeeded, he did so quietly, without fanfare.

When he failed, he handled that quietly, as well.

By the time all that had flitted through Aimee's head, Matt's initial shock had faded.

He leaned forward and kissed her back. As fully and enthusiastically as she'd kissed him. He didn't waste any time hesitating or testing her reaction.

He *kissed* her.

And she discovered that beneath Matt's ordinary-guy veneer ran an undercurrent of passion, need and sexual hunger far greater than she'd imagined. His heart beat strongly, rapidly, vibrating through her as his mouth moved over hers with authority and exquisite gentleness. A thrill of unexpected desire pulsed through her all the way to her core. She leaned closer, yielding to the promise of his kiss.

But then he stopped. He lifted his head and hovered there, his lips so close to hers that their warmth still lingered on her mouth.

"Matt?"

He was frowning, his eyes as black as coals. "What are we doing?" he whispered.

Chapter Nine

SATURDAY 1700 HOURS

A twinge of uncertainty embedded itself beneath Aimee's breastbone at Matt's question.

Don't ask what we're doing, she wanted to say. *Don't make it more than it is—or less.*

But she didn't have the courage to say that, so she tried to make light of it.

"Staying warm?" Her eyes had adjusted to the darkness, so that she saw the uncertainty there.

He smiled, but the worry didn't leave his eyes. His gaze roamed over her face, as if he were searching for something. "I'd really like to talk to you about—"

Aimee put her fingers over his mouth. "Please don't. Not now. I need to concentrate on William."

"Sure. Of course." He pulled away. "Sorry."

"Don't do that. Don't get all honorable and responsible on me."

"I'm confused," he said. "I'm not sure what you want from me."

She took a deep breath. "I'm tired and cold and

scared, and I'm feeling very alone." She nibbled on her lower lip for a second. "Is it possible I want the same thing from you that you want from me?"

Matt's eyes widened, and then narrowed. He sat unmoving for a moment, and then touched her chin with his forefinger. "I never meant to come on to you. I didn't intend to let this happen."

"I know that. Me, either. But it's happening." She looked down. "At least it is for me."

"Aimee—"

She looked at him from under her lashes, hearing his unspoken plea. "Just hold me for a little while. Hold me and keep me warm."

"No problem," he said with a sigh. "No problem at all." He settled back against the rock and cradled her against his side. His other hand held her head against his chest, and she felt him press a kiss against her hair.

She could hear his heartbeat, steady and fast. After a few moments, Aimee felt his thumb sliding across her cheek in a rhythmic, sweet caress. She sighed and curled her fingers against his chest. When she did, his heart sped up and his breaths turned ragged.

He stiffened, and she knew he was aroused. If she stirred, or if he did, she'd find out for sure just how turned on he was.

IT SURPRISED HER just how much she wanted to find out.

She knew Matt almost as well as she'd known her own husband. Probably better than any other man she'd ever met. He wanted her. His body told her that. But he would never act on those feelings.

He valued honor and loyalty above all else. In his

mind, acting on sexual feelings for his best friend's widow was a betrayal of her trust in him.

If she left it up to him, the stolen kiss and this warm embrace were as far as he would go. But even if she regretted it later, right now she wasn't willing to stop.

Heaven help her, she wanted more. Much more. The thought of touching him sent a thrill of desire humming through her. Her breath caught and her pulse raced.

She turned her head and pressed a soft kiss to the sensitive underside of his chin, feeling a triumphant satisfaction when he gasped quietly. Then she shifted, to gain easier access to his mouth.

For an instant, he sat still and unyielding, but she persisted, kissing his mouth and cheek, wrapping her arms around his neck.

Finally, he dragged her across his lap and gave her back kiss for kiss, caress for caress, until both of them were out of breath.

Matt lifted her again, and somehow she ended up lying on her back with him hovering over her. After a searching look, he lowered his head and kissed her again.

She'd never experienced anything like the feeling of his mouth on hers, of his body pressed against hers. He was aggressive and gentle at the same time. Demanding and giving. He rested his weight on his elbows so he could look at her. His erection pulsed against her thigh.

She slid her hand down his ridged abdomen until her palm found his hardness. The feel of his erection, firm and vibrant against her fingers, even through the barrier of his clothes, sent desire thrumming through her like a drumbeat.

He shuddered, and she knew he was almost to the edge. He felt for the buttons on her pants while at the same time his tongue slid over the sensitive skin of her neck. When his teeth scraped her earlobe and his breath warmed her ear, her whole body contracted in erotic reaction.

By the time she realized her pants were gone, his fingers were sliding inside the waistband of her underwear. Before he even touched her, she was gasping for breath.

Then his fingers reached their goal. She cried out.

He stopped, but she moaned in protest. "Matt, please. I need to feel you, too."

His dark eyes searched her face. Then he sat up, disposed of his pants, and stretched his length against her again.

Her backside was cold, pressed against the poor insulation of a thin blanket, but Matt's legs, his torso, his groin, radiated heat. His erection, hard against her, burned her skin with a delicious heat that turned her insides to liquid fire.

She closed her fingers around him, feeling his velvety hardness jump in her hand. At the same time his fingers slid through her nether hair and raked gently along the folds that hid her center.

She arched, the pleasure almost painful in its intensity. Pleasure she hadn't felt for far too long.

He teased her there, circling and coaxing, dipping and withdrawing, again and again, as his mouth traveled from her neck to her collarbone and on, to find the tip of her breast and nip at it through the thin silk of her long-sleeved pullover.

Then he lifted himself and settled between her

thighs. His rigid shaft rubbed against her, driving her desire. She opened to him, oblivious of the chilled air and the icy cold ground.

Bending his head, he nibbled at her lips, then pulled back and looked into her eyes.

"You okay?" he whispered.

In answer, she arched her neck and reached for his mouth with hers. "I'm ready," she whispered against his lips, knowing what he would know within seconds. Her core was liquifying, flowing, preparing to receive him.

He looked deeply into her eyes as if searching for something, then with deliberate, torturous slowness, he sank into her.

She moaned as his full length filled her and spread exquisite longing like golden, fluid light through her body. Enveloped in a haze of erotic sensation, all she could do was feel.

He stayed there, buried in her, his face tucked into the hollow between her neck and shoulder, for an interminable time. The feel of his breath on her neck was, if possible, more intimate than the sensation of his hardness filling her. It was a gesture of surrender, of trust, she realized.

He was blind with his eyes tucked into the darkness. He was vulnerable with his neck exposed to possible enemies. He was open, undefended.

Her eyes filled with tears. She slid her hand around the nape of his neck, and turned her face toward his.

Then he moved, and her body spasmed, sending electric shocks of pleasure tumbling through her. He slid out, out, until he hovered at her opening, then in to fill her again. The slow friction increased her wetness and made each successive thrust easier.

Each time he pushed into her, he sped up slightly, his body coaxing hers to keep pace with him. He stayed suspended above her, watching her. She realized that he was gauging her response and tailoring his movements to hers.

When she thought she would burst with anticipation, when her breasts were puckered and tight and her entire body felt electrified, he sat back on his haunches and pulled her legs atop his thighs. Then he held on to her waist and thrust again and again, filling her more completely and more deeply than she'd ever imagined possible.

Faster, deeper.

At last, he wrapped his arms around her and lifted her upright. He held here there, suspended, until she whimpered with need, then lowered her onto him. His powerful thighs flexed as he thrust upward.

Aimee gasped and cried out as a place inside her that had never been touched shattered. Matt kissed her, swallowing her breathless cries. Then he came, too, violently and thoroughly, his jaw clenched and his eyes squeezed shut as he poured everything into her.

With one last powerful thrust, he rocked with her and against her, continuing the dance as their climax faded.

After a few seconds of sitting there, draped against each other in the afterglow of sexual fulfillment, he splayed his fingers over her back again and gently lowered her to the ground, following her and settling beside her.

She lay her head on his shoulder as tears filled her eyes and ran over the bridge of her nose.

He touched one with his thumb and smeared it across

her cheek. "What's happening here?" he said tenderly. "Is something wrong?"

She shook her head slightly. "No. Nothing."

He kissed her forehead while his thumb swirled over her skin, spreading and drying the dampness.

"Then why are you crying?"

She shrugged and bit her lip to keep from saying *because this is a special occasion.*

MATT WOKE UP cold and stiff. Something sharp was poking him in the back. Something soft and sweet-smelling was pressed against his chest and side. He'd been dreaming about Aimee.

Aimee. He opened his eyes and discovered that his dream had come true. She was asleep with her head on his chest. Her brown hair was wavy and soft, and it tickled his nose. He'd kissed that hair, that brow, those lips.

Carefully, he lifted his arm and glanced at his watch. Almost seven. They'd slept for over two hours. The realization disturbed him. He'd left himself—and, more importantly, Aimee—vulnerable and exposed. The makeshift shelter was a pathetic cover. Had anyone happened by, they'd have been caught or killed.

He lay still for a moment and listened. He heard nothing but the wind whistling through the naked tree branches, and the muffled silence of falling snow. Occasionally, he heard a branch crack and fall, weighted down by snow and ice.

Aimee stirred and murmured something in her sleep. Matt ran his palm lightly down her silk-covered arm as his heart squeezed in regret.

He'd done worse than leave her vulnerable by falling

asleep on watch. He'd taken advantage of her by making love with her. She was completely dependent on him to keep her safe. She was frightened for her baby. And he'd promised to take care of her.

Instead, he'd let his feelings get involved. He'd acted on his personal desire, rather than in her and her baby's best interest. He'd relaxed his vigilance and put her in danger.

Despite his self-recrimination, his brain replayed the highlights of those few stolen moments—the supple firmness of her skin, her heavy breasts with their swollen nipples, the way she opened to him as he sank hilt-deep inside her.

To his dismay, his erection grew and strained, the physical symbol of his betrayal of her. He'd never allowed himself to be close to her, afraid that she or Bill or someone who knew them would see the truth in his face—how smitten he'd always been with her. He'd never even admitted to himself how much he'd wanted her.

Until now. He closed his eyes and clenched his jaw, forcing his brain back to his mission. Carefully, he slid his arm from around her and sat up.

She stirred, so he pulled the corner of the mummy bag over his lap to hide his erection, disgusted with himself.

She opened her eyes and looked at him in sleepy confusion. Then her eyes widened. He stared, mesmerized by the myriad emotions that flitted across her features.

To his surprise, she didn't turn away in disgust, or scream for help. Finally, she scraped her lower lip with her teeth and dropped her gaze.

Embarrassed? Humiliated? *Afraid?*

"Aimee, I'm sorry."

Her eyes snapped back up to lock with his. "Sorry?"

He nodded miserably. "We need to dress. It's almost dark, and I want to watch the cabin for a while before we make our move."

She shivered, and then ducked her head, searching around the cramped space for her clothes.

Matt turned the other way and dressed. Then he checked his MAC-10 to be sure it hadn't gotten wet, and loaded it. He did the same with the Glock and handed it to Aimee, handle first.

"Remember. From this point on, there's a chance you'll have to shoot someone to save your life or William's. You have to decide now whether you can do it. Don't aim if you're not prepared to shoot. And don't shoot if you're not prepared to kill."

She nodded, accepting the gun and sliding it into the paddle holster she'd already put on. As soon as she'd finished dressing, she started rolling up the blankets.

Matt stuffed them into his homemade pack and then took the mummy bag's stuff-sack from Aimee and packed it.

The sound of a motor starting up echoed across the canyon. He froze, listening. The motor revved once, twice. He touched Aimee's arm.

"Stay right here."

"Matt—"

"Stay here, and don't make a sound."

He carefully pushed the blanket aside and slipped out. When he'd sneaked as close to the edge of the overhang as he dared go, he used his eyes like an eagle or a hawk would to strafe the ground and search for prey.

Down below, Kinnard was on the snowmobile. As he watched, Kinnard revved it again, then turned off the engine. He cursed as he climbed off the vehicle and stomped back toward the cabin.

Had he forgotten something?

Without moving a muscle he didn't need to, Matt groped in his backpack until his hand closed around his binoculars. He pulled them out and watched Kinnard mount the snow-covered steps.

As the kidnapper reached for the door handle, a loud crack rang out, practically over Matt's head.

Kinnard whirled and looked in their direction. Matt didn't move. A huge branch crashed noisily as it fell through lower branches. It hit the ground not ten feet away from him with a deafening thud.

Kinnard stood perfectly still, watching and listening. His head was raised and his gaze was on the trees that were still swaying as they rebounded from being hit by the falling branch.

Matt knew that where he sat was partially obscured by tangled underbrush. He also knew that if he moved, Kinnard's brain would separate his gray-and-green-and-white camo from the surrounding natural foliage.

Behind him, he heard Aimee stirring.

It took every ounce of willpower he possessed not to move or speak.

Stay still, Aimee.

Matt didn't take his eyes off Kinnard as the man squinted up at the place where the branch had fallen. Behind him, Aimee continued to move. If she decided to push the blanket aside, they'd be sitting ducks.

Finally, the kidnapper's rigid stance relaxed. He

glanced around, then went inside the cabin. Matt didn't dare move. If Kinnard was just retrieving something he'd forgotten, he'd be out within seconds. Sure enough, Kinnard appeared again almost immediately, climbed on the snowmobile, started it up and headed northeast. Matt got a glimpse of the rifle in its scabbard, attached to the right side of the vehicle.

His breath hissed out between his teeth. He lifted the binoculars again and examined every inch of the cabin. As he was studying the layout and trying to remember anything he could about the couple of trips he and Bill had made up here when they were kids, a dim light came on in one of the windows.

His pulse sped up as a young woman appeared, holding a baby. She was rocking from one foot to another and bouncing the boy in her arms. As he watched, she bent her head and kissed him on his forehead.

A frisson of relief slithered down his spine. The woman's stance and demeanor were that of a caregiver. A nanny, maybe. Or a mother. She was obviously caring for William.

Aimee's baby was in safe hands—for the moment.

He sent up a brief *Thank You* prayer as he turned his gaze back to the northeast. The hum of the snowmobile's motor was waning. Kinnard was gone, at least for a while.

They needed to make their move now.

He detached the blanket from over the shelter opening and rolled it up. Aimee had searched the inside of the shelter to make sure they weren't leaving anything.

"Got everything?" he asked, looking around.

"I think so. What was that motor?"

"It was Kinnard on his snowmobile. He just took off

on it." Matt took her arm. "Aimee, as far as I can tell, right now William is in there alone with a young woman who appears to be taking *very* good care of him."

"Really?" Her gaze zeroed in on the cabin. "You saw him? He's all right? Can I see? Oh, Matt. Can we go now?"

"Listen to me. We've got to act fast. Kinnard headed north. He may be planning to hide up there and watch for us."

Matt rubbed his thumb across his lower lip and looked up at the sky. "The snow is coming down harder, so that's on our side. If we circle around to the south side of the cabin, and the snow keeps up, we should be able to sneak into the cabin without him seeing us."

"What about the girl?"

"When I saw her, she didn't act as if she were being watched. There didn't appear to be anyone else there, either. She was totally concentrated on the baby. But we have to go in as if there were armed guards in every room." He set his jaw and looked Aimee straight in the eye.

"That means you can't go rushing to William. You have to stay with me and do exactly as I say." He gripped her arms. "Can you do that?"

Her eyes glittered with dampness. She opened her mouth but nothing came out.

"Can you?" he growled. "Because if you can't, you're going to have to stay up here, hidden, until I can get him. I can't take care of both of you at once."

Chapter Ten

SATURDAY 1900 HOURS

Aimee closed her eyes and took a deep breath. Then she lifted her chin. "I can do it."

He pushed away his need to touch her, to pull her close and kiss her and promise her that everything was going to be all right. This was a mission—he needed to act like a commander. And somewhere inside him he had to find the detachment and focus that made him good at his job.

And Aimee had to act like a soldier.

"This is a covert operation, Aimee. I'm the commander and you're my team. You follow my orders. If I say *abort*—then we abort the mission and retreat. Is that understood?"

Her lower lip trembled visibly, and her eyes glittered with unshed tears. But she nodded.

"Are you sure? Because if I give the order, you have to leave William and do what I tell you. Can you do that?"

Her chin lifted. "Yes, sir."

Fierce longing and aching compassion took his breath

away. For one instant, he abandoned his Special Forces training and allowed himself to be just a man. He cupped her cheek and leaned in to kiss her trembling lips.

When their lips touched, a thrill swirled through him that nearly buckled his knees. "I swear to God, Aimee, if you can trust me, I will save your baby."

She pulled away and gave him a solemn look. "I trust you," she whispered.

IT TOOK THEM forty minutes to trudge down the hill and around to the south side of the cabin. Despite what Matt had told Aimee, he was hampered by her. If he'd thought for a minute he could have safely left her in the shelter while he rescued William, he'd have done it.

If he'd thought he could wait until he could get a message through to Deke to fly a man in to help him, he'd have done that. But he had no time, and more importantly, no intention of leaving Aimee to fend for herself for even a short while.

He had to rescue them both.

So he clenched his jaw and moved at a pace far slower than he wanted to. As they approached the south, downhill side of the cabin, he quickly repeated his instructions to Aimee.

"I'll go in first. You wait for my hand signal. I'll wave you on as soon as I can verify that the room is clear. If you don't see me, you stay right where you are until you do." He looked at her evenly.

"What do you do if I don't come back out?"

She swallowed. "After ten minutes, I head for the door and—and give myself up." She paused. "Matt—?"

"No. No questions. You give yourself up."

She nodded reluctantly.

"Okay, once we're inside—do you remember what I told you about the layout?" He was going by what he remembered from his early teens. He hoped to hell he was at least partly right.

"The big room is in front. The right-hand door goes to a bedroom, the left-hand door goes to the kitchen."

"Right, and the kitchen is where I saw the girl holding William."

"You're going through the bedroom and around to the kitchen from the north side. You'll wait until I go in through the south door and surprise her. When you hear me speak, you'll come through the north door."

"Good. After that, just listen to me. I'll tell you what to do."

She nodded.

He looked at her and sent her what he hoped was an encouraging smile. "Ready?"

Aimee's throat closed up, but she nodded. A week ago, if anyone had told her she'd be part of a mountain rescue mission to save her own son, she'd have called that person insane.

Now, here she was, ready to stage a dangerous rescue at the side of a Special Ops soldier who was one of the best search-and-rescue specialists in the country.

They were about to rescue her seven-month-old son from kidnappers.

A trembling started deep within her and quickly spread out to her hands, arms and knees. She held on to the Glock with both hands, hoping it would give her strength and courage.

In front of her, Matt stole forward, his entire body

tense with expectation. He was ready for anything. His broad shoulders looked strong enough to support the world. His body, even in the bulky coat and camo pants, moved with the powerful grace of a big cat—a leopard maybe, or a cougar.

He was so strong yet he could be so gentle. She knew if anyone in the world could save her baby, Matt could.

Dear heavens, she trusted him. And she believed him—believed every word he said. She hadn't wanted to. She certainly didn't want to believe that he couldn't have prevented Bill's death. It was so easy to blame someone.

He turned his head and glanced at her over his shoulder, his profile strong and assured as a warrior. Then he gestured, waving her forward and pointing to an evergreen.

She rose to an uncomfortable crouch and eased forward, staying in the shadow of the tree. Her pulse sped up and her mouth went dry. She reached behind her and seated the paddle holster, making sure it was secure.

Matt shifted his weight to the balls of his feet, then held up his hand, thumb and first finger forming an O for OK.

She sent him the same gesture back.

He pointed to his own head and then forward.

He'd given her the five-minute crash course in signals, so she knew he was telling her that he was about to move forward. He didn't look back at her, so her responding nod was wasted.

As he half crawled, half crept toward the two steps that led to the cabin's door, she waited. Her limbs twitched with the need to move, and her pulse sped up.

She fought to keep her breathing even as she watched him unlock the door and slip inside. He'd warned her that once he'd disappeared into the house, she'd feel an almost uncontrollable urge to follow him.

It's the hardest thing to learn about stealth reconnaissance, he'd explained. *When your commander gives you an order, his life and yours rest on him being able to trust you to carry out that order, even if all it means is that you stay still.*

She'd thought she understood. But he was right. She burned to move a few steps forward, enough to be able to see through a window.

She set her teeth and clenched her fists. She would not move. As much as it was killing her not to be able to see what he saw, not to be able to lay eyes on her baby. Her scalp burned, and despite the cold air, a drop of sweat ran down her back.

"Come on," she muttered. "Hurry up."

MATT STOOD in the front room of the cabin, listening. He heard water running, and a feminine voice talking in low, soothing tones. Then he heard a giggle and a splash.

The girl was giving William a bath. The excruciating tension in his shoulders and neck relaxed, sending a rush of relief through him all the way from his head to his feet.

William was safe and happy.

He needed to take a look at the kitchen before he gestured Aimee in. He didn't want to leave her outside any longer than he had to, but he'd ordered her to treat this like a mission, and he had to do the same thing.

It was dangerous to leave her out there undefended, but that's how he would handle it if she were a BHSAR specialist. Except that if she were a specialist, she'd know how long to wait and when to move, even if she didn't get a signal.

Matt glided forward a few steps and peered in past the door hinges. Although the light given off by the oil lantern was dim and flickering, his narrow view caught the edge of the sink. He saw William's arms waving, and the girl's hand gliding a soapy washcloth over his pink, new skin. She laughed. She sounded young, maybe not far out of her teens.

Hopefully that was a good sign. If she were young and enchanted by William, chances were she'd be easily manipulated into talking about Kinnard.

He angled his head enough to get a view of the rear door to the kitchen. In the dimness it was impossible to tell if it was unlocked, but at least he'd remembered the cabin's layout correctly. There *were* two doors to the kitchen.

He retraced his steps across the room, thankful that the floorboards were solid, not creaky. He slipped through the front door and closed it. Then he gestured for Aimee.

She rose and moved stealthily forward and up the steps. He let out the breath he'd been holding. Thank God she was all right. He'd only taken a few seconds to reconnoiter, but he knew all too well that it took only a few seconds to kill.

"They're in the kitchen," he whispered in her ear. "She's bathing William and he's happy. He's splashing water everywhere."

She swallowed and then nodded. "Bath time is his

favorite time of day. He thinks it's funny to splash water on me—" Her voice cracked.

"It's okay, Aimee. He's right there and he's safe. Now—I'm going around through the bedroom. Give me sixty seconds and then step through the left door—that's the door to the kitchen—get the drop on the girl. And be careful."

She hadn't taken her eyes off the door. He understood why. Her baby was on the other side of it. "Don't take your eyes off her for an instant and—" he touched her chin, forcing her to look at him "—don't let yourself get distracted by William. It's important, Aimee. Your life and his depend on it. Our mission is to rescue him. Right now you've got to be a soldier, not a mother. Do you understand?"

Pain lit her eyes, but she nodded.

"By the time you get the drop on her, I'll be coming in the rear door and we'll have her in a cross fire. Okay?"

"How will I know sixty seconds?"

He counted for her. "Count like that. Don't let your anxiety let you speed up the count."

She nodded. "Okay."

"One final thing. Get her to sit down. Keep away from the window. I saw her. That means Kinnard might be able to see you. Let's go." He peered around the door and then pushed it open. He gestured for her to go to the left door and he'd go to the right.

He pointed at his watch, indicating that she should start counting.

She nodded.

He slipped through the door and took a couple of

precious seconds to study the bedroom. He'd give just about anything to find something that identified Kinnard's first name or any information about him or the girl. But the most remarkable thing about the room was the pile of pillows on the bed.

He crossed to the bathroom, which led from the bedroom onto the enclosed back porch.

Good. He'd remembered the layout.

The porch had a half-paned door and two windows. Directly in front of the back door was the door to the kitchen. Through it he could hear the girl talking to William, but he couldn't make out what she said.

Come on, Aimee. He looked at his watch and saw that she had twenty more seconds. He itched to get in, grab the baby and handcuff the girl before she knew what hit her. But he needed Aimee there to take her baby.

So he waited and watched the second hand crawl around.

FIFTY-NINE, SIXTY. Aimee took a deep breath, trying to control her anxiety. She adjusted her two-handed grip on the Glock, laid her shoulder against the door and took a deep breath.

"Here we go, pretty boy," the girl said. William gurgled happily.

Aimee's throat spasmed and her heart squeezed so tightly it hurt. *Her baby.* She almost cried out loud. Closing her eyes, she drew in another deep breath, and shouldered the door open, leading with her weapon.

"Don't move!" she snapped.

The girl shrieked and clasped William to her chest. "What? Who—?" She stepped backward.

"I said—don't move." Aimee's nervousness was completely overshadowed by the horror of what she was doing. She swallowed against the bile that rose in the back of her throat. She'd never aimed a weapon at anyone in her life. Yet here she was, threatening a pretty young woman who was holding *her* baby.

She was aiming a loaded gun at William—her own son. The thought and the action made her physically ill. She looked at the door behind them, absently noticing a pair of snowshoes hanging on a hook.

Where was Matt?

The woman shifted William to her other arm. "Who are you? Where—where did you come from?"

"I'm asking the questions," Aimee snapped. "What's your name?"

In the flickering lantern light, Aimee could see that the young woman's hair was a flat beige color, and her shocked dark eyes were rimmed with pale lashes, which made her look younger than she probably was. She opened her mouth but nothing came out.

"I asked you what your name is."

"Shellie," she said, her voice rising in pitch. She hugged William tighter. "It's Sh-Shellie. What's going on? Who are you?"

Aimee gestured with the barrel of the pistol. "Sit down."

Shellie started around the table.

"No. Sit here." Aimee glanced at the window over the sink, where tie-back curtains hung. She needed them closed.

"Hold it," she snapped.

Shellie froze.

"First, close the curtains." She gestured with the gun.

Watching her warily, Shellie tucked William into the crook of one arm and reached for the curtain ties with the other.

As soon as the fabric fell into place, obscuring the window, Aimee gestured again.

"Now sit."

Shellie obeyed. She bounced William on her lap.

Aimee's sore heart filled to bursting with equal amounts of joy and pain. Joy because her baby was obviously safe and happy. But her arms ached to wrap around his soft, plump little body.

She shivered. The kitchen was much warmer than outside, but she could feel a chilly breeze. "Why aren't you using that generator?"

Shellie looked from the baby to her and back again. "I had it on earlier. We're low on fuel."

Aimee glanced at the door to the porch. What was Matt doing? More than anything, Aimee wanted to lay her weapon down and take William away from Shellie, but she'd promised Matt she'd act like a soldier.

He'd given her an order, and he expected her to carry it out. She had to hold Shellie at gunpoint until he came in.

She quickly glanced around the kitchen, squinting in the dimness. Near the cabinets on the other side of the stove was a step stool. She lowered her head and crept across in front of the window, then nudged the stool closer to the kitchen table and sat on it. Her hands were getting tired, so she set the gun on her lap and rested one hand on the grip. The barrel was still aimed at Shellie.

Matt hadn't told her to talk to the girl, but he hadn't told her not to, either. "Who hired you?" she demanded, her gaze still hungrily assessing every inch of her son's body, to make sure he was all right.

Every time she spoke, his blue eyes turned her way. It was the hardest thing she'd ever done not to look at him. If he started crying, she didn't know if she could stop herself from picking him up.

"Hired me? I don't—"

"Don't lie to me." She picked up the Glock and aimed it at the girl's head. "Who brought you up here and left you to take care of—" Aimee paused. "What's the baby's name?"

She didn't want Shellie to know the baby was hers. If the woman knew that, it would give her a weapon that Aimee couldn't counter.

Shellie licked her lips nervously and lifted William to her shoulder. She patted his back. "I don't know his name. My boyfriend brought me up here. Listen, please don't hurt the baby."

Aimee uttered a short, ironic laugh. "Don't hurt the baby? Oh, don't worry, Shellie, I'm not going to hurt the baby. But if you don't give me some straight answers, I am definitely going to hurt you."

"Okay, okay." Shellie licked her lips again. "My— my boyfriend told me he needed me to watch his—his niece's little boy for a few days. She's sick, and—"

"I said, the truth!"

"But that *is*—"

"You really believe you're up here on the top of a mountain in a snowstorm because your *boyfriend's niece* has a cold?"

William's big bright eyes widened. He turned his head to look at her and frowned and began to whine.

Shellie's eyes grew wide and filled with tears. She sniffed. "You don't understand. When Roy tells you to do something, you don't get in his face about it, you know? I mean, he's been real good to me, but when he says do something, you just gotta do it." She shrugged and took her hand off William's back to wipe her nose on the sleeve of her sweater.

"Who's Roy?"

"He's my boyfriend. I told you."

"Roy who?"

Shellie's eyes narrowed, as if she were weighing the advisability of telling a stranger Roy's full name. Then her gaze dropped to the Glock and she swallowed. "Roy Kinnard. Look, did he do something wrong? 'Cause I didn't know nothing about it if he did. I just watch the baby."

Aimee lowered the gun again. It sounded like Shellie was completely in the dark about Roy's activities. But slim as it was, there was a chance that she was acting. Aimee's instincts told her to believe Shellie was telling the truth. But she couldn't trust her instincts. Not with her baby's life literally in the woman's hands.

"Oh, he's asleep," Shellie said softly.

Fierce longing arrowed through Aimee. She tamped it down. "Where does he sleep?" She kept her voice as hard as she could make it.

"In—in the bedroom. I pile pillows around him so he won't fall off the bed."

"You have children?"

Shellie laughed. "No, but I practically raised my two little brothers. I know all about babies."

Aimee wanted to call out to Matt, but she knew there must be a reason he was keeping quiet. What if something had happened? He'd told her to give herself up if he didn't show.

Apprehension stole her breath. She couldn't do that. She was here, in a warm, safe house with no one but a skinny girl standing between her and her baby. Right now she was in charge. She had the advantage, and she had to keep it.

"Put him to bed." Aimee aimed the gun at Shellie again.

Shellie stood carefully, still patting William on the back. She started toward Aimee, toward the closed door where Matt was supposed to be.

"No!" Aimee snapped. "The other way." She stood and blocked the door.

Shellie looked surprised, but she turned and stepped through the doorway into the big front room and across to the bedroom door.

Aimee was right behind her.

Shellie shifted William and reached for an oil lamp.

"No light." Aimee took a deep breath. "You do what I tell you to—nothing more," she ordered the girl. "I don't want any lights turned on. Just put Wi—the baby—to bed."

Shellie obeyed.

It broke Aimee's heart to watch another woman do the things she always did for William. Her heart twisted in agony to have him so close, and yet too far, in every sense of the word, for her to touch.

"There you go, darlin'," Shellie cooed. "Sleep

tight." She leaned over and kissed William's round pink cheek.

Aimee nearly lost it. She bit her lip—hard—to stop herself from moaning aloud. "Sit down, on the foot of the bed, and keep your hands in your lap, so I can see them."

She didn't want Matt to come into the kitchen and find nobody there, but she wasn't sure how concealing the kitchen windows were. Besides, she didn't think she could leave William alone, not even for a moment, now that she'd found him.

Aimee sat at the head of the bed, near William. She leaned back against the headboard and rested her gun hand on her lap.

"Now, how about telling me who Roy is and who he works for."

MATT PRESSED HIS BACK against the wall next to the half-paned door, his MAC-10 in his hand. He'd been about to burst in on Aimee and the girl when the clouds had parted, allowing the moon to light the snow-covered landscape.

Aware that Kinnard was still out there, probably waiting for a chance to ambush him, he'd flattened himself against the wall, and carefully surveyed the clearing around the cabin.

He wasn't worried about Aimee. As he'd listened to her barking orders and questioning William's caregiver, he'd smiled and his chest had swelled with pride. She was handling the girl like a pro.

He was relieved when Aimee directed the girl to take the baby into the bedroom. He would have much more freedom to handle Kinnard knowing that Aimee and William were out of the way.

Just as he'd decided it was safe to move across the porch to the kitchen door, he detected movement out of the corner of his eye.

He angled slightly, just enough to check the area close to the house. Nothing. Maybe he'd seen a rabbit or a deer, or even a wolf, but he didn't think so. His instincts, honed by four years in Air Force Special Forces, told him it was a human predator.

Crouching down, he crept across the porch to the door. He was taking a chance. If Kinnard saw the lantern's light, he'd know someone had opened the door.

But Matt would rather lure Kinnard to the kitchen than take a chance on him circling around to the front door. He wasn't about to get himself in a position where Aimee and William were between Kinnard and him.

Matt slipped into the kitchen. The lantern was still lit, although it looked low on oil. The curtains were closed but he knew his silhouette would be visible if he stood. So he slinked across the wooden floor to the table and extinguished the lamp.

He pulled his infrared glasses down from his forehead. He figured Kinnard was likely to have infrared glasses, too, so he stayed hidden as much as possible while he slipped back over to the porch door and opened it. Staying in the shadow of the open door, he rose enough to look out. The moon was still bright.

Then he spotted a figure sneaking down toward the house from the north. Matt recognized Kinnard's burly silhouette. His weapon was slung over his shoulder as he carefully picked his way across the snow from tree to tree.

Matt waited, watching. Once Kinnard got to the clearing, he'd have to step into the open to come any closer. Matt's fingers tightened on the MAC-10. He could take Kinnard out at any time. He'd used deadly force a few times as an Air Force Special Op, but always as a last resort. A *dead* last resort.

No, he wanted Kinnard alive. He wanted to find out who had hired him, and why. He knew he was capable of extracting every bit of information Kinnard had, if he were willing to apply the necessary impetus.

Still, to be safe, he kept a bead on the man as he paused at the edge of the trees. As Matt watched, the kidnapper pulled on a pair of infrared glasses, swung his rifle off his shoulder and held it ready as he stepped into the clearing.

As if on cue, clouds covered the moon. Without the glasses, Matt would be blind in the cloudy darkness. Yet he could see Kinnard's heat silhouette, and he tracked him across the snow-covered ground through his gun's scope.

Kinnard swung the rifle slowly across the windows and doors of the cabin. Matt ducked back into the shadow of the doorway as Kinnard swiveled the barrel his way.

He waited, counting the seconds, considering what he would do if he were the other man. After enough time had passed that the man should have moved on to survey the next window, Matt took a chance and peered out.

Sure enough, Kinnard was aiming at the far west window as he eased forward, his shadow crawling across the moonlit snow.

Matt took a deep breath and rapidly crossed the door's opening, flattening his back against the left facing. Now he was in a better position to shoot, if he had to.

He angled around the facing to get a better look at Kinnard's position.

A shot rang out—cracking the cold, silent air.

Kinnard went down.

Chapter Eleven

Aimee shot straight up off the bed at the sound of the gunshot. Before her brain could process the meaning of what she'd heard, several other shots followed—each one quieter than the last. *Echoes,* she realized.

But echoes of what? Matt's gun? Or Kinnard's rifle? Matt's gun was fully automatic, but she'd only heard the one shot and some echoes. That scared her—a lot.

Had Matt been shot?

William started to whimper. Shellie jumped up, reaching for him.

"Stop!" Aimee barked, pointing the barrel of the Glock at Shellie's head.

Shellie froze, her hands out, fingers spread.

"Don't move a muscle," Aimee whispered.

"That was a gunshot. It scared him," Shellie protested.

"Hush!" Aimee dared a quick glance at her baby. He hiccoughed and stirred, probably as much disturbed by the tension in the room as by the gunfire, then settled back to sleep. She held her breath and listened.

She didn't hear another shot, but a low deep rumbling rose from somewhere.

Shellie raised her head.

"What's that?" Aimee asked.

When Shellie didn't answer, she took a step toward her. "I asked you a question."

"It sounds like snow moving." Shellie licked her lips. Her fingers twitched, and her eyes darted back and forth from the gun in Aimee's hand to the baby.

Aimee moved away from her, toward the door that led into the living room. She didn't want to take a chance that Shellie would try to rush her and take her gun away. "You mean an avalanche?"

Shellie's dark eyes met hers. She nodded. "A small one. That gunshot may have dislodged the wet snow."

Panic fluttered in Aimee's throat. "Is it coming this way? What happens if it hits the cabin?"

Shellie shrugged. "This late in the year, when the weather's getting warmer, slides happen a lot. Can I pick up the baby? He's going to be scared."

Aimee looked at her son, then back at Shellie. *No,* she wanted to say. *He's my baby. I'll pick him up.* But the only thing she knew about this woman was that she cared for William. She wouldn't hurt him. What she would do to Aimee if she let down her guard, Aimee didn't know.

Doing her best to keep her face expressionless, Aimee nodded. "Have you got a safety seat?"

Shellie nodded. "Right there in the corner."

"Don't move. I'll get it." Aimee backed toward the corner and grabbed the child safety seat. She sat it on the foot of the bed near Shellie then backed away.

"Put him in it."

"Uh, ma'am? You're his mother, aren't you?"

Aimee froze. Was she that transparent? "Why would you say that?"

Shellie smiled as she strapped William safely into his seat. "I can see how he reacts to your voice. And you can't keep your eyes off him. I don't exactly know what Roy's doing, but I do know this baby needs his mama." She pushed the seat toward Aimee. "Take him. I know you're dying to."

Aimee forced herself to keep her eyes on Shellie. "No. I can't." She'd promised Matt that she could be a good soldier. William was safe. She didn't have to hold him to know that. Her hands tightened on the Glock's handle and she shook her head.

"He knows I'm here. And I know you've taken good care of him."

"I've been waiting for someone to get here. I called the police this morning, before Roy got here." Tears formed in Shellie's eyes and slipped down her face. "I know you don't trust me, but I did take care of him."

"You made the anonymous call?"

"Please don't tell Roy. He gets mad. But I was afraid something would happen to the baby."

"Thank you, Shellie," Aimee said, just as another deep rumble filled the air and she felt a shudder—she had no idea if it were the cabin floor or her own legs shaking, until she saw the lantern's flame waver.

Her fingers tightened on the Glock. First the gunshot and now an avalanche. Her head spun with panic and worry. Matt was out there. What if he'd been shot?

Had she found her baby only to lose Matt?

KINNARD HADN'T MOVED. Matt kept the MAC and his eye trained on the kidnapper's torso. Even with the infrared glasses, he couldn't tell if any of the shadows he saw were blood. And he couldn't risk going out to check.

Because the gunshot hadn't been from a Glock semiautomatic, or any other kind of handgun. That shot had come from a rifle at least as powerful as the one Kinnard carried. A gun he'd heard firing before.

It had to be Al Hamar, Novus's man who'd followed Matt back from Mahjidastan.

Kinnard had shot him back at the ransom drop point. Matt had seen the blood. But obviously Al Hamar's injury wasn't serious. It certainly hadn't kept him from following them.

Now he was trying to kill Kinnard. Matt had to assume it was because Kinnard was trying to kill Matt.

He'd be happy if Kinnard and Al Hamar got into a cross fire with each other, leaving Matt free to get Aimee and William to safety. But he knew it would be dangerous to let down his guard, so he crept back through the kitchen and into the front room. He wanted to check out the downhill side of the cabin and try to pinpoint Al Hamar's location.

Just as he started across the floor, he heard Aimee's voice, ordering the girl to precede her out of the bedroom.

As soon as he saw her, he spoke quietly. "Aimee."

Both women jumped.

"Matt! Are you okay?"

"Yeah. Shh. Get down, both of you."

"Where did that shot come from?"

"South. Below the cabin. I think Kinnard took a bullet."

"Roy?" the girl cried. "Roy's shot? Oh my God!" She set the baby seat down on the floor. One hand went to her mouth and the other pressed against her tummy.

"Calm down, Shellie," Aimee snapped at her. "Don't move."

Matt pushed his infrared glasses up onto his forehead and watched the two women's silhouettes.

"Is William okay?" he asked.

"He's fine. Shellie took very good care of him. Matt, she's the one who called in the tip."

"What? She called the police—?"

"Where is he? Where's Roy?" Shellie sobbed. "Is he in the kitchen?"

"He's outside," Matt said. "Settle down. We'll check on him as soon as I can be sure Al—the shooter—is gone."

"No! No!" Shellie ran for the front door.

"Shellie, wait!" Aimee cried.

"Hold it!" Matt said. "I need to ask you some questions about the kidnapping."

"No! I have to get to Roy! How could you shoot him?" Shellie broke for the door.

Matt dove for her but she got to the door first and slipped through, shoving it wide enough to block Matt and slow him down.

"Matt, stop her! She'll get killed." Aimee headed for the door.

"Aimee, no!" He stepped in front of her and caught her against his chest. "Get down! Get William."

Aimee immediately dropped to her knees and crawled back to the baby.

"Stay here. That's an order." Matt slid through the open

door and onto the front porch. Falling to his stomach, he held the MAC-10 ready to fire. He couldn't see anything.

He crept to the side of the porch, watching every direction. He didn't want to end up shot or captured. He still had work to do. He had to get Aimee and her baby off the mountain.

Shellie's voice sounded muffled and far away as she screamed for Roy. Matt needed to see around the side of the cabin, but the porch didn't extend to the corner.

He pulled down his infrared glasses again and scanned the area to the south. Nothing stood out that looked like a human. Sliding off the porch, he crawled westward along the cabin's wall, staying as much in the shadows as he could, keeping an eye out to the south for the shooter.

By the time he reached the southwest corner of the cabin, he could hear Shellie crying. Flattening himself against the cabin's wall, he peered around the corner and saw her crouched beside Kinnard, who was stirring.

He breathed a sigh of relief. Shellie was okay, and Kinnard was still alive. He needed to question them both.

While he watched, Kinnard sat up with Shellie's help. Matt saw a patch of black on the front of his winter camos. Blood. He must have taken a bullet in his shoulder, because he was moving pretty well. If he'd been hit in the chest, he wouldn't be upright.

Shellie rose to her knees, still holding on to Roy.

A tiny red dot appeared on the side of her head.

"Look out!" Matt yelled, breaking into a run. He risked a glance behind him, but didn't see anything.

He pushed his legs to pump as fast as possible through the wet snow. "Get down!"

He was about four feet away from the two of them

when Shellie turned her head in his direction. The red dot was centered on her forehead.

"Down!" Matt shouted. "Look out!"

Kinnard reached for her to try to pull her to the ground.

A loud crack drowned out all other sound. Shellie's head jerked, then slowly she toppled over.

"Shellie! Oh God!" Kinnard yelled, trying to get to his feet.

Matt saw the red dot slithering up Kinnard's chest and neck.

"Kinnard, duck!"

The kidnapper hit the ground and rolled sideways.

A second crack. Snow puffed as the bullet plowed into the ground barely two inches away from Kinnard's shoulder.

Matt dove into the snow and immediately raised up to shoot, but he knew his MAC wasn't powerful enough to reach the terrorist. So he hurled himself across the snow-covered ground and grabbed for Kinnard's rifle, but the sling was twisted around the other man's arm.

A third shot zinged past Matt's head. At the same time, Kinnard rolled again and sat up, trying to untangle the rifle sling. After a couple of seconds, he got it loose and raised the weapon to his uninjured shoulder.

"You SOB, your man shot Shellie!" Kinnard yelled.

"Not my man," Matt said. "You don't know him?"

"Hell, no. Who the bloody hell is he?" Kinnard bellowed.

"Tell me who hired you, and I'll get you to the cabin."

"Go to hell." Kinnard brandished the rifle in Matt's direction, but Matt grabbed the barrel and twisted it sideways, then shoved the end of it into the snow.

"Listen to me. Do you know who hired you?" Matt growled, aiming the MAC-10 at him. "Was it Margo Vick?"

Kinnard let go of the rife with a groan. "All I know is I was told where to go, when to get there, and how long I had to grab the kid before the alarm went off."

Another shot rang out and Matt and Kinnard both dove for the ground.

"You had to know who you were dealing with. You made the ransom call."

"I didn't do nothing but grab the kid and bring him and Shellie up here. The same guy who hired me told me to meet you for the ransom. He told me to kill the woman and the baby once I'd captured you. But Shellie wanted the baby—" He stopped. "Shellie!"

Just then a low rumbling that Matt hadn't noticed grew louder. He felt the ground beneath them tremble.

"Snowslide!" he shouted, scrambling to get his feet under him. He had to get to the cabin.

Kinnard cursed and began crawling toward the trees.

The rumbling grew in volume. Matt looked to the north, toward the peak of the mountain, and saw the white cloud foaming upward toward the heavens, obscuring the moon's light.

He was at least forty feet from the cabin. But about eight feet uphill was a sturdy-looking evergreen. Its trunk looked just about right for him to be able to hook his arms around.

He lunged forward, scrambling to get a foothold in the wet snow. He managed to shove his way through the branches and wrap his arms around the trunk as the first billowing drifts of snow reached him.

He ducked his head and locked his hands around the barrel of the MAC-10, praying that the steel and his fingers would hold.

But he was pretty sure he was going to be buried anyway.

Dear God, he prayed. *Let Deke find Aimee and her baby. Keep her safe.*

AIMEE HEARD THE ROAR and felt the ground shake.

Avalanche.

Muffled thuds jarred the walls and windows, rattling the glass. It was snow slamming into the cabin's walls.

"William!" she cried, throwing herself across the remaining foot or so of hardwood floor and grabbing his seat in her arms.

A vague memory from childhood tickled the edge of her brain. A children's education piece on what to do in a snowslide. The most important thing, she recalled, was to keep a pocket of air in front of one's face, and of course, not to panic.

She and William were inside, and probably safe, even if the cabin was buried, but what about Matt?

Dear heavens, he was out there with no protection.

She heard his voice as clearly as if he were next to her. *Take care of William. I'll take care of myself.*

You'd better, she answered silently. Holding on to William's safety seat, she crawled across the floor to the central wall that divided the kitchen from the bedroom. It seemed like it would be the strongest place to wait out the slide.

Provided the snow was heavy enough to crush the cabin, they might survive.

She lay down against the wall and cradled William's seat against the curve of her body.

"Hi, William Matthew Vick," she whispered, touching his cheek for the first time since he'd been kidnapped. "Smile for me," she coaxed. He waved his arms and cooed.

She leaned forward to kiss his little face. "That's right. I've been waiting a long time to see you, too." Her eyes filled with tears. She blinked and one fell on William's forehead. She wiped it away.

"Hang in there with me," she said softly. "I've got someone I want you to meet. He's a brave man. He took care of your daddy and he took care of me."

As she spoke the words, she realized that she meant them. Matt would have done everything in his power to save Bill—even sacrificed himself if it meant Bill could have lived to see his son. That was the kind of man Matt was.

She smiled sadly and blinked away her tears. "A very brave man," she whispered as the rumbling of the cascading snow grew louder and the cabin's timbers creaked and groaned.

Behind her, glass shattered. She pulled William closer and covered his seat with her torso and arms.

As THE SNOW PILED UP around Matt, he pondered whether the latest theory of surviving a snowslide made sense. It was called the Brazil nut effect. The theory was that, when shaken, larger and less dense objects rose to the top of water, snow or, in the case of Brazil nuts, the contents of a can of mixed nuts.

The idea was to let the moving snow shake you to the top as more dense rocks and limbs were plowed under. Many experts felt it made more sense than the theory of trying to swim by flailing one's arms.

The snow was piling up over his head, and his arms and legs were trembling, they were so tired. The tree's trunk was bent almost double and its roots were coming loose from the ground.

Matt figured that if the Brazil nut theory were wrong, he had two chances—slim and none. But he opted for optimism.

With a deep breath, and gripping the MAC-10 as tightly as he could with his exhausted, frozen right hand, he let go of the tree and let the snow carry him down the mountain.

Take care of William, he whispered silently to Aimee. *Don't worry about me.* As the snow billowed around him and he covered his nose and mouth with his left arm, warm tears mixed with the freezing crystals on his cheeks.

SUNDAY 0700 HOURS

MATT WAS FREEZING. He was afraid to move, afraid of finding out that he couldn't. For a few minutes, he lay doubled in on himself like a fetus, figuring that eventually he'd get up the courage to move. And he'd count himself lucky if his fingers and toes didn't break off when he wiggled them.

The sun was up. That surprised him. The last thing he remembered was floating on snow in the darkness. Now the sun felt warm on his shoulder and back. But strangely, there was also warmth below him. Warmth and sticky wetness.

Don't let it be blood.

Not yet brave enough to move, he assessed his position. His head, covered by his parka's hood, was tucked between his shoulders, and its hem was pulled down as far as it would go over his butt. He didn't remember doing any of that.

All he remembered was letting go of the tree and floating downhill on a wave of snow.

And praying that Aimee and her baby were all right. *Aimee!*

He straightened—or he tried to. He couldn't move, and it wasn't just because his muscles were ice-cold.

Something was on top of him, weighing him down.

Snow? He took a deep breath, preparing to push against the weight, and his nostrils filled with the unmistakable spicy smell of evergreen needles.

When he tried to move, pain shrieked along his nerve endings.

Nausea engulfed him. Sternly, he forced his brain to rise above the pain and think rationally.

One part of his body hurt more than all the rest, but for the life of him he couldn't figure out which part it was. The pain seemed to be everywhere at once. And the nausea was making it worse. He stuck out his tongue and lapped at a few snowflakes that were caught on his lips.

Then, carefully, he flexed his ankles, relieved that his brain still had that much control over his limbs, and waited. They weren't causing the nauseating pain.

After a few agonizing seconds, his cold calf muscles responded and relaxed. Matt blew out a breath. One by one, he tested each muscle without actually moving. Each time, he cringed and braced himself for the shrieking pain. It was a slow, excruciating process.

Finally, he concluded that his feet and legs weren't the problem.

Then he realized he hadn't opened his eyes. When he did, he saw the crisscrossed shadows of evergreen branches. Inhaling carefully, he smelled wood, evergreen—and blood.

Oh, hell. The sticky stuff was blood. Trying not to move his head, he looked down at himself, and saw where the blood was coming from.

A small branch was embedded in the meaty part of his left forearm.

He gagged and his mouth filled with acrid saliva as his stomach heaved. Icy sweat beaded on his face and trickled down the side of his neck. What if that wasn't the only branch that had impaled his body?

What if he couldn't get to Aimee and William?

Lying still, Matt racked his brain for a way to free himself from the tree.

He had a small handsaw in his backpack. He groaned in frustration. The backpack had burned up in the Hummer. What did he have on him?

A knife. In a scabbard attached to his belt. Now if he could just get to it.

In between several bouts of nausea and a couple of periods of unconsciousness, he finally worked the knife out of its scabbard with his right hand without ripping the stick out of his arm.

Once he had the knife in his hand, it was only a matter of about a half hour of excruciatingly slow and careful sawing to cut the thin stick loose from the branch. And then another thirty or forty minutes to extricate himself from underneath the branch. Afterward, he barely remembered anything about it, except for the awareness that he was taking much too long and bleeding a lot.

All in all, it was a miracle that he lived through it. And a miracle that the thin branch hadn't broken a bone. He shuddered, hoping the miracles didn't run out too soon, because he was pretty sure he was going to need a few more of them.

And as hard as he tried to pretend that it wasn't a problem having his forearm skewered on a stick, he knew better.

So much for miracles. With only one arm, he wasn't sure even a miracle could help him save Aimee and William. But he had to try.

As he put his right glove back on, he heard something.

It was a baby—crying.

William!

He was close. At least he was close to them. His eyes filled with tears. Now all he had to do was figure out exactly where he was in relation to Aimee and the baby.

Looking around, he noted that whatever he was sitting on, it was a few feet above the surrounding snow. He blinked, trying to get his bearings. Maybe if he stood...

He tried to tuck his left arm against his chest, but the stick was in the way.

With a sick desolation, he faced the truth. He couldn't do anything until he got rid of the piece of wood. The good news was that it was barely more than a twig—maybe a half inch in diameter and around four inches long. The bad news was that four inches was hardly enough to grip.

With his right hand, he picked up a twig lying nearby

and put it between his teeth, then tried to view his impaled arm detachedly, as if it were someone else's.

For a few minutes, he bathed his forearm in snow, numbing it with cold.

Then, biting on the twig, he carefully wrapped his right hand around the two inches of bloody wood protruding from the inside of his arm. He took deep breaths until he was drunk on oxygen. Then with a roar, he slowly and deliberately pulled the stick out of his arm.

And passed out.

Chapter Twelve

Matt's arm hurt like hell. He opened his eyes and looked at the matching holes on either side of his forearm, where the stick had been.

He frowned. *Stick?*

Eventually, he remembered that his arm had been impaled on a small sharp branch, and that he'd pulled it out himself. Maybe it was a good thing that he didn't recall the specifics.

The two holes on either side of his arm were oozing blood. Another miracle. The stick hadn't shredded an artery.

He licked his dry, chapped lips and tried to sit up. Reflected sunlight nearly blinded him.

He looked down. He was sitting on something metallic. He brushed snow away to reveal a slab of tin.

A tin roof. He was on top of the cabin!

His whole body trembled in relief. That's why he'd heard William crying. Aimee and her baby were directly below him. All he had to do was get to a door or window. Then he could get them out and get them to the next rendezvous point and they'd be safe.

Rendezvous point. Deke.

Matt shook his head as trepidation churned in his stomach. How was he going to get them to the rendezvous point? He wasn't even sure he could stand up.

He'd arranged for Deke to put down near the peak at 0900 hours. But since the last storm and the avalanche, he had no idea what conditions were like there.

He needed to talk to Deke.

Awkwardly digging into the inside pocket of his parka with his right hand, he pulled out the satellite phone. At least the sky was clear this morning. He pressed the call button on the phone. The light came on. Thank God the battery wasn't frozen.

He read the time on the phone's display. After 0800 hours.

He punched in Deke's number.

"Matt!" Deke's voice was distorted by static. "Son of a gun! What the hell's going on?"

"Deke." His voice was hoarse and shaky. He cleared his throat. "Are we on for 0900?"

Static filled his ear. He turned his head, trying to get a better signal.

"—don't know if I can—put down—"

"Deke," Matt shouted. "0900. 0900. Be there."

"—firmative—"

Deke was worried that the new snow would make it impossible for him to set the helicopter down near the peak, but he would be there.

It was up to Matt to make sure Aimee and William got there. Between them, he and Deke would figure out how to get them into the helicopter.

Matt checked the battery life of his phone. Not good.

It was down to one bar. He pocketed it and awkwardly pushed himself to his feet, holding his throbbing left arm close against his chest. The first thing he saw was the barrel of the MAC-10, sticking out from under a dusting of snow and partially hidden by the tree.

He grabbed it, wondering if the cold had rendered it useless. Then he scanned the landscape, assessing the slide's wreckage.

The slide had deposited what looked like about two feet of powder over the snow that had already fallen.

About twenty feet away, something stuck up at an odd angle from the snow. Matt shaded his eyes and squinted. It was a body, clothed in winter camo.

Kinnard. Damn. Based on the angle and rigidity of his body, he had to be dead and either frozen or in rigor.

Turning toward the south, he searched for any sign of Al Hamar, with no luck. His best estimate of when Al Hamar's rifle shots had come from put the terrorist beyond the worst of the piled-up snow. If he'd stayed put, he was probably unhurt.

Matt couldn't afford to assume that Al Hamar was no longer a threat.

Matt had to proceed as though the terrorist had survived the storm. He surveyed the whole visible landscape, but didn't see any new footprints, any disturbance of the new snow. He saw no sign that suggested anyone had been there.

Kinnard was dead. But Matt had to assume that Al Hamar was still out there somewhere. That meant Aimee was still in danger. Because although Novus needed Matt alive so he could be questioned, he had no use for Aimee or her baby.

Matt looked back at Kinnard's frozen body. This time he spotted the assault rifle, half buried in the snow. He needed that rifle. So he used a few precious minutes to trudge through the snow. He confirmed that Kinnard was dead. Then he dug the rifle out of the snow with his good hand.

Turning back toward the cabin, he examined the tree that had fallen onto the cabin's roof, and onto him. Its roots were still partially embedded in the ground. And that meant that only part of the tree's weight was resting on the cabin.

At that instant, the tree creaked and settled, shaking the cabin. Its movement drew his attention to a branch that had penetrated the roof in the same way the stick had penetrated his arm.

Dear God, don't let Aimee or William be hurt.

Matt cautiously approached the downhill side of the cabin. As he got closer, he saw the damage the big tree had caused. The sides of the cabin had been crushed.

The slight bump he saw in the roofline told him the central portion of the structure had withstood the weight of the tree better than the sides. But the way the tree was creaking and moving, its roots might give way at any minute, and its full weight would flatten the cabin.

He had to get Aimee and her baby out of there.

Cradling his hand, he climbed over the snowdrifts and landed on the porch with a thud, jarring the hell out of his arm.

The pain was like a punch to his gut. For a few seconds he couldn't get his breath as dizzying nausea racked him.

Then he heard William crying again. He couldn't tell

exactly where the sound was coming from, and ice crystals had formed on the panes of the door. He rubbed them away, trying to see inside.

"Aimee!" he called. "Aimee! Are you okay?" He couldn't see anything through the glass panes. The inside of the cabin was pitch-black.

"Aimee! Answer me!"

SUNDAY 0900 HOURS

THE HEAVY TREE that lay on top of the cabin shifted as the snow melted around it, and the roof creaked and groaned. Aimee shook her head as she stared at the huge branch that had speared through the cabin's roof right in front of the wall where she'd huddled with William. It had missed them by several feet, but somehow that wasn't comforting.

She jumped and cringed as a thud reverberated through the cabin. Another tree falling? She wasn't sure. All she knew was that the loud bang was the latest in a long night full of very scary sounds. Many of them from the cabin itself. The center wall where she'd huddled with William had turned out to be a very good choice.

When the tree had hit the cabin, glass had popped out of the windows and studs and logs had cracked loudly. Nails screeching against wood, and logs crunching under the weight of the tree, had continued all through the night.

Every screech, every crunch, had Aimee cringing and hovering over William to protect him, terrified that the cabin's structure wouldn't hold for another second.

She clutched William closer and whispered to him. "I know, William, I know. You're so uncomfortable.

Your mommy isn't taking very good care of you." She took a shaky breath. "You're wet and hungry, and all I've got is this cold bottle of formula."

Earlier, she'd dared to leave William long enough to weave her way into the kitchen around the debris. She'd found a bottle turned upside down on the drain board, with its top beside it. Further searching had yielded two cans of baby formula.

William had taken a little formula, but he scrunched up his face, making sure his mommy knew he didn't like it. That, plus his reaction to her fear, made him fussy.

She'd held him through the rest of the night, singing lullabies and trying to pretend for his sake that she didn't believe they were the only survivors of the snow-slide. Trying to believe that Matt was out there some-where, trying to get to them.

"Aimee!"

She stopped murmuring to William and listened. She'd dozed a few times during the night, only to wake up thinking she heard Matt calling her. But it always turned out to be the wind howling or the timbers of the house rubbing together.

"Matt?" It was foolish, she knew, to answer the wind, but there was nobody to hear her except William.

"Aimee? Are you all right?"

That sounded real. She held her breath, listening. Hoping with every fiber of her being that it really was Matt. At the same time fearing she was hallucinating. She was desperately afraid that he hadn't survived.

Then she heard a pounding on the door. She looked up, squinting against the glare of sunlight on snow.

Pushing herself to her feet, still clutching William to her chest, she forced her stiff muscles to move.

She had to thread her way around the limb that had impaled the roof, and between fallen beams and broken glass, but she finally got to the door. She rubbed frost off the glass. "Oh, dear heavens, Matt! It's really you."

"Aimee."

Standing in front of the door with the sun and bright snow behind him, he looked like an angel. The parka's hood was pushed back. His ears were bright red, his cheeks were chapped, and his mouth was compressed into a thin line, but he was there. And he was beautiful.

He grabbed the doorknob and pushed. It didn't move.

"Matt, the cabin's crushed—"

"Get away from the door." He put his right shoulder against it and shoved.

Something cracked, and a broken board fell, barely missing his arm.

"Matt, stop! You're going to get hurt." Aimee had never seen him so desperate.

He kicked away the board and pulled his MAC-10. "Get as far back as you can. I'm going to break the window."

"Wait!" Aimee yelled.

He stopped, surprised.

"Matt, the door's stuck, and the cabin is collapsing. Slow down. We need to figure out what to do."

He pressed a gloved hand against the glass. "Listen to me. We don't have time. Deke is going to be at the peak in less than ten minutes. I've got to get you and William up there."

Her first reaction was excitement. "Deke's coming?" They were safe.

But Matt's face told a different story. He looked exhausted, desperate, defeated.

Shifting William's weight to her right arm, she laid her left hand against his right on the other side of the cold glass.

"What's wrong?" she asked softly.

He laid his forehead against the glass. The corners of his mouth were white and pinched. "My phone is almost dead. I won't be able to contact Deke again."

Aimee heard what he didn't say. This was their last chance. "Break the windows," she said, and backed away.

He met her gaze. She wasn't sure what he was looking for in her eyes, but she knew by looking at him that his goal was the same as hers.

Get William to safety.

He swung the handle of the MAC-10 at the panes of glass.

She wanted to cry at the weakness of his swing. He was exhausted. He'd spent the night out in the freezing cold. He'd fought to get to them. She was terribly afraid that he was using up the last dregs of his strength to save her baby.

And she was going to let him do it.

Several blows later, there was a fair-sized hole in the door. Not large enough for her to get through, but plenty of room for William's safety seat.

"Matt, stop! That's enough." Without waiting to hear his response, she ran back to the wall and secured William into his safety seat. Then she took one of the blankets she'd used for warmth, and wrapped it around the seat.

When she looked up, Matt was bracing himself to swing again. "Get back," he shouted.

His hoarse voice and his pinched face attested to his exhaustion. He was hovering at the end of his strength.

Would he make it to the peak? She had to believe he would.

"Matt. There's no time. Here."

"What are you doing?" Matt cried. "Another couple of minutes and I'll have enough room to get you out."

"No. There's no time."

He stared at her as if he didn't understand what she was saying. After a second, he nodded.

She kissed William and took a precious few seconds to whisper to him. "I swore once I got you back in my arms I'd never ever let you go. You're the most important thing in my life. You *are* my life. But I can't keep you safe here."

She touched his chin and he giggled, which brought tears to her eyes. "That's right. It's too cold here. So Matt's going to take you someplace where you'll be safe, and I'll see you soon, okay? You can trust him. I do."

She kissed him one last time, then covered the seat with the blanket, and handed it through the broken panes to Matt.

When he reached out his right hand to take the baby seat's handles, Aimee saw the blood that stained the left sleeve of his parka.

"Matt, you're bleeding."

He shook his head. "Not so much anymore."

"You can't make it to the peak like this. What happened?"

His grim mouth flattened. The only color in his face came from the bright spots on his cheeks. "I'll make it. Stay inside. Stay warm. I'll be back for you," he rasped.

She blinked away tears. She touched his hand. "I know you will."

Gripping William's seat, he turned away.

"Matt," Aimee called.

He looked over his shoulder at her.

"I trust you."

For an instant, his gaze held hers, then he nodded and turned. He carefully maneuvered the sloping hill of snow in front of the cabin, holding tightly to the baby seat with his right hand.

Aimee watched him as long as she could. Finally, she had to accept that no matter how hard she strained, she wouldn't get another glimpse.

The man she'd once thought she could never count on now held her baby's fate in his hands. And she'd told him the truth.

She trusted him to keep William safe.

She moved back to the center wall, wrapped herself in the remaining blanket, and sat down to wait for Matt to return.

She didn't allow herself to consider that he might not make it back.

Above her, the snow-laden boards creaked ominously.

MATT HEARD THE HELICOPTER long before he saw it. The rhythmic drone of the propellers was strangely soothing. He matched his pace to the engine's cadence.

At least he was warming up. Probably the combined efforts of climbing and maintaining his balance with only one arm. Setting the baby seat on a downed tree trunk, he lifted the blanket slightly to check on William. It was the third time he'd peeked.

But no matter how much he lectured himself that he needed to keep the blanket in place so William didn't get cold, he found it impossible to go more than a few minutes without checking on him.

William was fussy and unhappy, but he'd stopped crying. That worried Matt.

Like he knew anything about kids.

He figured the baby was wet or hungry or both. He hoped that was all that was wrong. But as fussy as William was, whenever Matt checked him, his blue eyes latched on to Matt's and widened.

"Do you have any idea who I am?" Matt whispered. "I'm your godfather. Not that I deserve to be. I haven't done a very good job of taking care of you so far, but I'm hoping I can fix that in just a couple of minutes."

William waved his arms and whined.

"I know. It's cold. But you're about to have an adventure that possibly no man your age has experienced."

His mouth twitched. "That's right," he said. "You *are* a man. A little man right now, but a man. A brave, good man, just like your daddy."

At that moment, Matt noticed that the sound of the helicopter had gotten louder. The propellers appeared from the other side of the mountain, rising up like the cavalry coming over the hill in a B Western movie.

Matt sat the baby seat down and waved with his right hand.

Deke, in his supercool sunglasses and his helmet and earpiece, waved back. He maneuvered the bird so that he was hovering almost directly over Matt's head. The downdraft created by the propellers whipped around, lofting the blanket that protected William.

Matt knelt and tucked the corners of the blanket securely around the baby.

When he glanced up, Deke was holding up his satellite phone. Matt reached for his, hoping the battery hadn't died.

To his relief, he saw that its light was on.

"I'm glad to see you're still upright. The weather service reported an avalanche, and I could see the results when I flew in." Deke's voice was cut by static.

"I rode it. Kinnard and his girl didn't make it."

"Damn. Aimee and the baby okay?"

Matt nodded. "Drop a basket," he yelled into the phone. "You're taking the baby."

A surprised expletive slipped from Deke's lips. Then he recovered. "You got it. Be right back." The helicopter rose and angled away from the mountain peak.

Matt knew what he was doing. He needed room to hover on autopilot while he secured a rescue basket to a rope.

While he waited, Matt made sure that William was snugly strapped into his safety seat. Then he tucked the blanket in tightly. "Okay, William Matthew Vick. You ready for your great adventure?"

To his utter shock, William giggled. Matt couldn't stop himself from smiling. He pulled off his glove and traced the baby's plump cheek with his forefinger.

"You're as beautiful as your mother," he whispered, surprised when his voice broke.

Above him Deke was back, maneuvering until he

hovered directly over them, blasting them with down-draft. Then he lowered the heavy metal basket. Matt grabbed the cold steel.

Even the slightest movement made his arm shriek with pain. But the only way he could hang on to the basket was to embrace the line with his left arm.

He picked up William's baby seat and lifted it over and in, then grabbed the bungee cord that was attached to one side and ran it through the handles of the baby seat and secured it to the other side. By the time he completed those maneuvers, he was dizzy and sick with pain.

He looked up, still holding on to the cage, and waved at Deke, who gave him a thumbs-up.

Matt watched, not breathing, as Deke activated the crank that raised the basket. When it was close enough, Deke leaned out and grabbed it, lifting it in through the open door. Once the basket was safely inside, Deke sent Matt another thumbs-up, then held up his satellite phone.

Matt retrieved his phone.

"—the hell's wrong with your arm?"

"Forget it," Matt growled. "Get the baby out of here."

"What about you and Aimee—?"

"You'll have to put down."

Deke nodded. "Six hours?"

Matt had racked his brain about where Deke could safely set the helicopter down. The original secondary rendezvous place was a clearing two miles southwest from the cabin. It was probably the best choice.

"Secondary rendezvous," he yelled into the phone.

Deke shook his head and shrugged. "Wha—?"

The static was growing. Matt knew his phone was

about to go dead. "Secon—dary ren—dez—vous," he enunciated slowly.

Deke ducked his head, listening. Then nodded. "—dary—"

Relief nearly buckled Matt's knees. Deke had heard him.

"Deke," he yelled. "Anything on the sabotage?"

Deke shook his head and spoke, but all Matt got was static. He looked at his phone's display in time to see the battery light go out. It was dead. That was it. This would be the last communication until they were rescued.

If they were rescued. He waved the phone and shook his head.

Deke frowned and then held up six fingers.

He wanted confirmation of the time. *Six hours.* Enough time for as much snow as possible to melt.

Matt nodded and gave Deke the thumbs-up.

Deke returned the gesture, grinning. Then he held up his forefinger, followed by five fingers, then his closed fist, and his closed fist again.

1500 hours. Three p.m.

Matt repeated the signs with his right hand.

Deke mimed a salute, turned the helicopter and flew off.

Matt watched until it disappeared over the edge of the peak. Then he fell to his knees, his stomach heaving and clenching, although he had nothing in it. Then he raked up a small handful of snow and let it dissolve on his tongue, hoping the chill would chase away the queasy dizziness.

The pain in his forearm had become a constant

agony, made worse by the numbness in his fingers. He unzipped his parka and tucked his hand inside, hoping to warm his fingers without having to move them. He felt warm blood trickling down his cold arm. He shivered.

Then he staggered to his feet. He had to get back to Aimee. She'd be happy to know that William was safe.

He'd be happy if he could get her safely to the rendezvous point before he collapsed from blood loss.

Chapter Thirteen

SUNDAY 1100 HOURS

It had been almost twenty-four hours with no communication from Kinnard. He hoped to hell the jerk hadn't run off with the money. He trusted him, but only so far.

He tried Kinnard again. No response. It wasn't the storm this time. The skies were clear. He tried Kinnard's girlfriend, too, but no luck there.

Maybe Parker had killed them.

He drummed his fingers on the computer table. Parker could certainly have killed Kinnard. From what he'd seen in the years he'd worked for Black Hills Search and Rescue, it was pretty obvious that Parker would do anything for one of his oath brothers—or for Aimee Vick.

But killing the girl who'd been brought in to take care of the Vick baby—that was another matter. Parker wouldn't have the stomach for that.

He stood, kicking his desk chair backward. Looking out the window at the Black Hills, he doubled his hands into fists and forced himself to stay calm. Hopefully, Kinnard and the girl were dead. If they'd turned tail and run, all his careful plans could be in jeopardy.

He picked up his prepaid cell phone and looked at it. He did not want to make this report, but he had to.

AIMEE SQUINTED against the glare of the sun on the brilliant white snow outside the cabin door, and swung the stick of firewood at it one more time. To her relief, the pane of glass finally broke.

The stick of firewood she wielded in her gloved hands was heavy, but the cabin's door was solid wood and the frames that held the six panes of glass were solid. Even the glass seemed to be reinforced.

She'd been working ever since Matt had left. She didn't have a watch, but she knew it had been a long time—maybe too long.

No. She wouldn't—couldn't—worry about William. Matt would die to save him.

She swung again, letting the reverberation of the blow shake that thought from her mind.

"Matt—won't—die," she muttered as she swung again and again. He'd promised her he'd be back. She believed him.

"He—won't—die." She dropped the log from her aching hands and blew out a breath.

She eyed the hole where the glass panes had been. It was big enough for her to crawl through—probably. But if she climbed out now, she'd have nothing to do but sit in the snow and wait for Matt to show up.

The roof creaked again, and Aimee cringed. The fear that had dogged her ever since the sun had begun beating down on the snow sent her pulse skyrocketing. What if the roof collapsed?

Maybe it was a good idea to go ahead and climb out.

She could wait for Matt outside in the sunshine, away from the possibility of being crushed when the tree's last clinging roots let go and dumped its full weight on the cabin roof.

She grabbed the daypack, and then remembered the food and drinks she'd seen in the kitchen. Running into the kitchen, she chose a few things to put in the daypack. Too much and it would be too heavy to carry. Then she went through the kitchen drawers, checking to see if she saw anything that might come in handy. She found a couple of odd-shaped pieces of metal that she assumed were key rings, a small can opener with no handles. She had no idea if it was broken or if it was made that way, but she stuck it in the bag anyway.

One of the drawers seemed to be dedicated to first aid supplies. She grabbed antibiotic ointment, gauze, tape and a small bottle of alcohol. Then she saw a pair of scissors and stuck them in the pack, as well.

Lifting the pack, she grimaced at its weight. "I'll ask Matt," she told herself. "He can dump whatever he thinks we don't need."

Back in the front room she examined the hole in the door and brushed away all the glass shards and splinters of wood she could see. Folding the blanket several times, she lay it over the bottom of the jagged opening.

Outside, drifts of snow glistened with water where the sun hit them.

She went back to the kitchen and grabbed a chair to drag over to the door, but stopped when she heard something. She glanced up, cringing. Had the tree's roots finally let go?

"Aimee?"

A thrill lanced through her. "Matt?" She whirled. There he was, on the other side of the broken door. Spots of color stained his cheeks, standing out against his pale skin and pinched mouth. His left hand was tucked inside his unzipped parka, and blood stained the sleeve—more than before.

"Matt!" She was stunned at his appearance. His face was set, with lines of pain etching it. His eyes were too bright, and appeared sunken. And his face was horribly pale. She pasted a smile on her face, trying not to show how worried she was about him. "Is William—?"

He nodded and a tight smile lightened his drawn features. "He's safe. Deke's got him." His voice was hoarse, and he was obviously trying to sound upbeat.

"You put him in the helicopter?"

"Actually, he rode up in a basket."

"A basket?" she repeated, horrified at the picture his words evoked.

"These are specially designed for rescuing people. Like the ones they used down in New Orleans during Katrina."

"Oh." She wasn't convinced about the safety, but if William was fine, then that's all that mattered.

He coughed. "I see you found something to do. You finished breaking in the windows."

"I figured it was about time for me to chip in."

"Let's get you out of there."

"You just stay back. I can do this myself."

He lowered his gaze and complied. That sent an

arrow of hurt through her. Not because she needed his help, but because he knew he was too weak to offer it.

She grabbed the daypack and lifted it through the broken window. Lowering it by one strap, she let it fall to the ground. Then she pulled the chair over.

Standing on it, she climbed through the broken panes and hopped to the ground. Then she picked up the blanket, shook it out and rolled it up.

"Leave it," he said.

"Are you sure? Because I can carry it—"

"Leave it."

She tossed the blanket back inside. "How far are we going?"

"About two miles."

"Two miles? That's not bad. Deke's going to meet us?"

He nodded. "At 1500 hours. Three o'clock."

She frowned. "Isn't that a long time?"

"Not really. About five hours from now. He needs time for the—sun to melt the snow," he said raggedly. "And we need time to get there. Let's go."

"No." Aimee crouched and unzipped the daypack. She dug in it for the first aid items. "We're not going anywhere until I take care of your arm. You're still bleeding. What did you do?"

He caught her arm. "No."

"Matt, yes! You're about to collapse. You can't go any farther until we stop that bleeding."

"Not here. The tree—"

As if on cue, the branches creaked and scraped across the tin roof.

Of course. The tree. They had to get out of the way, in case it fell. "Come on, then. Let's get away from here."

"Go on," Matt said tightly. "I'll follow."

"Oh, no, you don't. You took care of me when I was hypothermic. It's my turn."

She zipped up the daypack and slung it onto her back, sticking her arms through the straps. "Will it help you to lean on me?"

Matt's mouth turned up in a wry smile. "I already am," he muttered. "More than I should."

After a couple of seconds, he shook his head. "No. Please go on. I'm going to be slower than—than you."

Aimee could tell his voice was getting weaker. *Don't quit on me,* she wanted to say. But that wasn't fair. He'd pushed himself further than she ever would have been able to. He wasn't quitting.

His wounded body was betraying him.

So she headed south for about fifty feet, stopping at a fallen tree trunk that was about the right height for sitting. She brushed snow off and sat to wait for him to catch up.

He walked slowly, doggedly, as if all that was keeping him on his feet was sheer determination. It broke her heart to watch his struggle. It took all her self-control not to run to help him.

Her eyes burned and her throat closed, but she busied herself with unloading the first aid supplies.

When he got to her she looked up, masking her feelings with a smile. "Sit down and let me see your arm."

He didn't even try to argue. He propped the rifle against the tree trunk and slid his parka off his right arm. Then he carefully peeled the sleeve off his left arm, doing his best not to move his arm.

His sweater was soaked with blood. Aimee swallowed against the nausea that rose in her throat. "Sit," she said as evenly as she could.

She took the scissors and cut the sleeves off his arm. "Oh, Matt. What happened? Is that a gunshot wound?"

His back was straight but his eyes were closed. "No," he muttered. "A branch."

"It went—" She twisted his arm slightly so she could see the underside, grimacing when he moaned. "It went all the way through?"

Dear heavens, don't let me hurt him. She knew that was a wasted prayer. She had to clean and wrap his arm. Everything she did was going to hurt him.

"I've got to get your watch off." His hand was swollen and discolored, and the watchband looked unbearably tight. "Please, believe me. I don't want to hurt you, but it's got to come off."

It wasn't easy, and Matt was wheezing in pain by the time she was done, but she got the watch unfastened. She put it on her wrist and buckled it in the last hole.

"Aimee—" he gasped. "Before you—get started, hand me the rifle."

"It's right next to you—" She stopped as understanding dawned. He knew where it was. He just couldn't lean over to get it. Every bit of strength he had was devoted to keeping himself upright. She couldn't imagine what it had cost him to ask her to pick up the rifle and put it in his hand.

She grabbed it and held it so he could get his right arm around it and his finger on the trigger. "Thanks," he breathed.

"I don't have anything to give you for pain," she said as she sat back down and gently touched his arm.

"Just hurry."

As quickly and as gently as she could, she poured alcohol over the top of his arm and caught it with gauze pads underneath. She cleaned both awful, gaping holes as well as she could, doing her best to ignore Matt's harsh breathing and frequent grunts of pain. By the time she was done, sweat was beading on her forehead and Matt had gone quiet.

"I don't know how doctors stand it," she muttered as she squeezed antibiotic ointment onto a clean gauze pad, applied it to the upper wound and did the same with the wound on the underside of his arm. Then she took a roll of gauze and wrapped it around his arm.

"Is that too tight?" she asked.

Matt raised his head a bit and he carefully moved his fingers. "Okay," he said shortly.

She secured the ends of the gauze with adhesive tape.

When she finished, she straightened and examined his face. His skin looked tight and drawn across his cheekbones. His mouth was compressed into a thin line, his nostrils and the corners of his lips were white and pinched. And sweat glistened on his forehead and neck.

"I'm done," she said. "Are you okay?"

"I will be."

She took a last gauze pad and wiped his face and neck, noticing that he was trembling.

"Okay, I've got something for you." She pulled out a self-heating container of hot chocolate. "I figured if I asked, you'd tell me to leave it because it was too heavy. But I think you're going to be glad I have it. I found it in one of the cupboards."

Pressing a button on the bottom of the container, she activated the chemical reaction in the container's sleeve that heated the chocolate drink inside.

"In about ten seconds, this is going to be hot chocolate. You need to drink it."

"We need to go."

"No. You're not going anywhere until you drink this." She waited until the container felt hot in her hands. Then she popped the tab and firmly pressed it into his right hand. "Drink."

"You need—"

"Listen, Matthew Parker. I haven't been out in the snow all night, and I didn't just single-handedly save a helpless infant. And I haven't lost pints and pints of blood. That chocolate's all yours. Besides, I had some already. I'm full."

She didn't miss his sidelong glance. She was lying, and he knew it.

Even though nothing but the nylon shell of her parka was touching the shoulder of his sweater, she felt the shudder that racked him as he swallowed the hot, sweet liquid.

Something shook loose inside her, and tears filled her eyes. Strangely, that had been happening a lot the past few days. She knew what Matt would say—probably what most people would say.

Your child's been kidnapped. It's natural to cry.

But that wasn't true—not for her. She'd decided a long time ago that for her, crying equaled losing control. For her entire adult life she'd prided herself on never crying.

All those times when control had slipped through

her fingers, leaving her feeling helpless and impotent—her parents' deaths, Bill's illness and tragic death, even William's kidnapping—at least she could say she didn't cry.

Ever since she and Matt had joined together to rescue William, she'd begun to look at tears differently. They had more to do with relief and joy and even sadness than with failure on her part.

Right now her tears reflected a poignant concern for Matt and a deep-seated satisfaction that, finally, she was able to give him back a fraction of the help he'd given her. She only hoped the energy in the chocolate drink would be enough to carry him to the rendezvous point. She watched him to make sure he drank every drop.

Matt's first swallow of hot chocolate spread through him like a flame of desire. As soon as it hit his stomach, however, a deep, bone-rattling shudder had racked his body. Partly a result of the hot liquid flowing through his chilled body, warming his insides. But also the clenching response of his empty stomach suddenly being hit with the sugary substance.

Once the initial queasiness passed, he actually felt a little better. The unrelenting pain in his arm was the same, but each throb didn't plaster black-edged stars before his eyes or trigger his gag reflex.

"Why don't you eat an energy bar?" Aimee said. "I've got several."

He squeezed his eyes shut and moved his head a fraction in a negative direction. He knew his gut wouldn't accept the chewy, fiber-rich bar.

"We need to get going." He stood. For a second, the

black-edged stars blinded him again, so he stood still, waiting for them to fade. He wasn't going to get far if the pain in his arm kept up. Just standing jarred it.

"I need you to do something else for me," he said.

Aimee looked up at him. "Anything," she said.

"Do you have any more tape or gauze?"

She looked into the bag. "Both, why? Are you hurt somewhere else?"

"I need you to immobilize my arm against my middle. If it starts bleeding again, I'll probably pass out, so I need to keep it as still as possible."

Aimee cut the left arm of his sweater and his long underwear, all the way up to the neck. Then she wrapped gauze around his wrist and back until his forearm was sealed against his torso. "I don't know how we're going to get your sweater or your undershirt back on."

He shook his head. "Just hand me the parka."

Finally, once he had his parka up over his right shoulder and draped over his left, he cautiously lifted his head, steeling himself against nausea and dizziness.

A flicker of light caught the edge of his vision. He squinted in that direction, but didn't see anything except snowdrifts and fallen trees. Was it his weakness, playing visual tricks on him?

He moved his head back and forth, trying to catch the reflection again. It could have been a piece of ice that caught the sun just right, or a tiny scrap of metal turned up by the snow.

Or it could have been something more ominous, like sunlight glinting off binoculars—or the barrel of a gun.

"Do you need to rest for a little while longer?"

"No," he said, rubbing his temple with his right hand. If someone—Al Hamar—was watching them, he didn't want him to think he'd spotted him.

And he didn't want Aimee to know his suspicion. She wouldn't be able to keep from looking behind them, and that could be fatal. He was still counting on Al Hamar needing him alive. All he had to do was make sure the terrorist couldn't get a clear shot at Aimee.

The only way he could do that was to stay so close to her that Al Hamar couldn't shoot her without running the risk of hitting him.

"I need something else," Matt said.

Aimee looked at him in surprise. "Sure. What do you need?"

"I need to lean on you." He held up Kinnard's rifle. "Hook the rifle over my right shoulder. Then I'm going to put my arm around your shoulders, just to keep me steady."

Aimee bit the inside of her cheek, doing her best not to cry. She saw in his face that he wasn't used to asking for help. "No problem," she said, putting a false brightness into her voice. "I might even get the chance to cop a feel."

She stepped in close enough to him so he could put his arm around her shoulders. "Can I put my arm around your waist without hurting you too much?"

Matt's breathing was fast and short. "I'd be—insulted if you—didn't."

Gingerly, she slid her hand under his parka and wrapped it around his middle, feeling the hard muscles of his back. Even covered by layers of clothes, they felt like long straps of steel.

It terrified her how frail and breakable the human body was. Not many hours ago, his lean, rock-hard body had covered hers, strong, demanding and unbearably sexy as they'd made love.

A thrill tightened her stomach at the memory. It seemed unreal now, like a fantasy, or a dream. It was a moment stolen out of time.

This was reality. Matt injured, needing her support.

Although the arm clutching her shoulders was corded with muscles, he leaned on her heavily, at this moment needing her more than she needed him.

It took a long time to figure out how to walk with Matt so close to her. Finally, once they found a rhythm, it seemed as if he were hardly leaning on her at all.

AIMEE LOOKED at Matt's watch on her wrist. It was two o'clock. She'd been denying the truth for over an hour. But the fact was that Matt was getting weaker—much weaker.

After he'd drunk the chocolate, he'd started out walking strongly, barely even resting his arm on her shoulder.

But the farther they went, the heavier he got. He was losing strength fast. She'd tried to get him to stop and eat something, but he'd refused. She'd forced him to drink a few of sips of water, but the last two times she'd held the bottle for him, he'd shaken his head doggedly and refused.

She was pretty sure her makeshift bandage had stemmed the flow of blood, but not in time. She knew he'd lost too much already. She knew nothing about blood loss or first aid, but it made sense that if he was losing blood he should be drinking water.

"Matt, here. Have some more water."

He shook his head. "Not now," he whispered.

It was the same answer he'd given the last three times she'd asked.

He turned his head to look behind them, as he'd done a number of times. Even though he hadn't said anything, she knew what he was doing. He was worried that someone was behind them, following them.

"I know there's someone following us," she said.

He didn't comment, but she felt a deep breath shudder through him.

"It's the terrorist, isn't it? You told me you found Kinnard dead, so it's got to be Al—Al—?"

"Al Hamar."

"So how do you want to handle him? Just keep ignoring him? It's after one o'clock. We should be getting close to the rendezvous point."

He nodded. "Half a mile—maybe." His voice was nothing more than a raspy whisper.

Half a mile. They'd only come three-fourths of the way? It felt like they'd been walking for hours.

And Matt sounded so weak it made her want to cry. But crying wouldn't accomplish anything. He'd been so strong for her. It was her turn to be strong for him.

"Matt. I'm not taking another step until you drink some water. You of all people should know that if you're losing blood, you should be drinking water." She uncapped the bottle and held it out.

"Drink," she commanded.

He took the plastic bottle, but all he did was fill his mouth. He acted like it was agony to swallow.

"Are you nauseated? Do you want another hot chocolate?" She tried to give him a smile. "It'll do you good."

He shook his head and swallowed the mouthful of water with difficulty. Then he blew out a hard breath, as if the mere act of swallowing had exhausted him.

His face had turned from merely pale to a very scary gray color. And she knew gray-tinged skin was not a good sign.

He wasn't going to make it.

As soon as that thought crossed her mind, her brain screamed in protest.

No. Matt couldn't be dying.

Oh, yes, he could, her rational brain answered her back.

The water bottle fell from his hands.

"Oh, no. That's all we've got!" Aimee let go of Matt and reached for the bottle, which had rolled away. The water represented life to her. If she could get him to drink the water, he'd be okay.

"Aimee!" Matt rasped.

She grabbed the bottle. "We only lost a little bit. It's still half-full."

She turned, holding the bottle up.

But Matt had gone down on one knee. His head was bent and as she watched, the rifle slipped from his shoulder.

"Matt! Oh, I am so sorry." She stood.

He lifted his head. "Get down!" he yelled hoarsely. "Now!"

She dove for the ground, her hands plowing snow in front of her.

Then she heard the gunshot.

Chapter Fourteen

SUNDAY 1500 HOURS

Matt heard the bullet whiz by his ear. His entire body clenched at the sound of the shot.

Ignoring the pain that throbbed through his injured arm, he grabbed the strap of Kinnard's rifle and crawled toward the pile of snow that marked where Aimee had fallen.

"Aimee," he whispered desperately. "Are you okay?"

He saw the top of her head.

"Keep down," he snapped, expecting another shot at any second.

He slithered like a snake across the melting snow until he was close to her. Then he flipped over, so he was facing the shooter.

He was going to have a hell of a time shooting with only one arm, but he could do it if he had to.

Aimee was in danger. He had to take a shot.

Lifting his head up over the top of the snow, he scanned the clearing, but didn't see anything.

"Matt?"

"Don't move." He knew he could outwait the other man. It would be hell to lie in wet snow with the pain in his arm stealing his breath and his fingers going numb again, but he was only minutes from getting Aimee to safety. He wasn't about to give up now.

Clammy sweat stung his eyes and rolled down his neck. His empty stomach cramped, sending nausea crawling up his throat.

There. A flash of sun on metal. He lifted the rifle with his right hand and looked through the scope, but he couldn't focus.

His eyes were blurry. He lowered the rifle and bent his head to wipe his eyes on his sleeve, but his sleeve was wet.

"Here," Aimee said. From somewhere, she pulled a dry piece of cloth and handed it to him.

He wiped his eyes and face. She took the cloth back. "Can I do something to help you hold the rifle? I could lie down and you could prop it on my back."

Matt barely heard her. Something else had grabbed his attention. He cocked his head and listened. He wasn't sure if he could trust his ears. He'd already found out he couldn't completely trust his eyes.

He rolled onto his right shoulder and looked up. He had heard the rhythmic whup-whup of helicopter blades.

Aimee followed his gaze. She gasped. "Matt! Is it Deke?"

Without waiting for him to answer, she waved her arms. "He's here! Deke!" she cried.

"Aimee, don't!" His left arm jerked, an instinctive move to try and grab her. He couldn't stop an involuntary cry. He sucked in a breath.

"He sees us."

Just as she pulled her arms down, another shot rang out.

"Ow!" she cried, grabbing her hand.

Matt pushed himself up onto his right elbow. "Aimee! Are you hit?"

She looked at her hand. "I felt something hot—but I don't see anything."

"Give me your hand."

He examined it closely. There was a tiny red scrape along the flesh of her palm below her little finger. "Looks like the bullet barely missed you."

He closed his eyes for a second, willing away the dizziness and blurred vision. Then he glared at her. "Could you please stay still, and do what I tell you?"

She bit her lip and her cheeks turned pink. "Yes, sir," she whispered.

"Bastard's desperate. He knows once Deke lands he's got no chance to kill you or capture me." He raised his head again, scanning the area for the shooter. "We've got to stay down until Deke lands," he told Aimee. "If Al Hamar starts shooting at the helicopter, Deke will have to abort."

"Abort?"

Matt nodded grimly. "We can't afford to lose the helicopter, or Deke. But don't worry. He's got a high-powered rifle on board. Maybe even a machine gun. He'll be back, loaded for bear."

She nodded, but her eyes were wide with fear.

"Our job is to stay down until he can put down. If I can, I'm going to take out Al Hamar when he tries to shoot the helicopter again. I'd like to take the SOB alive, but that may not be possible. The most important thing is to get you out of here."

"No," she snapped. "The most important thing is to

get *you* on that helicopter and to a hospital. I'll take my chances."

Matt felt his chapped, cracked lips widen in a smile. It hurt but he didn't care. He raised his brows. "You'll take your chances…"

Her cheeks got pinker, but she lifted her chin. "That's right. In fact, why don't you give me that rifle and I'll take care of Al Hamar, or whatever his name is."

The terrorist was shooting again, this time at the helicopter. Over the sound of the rotors, Matt heard the zing of a bullet ricocheting off metal.

Deke took the bird up a few dozen feet, but he didn't turn away.

Matt squinted up at him. "Come on, Cunningham. That's just stupid."

"What? What's the matter?"

"Deke's drawing his fire." Matt swiped his forehead on the sleeve of his parka again and flipped over onto his stomach, suppressing a groan.

"Why?"

Matt swallowed the bile that was threatening to erupt from his throat. He felt like he was about to puke his guts up. The good news was that his arm had quit hurting. It was just numb.

Or was that the bad news?

Pushing away those thoughts, he lifted the rifle and sighted through the scope. "He knows our terrorist friend's got to come out from his cover to get a shot at him. He's drawing him out so I can shoot him." He blew out a harsh breath. "I hope I can."

Aimee scooted over closer to him.

"I told you—"

"Matt, lean on me. Use me to brace the gun."

Matt's right arm was shaking with fatigue and weakness from loss of blood. He shook his head. "I can't even figure out what you're talking about."

"Here. Move over." She crawled around until her body was perpendicular to his. "Now let me lie down in front of you and you can brace the gun on my back. Won't that work?"

He didn't want to tell her that most of what she'd just said sounded like gibberish to his buzzing ears. He just watched as she lay flat on her stomach in front of him. "Now, can you brace the barrel of the rifle on me?"

Slowly, his brain processed her words. "Maybe so," he whispered. "I can try."

"Listen," Aimee said. "Deke's coming lower. Al Hamar will probably shoot at him." She took a long breath. "Get ready."

Matt set the barrel of the rifle across her shoulders and pushed himself forward until he could see through the scope. "Aimee?"

"Yeah?"

He blinked sweat out of his eyes, and swept the scope back and forth, looking for the terrorist. "I love you."

Her body stiffened, making the scope wobble. "Hey. Stay still. I almost had him."

"Are you okay?" she asked, a worried tone in her voice. "You sound like you've been drinking."

"Hold still." He concentrated all the energy he had left in him on watching through the scope. Then he saw him. Al Hamar. He'd slipped out from behind a tree to get a shot at Deke. He'd braced himself and was aiming at the helicopter that loomed over their heads.

"Don't move," Matt whispered. "I've got him." His vision wavered, but hell, it was a short shot. And the guy was presenting a perfect target, the way he stood with his feet apart. It was a sucker shot.

Slowly, carefully, Matt squeezed the trigger. He saw the man jerk, saw blood blossom on the leg of his pants. As he watched, the terrorist dropped to his knees.

Then the man turned the rifle on Matt. For an instant they were scope to scope, then Al Hamar shifted his barrel downward. He was going to shoot Aimee.

Matt pulled the trigger again and again and again.

The last thing he remembered was a burst of bright stars before his eyes.

SUNDAY 2000 HOURS

THE CLEAN WHITE SHEETS and pillow felt like heaven to Aimee's exhausted muscles and chapped skin. Even the cotton hospital gown couldn't have felt better if it were the finest silk.

But what felt better than all that, even better than the warm bathwater or the delicious hot soup they'd given her, was the tiny bundle that was nestled into the crook of her arm.

She looked down at William. He was asleep. He'd seemed singularly unconcerned that she'd been gone. As soon as she'd stopped kissing him all over his face and touching every tiny perfect finger and toe, he'd fallen right to sleep.

"Must be nice," she murmured drowsily, "to be so sure that everything's fine in your world." She chuckled softly. "Know what, William? I think they gave me something to make me sleepy." She reached for the cup of water on the bedside table and took a small sip, letting the cool wetness slide down her throat. "I'm just going to take a little nap while you're sleeping. Then when I wake up, we'll go find Matt."

Matt. Her heart gave a slight jump. Deke had told her he was going to be fine. Hadn't he? Her eyes drifted closed. Or had she dreamed it?

She didn't remember much after Deke got them into the helicopter. Just his deep, reassuring voice, saying everything was going to be all right.

But what else was he going to say in that situation? *Sorry, guys, looks like you're not going to make it?*

Then he'd put the helicopter down on the roof of the hospital and all kinds of mayhem had broken out. Men and women dressed in blue with rolling tables had rushed out into the wind and grabbed Matt.

Aimee remembered trying to see where they took him, but more people ran out and grabbed her. Somebody leaned over her and said something, and that was all she remembered until she woke up while a nurse's aide was bathing her.

Nurse. The nurses could tell her about Matt. She reached for the call button. Her movement disturbed William and he whimpered.

"Sorry, baby. I'm just going to call the nurse." But her arm was tired, and her eyelids were heavy. "In a minute," she whispered and tucked her arm closer around her baby.

THEY WERE BACK. Parker and Aimee Vick. According to a brief message from Irina, Parker was in surgery and expected to be okay, Aimee was fine, and she and her child had been reunited.

He couldn't deny that he was relieved that the child hadn't been harmed.

But how the hell had Parker managed to outsmart Kinnard at every turn? Kinnard knew these hills and conditions better than anyone he'd ever known. Parker was supposed to be a weather specialist and something of a survival expert, but Kinnard had at least three inches and fifty pounds on him, plus all the time Parker had been overseas in the military, Kinnard had been roaming the mountains, learning how to survive. Having been a Marine, he already knew how to fight.

He had to find out what had happened out there.

His cell phone rang. He glanced at the display. It was Irina's administrative assistant, Pam Jamieson.

"There's a briefing in the conference room in twenty," she said, all business as usual.

"Got it," he responded.

Good. He'd have information to pass on tonight. He glanced at his watch. He had just enough time to check on the next phase of the plan. With any luck, by this time tomorrow, Deke Cunningham would no longer be protected by the security surrounding Castle Ranch.

MATT JERKED. The terrorist! He was shooting at Aimee! Matt tried to pull the trigger, but he couldn't. Something was wrong with his hand.

He opened his eyes. All he saw was blue and white. Blue walls, low blue light. White sheets.

Sheets?

He looked down at himself. He was covered up to his chest by a white sheet. His left arm was wrapped up like a mummy and his right arm was strapped down, with tubes running in several different directions.

What the hell? He felt drugged. The way he'd felt years ago when he'd woken up from an emergency appendectomy. His eyes burned and his mouth was dry, but not as dry as it had been. His arm hurt, but not as badly as it had before.

Before what?

Closing his eyes, he tried to wipe his mind free of all the confusing and disturbing images that were clicking through it like a slide show gone out of control.

—Aimee, lying so close to the spreading pool of gasoline.

—Kinnard pointing that assault rifle at her.

—His own arm impaled by a sharp piece of wood.

—Kinnard's girl jerking as the bullet hit her head.

—Deke hauling up the basket carrying its precious cargo.

Matt growled and opened his eyes. Closing them had only sped up the slide show. He stared at the ceiling, counting off the pictures as they flashed across his inner vision, trying to pick out the latest ones and shuffle them into some sort of order.

He remembered Aimee waving at Deke, and the horrifying sight of the red dot wavering on the front of her parka.

He remembered her lying down in front of him so he could use her as a prop for the rifle barrel. He remembered pulling the trigger again and again and again.

But for the life of him he couldn't remember anything after that. What a weakling he was. Some rescuer he was. It was pretty bad when the rescuer himself had to be rescued.

It was a good thing Deke was there, because if it had been left up to him, Aimee would probably be dead now.

Aimee. He had to find her—check on her. He looked around for the nurse call button, and discovered that someone had had the foresight to put it next to his right hand. With more effort than he'd have thought he'd need, he lifted his hand enough to get his finger on the button and pressed it.

"—help you?"

"Get me a nurse now!" What he heard in his ears was nothing like what he'd intended. He'd barked a command, but a raspy whisper was all that had come out of his mouth. Plus the very act of punching the button and speaking had started his heart hammering and his head pounding.

He closed his eyes and pretended that the dampness that leaked out from under his lids wasn't tears.

"Mr. Parker, are you all right?"

He turned his head enough to see the pretty young woman dressed in some kind of smock with dogs and cats on it.

"Get me unhooked from all this stuff. I've got to check on Aimee."

The young woman smiled as she stepped over to the bed and patted his hand. "I'm glad to see you're awake and feeling better, but you're not going to be able to get up for a while. You've only been out of the recovery room for an hour or so."

"Recovery room?"

"The surgery on your arm." She punched some buttons

on the monitor that was beeping behind his head, and checked the bag of fluid that hung on a pole beside him.

"Everything looks good. You have some visitors who have been waiting for you to wake up. They're down in the coffee shop. I'll call them, and in a few minutes, I'll bring you a sleeping pill."

"Visitors? Is it Aimee?"

"Aimee? The young woman who was brought in with you? No." She pulled off gloves he hadn't noticed she had on and pumped a bit of antiseptic gel on her hands from a dispenser hanging on the wall.

"Wait a minute. Where am I?"

She pointed at a whiteboard, hanging on the wall directly across from his bed, where the name of the hospital, the date and the names of his nurses and aides were written. "You're in Crook County Hospital. Today is Sunday and my name is Jean. I'll be back soon."

Matt studied the tubes and needles that were sticking out of his right hand, trying to decide how much it would hurt to pull them out. He wanted to look more closely at them but for some reason he found it very hard to lift his arm. So he turned his attention to his other arm. He still had his hand. It was sticking out from the huge roll of bandages. It looked swollen and discolored, but at least it was there.

Before he had a chance to wonder what the surgeons had done to it, the room door opened and Irina Castle came in, followed by Brock O'Neill and FBI Special Agent Schiff.

"Matt! Oh my goodness, you look awful!" She laughed self-consciously as she stepped around to the far side of the bed and patted his hand. "I mean, you look wonderful, given all that you've been through. How are you feeling?"

Brock nodded and scowled as if he were irritated to see Matt alive. But that was his usual expression, so Matt merely nodded back.

"Where's Aimee?" he asked Irina.

"She and William are doing fine. Aimee's been admitted overnight, but they should be able to go home tomorrow." Irina looked at Schiff.

He stepped forward. "Sorry, but we need to talk to you."

Matt ignored him. "Irina, Aimee can't go home by herself. She's been through too much. Can you do something? I don't think it's a good idea for her to have to depend on Margo."

"Don't worry. We're going to take good care of her." She picked up the cup of water and held the straw to his lips. He took a couple of swallows and coughed.

"Margo Vick won't be going anywhere near Aimee," Schiff said. "Not anytime soon. I can promise you that."

"What are you talking about?"

"Once we found out that the baby was being held at the Vicks' hunting cabin, we got a warrant for Mrs. Vick's financial and telephone records, and her home. We found that a million dollars had been liquidated within the past week. Mrs. Vick and her accountant claim to know nothing about it. There were also two calls to Margo Vick's home telephone from a survivalist group of which Kinnard is a member."

"*Was* a member," Matt said.

Schiff's eyebrows rose.

"Kinnard's dead. I'll give you a statement, and I can

pinpoint the location of the body within a few yards."
Matt didn't mention Shellie. He'd give a formal, complete statement later.

The FBI special agent pulled a PDA from his pocket and made a quick note, then continued. "The telephone calls from the survivalist group were short, less than a minute. Mrs. Vick stated that she received a couple of calls in the past week, and she was asked to hold. She said she held for a short while, and then hung up."

Matt cut his eyes over to the FBI special agent. "It's possible she was framed."

"I know. It's beginning to look that way."

That surprised Matt. He lifted his head and immediately regretted it. The movement hurt his arm and he felt queasy. "What do you mean?" he asked softly.

"We picked up the body of the second man who was following you. Cunningham gave us the coordinates. He was carrying a cell phone, with a message from an unidentified number. The message was in Arabic. We got it translated. Basically, it said—" Schiff looked back at his PDA "—KILL KIDNAPPERS. NO SURVIVORS TO ID US."

Matt's pulse jumped. "The kidnapper *was* hired by Novus."

"Novus?" Schiff frowned. "The terrorist Novus?" He turned to glare at Irina.

When he did, Brock took a step closer to her.

"I figured the dead guy might be somehow involved with your search for your husband, but *Novus Ordo?*"

Irina gazed at him evenly.

"Well, that explains a lot. Not everything, but a lot. We had the voice of the caller who set up the ransom drop analyzed. There were certain inflections and idiomatic inconsistencies that indicated that English may not have been his first language."

"May not?" Irina repeated.

Schiff nodded. "The results were inconclusive. My expert said it was possible that the caller was trying to alter his phrasing to make us think he might not be American."

Matt closed his eyes and sighed. "So we can't prove whether the whole thing was engineered by Novus or not."

"It would help if all the people involved in the kidnapping weren't dead. Couldn't you have left one of them alive?"

"Agent Schiff," Irina broke in. "Matt needs to sleep. He's still under the effects of the anesthesia from his surgery."

Schiff sent her a sharp glance. "Fine. I'll get his statement tomorrow, when he's feeling better. Mrs. Castle, may I speak to you after we're done here?"

She put her hand on Matt's forehead and brushed his hair back. "We'll see."

"Irina, what about—what about the sabotage?" Matt whispered.

Irina leaned over. "We'll talk about that later," she said softly.

Just then the nurse came in. "It's time for Mr. Parker's medication."

Irina kissed him on the forehead. "Don't worry about Aimee," she whispered. "I'll see you tomorrow."

Brock hadn't said a word the entire time. In fact, he'd hardly moved, except when he'd intercepted Schiff. He'd just listened intently to everything that was said.

As Irina and Schiff left the room, Brock met Matt's gaze and nodded, the scowl still on his face.

The nurse injected something into the IV tubing that ran from the bag of fluid down into his hand. "There you go, Mr. Parker." She peeled off her exam gloves, then turned and looked at him.

"Who was that man?" she asked, her eyes wide and her cheeks flushed.

"The guy in the suit?"

"No. The one with the eye patch. The dangerous-looking one. Who was he?"

Matt's eyelids were getting heavy. "You mean Brock O'Neill?" he muttered. "That's a real good question. I'm not sure any of us know who he is." He peered at her. "You want me to introduce you?"

She laughed and shook her head. "Oh, no. I was married to a dangerous man once. I'll never make that mistake again. You get some sleep and I'll be back later to check your vital signs."

MONDAY 1100 HOURS

THE DOOR TO MATT'S hospital room was closed. It had taken Aimee much longer than she'd anticipated to be discharged, although the doctor had promised her yesterday that he was only admitting her overnight for observation. The nurses on her floor had brought her a set of scrubs to wear and had outfitted William with clothes from the pediatric floor.

But now, finally, she was here. She was supposed to be waiting downstairs for a taxi that the floor clerk had called, and she felt slightly guilty for leaving the driver sitting there, but she had to see Matt.

She shifted William's baby seat to her left hand and started to knock. But she hesitated. What if he were asleep? Or being given a bath? Or what if he didn't want to see her?

She took a deep breath. No matter what he wanted, she *was* going to see him, if only for a few minutes. She wasn't about to leave the hospital without making sure he was okay.

"If he's asleep, we'll go," she whispered to William. Instead of knocking, she gently pushed the door open.

The room was dark. The curtains were closed. The only light came from the weak, recessed fixture above the bed. He was asleep.

She knew she should turn around and leave, but she couldn't take her eyes off him. She'd been so afraid he wouldn't make it. They'd taken him away so fast once the helicopter had landed.

She moved carefully over to the bed, hoping that William would stay quiet. The shadows cast by the dim light emphasized the pain lines etched between his brows and around his mouth.

His hair was a little bit tousled, enough that she wanted to reach out and brush it back from his forehead. And his mouth was as straight and grim as it had been the last time she'd seen him, right before the emergency doctors had taken him off the helicopter and rolled him away.

"I'm so sorry," she mouthed, not really sure why she was apologizing. Mostly that he'd been hurt so badly for trying to help her, she supposed.

"You've got nothing to be sorry for," he whispered.

She jumped, jostling the baby seat. William made a tiny whimper of protest, but Aimee couldn't take her eyes off Matt.

He opened his eyes, those deep, dark eyes, and looked at her.

"Matt," she breathed, her pulse hammering in her throat. "You're—okay?"

His mouth curved up slightly. "Depends on what you mean by *okay*. I'm here, and essentially in one piece." He lifted his right hand, which was attached to what looked like a tangle of tubing, and pressed a button on the bed. The head of the bed raised up.

He winced slightly, and Aimee's gaze went to his left arm, which was covered by a fat bandage. "What— what did they say about your arm?"

His long, dark lashes swept downward. "The doctor came in earlier. He said all I needed to know was that they cleaned the wound, sewed some muscles and tendons back together, and stitched it all up." He looked down at the bandage. "He said it wouldn't be pretty, but with a little luck and a lot of physical therapy, it would probably work okay, thanks to whoever cleaned and bandaged it."

Aimee took a long breath. "I'm so glad."

"Me, too, although I have a feeling he really meant a *lot* of luck." He raised his gaze to hers. "How are you? You look good."

"I'm good," she said, nodding. "I'm fine. I brought someone to see you."

"William—?" Matt's voice broke, and Aimee's heart felt like it was cracking in two.

She smiled. "He wants to say thank you." She swallowed the lump that had risen in her throat.

"Let me see him."

She set the baby seat down and took William into her arms. "Can I sit down?" She nodded toward the side of his bed.

"Sure. Bring him over here."

She bounced the baby in her arms as she walked around and sat gingerly on the edge of the bed. She propped William on her lap.

Matt lifted his right hand, then checked his gesture. "Think the tubes will scare him?"

As if in answer, William cooed and waved his arms.

"I don't think anything about you could possibly scare him. He's happy to see you."

"Yeah?"

"William? You know who this is? Remember Matt? He's your godfather. He saved you."

"Aimee, don't—" Matt's hand fell back to the bed.

"Don't what? Tell my son the truth? You did save him. You saved him and me."

Matt leaned his head back and closed his eyes. "If you're going to tell him the truth, tell him the whole truth. Tell him what happened to his father. Tell him that I didn't have the sense or the courage to refuse to take Bill skydiving. I didn't have the good sense to make him take some practice runs or do a buddy-dive."

"Bill had skydived before. His carelessness wasn't your responsibility."

Matt blinked. "Why have you suddenly changed your mind?"

"Changed my mind? What are you talking about?"

"Are you feeling sorry for me? Is that it? What happened to blaming me for letting him die?"

"I never blamed you."

"Hah." He squeezed his eyes shut and shook his head. "I saw how you looked at me when I brought his—when I brought him home."

"Matt, I can't remember what I did or said or even thought that night. What I do remember is what Bill always told me. 'You can count on Matt.' He said that the day before you and he left on your trip. 'Matt's safe as houses.'"

Matt lifted his head and looked at her. "I don't know why he thought that."

"I do, now."

He stared at her, his dark eyes glittering with unshed tears.

"It took me a while to understand what he meant. He knew you, maybe better than anyone. He knew you'd die, if by dying you could save an innocent life."

He shrugged and winced. "For some reason, Bill always believed in me."

William was getting restless. He began to fret. "I guess I'd better put this little guy back in his seat."

"Can I—?"

Aimee knew what Matt was trying to ask. She held William close enough that Matt could press a kiss to his fat little cheek. "Hey there, William," he whispered. "Are you glad to see your mom?"

She turned to fasten William back into his seat.

"Aimee?" She didn't look up. She was busy blinking away the tears that she couldn't stop. Seeing Matt kissing her little boy had shattered the last fragile pieces of her heart.

"Aimee—"

She lifted her head without really looking at him. "I'm listening. I just need to get William Matthew settled."

"Could you—maybe one day—give me a chance?"

She froze for an instant, wondering if she'd heard what she thought she had. Then she tested the last strap, to be sure William was safe in his seat.

Slowly, she raised her gaze to his. "Give you a chance?"

The muscles of his jaw worked. "I—" He swallowed. "I love you."

She gasped softly. "You said that before. I thought you were hallucinating."

He shook his head. "I wasn't hallucinating." Then his gaze wavered.

She'd seen him face killer snowstorms, assault rifles, gasoline fires, a horrible injury, but this was the first time she'd seen him nearly paralyzed with fear.

Her mouth stretched into a grin, even as fat tears slipped from her eyes and plopped onto her hands. "I am—so glad," she said, her voice shaking with sobs. "Because I wasn't sure how I was going to—tell you that I fell in—love with you the minute you bullied me into letting you go to the ransom drop with me."

"You did?" he said, his brows shooting up.

"Well, it didn't hurt that you made the supreme sacrifice of warming me with your own naked body."

"Anytime," he said, smiling at her.

"Promise?"

"You—" He paused. "You're okay with me being William's stepfather? I mean—are you saying you'll—you know?"

"I have something to tell you. When Bill found out he had cancer, he made me promise him something."

"Yeah? What?" Matt still looked scared.

"He made me promise that when I was ready, I'd think about you first."

She'd done pretty well so far, but remembering Bill's words and thinking about how prophetic they were, she looked at the man she knew would keep her and her son safe. Love and desire welled up inside her, and pushed away the last bits of the rigid control she'd always clung to like a lifeline. For the first time in her life, she broke down and sobbed.

Matt lifted his hand. "Aimee, are you okay?"

"Sure." She sniffed.

"You're crying."

"I know," she wailed.

Matt's mouth curved into a smile. "Does that mean this qualifies as a special occasion?"

She leaned over and kissed him on the mouth as tears streamed down her face. "I think it qualifies as the first in a lifetime of special occasions."

THE NIGHT SERPENT

BY
ANNA LEONARD

Anna Leonard is the nom de paranormal for fantasy/horror writer Laura Anne Gilman, who grew up wondering why none of the characters in her favourite gothic novels ever seemed to know a damn thing about ghosts, vampires or how to run in high heels. She is delighted that the newest generation of heroines has a much better grasp on things. "Anna" lives in New York City, where either nothing or everything is paranormal…

She can be reached via http://www.sff.net/people/lauraanne.gilman/ or http://cosanostradamus.blogspot.com/.

For KRAD and TO

May your life together be filled with love,
joy, satisfaction and success.

*E*ight times before she had traveled this dream-road; traveled, and been lost. Eight times before, the same sensations haunted her sleep. The feel of the sun's intense heat between her shoulder blades, the heavy slip of linen across her shoulders, the sweat of fear down her neck. The sound of scorn in his voice as he cast her aside. Most of all, the low vibrating purr, the gentle rumble that chilled her, made her eyes scrunch closed and pray to a vengeful goddess that mercy would at last be granted her....

And the Voice, echoing forever in dream-memory. "As you destroyed, so must you repair. Until then, child-of-mine-no-longer, walk these sands as one forgotten, never to be judged worthy, never to rest—"

"Mother, please..." She wasn't sure what she was asking for. Forgiveness? Absolution? A chance to explain, to make an excuse?

No matter. It did not matter. It never mattered.

Eight times she bowed her head to the inevitable, knowing there was no excuse she could make, and no explanation she might offer that would wash the blood from her hands. Her birth and position would save her from public humiliation and shame, but inside, in her ka, *she would always know. Always remember.*

"Mother, I am sorry. My children, I am so very sorry...."

A soft touch against her skin, fur stroking skin. She flinched from the comfort, welcoming the pain that followed. Agony, the sharp downward stroke of betrayal, over and over and over again. Then... darkness.

When she woke, she would remember none of it. She would forget.

Eight times, she always forgot.

This was nine.

Chapter 1

Lily Malkin undid the barrette holding her hair out of her face. The thick black curls slid past her shoulders, and she reached up to run her fingers against her scalp, feeling herself relax. The headache that had haunted her all morning, residue from her usual insomnia, eased a little more.

"Mrrrup?" A tiny paw batted against her knee, demanding attention, and the chance to claw those curls.

"Hello, Rai." Lily scooped the tiny silver tabby up in one hand, easily keeping the needle-tiny claws away from her hair. The kitten complained, and she soothed it by stroking the soft head until the outraged expression was replaced by heavy lids and a gentle purr.

Lily could almost feel her own eyelids lowering in

response. Kitty nap-vibes, the other shelter volunteers called it: the sincere conviction that everything in the world could be made better by stopping to nap in the sun. Oh, if only that were true. She raised the kitten higher and touched her nose to the little pink one. "There you go. Life's not so bad. And it will only get better for you now, I promise."

The kitten, secure in her grip, kneaded its claws sleepily against her skin, but didn't otherwise respond. Lily only wished that her problems were that easily solved. Never a particularly good sleeper, she had been averaging less than four hours a night for the past month, and it was taking its toll.

Madness takes its toll. Please have exact change ready. The old joke was even less funny now than it had been in college, she thought. At least then, she had exams and a social life to blame for her exhaustion. Now... Now there were only dreams that she couldn't remember, and a sense hanging over her that there was something, somewhere, she needed to do. Something important.

The sad truth of the matter was that there wasn't anything really important in her life. Not in the way that niggling dream was telling her.

Maybe it was time to go back to therapy. Or visit a psychic. Or start taking sleeping pills. Something.

Rai dug tiny needle-claws into her hand, informing her that the petting had stopped, and why had the petting stopped? An obedient human, Lily stroked the downy head again, until the claws relaxed.

A deep voice above her, filled with laughter, broke

her concentration on the tiny animal. "You, Lily Malkin, are a miracle."

"Me?" Surprise made her voice rise, making the word even more of a question, but she kept her attention focused on the kitten, afraid to startle it and ruin the progress they had made. She felt like many things right now, but none of them were miraculous.

"You, yeah. Three years ago, just looking at a cat made you break into a cold sweat. Now?" Ronnie, the director of the Felidae No-Kill shelter, sat down on the floor next to Lily, where a pair of inquisitive kittens immediately pounced on her. The two women were in the middle of the "socialization" room, a space filled with climbing trees, catnip mice and rope nets—and almost a dozen cats and kittens in various stages of sociability. "And now? Now you're our very own 'cat whisperer.'"

Lily made a face. She hated that nickname, and "cat talker" and "cat lady" and all the other terms the other volunteers and media people had stuck on her. But there didn't seem to be any way to get rid of it, now.

It was ironic, really. Despite her last name having a traditional, if unfortunate connection to cats, from the time she was a child being around cats had made her uneasy both physically and emotionally. Physically, she got dizzy, sweaty palmed and nauseated. Emotionally…she had nightmares triggered by something as simple as hearing a cat meow.

Despite that, cats still seemed drawn to her, climbing in her lap and weaving in and out of her legs at the slightest chance.

"It's because you're scared and sit so still," people had told her, as though that made it all right. And, in truth, she had always—from a distance—admired cats, with their easy strides and poised gracefulness, and the way they could curl up, nose, toes and tail, and be instantly comfortable anywhere. But the unease kept growing, to the point where she could not visit homes of friends with cats, or even watch a cat-food commercial on television without changing the channel.

Over the years, that unease had transferred to people, too. She watched them the same way she watched cats, wondering what they wanted from her, what they expected, and when their demands would overwhelm and consume her.

It wasn't rational, but nothing Lily had read about phobias over the years indicated that rational thought was involved.

When she had moved to Newfield three years before, it had been with the plan to make a new start after the collapse of yet another relationship, her fourth since graduating college. This time, she had told herself, she would not make the same mistakes. New town. New start. Except that she didn't know how to begin.

Her problems had started with cats—she thought maybe she could start there, and work her way up to people. A helpful therapist and a lot of pep talks had gotten her to the door of the Felidae No-Kill shelter, meaning simply to volunteer in the front office, maybe greet people when they came in, help maintain their Web site, or…

It hadn't quite worked out that way. The fact that she

was where she was, the ranking volunteer with the most responsibility...

Maybe Ronnie was right. Some days even she could barely remember the person she had been the first time she set foot in the doorway two and a half years ago; shaky, sweaty and ready to pass out at the sight of the first inquiring whisker. It had been that much of a change.

With cats, anyway. Lily still had trouble with really connecting to people beyond casual friendships and working relationships.

But she didn't speak cat, or have any kind of supernatural connection with them, the way some people seemed to think. Cats were just easy to understand. The things they wanted were simple: scratching, and feeding, and a warm place to sleep and to be left alone when they were enjoying all those things.

People? People always wanted more, and they never seemed able to just come right out and ask.

"I think this guy's going to be ready to adopt soon," was all she said, lifting the tabby and putting him next to a large orange tom named Willikers, who promptly started grooming the kitten. "And he'd be fine in a house with older cats. Maybe even a dog, if he was used to cats." Talking about cats—and their adoption chances—was easier than talking about herself.

"I'll note that on his chart," Ronnie said, accepting the change of subject. "In the meanwhile, you should try to scrape off some of that cat hair. There's someone here to see you."

"Me?" Again, her voice rose, this time almost to a

squeak. Maybe that was what she needed to work on next, not sounding so anxious when people noticed her.

Her boss nodded, absently petting the calico she had chosen. "Your faithful mechanical Mountie just stomped in, looking for you."

Oh, Lily thought. Then, uh-oh. She knew what that meant.

Resigned, Lily stood up and brushed without much hope at the denim of her jeans. She had quickly learned not to wear wool or corduroy at the shelter, but cat hair could stick to anything, and with the multicolored cats they were currently housing, there wasn't a color you could wear that wouldn't show the inevitably shed fur. Giving up, she gave her cotton sweater a tug, ran her fingers through her hair to get the overlong curls off her face and went out of the glass-enclosed socialization room and into the lobby.

Two men were waiting for her. One was an older man, craggy-faced, wearing casual slacks, a button-down shirt and a gray blazer that had seen better years.

"Detective Petrosian." Formal in the presence of a stranger, for all that they had known each other for two years now.

Aggie—Augustus—Petrosian looked up, and Lily knew for certain that she wasn't going to want to hear what he had to say. It was going to be worse than her usual calls, which were more along the lines of removing a litter of kittens from the inner walls of a building that was being torn down, or getting someone's illegal pet—last month it had been a half-grown ocelot—out of an apartment without anyone getting bitten. When he showed up with those sorts of problems, Aggie never looked as grim as he did right now.

"Lily. Thank you."

She smiled at him. He always said that, as though she was going to hide in the backroom and pretend he wasn't there.

"Lily Malkin, this—" and he indicated the man next to him "—is Special Agent Jon T. Patrick. He's with the feds. Visiting us here in the burbs to help out on a case."

"Patrick" as a surname sounded as Irish as it got. This guy, Lily thought immediately, wasn't even remotely Irish; not unless they had packed up and colonized somewhere more exotic when history wasn't looking. Intense black eyes looked out from deep-set sockets. Those rather amazing eyes, emphasized by a thick, short cap of black-and-gray curls above and the high brace of cheekbones below, were all you saw at first. Lips were thin, ears ordinary and skin a soft golden tan that gave her the urge—briefly—to lean forward and find out what he smelled like. Sandalwood, she thought, without knowing what sandalwood actually smelled like.

Oh. Also, oh. If she were a shallow woman, her mouth would be watering right about now.

All right, so she was a shallow woman on occasion. It wasn't a crime.

He looked her up and down and then directly in the eyes, and the intensity of that gaze felt as though he was undressing her almost casually, as though he had the right to do so. That kind of arrogance pissed her off, so she stared back at him, daring him to continue. At least she had been discreet in her observation.

You're not that *hot, pal,* she thought, now annoyed by how quickly she had responded to him. It hadn't been *that* long since she'd… All right, maybe it had. That was still no reason to react like a tabby in heat.

Detective Petrosian finished the introductions quickly, as though he sensed the undercurrents. "Agent Patrick, this is Lily Malkin. Lily's our local cat expert."

Her lips quirked at Aggie's words, despite her irritation. Between him and Ronnie… She wasn't any kind of expert, really, just cheaper and easier to get hold of than any specialist they could afford to hire, even if one were available. Newfield was a small city, as cities went, and they had an equally small budget to cover a lot of far more urgent needs.

Agent Patrick didn't seem too impressed, by either her or her credentials or his surroundings. His gaze was still on her, but it had become a polite, indifferent look, and his mouth—too thin, she decided, and not to her taste—was held flat, as though he was biting back a comment.

So much for her federal rating, she thought. He probably preferred athletic blondes. Not that he was her type either—she preferred her dates to be a little less obviously high-maintenance.

Agent Patrick did dress well, though. Or maybe that was in contrast to Aggie's familiarly rumpled self—the gray suit and white shirt was probably issued in bulk at FBI headquarters, but it fit Agent Patrick's tall but solid form, and his tie was not the usual power red, but a dark gray-on-gray pattern that was both stylish and surprisingly soothing.

The agent hadn't looked away from her yet, despite his disapproval, and Lily felt the back of her neck prickle under that steady regard. He needed to blink, at least. If she had been one of her four-legged charges, she might have hissed and arched her back to look more fearsome and drive him away.

"Lil." Petrosian was speaking again. "Lily, I'm sorry, but I gotta ask you to do something ugly."

Her attention left the fed and narrowed to the expression on Aggie's face: regretful, but determined. She had been right. Whatever it was, it was going to be bad, especially if a federal agent was along. Lily had no idea what she might be able to help with, at that level, but she trusted Aggie Petrosian as much as she trusted anyone. He was, maybe, the only person she truly did trust. He asked of her only what he asked, and nothing more. No hidden agendas waiting in the shadows. He had always been up front with her. Like a cat. And because of that, if he needed her to do something, she would do it. It was that simple.

Even if it meant being in the company of this Agent Rude-stare Patrick.

"All right."

Special Agent Jon T. Patrick wasn't usually so obvious when he checked someone out; contrary to popular opinion, the bureau did install some couth and control in their people. And his mother would have slapped him over the sofa if he was rude to a woman. But from the way this woman—Ms. Lily Malkin—was shying away from him, he'd been both obvious and obnoxious about it.

Nice move, smooth guy, he thought in disgust. But she had taken him totally by surprise.

When the detective had collected him at the airport, Patrick had expected that they would go directly to the site, since it was still relatively fresh. Instead, as he loaded his bags into the back of the unmarked sedan, Petrosian had informed him that they were going to make a stop along the way, to pick up another consultant.

Patrick bristled at being called a consultant—if he wanted to, he could have used his credentials to argue for the lead in this investigation, and the detective knew it—but instead he merely nodded and let his gaze rest on the scenery. Newfield wasn't much to look at; the airport was just outside city limits, and they were passing the usual patch of warehouses, followed by blue-collar neighborhoods of two- and three-family houses, then into the city itself. He thought they might stop at the university, or maybe the police department.

The last thing he had expected was to find himself in the lobby of a run-down animal shelter, being introduced to a black-haired, peach-skinned pocket Venus wearing faded blue jeans and a black V-neck sweater that made you want to run a finger down the crevice…

He jerked his attention back to the woman's face as Petrosian asked her to accompany them. Her skin was smooth, with wide-set hazel eyes, a sweetly rounded face and a chin that was just blunt enough to keep her from being cute. Malkin. An old, useless bit of information filtered through his magpie memory and into recall; an old slang term, meaning a slatternly woman, or a scarecrow. It also, ironically, had been used to mean both rabbit and cat. She had the nervous posture of a rabbit, but the sleek lines of a cat.

And Lily? Lilies had long necks, like…

Patrick shut that line of thought down, aware that his brain could sometimes go off on totally random tangents. Work related: that was good. Libido related? Less so. Keep it official. Keep it on business.

The detective didn't explain to Ms. Malkin what was up when he made his request, and she didn't ask for details, indicating that they had done things like this before.

Patrick was reassured by that, the familiarity and the trust, both. Consultants, in his experience, usually asked too many questions up front. That prejudiced their read of the site before they even got there, making their evaluations useless. So she was not only sexy, but smart. And, apparently, from the coolness in her hazel eyes while she looked at him, wanting nothing to do with one special agent.

Blew that before you even knew you were doing anything, didn't you, Jon T.? He could hear his mother scolding him, across seven states and two time zones. *How will you ever meet a nice girl if you scare them all off?*

Yeah, yeah, Mom, I know, he told the voice. *Very* smooth. I'm a moron.

Not that it mattered. He was here on business. The case—ordinary enough on the surface—might be nothing more than a garden-variety cat killer howling at the moon, which he could leave for the locals. Or this guy might in fact be an embryonic serial killer just starting his progression: if so, finding what triggered him would support his own personal theory, and stopping the guy would help cement his standing in the bureau. A federal officer's career was all about reputation: making it, and keeping it.

It was never good to alienate a local expert, however dubious her standing, this early on, though. Petrosian thought enough of her insight to make a special trip to ask for her assistance, and the cop had come across as a pragmatic, by-the-book guy.

Patrick rubbed his chin thoughtfully. Well, if he suddenly needed to borrow the brain inside that lovely casing, then he'd pull out the professional charm and make her forget that she'd ever thought badly of him. The fact that she rang his bell would just make that job pleasant, rather than a chore.

"Let me get my coat, I'll be right back."

"Patrick." The cop got his attention with a thick, stubby finger waved under the agent's nose. "Don't underestimate her," Petrosian warned. "She may look like a little girl, but she's smart. And tough."

Patrick raised his eyebrows at Petrosian's wording. The last thing he would ever describe that woman as was "little girl."

"Aggie. You driving?" She was back, a denim jacket pulled over her sweater. Clearly, the chill air outside didn't bother her at all. Spring in New England, ha. He was already homesick for D.C.'s milder weather.

"Yeah. I'll bring you back after, okay?" Petrosian was already herding them out the door. That was fine by Patrick—the crime scene wasn't getting any fresher while they stood here. The sooner he got to it, the sooner he could determine if he had any business being here at all.

The dark green sedan slid through traffic, heading away from the downtown area into more residential blocks. Petrosian left the radio muted to a quiet squalk and their cat lady didn't seem inclined to talk, so Patrick took advantage of the time, sitting in the backseat, to go over his notes and compare them to the official file on this incident. There wasn't much in the update Petrosian had given him at the airport, and he closed it without having made any more progress than he had since getting the original material via the local bureau office the night before. The information was too slim: he needed to see the site himself, form his own impressions. That was why he was here: his skill was in transforming direct observation into a working and workable theory. Someone else's observations, with their inevitable biases, were useless to him.

"Please, don't let anyone have fubar'd the scene."

"What?" Petrosian raised his eyes to the rearview mirror to look back at him.

"Nothing," he said, gesturing at the files in explanation. Thankfully, Petrosian just nodded and went back to his driving. Bad form to tell your host that you expect his men to be incompetent. No, Patrick thought ruefully, he was not getting off on the right foot with anyone here so far.

Ten minutes later, they parked outside a small storefront, a single-story corner convenience store in a neighborhood of small, neatly maintained houses with neatly, if unimaginatively, tended lawns and a grade school down the block. There were two squad cars out front, but no yellow tape to be seen anywhere. Ms. Malkin got out of the car and waited for Petrosian, who gestured her toward the front door. She nodded once, her body language changing from uncertain to aggressive, and moved up the walkway. Another thing to like, Patrick noted: she took possession of her scene like a pro. It took them a year to hammer that into cadets at the academy, and some of them never learned how to do it.

Lily had been aware, the entire ride, of Agent Patrick's presence directly behind her. Oh, he hadn't done anything, hadn't said anything, but she could practically feel him looming behind her.

All right, "looming" was overstating it. He was sitting normally, going through an official-looking file of papers and photos, barely even glancing up as Petrosian took corners too quickly, only once muttering something she didn't quite catch. But when he did look up, she felt his gaze like a physical touch, as soft as a cat's tail flick and just as unmistakable. It wasn't unpleasant, exactly…but it made her uncomfortable.

He made her uncomfortable. And it wasn't just because he was good looking. Or even because he was arrogant. Lily had seen better and worse examples before, both on her job and in dealing with the cops and the press. But there was something about this guy that was putting her on edge.

Or maybe it was this…whatever it was that Aggie had called her out for, and Agent Patrick was just catching the fallout. She wished that she had asked for more detail before agreeing, but...

It didn't matter, not with regard to Agent Attitude. Either way, it wasn't as though she was going to have to deal with him for long; she could put up with the arrogance and just enjoy the eye candy while it lasted.

When they arrived, she got out of the car before Aggie had even finished parking, looking around curiously. She had lived in Newfield for three years, but she didn't know this neighborhood. It seemed a little run-down, but reasonably safe. Although, she admitted, that might have had something to do with the noticeable police presence on the street.

"Up here," the detective said, waving her toward the storefront. She swallowed hard and went inside, passing a uniformed officer in the doorway.

There was no warning: one moment she was moving forward, and the next she was knocked back on her heels, a full-body slap.

Aggie had said it was ugly. *Ugly* wasn't the word for it. Lily stopped just inside the doorway and blanched, the back of her hand pressing against her mouth while she swallowed, hard, and tried not to breathe.

"Oh God."

The inside of the front room was splattered in red; walls, counters and empty glass-fronted display cases. In a photograph it might have looked like paint; the smell told the real story. Some atavistic sense in the back of her brain told her what the tinge in the air was, and what the spray, by default, had to be: blood, with the undercurrent of meat starting to go bad.

But the floor was what caught her attention: a cleared space in the middle of the room, the pale green linoleum tiles covered with a black cloth about four feet square. On the cloth, seven still, limp forms were arranged in an odd-shaped circle, nose to tail.

Cats.

And, without warning, she was back in the echoes of a dream. *Cats, sprawled as though basking in the sun. Only there was no sun, and their heads turned wrongly, their tails stilled, their voices silent.... A shadow rose behind her; despair and terror flooded her throat....*

"Oh, the poor moggies," she heard Agent Patrick say behind her, and the faint flash of not-quite-a-dream shattered. Her mouth was dry, her skin clammy. Where had it come from, that flash, that overwhelming, painful visual? It wasn't a memory, nothing she had ever seen. She would remember something that horrible. But where had it come from, then? Television, maybe, or something she had read?

It didn't matter, she decided, trying to shove it away. The here and now was disturbing enough.

"Who did this to you, little ones?" she heard the agent ask, obviously speaking to the cats, and the discomfort she had felt in the agent's presence earlier was diluted by an instant and unexpected kinship with him. Arrogant as he might be, there was real sympathy in his voice. They weren't just animals to him—they were victims.

"I'm going to need photos from every angle," he barked to Aggie, taking command of the scene as if it had been deeded to him. Clearly, no matter how much he might have felt for them, he was all business now.

The arrogance that had annoyed her earlier was reassuring now. Attitude was much more appealing when matched with clear competence.

Lily took a shallow breath, and regretted it. The bodies weren't fresh. More than a day, from the smell, but not much longer, or it would be worse. She thought it would, anyway. Actually, she had no idea, and wasn't able—or willing—to turn around and ask Aggie for an answer.

"You were the one who found the bodies?" Patrick was now asking the young cop nearest him, who nodded. The man—a boy, really—looked as ill as she felt.

Intellectually, Lily knew that people did things like this. The first year she worked at the shelter, around Halloween, she'd been asked to help with two black cats that had been tortured by a couple of wannabe Satanists, to see if the cats could be used to identify and hopefully convict their abusers. It had been a slow news week, and the media had gotten hold of the story. The shot of her leaving the scene with one of the cats clinging to her, his triangular head hidden in her hair, had run every time they touched on the story. That had been what started the "cat talker" nickname. The press had hounded her for a week afterward, even though she refused to give any interviews or sound bytes. Petrosian had sworn to run interference with the press from then on.

Lily didn't like being in the spotlight. It made her nervous, the same way the unblinking scrutiny of cats once had, as though someone was judging her, finding

her lacking, unworthy. Not the way Agent Patrick had,
but deeper down, where it mattered. Where you couldn't
avoid it. Connection, a therapist had told her once. She
wasn't good at maintaining connections. The responsibility made her nervous, made her wonder how she had
failed, even when she knew that she hadn't, couldn't
possibly have.

But nobody was watching her now. Even Aggie had
turned away, joining Agent Patrick in talking to the
cops on the scene, giving her a moment to regain self-
control.

"Your people have already been through?" Agent
Patrick, his voice still and intense again, as though the
lapse into emotion had been a—well, a lapse.

"Last night, yeah, when we made the discovery of
this new source." Aggie's gravelly rumble was soothing
by comparison. "Everything's been documented and
swabbed, but since no humans were involved, we left
the scene itself intact, as per your request. As soon as
you're done here, we'll bag and tag it."

Lily stood over the circle, wondering what she was
doing there. Normally, at a scene, there was a live cat
present, of some breed or another, that she could ob-
serve and interact with. Normally there was something
she could *do*. Now, all she could do was to take in the
details, look at the still, unmoving, cold bodies, and
wonder who could have done such a thing.

God have mercy on them, the poor innocent beasts,
she thought. She wasn't much for religion—going to
church had always left her feeling more empty than ful-
filled, and her brief foray into Buddhism during college

wasn't much better, but there had to be *someone* who looked after those so ill used....

She swallowed hard against the surge of emotion, willing herself into professional behavior. Thankfully, some coolly analytical portion of her brain came forward, sorting the scene into dry facts, something she could process, the way she handled numbers at her day job at the bank. All right then. Aggie wanted her here for some reason. She knew cats. So she would study the cats.

Seven bodies, all spotted tabbies, their silver, gray and white coats covered with black thumbprint-size spots, tails striped with wide black marks. Young, male. Not at their full growth yet, they weren't, with tails too long for their bodies and ears too large for their heads. There was a slice across each throat, a puddle of red underneath where each one had bled out. Where had the blood on the walls come from, then? How much blood was in a single cat, multiplied by seven?

No, don't go there. Keep the thoughts all clinical, detached, distanced, and unreal. Safe. Like counting out money, entering numbers. Important but not emotional. Not anything that could make her chest hurt for the horror of it. Lily was good at being practical, at making the world make sense, especially when it didn't. She only wished she'd had more sleep last night.

The headache was back, sneaking up like a bully with bad intent, and Lily wished she had taken her own car, which had painkillers stashed in the glove compartment. She reached up to rub the ache between her eyes, allowing her concentration to slip.

That was a mistake: the separate details clicked into

a whole picture, the smell and texture and reality of it slamming into her. *Wrongwrongwrongwrong!* A sheen of red to match the blood on the floor and walls rose over her vision, and her hands shook until she clenched them together. Someone had done this to cats—to *kittens.*

The headache was swamped, disappearing under the onrush of rage. Anyone—any*thing*—that could do that needed to be stopped. Punished.

She felt someone coming up behind her, the heavy tread and swish of wool uniform slacks telling her who it was even before the smell of stale cigarette smoke that hung around him reached her, mingling with the smell of blood and meat and, oddly, settling her stomach before she even realized that it was upset.

"What do you need me to do?" she asked Petrosian, not taking her eyes off the scene. If he heard the rage in her voice, either he had been counting on it, or he didn't want to call attention to it, because he didn't flinch or make any movement to try to soothe her.

"I don't know," he said instead. "I'm hoping you can tell me. Tell us what's going on. What happened here."

She looked over her shoulder, then looked back at the cats, and then up at the ceiling, which, she noted now, had been painted black. The paint looked oddly flat, under the fluorescent lights, as though it had been meant to reflect softer, kinder lights. None of the blood had reached that high, she noted. "Other than animal abuse?"

"That much we got. But that's Patrick's problem, what he's here to study. What I want you to take a look at is back here." Petrosian's thick-fingered hand came down on her shoulder, steering her past the grisly tableau, the only apology for putting her through this that he could give her, the only one she would accept.

Out of the corner of her eye she saw Agent Patrick kneeling by the bodies, pulling on a pair of latex gloves before reaching out to touch one of the kittens gently.

He looked up and met her gaze. A spark seemed to jump between them, invisible electricity that she felt through the palms of her hands, running like a ribbon of warmth all the way to her feet.

He looked away first, and in another place, another time, she might have felt a flush of feminine triumph. But not here.

There was another room behind the first one, and that was where the smell was coming from. Ten mesh cages, each one with a water dish—most dry—and spilled dry kibble. A small plastic box in each, half filled with uncleaned litter.

"Nobody touched anything once we found it. How many cats, Lily? How many cats were here? Tell me what this guy was doing with them."

Usually she had to listen to the cat's vocalizations, watch its body language, before she got a read on the situation, on how it had been treated. Not this time. This time it came out of the empty space, swarming her, almost knocking her over.

Crowded. Anticipation. Fear. Hunger. Lust.

Even without the cats, she could feel the emotion still in the room, could almost hear them meowing, scratching at the wires of their cages, scratching at the metal floors, the rasping of their tongues as they tried to keep fur clean and claws sharp…. Not a bad dream. Not something she could block, ignore or forget.

She gagged at the strength of the knowledge, forcing the words out carefully. "More than ten. More than… there were kittens here. Litters."

That was the smell she had picked up, even over the blood and shit. Pheromones. The scent of a female cat in heat. The thought made her ill, where the killings had only made her angry.

"He was breeding them. This wasn't just storage, it was a cattery."

"Go, do your thing," Petrosian had said to him when they got out of the car. The cop hadn't said it rudely, or mockingly, the way some did; more along the lines of "you do your thing and I'll do my more productive thing." Profiling was still looked at sideways and suspiciously by a lot of folk, especially outside the agency. Hell, Patrick knew that he occupied a strange sort of niche within the FBI hierarchy itself: he had a master's in psychology, but he had never been interested in profiling, preferring to play a more active role in chasing down criminals. He might have had a very traditional career; fieldwork landing him in a desk job leading him all the way to retirement and possibly a teaching job after that, except that during his second year in the field he had discovered in himself an odd fascination for—and affinity for solving—a particular kind of crime, specifically animal mutilations, and the criminals who perpetrated them. Those acts, along with a few others, often heralded the beginning career of a serial killer.

A profiler got into the head of an unsub—bureauspeak for an unknown subject of an investigation. He tried to feel where they were going, mentally and emotionally, and sense how close they were to breaking out to human victims. Patrick was less interested in what went on in their heads than in the end result; the instinctive reaction response to that internal stimulus. His skill might have ended up simply as a side talent, except that he was very very good at finding those patterns, even where none seemed to exist. And so, whenever a case with certain elements—domestic animals, ritualistic injury—came up in the reports, the agency tapped him to immediately take a look. Catch an unsub when he was still targeting animals, and save human lives later.

That was the theory, anyway. There was no quantitative proof either way. It could all be hand-waving and luck.

Patrick had, in self-defense, come up with his own theories about sociopaths and the making thereof. Forget the psychology, the biochemistry, the sociology. Jon Patrick was a believer in *intent*. Not that someone chose to be a stone-cold killer, but that they always had a trigger, something to make all the parts come together from where they lay latent in every single human being.

He focused on the ritual aspect rather than the actual violence—violence was universal in the end, while the steps chosen to get there were individual. Identify a strain of ritual, and determine where that particular mind might go, criminally. Find the pattern break the pattern and prevent a killer from being born.

The problem was that, without enough distinct data points to prove or disprove his ideas, he couldn't get anyone to take them seriously. And being taken seriously was what Agent Jon T. Patrick was all about. Being taken seriously, and getting serious results.

He was damn good at his job, though, and even if his ideas were unsubstantiated, his results were getting him some notice at higher levels; the bureau cared less about theory than they did about getting results they could use. The suits back in D.C. were marking him as a player of note, and Patrick had goals above and beyond being a field agent with nightmare memories and a passable retirement package at the end. Ambition, to him, wasn't a dirty word.

His career, if he didn't screw up, was looking good. It was all good.

This, though…this wasn't good. He made a circuit of the scene, aware of the technician taking additional photographs and jotting down measurements, observations and verified facts. Good—he would need the daylight shots, too. He knelt beside the small, still bodies, careful not to disturb the black cloth or the blood splatter around it, and pulled a pair of latex gloves from a pocket, sliding them onto his hands His last girlfriend had referred to them as fingercondoms. He had been amused by that: a pity that had been the extent of her sense of humor.

"Poor moggies," he said again, reaching out to touch one of the bodies. The flesh was firm even in death, meat and muscle over the ribs. The cats hadn't been abused before being killed. Small mercies. But that put a different spin on the scene, and his unsub. Usually animals were tortured before they were killed. It was all about power in most cases. Power, control, authority. To kill animals that, although helpless, were undamaged, especially in such a methodical, almost ritualistic manner? All it lacked was an athame—a ritual knife—and some candles, and the press would be screaming black magic.

He didn't believe in magic, black, white, pink or polka-dot. He did believe in the power of belief, though. Believe something, and you could take power from it. Believe in it strongly enough, and it took power over *you*.

Normal people with normal emotions didn't kill small cute cuddly animals. This killer was bent at best, and possibly a textbook sociopath, working his way up to more of a challenge.

Despite the violence inherent in the act, though, Patrick got the feeling that this guy wasn't acting out of unformed rage or irrational fear. He wasn't striking out in any desperate attempt to be heard, or regain control or any of the usual textbook profiles. There was a cooler, more rational mind behind this. A mind with a list, maybe, or a plan.

Intent. What was his intent? What triggered him to take cats, care for them, kill them, arrange them this way and then just leave them here?

"Is this guy just your everyday boring psychonutter," he said, sitting back on his heels and looking at the bodies. "Or is there something else going on? And if so, what? Where is he coming from, that this is a logical progression?"

What he wouldn't give to be able to talk to this guy,

to unpack his brain and see where the wires went and which ones were crossed....

A noise behind him made him look away, up and toward the door to the backroom. Petrosian and the woman—Malkin—were coming back. The cop looked a little grim around the mouth, issuing soft-voiced directions to the painfully young uniform who had been first on the scene. Ms. Malkin—he tried to read her expression, and failed utterly. It was as though a stone wall had come up, leaving him no opening to see through. Even his charm might not be enough to win her back, if he needed her help with this case.

Then she looked up, and he almost recoiled. Even under the fluorescent lights overhead, there was no mistaking the fury in those wide-set eyes. He had never bought into that whole cliché of flashing or sparkling eyes—eyes were just bits of meat and veins, and they did not shoot anything except glares.

But he would have sworn an oath that Ms. Lily Malkin's hazel eyes filled with dangerous green sparks as she stared at the dead cats under his hand.

It was scary. It was also, he admitted to himself, pretty damn hot.

Chapter 2

Lily had gone outside to get some fresh air. She was waiting there, watching the cops canvassing the neighborhood, when Patrick and Petrosian finally came out. It was close to 4:00 p.m., and dusk was falling. She loved winter, but getting to it… Autumn just depressed her. She shivered, crossing her arms over her chest, less from the evening chill than the inner one. The spark of attraction that had warmed her earlier was long gone.

She tilted her head, looking for the first evening star. It was an old habit from her childhood, stargazing. But no matter how many times she looked, however much she read about constellations, the sky never seemed quite right to her, the ancient drawings in the sky never familiar. She kept looking, hoping that one night the patterns would suddenly make sense to her. They never did. They didn't tonight.

"Sorry, took longer than I expected," Petrosian said, breaking her concentration. "I just need you to give a report, and then you're done. Okay?"

Normally she did whatever they needed her to do, and went home, or took the cats involved to the shelter for processing. This was different. Everything about this was different. Knowing that there were people who were cruel, who could do things like that; it was different actually seeing it. Experiencing it.

It made her ingrained distrust of the world suddenly seem like a good idea, not a handicap.

"Lily?" Petrosian was watching her, his careworn face filled with regret. "I'm sorry. I needed you to go in without any knowledge beforehand…." He had apologized more to her tonight than in all the time they had known each other.

Aggie and his daughter, Jenny, had adopted three cats from the shelter, two since she had worked there. Max, a red tabby, and Wilma, a calico shorthair. He had been the one to suggest her name when the department first needed a cat expert and had been her contact person ever since then. He knew more about her, simply through observation, than even members of her own family. He knew what he had asked her to do.

"Yeah. Me, too. Sorry, I mean." Only she wasn't sorry. She was angry. But without knowing where to direct that anger, it weighed her down and simply made her tired. And cold. The crisp night air seemed to cut into her bones. "It's okay, Aggie." No, it wasn't.

It was very much not okay. But it wasn't Augustus Petrosian's fault. "Let's go."

There were two police stations in Newfield, one uptown and one down. There was a substation, Lily knew, that was closer, but Petrosian took them to the uptown station instead. Agent Patrick excused himself the moment they arrived to make a phone call, and the detective handed her over to a sketch artist, a tall, rounded woman with a ready smile and ink stains on her fingers and a smudge on her freckled snub nose that made her look too young to be working in the police department. She introduced herself as Julia, and brought Lily to a square table in a small room off the main hallway, out of the flow of traffic. There wasn't a door to the room, but the chatter, slams and creaks of station activity flowed around them, turning into a babble of white noise.

"All right. Detective Petrosian says you've got a scene for me?"

"I thought sketch artists did faces?" Lily didn't really care, she felt too exhausted by what she had seen to worry about anything else, but it made for conversation. Conversation was easier than thinking. Kinder than thinking.

"Mostly, yeah. But we do whatever it takes to close a case, same as everyone else here. So. What've you got for me?"

So much for not thinking. Worse, they wanted her to *remember*.

Lily sat down at the table, in the chair Julia indicated, and closed her eyes. She had thought—had hoped—that once away from the site, the visual would fade. But the moment she shut out the distractions around her, it came back, and she began to describe it, slowly, trying to hit as many details as possible. Something stuck in her throat as she talked, and hurt, like it was hard-edged and heavy, and the more she talked, the worse it became.

"All right. I think I've got it."

Julia's voice seemed to come from far away, down a long tunnel. Lily opened her eyes, resurfacing into the noise and bustle of the police station. Julia was putting down her pencils and Agent Patrick was standing behind her, looking down at the sketch with a fascinated expression.

"This is what you saw?"

Lily frowned, confused by his question. He had been there, why was he so surprised? Julia turned the pad around and slid it across the table so that she could see. It was the cattery, but not abandoned now. Each cage was filled with four or five shadowy bodies: adult cats in some and kittens in others, almost all of them with dappled coats. Dishes overflowed with dried kibble, and water was slopped carelessly onto the counters. There was a figure in the middle of the room, but so roughly drawn that it was impossible to determine if it was male or female. Tall and lean: hunched over slightly as though expecting a blow.

"You saw this?" Agent Patrick asked again, his voice intent on the question. She responded almost unwillingly to the urgency in his voice.

"No. Not really. The room was empty." He knew that. He had been there, too.

"But you described it. Every detail." His voice wasn't exactly doubting, but it was skeptical that she could have managed it without prior knowledge, something she wasn't telling them.

Lily was too shocked to take offense. She looked at Julia, who nodded. "I don't add anything the witness doesn't tell me, not until we go to the next stage. Everything there's what you told me to put down."

Lily looked at the sheet again, and a sense of familiarity moved through her. Yes. This was what the room looked like. The cats, restless and calling each other. The figure moving among them, taking them away and—sometimes—bringing them back. The smells of food and urine against the stainless steel of the cages, the hint of antiseptic…

There was no way she could know any of that. But she did. As much as she knew anything that happened today. She could even pick out the shadowed forms of the cats that had been selected for death, there, in the far cage, segregated from the others.

"You psychic?" Agent Patrick's voice had evened out, not making judgments in a way they had to teach in the academy. "Humor the crazy person, and then disarm them" would have been the motto of that class, no doubt. He probably got an A. It should have rankled, but looking at the sketches, Lily just felt tired. He was only doing his job, and part of that job was to doubt everything.

"No." She looked at him, then down at the drawing

again. "It was just how everything was laid out. This is the only way it could have been."

That didn't satisfy him, she could feel it in his gaze, in the way he looked at her, and then at the sketch, and then at her again. He didn't accuse her of lying, but he didn't quite believe her, either.

She couldn't explain it. She couldn't prove it was true, what she described. But it was.

"All spotted cats," Julia noted.

"Yes." She was certain of that, too.

"Tabbies, mostly. The slaughtered animals here had white paws. How common is that?" Patrick was staring intently at the drawing, clearly trying to work something out in his mind. He had put aside the question of her accuracy, and was working with the available evidence, no matter how dubious.

"What, mitting?" Lily said. "It's pretty common, no matter what the coat's color. Especially if he'd been breeding them—there weren't that many queens in the room, so the gene pool was small."

"Queens?" Julia asked.

"Breeding females," Patrick said, surprising Lily with his knowledge. "A queen can breed every four months, anywhere from three to seven kittens in a litter."

For a moment, Lily felt that spark running between the two of them again, a spark that had nothing to do with his dark eyes or undeniably masculine appeal— or his interest in her. A cat person. Or at least, one who had done his homework. That tied in to the feeling she had gotten from him at the scene: that he saw more than statistics and splatter.

Aggie had said the agent focused on animal abuse cases, something about him psychoanalyzing killers the way they did on TV shows. But that made her wonder—why was an FBI agent, a profiler, investigating something like this? What made cats important enough to interest a federal agency?

Suddenly Lily felt herself deflate. Of course he was interested in her, a cat person. It was part of his job. Well, that was what she was here for; to help him, however she could, to catch this guy.

"He—whoever was doing this—didn't have more than three queens in the room, from the size of the cages. But a lot of kittens. You think he was trying to breed for a particular color?" Lily had never really thought about the genetic side of cats before; all she knew about different colors was what was more popular among adopters.

He shrugged. "I'm not ruling out any theories at this point."

"And what is that point, exactly?" *Why are you here?* she meant.

Julia touched the sheet, the motion drawing their attention. "I'm sorry. I need to run this over to the detective. Lily, if you want to wait, I can make sure an officer—"

"I'll make sure Ms. Malkin gets home safely," Patrick said, cutting Julia off, and then smiling at her to soften his rudeness. "I'd like to ask her a few more questions first, if we can use this desk?"

"Yeah, sure." Julia seemed flustered at being the focus of his attention, which Lily thought was odd, but then the artist gathered herself back into professional mode. "Will you want a copy of the sketch?"

"That would be wonderful, thank you."

Lily watched Julia's slender white hands gather up her pencils and the sketch, then disappear into the swirl of noise around them. Somehow, it seemed distant from her, even now. She had known about the queens, the female cats. How? How *could* she have known anything she had told Julia to draw? Extrapolation from a few cages and a smell could only go so far, but—

But, stop, she told herself, feeling the old, familiar, *unwanted* distress crawling back. *Stop.* Breathe, Lily. Breathe in through the mouth, out through the nose. Breathe, and be still. A lifetime of dealing with panic attacks—she might not need the technique on a daily basis anymore, but it still did the job. Her anxiety level dropped until she felt as if she could manage again.

"Why is the FBI investigating this?" she asked, once her breathing was under control.

"We have varied interests," Patrick said, sliding into Julia's seat with a grace that belonged to a more slender man. If he noticed her momentary distress, he didn't mention it. "Why do they call you the cat talker?"

She shook her head, too worn-out to be either angry or amused at his evasion or the appearance of her hated nickname. "Who told you that?"

"One of the uniforms. Said you could talk to anything feline, get it to do what you wanted."

"Anyone who said that knows nothing about cats." Lily looked up finally, and in doing so was caught again by Agent Patrick's gaze. Dark, yes, and intense, yes, and totally focused entirely on her, in a scary-nice sort of way. Oh. So that was what he'd done to the sketch artist. You could get lost in those eyes, just watching them watch you. It made her nervous. Something, hell *everything* about him was making her nervous. Like he thought she was one of his suspects, someone to be interrogated, bullied and pushed around.

"Oh?" His tone was smooth, inviting; much smoother than the look in his eyes. That voice was another thing the FBI probably issued its agents on their first day on the job, to go with the suits. And the guns, although she hadn't seen Patrick's yet. She didn't doubt he carried one. There was something about him. That intensity, it had a purpose beyond getting answers. Or undressing women visually. She had seen it before; he was a man with a long-term goal, and Lord help the person who got in the way.

All right, maybe that was unfair. But she could practically smell the ambition in him, and it made her wary. Lily didn't understand ambition. She had needs, desires, of course. Everyone did. But ambitious people carried a tension around inside them that made her tense up in return. She preferred the company of those who were comfortable where they were, who took days one at a time and who didn't ask too much of life.

"There's an old joke," she said, shaking off her reaction and responding to his earlier question. "'Dogs have owners, cats have staff.' Or, 'Dogs come when called. Cats have answering machines and might get back to you.' All true. A cat will do something you ask of it because it chooses to do so. It won't obey out of loyalty, or fear, or even love—merely choice."

Cats couldn't be used. Not that way. It was one of the reasons why she respected them.

Agent Patrick nodded, not laughing, or even smiling at her words. "And cats choose to listen to you?"

No. Cats chose to talk to her. They always had, even when she was a little girl and terrified of them. They would come to her, twine their lithe bodies around her ankles, look up at her as though she could solve great mysteries, and she would curl into a ball against the nearest wall and cry until her mother came and got her. She never got violent, the way some phobics did, and she never got angry—just sad to the point of over-whelming depression. She had *wanted* to like cats, in a way she never felt with people.

"My boss at the shelter claims I must smell like catnip, or something."

The look in his eyes suddenly shifted. Lily wasn't sure how, or why, but the interest deepened, his face changing slightly. It made her suddenly uneasy in a way even his previous intensity hadn't, as though she had suddenly been dumped somewhere unfamiliar, without warning. The other man, the FBI agent, she knew how to avoid, and why. This man, the one with the glitter-bright stare, he was... *Seductive* was the only word that came to mind. Seductive, and danger-ous, and appealing. Which were three words, but all meant the same thing. He was looking at her as if he wouldn't mind taking a roll in some catnip, himself, right then. Like he wasn't undressing her now, but was already inside her.

Lily knew herself pretty well. She was attractive, if you liked brunettes, too short, and had a reasonably curvy, if not stacked, body. Great hair, nice face. A

solid B-grade on all fronts. Nice, but nothing that quali-
fied for that kind of fascination. He was interrogating
her again, only with a different question in mind.

"Look, I don't know what Detective Petrosian
thought I'd be able to tell him, or what you think I can
do. I'm good with cats, yes. But—"

"Have dinner with me."

"Excuse me?" She should have been expecting that,
yet it still caught her off guard.

His thin lips curved in a smile now. The hint of white
teeth showed between the pale red flesh, but the intensity of his eyes was, if anything, even more focused on
her. Not undressing her, but getting inside her brain.
Inside her soul.

She recoiled, and then scolded herself for recoiling.
All right, Lily, stop that, she told herself. *You're tired,
stressed and overreacting. He's just a guy. A cute guy.
Why not have dinner with him?*

"I'm a federal agent, miss. You can trust me." She
must have laughed at that. "Seriously," he went on. "I
have a few questions I want to ask you, but I just hit
town and I'm starving. And we hijacked you out of your
job—the least I can offer is dinner, as a thank-you for
your help."

Lily was oddly flattered, but shook her head. She
wasn't much for dating, and even if she were, a guy who
was in town for two, three days tops? She needed more
time than that to make up her mind about a guy. Even
if he was as exotic as a Burmese, and friendly as a
Maine coon. And on the hunt sure as any big cat she'd
ever seen. "Thank you, but no. I'm just going to grab a

ride back to the shelter, pick up my car and go home. It's been a really long day and I'm not feeling particularly social. Detective Petrosian has my phone number and e-mail address, if you need to ask me anything more, but I'm sure there's nothing I can add."

She stood up, and then looked down at the agent, remembering that moment of sympathy she had experienced on the scene, over the bodies of the kittens. "Whoever did this, you'll find him."

It wasn't a question, and Agent Patrick didn't pretend otherwise.

"Yes, ma'am."

Petrosian found him half an hour later still sitting at the table, a notepad flat in front of him, the unlined paper covered with circles with words scribbled inside them.

"So what's the story?" he asked the cop, pushing the notepad away from him in disgust.

"The store was for rent. Last owner moved out four months ago, but market's been slow, hasn't even had anyone in to look at the space since then. It was the Realtor who found the bodies, called us in."

"Four months." Patrick reached for the pad and jotted that down as well. "We'll need a list of anyone who might have known about the space, had access to the keys, that sort of thing."

"Already have someone on it. Anything else you want us to dig into?"

Jon T. Patrick was smart. More, he was savvy. And he knew blue sarcasm when he heard it. So he dragged himself out of his thoughts and gave the detective his full attention. "You guys have it under control. I'm just working a side investigation, is all. A little project."

"Uh-huh." Petrosian maybe wasn't as smart, but he was plenty savvy too, so he let Patrick's comment go without challenge.

"Although…" Patrick knew it was stupid, but he couldn't resist. "Tell me about your specialist, Ms. Malkin."

Ms. Malkin. Lily. It wasn't a name that suited her: a lily was a delicate, overscented flower. Malkin's hazel eyes were tough, her body toned and muscled under the curves, her stride strong, and her scent…unscented. Powder and soap.

He usually liked perfume on a woman, liked placing his face against her neck and smelling the aroma rising off her skin. But perfume would be wrong on Malkin. It would be overkill.

He wanted to take her out to dinner. Nothing fancy: pasta maybe, and a bottle of decent wine. He wondered if she drank red wine. He thought maybe she did. Or maybe he was projecting. Patrick was amused at himself, despite the seriousness of the case. Profiler, profile thyself? Why was he so attracted to her? She was a hot little thing, yeah, but he'd seen better. But there was something about her that spoke to him, beyond the physical, and well beyond any use she might have to the case.

That attraction was bad. He couldn't afford to be distracted. He had a steady rule: no female distractions on a case. After, yes. But he would be on his way home by then.

Petrosian looked at him carefully, and then answered. "Lily's good people. She works as a teller down at West Central, that's a local bank. Volunteers at the shelter. Lived here, oh, three, four years? About that. Went to school on the West Coast, doesn't seem to have any family that she's mentioned. Straight up, all straight up."

"And she talks to cats." She also had skin the color of a sun-ripened peach. He wondered if all of her skin was that exact tone.

Petrosian snorted. "She does something, that's for sure. Years ago, I was a rookie, we had a cougar wander into town, get panicked. The local zoo sent over one of their people to try to get it back into a cage. Took us all night, half a dozen tranqs, and earned me a couple of nasty gashes before we got the damn thing cornered and caged. Last year? Lily damn near purred a big cat into walking on its own paws into the cage. Took maybe an hour, all told."

Patrick wasn't sure he entirely believed that, but they'd probably both seen stranger things in their years. "How does she do it?"

The cop shrugged. "Don't know, don't care, and she won't thank you for poking around."

Patrick sat back in his chair. It wasn't a warning-off. Quite. But he wasn't on the prowl; he wasn't going to do anything that would hurt her. His interest in her was about the case; he really *did* have questions he wanted to ask her. A traditional expert would be by the book. This case didn't feel by the book. The cats had been clean and well cared for, and killed with what could almost have been reverence. Maybe talking to the cat talker would give him the point of view he needed to understand how and why.

Petrosian looked at the schoolhouse-style clock on the wall. "I'm still on shift. I've got other cases to deal with before they let me out of here. A patrolman will take you to your hotel. If we catch any new info, I'll give you a call."

That was a clear dismissal. Slaughtered animals were a crime, but they weren't a high-priority one, not even in a relatively sleepy New England city. FBI man could do whatever he wanted, but the cops weren't going to hold his hand while he did it. That suited him fine, actually.

Still, Petrosian lingered. "You going to need anything else for your 'little project' before I sign off on the paperwork?"

"No, I think I have everything I need for now." Clearly, he was supposed to skedaddle, as his mother used to say. Patrick closed his notebook and stood, feeling the joints in his knees and hips creak distressingly. He wasn't getting old, just road-worn. He'd been on another assignment when the call came about this find. He'd barely had time to hand over his notes to another agent and throw some clean clothing into a case before catching his flight to Newfield. "I think I'll grab some dinner and do some more research."

"You do that."

Petrosian watched him walk out; Patrick could feel the man's gaze between his shoulder blades, like an infrared targeting mechanism. But he had been in cities where the cops were actively hostile, not just cautious, and he had learned not to take offense where none was intended.

The hotel he'd been booked into was pretty standard: a decent enough bed, small bathroom, inexpensive toiletries. But it had hot water, a desk he could work at and a twenty-four-hour restaurant next door. All the comforts of home. But somehow, showered and dressed, his notes spread out in front of him and covered with his scribbles and yellow Post-its, he wasn't in the mood to work, or to go downstairs and eat alone.

You're on the job, he told himself. *Don't be an idiot. The lady said no, and you shouldn't have asked in the first place anyway.*

Not letting himself think about it, he pulled out his cell phone and dialed the phone number he had jotted on the edge of his notebook before handing back the original file to the police clerk.

"Lily Malkin? It's J.T. Patrick. Agent Pa—yes, that's right. Hi. Look, I know you said that you weren't interested in dinner, but I really want to bounce some ideas off you, and…well, I hate eating alone. Especially when I'm away from home. In a new town. Save me?"

Chapter 3

Lily stared at the phone, not quite believing what she had just heard. Did he know how obvious that line of bullshit was? He had to; she could practically hear it in his voice: "Laugh at me, but laugh *with* me."

"Agent Patrick…"

She shouldn't. She really shouldn't. He was far too appealing, and her thoughts had been far too depressing. Against her better judgment, she said yes.

"Great. Nothing fancy—maybe there's a local Italian around here, a mom-and-pop place you could recommend? I'm craving ziti."

She knew exactly the place, and on a Tuesday night, it shouldn't be too crowded. "I'll pick you up in—" she looked at the clock on her desk "—twenty minutes?"

"Great. I'm at the Veis Hotel, over on—"

"I know where it is. Budget central—nice to know our tax dollars aren't going to Jacuzzis and wet bars."

He snorted into the phone. "Hardly. I'll see you in twenty."

She hung up the phone and stared down at the pile of bills she had been paying. Or trying to pay, as her thoughts had been more on this afternoon's scene than what she owed Visa and the electric company. "You. Are insane. And this is a terrible idea."

Ten minutes later she had gone through three different outfits, finally settling on a pair of black slacks and a dark red sweater, with her favorite boots with the heels that made her feel not quite so short. Jeans were fine for shelter work, but even a casual dinner with a good-looking guy seemed to call for something a little more. Or at least something not covered in cat hair.

She stared in the mirror, giving herself a once-over. A rub of blush over her cheekbones, and eyeliner and that was it. The look was casual, not too much effort, but looking good. Grabbing her keys off the hook by the door, she was in her car and on her way before she could second-guess herself.

Lily Malkin wasn't much for impulsive actions. She felt more comfortable on her own, when she could control the situation, and not have to do anything other than what she wanted. Her father called her selfish, but among all the men she had dated—and the few she had loved—Lily had never met anyone that she honestly felt that she could relax with; that she felt could accept her for who she was.

Probably because she was never quite sure who that was. An insomniac, not-quite-cat-phobic, detail-oriented female with trust and responsibility issues, to start. In short, a mess. On her own, Lily could deal with it. Bring someone else into the equation, and there were too many variables. Too many ways things could go wrong. So control was important.

After graduating from college, she had gone into banking because she wanted a job that would allow her to interact with people, but from a safe distance, and would allow her to leave the job at the office. Being a bank teller was perfect. She had moved to Newfield after a lot of thought, choosing it for low cost-of-living and a pretty environment.

Even working at the shelter had been part of a long-term planned goal. Tired of having responses to stimuli she could not control, she had finally gone to a therapist who helped her gain the courage to stop avoiding cats, and face the discomfort. It had worked, but the process had been slow, steady, and under her control every step of the way.

She was having dinner with this man because…

Lily knew the reason. Because she couldn't get the image of those kittens out of her mind, and he was the only way to get answers about who would do that sort of thing. And why.

If she could help him find this guy, then maybe this feeling of depression, of helplessness and failure, might go away.

It had nothing to do with the way his eyes were so dark, or intense. Really. It was all part of the long-term plan.

"And if he suggests dinner in his hotel room, you are out of there, federal agent or not," she told her reflection in the rearview mirror. Her reflection looked dubious, and she laughed at herself. Right now, she was so tired she'd probably fall asleep in the middle of anything, anyway.

To her relief, he was waiting outside the hotel's lobby when she pulled up, talking on his cell phone. He saw her and waved, then closed the phone and slipped it into his pocket. He had a slim leather briefcase with him, she noted, and when he slipped into her Toyota she noted there were a number of color-coded files sticking out of it. This really was going to be a working dinner, then. Lily almost laughed again at the wash of disappointment she felt.

They were seated quickly; as expected, the little Italian restaurant wasn't busy, and they had the corner to themselves. Patrick put the file on the table next to him and quickly buttered a bread stick. "Sorry. I'm a carb addict, if there's one thing I can't resist it's fresh bread."

"It is so unfair. Guys can eat anything and not gain a pound." Casual, almost stupid chitchat. They were doing it to keep from thinking about what they had seen that afternoon. Or at least, she was. If she could not think about it, she could keep it from being so real. If it wasn't real, maybe it wouldn't hurt so much.

I'm sorry, kittens, she thought again, feeling the wave of helplessness move through her. There was nothing she could have done, and yet she felt overwhelmed by the feeling that she was *supposed* to have done something, somehow prevented this.

He protested the implied slur in her words. "Pound,

shmounds. This particular guy has to keep up with the FBI regs for fitness. They don't let us relax until after we have seniority behind a desk. That's why we're all so anxious to get promoted."

She laughed, almost more than what the joke was worth. He glanced at her quickly, looked at the menu, then looked at her again, those dark eyes toned down for once. "Lily. Before we talk about anything else… I'm not a practicing psychologist, but it's okay to be upset. What you saw…most people never run into that kind of violence, and that's good. Nobody ever should, whether it's directed at them or someone or something else. And when you do see it, you shouldn't be unaffected. It's not healthy, or human, to be unaffected. Even us tough federal-lawman types."

She toyed with the corner of the menu, rubbing it between two fingers. "I know. It's just…how do you sleep? After things like that?"

He gave the faintest shrug, barely a jerk of his shoulder. "I catch the people responsible. Or I do my damnedest to try, anyway. That is why I need to pick your brains. I think you can help me."

She pursed her lips, weighing his words. "All right."

Something she hadn't even known was knotted inside her eased with those words. She only meant to agree to having her brain picked in exchange for dinner, but somehow it felt as though it was more.

Is this it? she wondered. Is this the thing I've been feeling I need to do? That easy? She doubted it. But it was something.

They placed their orders, and Lily ordered a glass of

wine—"None for me," Patrick said regretfully. "I'm technically on duty. On the plus side, that means I can expense this, so eat up!"

There was something about him, despite his practiced charm, despite his intensity, that almost made Lily forget her original discomfort. Almost. He cared about what he was doing. That made him likable. The fact that he was likable made her even more cautious. Charming men were men with agendas and ambition. Men with agendas and ambition were not to be trusted. It wasn't any one bad experience that had drummed that into her, although it was proved, more often than not. No, that knowledge, that wariness, was born in her, it sometimes seemed.

This wasn't a date, she reminded herself, wondering at his pleased smile at her choices. It was, as he said, a business meeting. Over food. So what if he had an agenda?

Everyone wanted something. Everyone had a secret. Even her.

"So why is the FBI investigating this?" she asked again, taking a bread stick for herself.

This time, unlike earlier that day, he answered her.

"The FBI normally gets called in for certain things. Kidnappings, bank robberies, crimes that cross state lines or involve national issues…. This…isn't really one of them." He cracked a crooked smile. "Except it falls in that gray area of 'might be of interest.' Courtesy of the twenty-first century and modern paranoia, just about every investigated crime gets entered into a national database. Mostly they just sit there, unless there's something in them that triggers an alert somewhere else. In my case, I look for tags that indicate animal-abuse cases."

He waved the remains of his bread stick at her, as though lecturing. It should have been annoying, but wasn't, mainly because his intensity was so real, and focused on a *thing,* not her. Whatever it was that he did, it meant a great deal to him. She admired that.

"Animal abuse is—it's one of the things we're taught to look for in the background of suspects. I'm working on a particular theory that, if I can prove it, could lead us to a way to identify and stop potential killers. So, if a police department reports a notable case of animal abuse it pings on my radar. If there are certain elements to the case, I follow up."

"Certain elements?" The waiter came with her glass of wine and his soda. Lily nodded her thanks, but kept her attention on Patrick.

"A level of ferocity, or indications of repetition. Something that suggests escalation."

"That whoever it is, is getting ready to move on to something bigger," she guessed. "Like humans."

"Exactly. Abuse, especially of cats, is considered one of the 'terrible triad,' of indicators that's often found in the background of a serial killer. That, and arson, are historically two of the major warning signs of serial killers before they turn to human targets. It's almost as though they're trying to vent themselves on weaker beings, or—by some theories—are working up their nerve to go to the next level. Nobody really knows for certain. It's an inexact science."

Lily was horrified, but fascinated. Everyone knew about serial killers, of course—even if you never watched the nightly news, you had to have heard of *Silence of the Lambs*. But she had never realized that there was a pattern, or a science, to it. Or that cats were so very much a target.

"And you try to find them before then. But how do you know that they're going to go to people next?"

"I don't. Most of the time they don't, either. But if I can stop them before that line is crossed, that's all that matters. Law enforcement isn't all about punishment. It's about being a deterrent, too."

She nodded. It made sense. "So this one incident brought you out here?"

He hesitated, taking a sip of his soda before responding. "No. Not the one. This goes no further than this table, Lily." He paused until she nodded her agreement. "Three years ago in the next town, there was a couple of scattered cases—cats being cut open and left, like some kind of sacrifice. By itself, that's nothing, unfortunately. Wannabe Satanists, or just one kid with a cruel streak, or even a budding coroner who wanted to start small. They wouldn't even have been entered in the system, except there was a small media fuss.

"And that was nothing, until now. The reason they called me is that here have been two incidents prior to this in the past two months. All involving cats. All young males. None of them quite so…formalized as today's offering. Whoever this guy is, assuming it's the same guy from three years ago—he's working out a pattern that satisfied him. If it was him three years ago…

he's on an evolving scale, an escalating one. And that's a major danger sign."

"So you think…" She shuddered involuntarily. "You think we have a baby serial killer right here in Newfield?"

She'd had nightmares about that; not often, maybe three or four times, but unlike most of her dreams they tended to stay with her even after she woke: of women dying, one after another, in terribly bloody ways. She hated those dreams, all the more so for never being able to figure out what caused them or how to prevent them.

"No." He shook his head, almost as though he regretted that lack of serial killerage. "The indicators I've seen so far suggest that he hasn't crossed that line. I'm not sure that's the direction he's going in, either. His pattern is… Different. Odd. Intriguing."

Lily cocked her head and studied him. "You find strange things intriguing, Agent Patrick."

He accepted the jab with self-aware good humor. "Nature of the job, Ms. Malkin."

The conversation was interrupted by the delivery of their meals, and the resulting pause to sort things out.

"No," he said again once they started eating. "I don't think he's a serial killer. The specifics line up—cats, violence, repetition. That's what pinged on my radar. But seeing it—the feel of it is all wrong."

"Intriguing?"

"To a person with my background, yes. Serial killers have a variety of reasons for acting the way they do, by their standards. The files—" and he made a gesture with his fork to the file at his side "—the first two cases, and now this one, they don't show the kind of…passion normal to a serial killer's buildup. This was…"

"Restrained."

He looked at her with surprised respect. "Yeah."

Lily didn't know why she had said that, but when she thought about it, it was true. The violence had been contained, the cats carefully tended, the scene almost designed, like a stage set….

Going back there made her insides queasy again, so she changed the subject. "So what's the third thing? You said there was a—terrible triad? You said two, so what's the third?"

"Bed-wetting."

Lily stared at him. "Bed-wetting."

"It shows up often enough in established serial killers that it's considered an indicator, yes."

She wasn't going to laugh. It wasn't funny. "But not a crime."

"No, not a crime. We don't investigate anyone on the basis of soiled linens."

"I'm not laughing," she told him.

"Nobody ever does," he assured her, his dark eyes creased around the edges with humor. "Joking is frowned on in the FBI."

Lily ate a few bites of her veal, letting the moment pass intentionally, and then looked up at her companion. "All right. You said you wanted to ask me something about the case. About the cats?"

He took a bite of his own ziti, chewed and swallowed before responding. Good table manners, she noted.

Another point in his favor, were she keeping any sort of list. Which she wasn't.

"Yeah. About the cattery that you said he had. You work in a shelter—it looks like you have a full house there?"

"Always. Females, unless they're fixed, breed regularly even when they have kittens already. Even if you could stop every stray from breeding tomorrow, there would be more cats in shelters than we could ever find homes for."

Lily felt guilt once again for not adopting one or two of her own. She had the room, and Lord knew she had gotten over her fear…but something held her back from bringing them into her own home. She still needed that distance, the place to retreat to, in case things went wrong.

"So why was he breeding them, if there are so many out there to adopt?"

"For color." No hesitation in her mind now, not after what Patrick had told her. "He—we're assuming a he?"

"For now."

"All right. He used spotted tabbies with white paws, all seven of them. The cats before, they were spotted as well?"

Patrick nodded. "According to the files the cops gave me, yes. Not all of them had the white paws, though. That was new."

"The spotted markings are common enough, but not so much so that you could find seven of them, all about the same age—not kittens, but less than two years old, I'd guess. And to find three…three batches of seven?

The combination of color and age, there's no way he could assume he was going to find them all at the same time. So it makes sense he'd try to breed them himself."

"That was my thought, too. This guy, whoever he is, wasn't flying off the cuff. He has an agenda. There was planning here, at least a year's worth to be breeding his own litters. More, since the first incident was two months ago, and the cats were about the same age."

"But why?" Why would someone do something like this? Why use cats? Why cats of that specific type? "And God, how could he breed cats, raise them and then *kill* them?"

Patrick poked his fork at the mound of ziti on his plate, and then looked up at her, his dark eyes now shadowed by more than exhaustion. "I don't know. But I'm going to find out."

Then he leaned back and smiled at her, clearly changing mental tracks. "But enough. You've confirmed what I suspected, and may yet be useful to the investigation, so this meal is hereby considered a justified expense. Therefore I'm not going to do anything right now except enjoy the lovely company, the excellent food and the fact that I'm not cooped up in a hotel room watching reruns of Fox shows I didn't like when I first saw them. And I insist that you do the same, just to keep me company."

Lily flushed, but smiled at him, and went back to her veal piccata, hyperaware of the fact that he was watching her every move, observing her the same way he had observed the crime scene. Charming, but ambitious, she reminded herself. Be careful.

"So. You volunteer with cats and work in a bank. And, occasionally, help out the local cops and wandering feds. What else does Ms. Lily Malkin do?"

Lily didn't play games, was what she didn't do. "I bake. I work out to burn off the calories I put on from baking. I sleep as much as humanly possible. I like modern art and Delta blues, an occasional glass of wine and really scary movies with buttered popcorn. I have no siblings, my father lives in Seattle where I grew up and my last relationship ended amicably. Anything else?"

He blinked, visibly thinking over her words. "No, I think that about covers everything, and then some. Your turn."

She didn't have to think about that at all. "What does the T stand for?"

"The letter T," he said easily, and she smiled reluctantly in return. Oh, charming. Very, very charming. But she still wasn't going to play.

Lily turned off the beeping alarm even before she turned on the light as she came in through the garage. Once the condo was plunged back into silence, she slipped her shoes off at the door, dropped her bag on the dining-room table and shuffled to the narrow spiral staircase that led to the bedroom. She had lived in a studio apartment when she first came to town, but on her morning run one day she had passed the row of town houses under construction and, on a whim, stopped in at the builder's office. Three months and most of her savings later, she had closed on her town house, and two months after that she had moved in.

It was the first place she had ever owned, the first real home she'd had since leaving her father's home for college sixteen years before. Her dad had choked up when she called to tell him the news. Her dad was a little weird: "not married? No problem, honey, you'll find someone some day. But this endless string of living in apartments? That can't be healthy!"

The condo wasn't large—a kitchen, living room and dining room downstairs, and a bedroom and bathroom upstairs—but it was all hers. Her refuge.

She stripped as she went into the bathroom, tossing her clothing into the hamper and turning on the shower. The two glasses of wine at dinner, plus a hot shower, might be enough to let her get to sleep—and *stay* asleep until the alarm went off. If she was lucky, and fate was kind, she might not even dream.

Or if she did, maybe they would be the hot and sexy kind. Lord knows, she had enough material to work with tonight.

"Don't get so caught up in secret-agent-man fantasies that you forget to finish paying those bills," she told herself, pulling her hair into a scrunchie and knotting it. She was on shift at the bank from ten to four, and if she didn't get everything into the mail in the morning, it would bother her all day.

The mirror was starting to fog, and she rubbed a spot clear to check her skin.

"Holy shit!" she shrieked, spinning around.

There was nothing there, of course. She had known there wasn't going to be anything there. It wasn't possible that there was anything there—the alarm had been on, no windows had been open. There was no way a cat could have gotten in.

There was no way she could have seen, reflected in that tiny corner of the mirror, a cat sitting on the shower ledge behind her, watching her with wide, rounded green eyes.

Mrrrrrai?

And there was no way she could hear the plaintive query of a cat, echoing off the tile of the shower, over the sound of the water and the rasp of her own breath.

Lily took a deep breath; slow in through her mouth, out through her nose. "I'm tired. I've had a stressful day. I probably should not have had rich food and red wine on top of that. I'm hallucinating."

Mrrrrraaw.

"And I don't need you laughing at me, either," she told the phantom cat, getting into the shower and, against her original intentions, pulling the scrunchie out and putting her head entirely under the falling water, letting the steam and sound drive everything else away.

"Just let me sleep tonight," she said: a prayer to whoever might be listening. "No dreams. No staring at the ceiling. Just…sleep."

Somehow, she didn't think that was going to happen.

Chapter 4

He didn't like it here. The basement wasn't a good place. It was too damp, and too cold, and the off-white concrete floor absorbed the smells no matter how much bleach was dumped on it. But he had run out of other options; after his last failure, the authorities were watching empty spaces too closely, and he dared not openly rent anywhere, not with all the beasts he would have to bring with him.

This would have to do.

He finished scrubbing the table, and paused to wipe sweat off his face. He smelled as bad as the bleach and piss combined. There was no way She would come to him smelling like this. He needed to be clean, oiled and scented, and appropriately dressed, or even the very best sacrifice would be in vain.

The creatures around him were listless, most with their bellies distended with pregnancy. God, they were disgusting. Too long to wait, and nowhere to find new ones. Only four males were right, and he needed seven, but he couldn't wait any longer.

The appeal had failed again. He was close, so close, and yet the key would not turn; She would not come. Three years he had waited, since waking: three years counting cycles and watching the signs. Only once each turning was it right, and the doorway was only open so long; if he didn't find the right combination, it would close and lock and he would be forever on the wrong side, all he hoped to gain gone for yet another year.

Seven times three was a lucky turn; this would be the time. Three times to be lucky.

Seven was the number, was a holy number, all his instincts told him so, the same way he knew he would know Her when she came. There were no books, no guides to show him the way: instinct was all he had to go on. Instinct had told him who he was, what he must do. Instinct was all he could trust.

He glanced up into the sky. The moon. The moon was key. The dark moon was coming, and all the steps had to be taken before then—when She waxed full again, it would be too late to try again until the cycle passed again. But the faster he worked, the less perfect the beasts. He needed to find some way around that, something to make the offerings acceptable. And soon, soon! When the final offering was made, it had to be perfect!

A cat *mrrrowed*, low and angry, and another answered, setting an entire cage of the things off.

"Shut up!"

It wasn't fair! He didn't understand the urgency that drove him, or the knowledge that filled him, but they were the only things that had any reality, any substance. Everything was *wrong* suddenly, since that moment three years ago when his old existence had disappeared and left him in this hell. There was nothing inside him now except for that urgency. His brain could focus only on the things he needed, the steps he must take. All sensation, all joy, was gone: he woke in the morning and the sky was the wrong shade of gray, the air the wrong smell, the speech of those around him the wrong sound.

Only when he drifted back into the dream was everything made right again. Only then did he feel whole. The dream of what was through the doorway, his rightful, long-denied prize. Her, and the knowledge She would bring.

Everything he did, the steps he went through, they were all toward that.

"Water, water, everywhere, all for the beasties to drink," he chanted. He poured water from the jug into plastic dishes, placing each one in a cage, careful to move so as not to actually come into contact with any of the creatures. The gleam in the beasts' eyes taunted him, made him dizzy. They judged, they always judged, the damn things, as though they were somehow better than he was.

Damn things. How he hated them. Hated them! They were cruel, and faithless, and they betrayed....

"Calm, calm," he crooned, his voice a deep, soothing baritone that made the cats' ears flicker to attention as he passed, his left hand reaching up to touch the palm-size amulet hanging under his sweatshirt. "Follow your courses and be thorough. They're only animals. They don't know a thing."

But they did. They were the keepers of the secret wisdom, the knowing of old. The ancient secrets he needed. Their blood would bring Her, and She would bring the way home.

Fantasy and myth, but there was truth at the bottom of it, he knew. "They don't know, but you do, yes, you do. You remembered, you did."

Three years before. Something came to him in the night, a sudden click in the brain that set him on this path. The first time he had faltered. But now, now all he needed was to find the right key, the right combination and he would be free of this wrong existence. No longer powerless and drab but allowed to claim what was his, what had always been meant to be his.

Whatever that was.

The doubt touched his mind briefly, and he shook it off. It had been within grasp once, before She failed him, denied him. Ruined it all. Not this time. The beasts were the way. The beasts knew the answer. The thought soothed him, calmed him enough that he could continue.

He finished his chores and made sure all the cages were locked, then closed the basement's door behind him, letting the silence enrobe him. Silence was so much better. He hated the sound the beasts made; it caused his skin to crawl. He would have torn their tongues out if something hadn't warned him against it.

Use them, yes. They were part of the key. But do not harm them. Never harm them. That would undo it all.

He climbed the stairs, the solid tap of his boots against the concrete forcing him to focus, to put the basement into a compartment and close the door, to replace the mask that he wore, so others would not know him until it was time.

A passing memory—red slipped against black cloth, harsh panting and white claws—confused him for a moment, but he shook it off. The past was failure. The future was still to come. The future was in his control.

He opened the door, and felt dawn's cool air on his face. It was moist with rain-to-come, and he lifted his face to better enjoy it.

"Hey. You!"

A guy with an apron, a broom in hand, staring at him. Why? His mask. He needed to replace his mask, pretend to be one of *them* again. But the panic hit him, and he couldn't remember how.

"You sick or something? Get out of there!"

The exit from the basement led to an alley next to the man's store. The ground was disgusting, filthy. Cold. The damp suddenly seeped into his bones, and he shivered. He was always cold.

Not daring to say anything to the man, he brushed past him, hunched into his jacket, walking away. His mask came back to him too late, and he lifted his face to stare back at the man, willing him to remember this face, not the other.

Someday soon he would find his way home. Then he

could show his true face, his gods-given face, and they would know what he was, and the power he wielded. Then they would treat him with respect. With *fear.*

Chapter 5

Lily shoved her face into the pillow, her shoulders hunching up to her ears, as though trying to make herself into a small, unattractive target. The sheets tangled around her while she dreamed, creating an almost mummy-like wrapping around her. Darkness. Pain. Loss. A sense of failure as endless as the night sky curving over her. She wept, despair settling over her, seeping into her bones, her very being.

Then, out of the darkness, a faint sound. A hint. A suggestion. For the first time, a lifeline.

Mrrauu?

Her head lifted, deep in the dream. This was different. This was new. *Yes, yes. I hear you.*

Mrrauu! Like a beacon easing her out of despair,

bringing her away from the pitiless sky. *Mrrauu!* Commanding, imperious, the call demanded attention be paid, and paid now!

Her shoulders relaxed, her entire body softening, easing into the mattress as the dream took her over, bringing her out of nightmare into something more pleasant….

A shadow danced impatiently ahead of her, green eyes glinting in the lamplight. Her laughter spilled out over the doorsill, the sound bright as moonlight over the still-warm sand. "I am yours to command, my beautiful. Only allow me to dress myself first, before you drag me into the night."

Mrrauu! *Now! The moon is dark and it is time to dance, silly two-legged one! But she laughed as well, a rumbling purr and a small pink tongue.*

A moment of peace, a moment only, and then a shift as often happens in dreams: the moonlight turned cold, the voices harsh and cruel. Lily moaned in her sleep, pulling her legs up to her chest as though to protect herself. Familiar territory, this: an old familiar dream, but not a friend, no.

The warm sands underfoot became unyielding: cold, root-strewn and treacherous. Soft linen became coarse cotton, scraping against wind-chafed and broken skin. The weight of metal draped around her wrists and waist, and only the comfort of a small soft body was the same.

Then the cat's cry elongated, filled with fear and outrage as that comfort was pulled from her grasp, and hard hands grabbed and pulled, shoving her forward

into darkness. The flare of fire in front of them brought
no comfort, but sparked a scream from feline and
human throat at the same time, as though they were
one and the same....

Lily sat upright, her throat scraped raw as though she
had strep, her eyes streaming and her sinuses dry as
though all the moisture had been sucked out of her
body. The horrific images wrapped around her, making
her shake and shiver despite the warmth of the room.

"My lady! My lady, forgive me!"

The sounds that came from her mouth were gibberish, and yet Lily felt that they were actual words, if she
were only able to understand them. And with the
sounds, the memories faded, not disappearing, but re-
treating enough that she was able to remember who she
was, where she was. That it was not her flesh aflame,
not her neck snapped, not her skin flayed from her body
while she yet lived....

Lily shoved the sweat-soaked sheets off her body
and hugged her pillow to her, waiting while her heartbeat slowed to a more normal pattern. The usual cool
comfort of her bedroom seemed unfamiliar, alien
somehow, and that was almost more disturbing than the
nightmare itself.

Lily had suffered from nightmares since puberty,
dreams that left her sweat covered and crying. Even on
nights when she did not dream, she slept fitfully, aware
that one could strike at any time. Sleeping aids only
made it worse, forcing her to sleep without the ability
to wake up when a nightmare came.

In self-defense, she had studied not only the science

of dreams but the subject of her own, as much as she could remember. Cats crying in fear, nighttime assaults, and flashes of rage and death. Over the years, she had come up with a theory: that she was dreaming about the witch trials, here in New England, and similar events in Scotland, England, France and Spain. Anywhere the fear of women and cats had grown into such murderous depths. She had read about them, at some point, maybe when she was in school. It was a reasonable theory, and all tied into her problem with cats somehow, or grew out of it, or something.

Knowing that should have made her able to get rid of the nightmares, or make them easier to deal with.

It didn't.

Lily let the sweat dry on her skin, and let the details slide ever further from her grasp. The truth was that she didn't want to remember. It was awful, whatever it was. But there had been something new in this dream, something…she didn't remember details, but there was a vague sense of it being…nice.

"Not fair," she told the ceiling. "I'd like to remember the good things, at least."

Her therapist had told her once that it was the sign of an organized mind, to be able to separate nighttime fancies from waking reality. If that was true, Lily wasn't sure how disorganized people managed it, dragging the memory of such things with them throughout the day.

Thankfully, she seemed to have been born with an organized mind. True to form, by the time she was in the shower, rinsing out her hair, the images had faded almost entirely, and when she walked into the bank, greeting the other tellers and setting up her cash drawer, the only thing left was exhaustion, carefully hidden under coffee and a decent breakfast.

Her job was routine but not unpleasant, and she enjoyed the small interactions with the bank's customers. The day passed normally: the branch was the only one downtown, so they got a lot of foot traffic, especially between eleven and two when most people came in during their lunch break.

A tall, angular, gray-haired woman with a face cut from granite came up to Lily's counter. "Hello, Mrs. J."

The quintessential little-old-lady librarian, Mrs. Jablonsky came in on the second and sixteenth of each month to deposit her paycheck. According to town gossip, she had been a volunteer when the library first opened its doors in 1928, and had never left the job. When she died, they said, she would still be behind the desk, sorting returns and shushing kids who giggled too loudly in the computer room.

Kids were terrified of her. Lily thought she was fabulous.

"Hello, my dear. I can't believe that you're still here."

It was their own private joke. Mrs. J. knew what they said about her, and had more than once scolded Lily about following in her path, staying too long doing one thing over and over again, especially once they made her head teller.

"Don't you dare talk Lily into leaving!" Leanna cried from the next window. Lea was new, still in training, and still nervous enough about making a mistake that she wanted Lily to double-check every transaction she made.

"That's not going to happen," Mark said from the third open window. "She actually secretly runs the bank, it's just nobody's told the branch manager yet."

Lily shook her head, and finished Mrs. J.'s transaction, wishing her a nice day and going on to the person next in line. Mark was right, partially: she wasn't going anywhere. There was comfort in knowing what she would be doing each shift, every shift, and a comfort too in the combination of chatter and distance that her teller's window gave her. But she did wonder, occasionally, if there wasn't anything else besides working and volunteering at the shelter and having the occasional date that never seemed to go anywhere.

When things slowed down, she made sure that everyone else was set, then closed out her drawer and went into the backroom. She had intended to work on the shift schedule for the next week, but the moment she sat down her mind went blank, and she couldn't focus on the schedule sheet in front of her.

It had been twenty-four days since Aggie came and got her, brought her to look at an empty room of cages, and the bodies of murdered cats. Two days since the kittens had been killed, and if that bastard had done it before, he would do it again. Agent Patrick thought so, too. Somewhere out there, someone was raising cats for the sole purpose of killing them. Young male spotted cats. Three different instances, seven cats each. Or were there? Seven each time? Lily frowned, her pencil tapping the schedule form. It was an important point, but she didn't know why. She hadn't asked Agent Patrick that, during their dinner. Once he had finished asking her his questions, the evening had veered away from the case, covering more casual topics, as though…

As though they had been on a date. Which it hadn't been. Because she wasn't interested in dating an FBI agent. Especially an FBI agent who was only in town for a short time. Right? Right, Lily?

Worrying about the fact that she had no interest in dating a guy who hadn't asked her out was a better place to be than fretting over a cat killer. But not by much. She made an incoherent growl of frustration, and squeezed her eyes closed, trying to banish both thoughts and settle her brain on what she was supposed to be doing.

A penny dropped in front of her, ringing on the polished wooden desk and rolling onto the paper she was supposed to be filling out.

"I'd offer more for them, but I can't imagine you've got anything really tempting going on in there, the exciting life you lead."

"Very funny." She handed the penny to Mark, who added it back to his cash box.

"Actually, you looked way too intense for someone just trying to figure out who has to take the Saturday-morning shift. Come on, spill."

Mark was twenty-two, hyper, and about as able to keep a secret as a Hollywood talk-show host when the cameras were rolling. Even if she had been looking for a confessor, he would not have been it.

"Not a chance," she told him sweetly.

He pouted. "Bah, you're no fun."

"I'm your supervisor. I'm not supposed to be fun. Go away."

He laughed, and obeyed. Lily watched him go into the break room, and then heard the sounds of the mini-fridge opening and shutting, then the clatter of Tupperware and the *ding* of the microwave turning on. The smell of spicy rice and meat drifted back to her, and her stomach rumbled; she had leftover veal piccata for her own lunch, but she hadn't been hungry until that moment.

Shaking her head at how fickle the body was, she turned her attention back to the schedule sheet. Mark wanted off on Friday. Carole was on vacation. She had promised to take the Saturday-morning shift at the shelter; they were having another adoption drive, and it could get a little crazy if they had a good turnout… Trying to make everyone happy was impossible, but there was always a way to make everyone feel as if they had been listened to, even if they didn't get exactly what they wanted. You just had to work a little at it.

With a little willpower and a lot of determined rein-pulling when her mind wandered, the rest of the shift went easily enough. Once the week's schedule was finalized, Lea's cash-out supervised and everyone's numbers tallied out, it was time to go home. Suddenly, her exhaustion came back with a vengeance.

Lily said good-night to her coworkers and walked into the dusk to her car, humming a tune that had been playing over the radio in the backroom, when a cat ran across her path and went under the cars parked nearest to her.

A shudder ran down her spine, involuntarily. She

wasn't superstitious, and she wasn't afraid, but something about the sight of the cat, its tail held high, triggered an old reflex. And if it was a spotted tabby… The shudder was back, brought on this time by the thought of what a stray cat might face if the cat killer found him.

Better check, she thought. You really won't sleep tonight if you think you left a cat out here at risk.

"Hey there." She bent down to see if she could get a better look at the cat; see if it was a stray, or someone's pet gone for an evening walk. "Hey, sweetie, come on out here."

The cat mrrowed once, a narrow, plaintive sound, and a strange sense of disorientation hit Lily. The call was familiar, as familiar as her own breathing, and yet somehow the sound itself sounded…wrong.

Do cats have accents? she wondered, a little giddy. Is this little one a transplant from somewhere else?

As soon as she thought that, the familiar parking lot fading out, replaced by something not familiar at all, and yet clear in every single detail….

The ceiling was far overhead, the walls open to the sun and wind, both soft today, thanks be to Ra. This would be difficult enough, without having to battle the elements as well as her heart.

"Bast's daughter." The shadow moved, scattering attendants like petals in his wake. "What news do you bring us, Priestess?"

The voice was deep and commanding, accustomed to both obedience and answers. She made a graceful obeisance as she drew forward. Her priestess rank might give her leeway within the palace's walls, but

respect must always be given where due, and antago-
nizing this man would not serve her purpose.

"You must do this for me," her lover had said as they
lay together on linen sheets, watching dawn slip over
the hills before them. "This one thing, and we shall reap
the benefits forever. Together."

A ping alerted Lily to the fact that she needed to get
gas. She made note of it as she backed her little Toyota
out of her parking space, and then stopped the car,
suddenly confused.

Hadn't she just been looking for a stray? She was
certain she had bent to look for the cat…but no, she was
in her car, everything in its place, and there was no cat
yowling a protest, locked in the carrier she always had
in her trunk, in case she needed to bring someone to the
shelter. The carrier that was still in her trunk, untouched.

Lily looked at the clock display on her dashboard: 6:42.

It had been six-thirty when she left the bank. She had
lost twelve minutes.

"You need a vacation, Lily Malkin," she told herself.
"Or more fresh air, if you're going to start losing time
like that." She rested her head against the steering
wheel, hitting it once, lightly, and then put the car in
motion again. It was just exhaustion, probably, and the
fact that her brain was still, inevitably, worrying about
the scene she had been exposed to the day before. She
had seen the cat, and…

And what? What had happened to the cat?

She waited at a red light and tried to remember.
There was nothing, a total blank spot, and then…
"Come on, kitten. Come on. *I don't have any sardines*

with me this time, I'm sorry. But I'll get you some later.
You know that you can trust me...."

You can trust me.

Then the noise came. Not a noise, a sound. A cat's
meow, echoing from under the car she was crouched
next to. An ordinary meow, not frightened or scared or
particularly hungry. Almost like a welcome-home
meow, a familiar greeting. And a request. From a cat
she had never seen before.

But there the memory ended, leaving her with a
sense of frustration and concern and a growing need
to *do* something.

First the cat in the shower, and now this. Either she
was heading for a nervous breakdown, complete with
aural and visual hallucinations, or...

She couldn't think of an "or" that made any sense.

The light changed, and the car behind her honked impatiently. "All right, all right, I'm going," she told the
guy, resisting the urge to flip him off. "And I'll call Aggie
when I get home, if he hasn't left a message. Obviously,
I'm not going to be able to relax until that guy's caught."

You could call Agent Patrick, a treacherous thought
snuck into her brain, and Lily squelched it. It had been
a lovely dinner. And that was that. She wasn't going to
give in to a foolish schoolgirl crush. Or even a foolish
adult crush. She would call Aggie; he would tell her if
anything new had come up.

The phone rang just as she opened the door from her
garage into the town house condo, and Lily felt her
heart race, just a little bit, with anticipation. She placed

the mail on the small table in the foyer and went to answer it.

"Yes?"

An obscure sense of disappointment flooded her when the caller turned out to be a telemarketer, rather than Detective Petrosian.

Or Agent Patrick, that treacherous voice said, practically pouting.

"Stop it," she told herself sternly, hanging up on the telemarketer midspiel. Yes, dinner had been enjoyable, despite the rather gruesome topic of discussion. But he was here on an investigation, and then he would be gone again. And she wasn't going to think about getting involved in a long-distance relationship after one dinner—and a working dinner at that!

"Especially since there is absolutely no reason to think that he's ever going to get in touch with you again," a different, more practical but equally annoying voice inside her head told her.

Lily laughed, and rubbed her face with both hands, smearing what was left of her eye makeup. "You're tired. And he freaked you out more than you realized with his talk about serial killers and whatnot." The fact that he didn't believe that the person who hurt those cats was, in fact, a serial killer, was reassuring…but she didn't like knowing that there was someone who thought it was okay, for whatever version of okay, to do that to innocent animals, either. And *why* had he done it? Not just once, but three times, if Agent Patrick was right, and all three incidents were linked?

Or maybe more than three times. The cops had found

three sites, but what Patrick had said suggested that these guys didn't just start out full blown. They started small, with one cat maybe. Then the thrill wore off, and they had to—what was the word?—escalate.

Part of being the city's unofficial official cat specialist meant knowing when to actually *act* like one.

She wasn't an FBI agent or a cop. She couldn't do anything to stop the guy. But there was something she *could* do.

Picking up the phone again, Lily dialed a familiar number.

"Felidae No-Kill Cat Shelter, Nancy speaking." Lily could hear the sounds of a cat meowing in the background—they must have let Jones wander the halls again. A twenty-pound panther-wannabe, Jones was too big to be easily adopted, despite her sweet personality, so she had ended up being the office cat.

"Nancy, it's Lily. Is Ronnie in tonight? Can you get her for me, please? Thanks."

When the director picked up the phone, Lily wasted no time getting to the point. "Ronnie, I need you to okay Halloween protocol, amended for any cat with a spotted coat. Effective immediately, and especially for breeding females and kittens."

The Halloween protocol was a ban on the adoption of any black or mostly black cats the last few weeks of October. Not every shelter did it, but the previous year's incident—the one that had landed her an unwilling guest spot on the news—had made them all deeply uneasy. Ronnie's feeling had always been that anyone who wanted a black cat on October 28 would still want it on

November 2, and she wasn't going to risk a cat on some crazy who wanted to sacrifice it to Satan or some other nonsense. The case just gave her the reason to enforce the ban.

"This has to do with your visitors yesterday?" Ronnie didn't know anything more than the fact that Aggie had come to ask her about something in an official capacity. There had been enough going on in the news last night to keep that relatively small story out of the limelight, and if it had been in the local paper, Lily hadn't seen it.

"Yes, and I can't say anything more, Ronnie, I'm sorry. But you might want to look and see if we adopted out any spotted tabbies, especially females, to anyone new in the past year. Especially someone new. Just in case the police need the information."

There was a slight hesitation, then Ronnie came through, making Lily let out a breath she hadn't realized that she was holding. "I'll have Mike go through the files tonight, if it's slow, Agent Patrick and I'll call the county shelter, too, let them know what we're doing. Is there anything we need to know that you can tell us?"

"Not really, no." Lily shrugged, even though the other woman couldn't see it. "I'm sorry. If I could, I would, really." Anything that affected the shelter was Ronnie's business, after all. But she didn't feel as if she could say anything more, at least not without checking with Aggie and Patrick first. "It's probably nothing. I'm probably just overreacting."

"Uh-huh." Ronnie's opinion of that came through loud and clear. They both knew that Lily—practical, think-it-through, measure-twice-and-then-measure-again Lily—didn't overreact.

Not unless there was cause.

"I'll see you tomorrow," Lily said, and hung up the phone. It was after 7:00 p.m. and Aggie was off shift. She'd make some dinner, and get some sleep, and talk to him tomorrow morning.

Chapter 6

"You're our Fibbie?"

Patrick managed not to wince at the shelter receptionist's breezy greeting. "That would be me, yes." He wasn't exactly nostalgic for the bad old days when "Federal Bureau of Investigation" made people shiver, but sometimes familiarity really did breed contempt. Or worse. And how the hell did they know—he hadn't exactly been flashing his badge in the shelter….

The tiny redhead seemed inordinately pleased with herself. "We pulled the file together."

Patrick relaxed a little. Lily must have told them it was a federal priority, in order to get the material he had asked for so quickly. It wasn't a problem.

"There's not a lot of stuff. Adoptions slowed down

after the spring, and we actually had a run on reds and tiger stripes, not so many spotted." The redhead paused in her babble. "Which is weird, actually. Like Mother Nature knew this guy was coming and dried up the available pool. I mentioned it to a friend last night, and he said he hadn't seen any spotted or even many striped cats out and about either lately."

He accepted the inch-thick manila folder with a restrained sigh, tuning her chatter out. They'd managed to keep the killings out of the media, but there wasn't much you could do to stop gossip short of issuing a gag order, and the only way to ensure that would work was to actually gag the participants. Somehow, Patrick didn't think Lily would go for being gagged. Although…

Right. Brain on the job, Agent Patrick.

"Nancy, I'm going to bring the new calico into the soci—oh."

Speak of the devil.

"Lily."

She was wearing jeans again, topped with a red sweater, and high-top sneakers. Her mass of dark, curly hair was pulled back into a high ponytail that brushed her shoulders when her head turned. God, she was adorable.

"Agent Patrick." Something in his expression must have changed, because her face softened, and she relented. "Jon. Here for the files?"

He lifted his hand to show that he did, indeed, have the information. "Thanks for getting it together." The shelter had been more help so far than the local cops. And cops gossiped just as much, if not more.

"I just made a phone call," she said, dismissing his

thanks. "The staff here put everything together. I hope it's useful." She half turned, as though to go back into the shelter, away from him. Something about the slope of her shoulder reminded him of the curve of a cat's tail, the way it dipped and rose, and that triggered another thought in his head. Trying to nail it down, he held up a hand to stop her from leaving before it coalesced.

"Yeah?" she asked, pausing with a look he couldn't quite identify. Not suspicion, but…

"I'm going to ask another favor," he said, suddenly seeing a possible lead to follow, a thread to pull. His brain did that sometimes, seeing A and J and somehow coming up with 42. That was what made him good at his job; even when the lead didn't pan out, it brought them closer to something that might. Or a dead end, but you never knew until you investigated.

That's why the I was in FBI.

"Yes?" She was definitely wary now. He plowed on, the more he spoke the more solid the idea becoming in his mind. Somewhere in his brain he knew that he was imposing, asking too much of her, but he shoved it aside.

"I need you to do some digging for me. You said something that first night about a crazy who tried to adopt a cat last year for some kind of nasty use?"

"Yes…I had the shelter freeze all adoptions of cats matching the description of the ones this guy's been using, for the duration."

"Excellent, excellent. But you have had a problem in the past?"

"Yeah. Only once for us. But it happens all across

the country." She leaned against the wall, watching him. Nancy was looking from one of them to the other, like a spectator at a tennis match, clearly entertained.

He noticed her watching, and shook his head. "Is there somewhere we can talk?"

"We are talking, right here." Her chin was set on stubborn, he noted, and wondered what he had done this time. And why he knew that the way her jaw firmed like that meant she was feeling mulish.

"Lily." He meant it to be cajoling. It came out slightly amused, with a note of pleading. It seemed to work.

"All right. Come on." She led him into the back hallway, past a glass-walled room where dozens of kittens and cats frolicked on ropes and platforms. She pushed open a door and ushered him inside.

It was about the size of a broom closet, but with a soft carpet underfoot, and a bench covered in the same carpeting.

She noticed him looking around, clearly curious. "Meeting room. Where people can bond with a cat they plan to take home."

He was, reluctantly, impressed. "You guys have it all thought out, huh?" He had to admit that he had never really thought about what went into adopting out an animal.

"We try. Giving cats homes, it's maybe not up there with saving the world, but…"

"No, it's up there. All the studies say that people with pets are happier, healthier—better adjusted. If everyone had a cat to go home to, maybe I'd be able to stay home more often too."

Something happened there, right then: he felt it. A tangible connection between the two of them, the same thing he'd felt when they'd had dinner together. From the startled expression on her face, she had felt it—something—as well. He was suddenly aware of the fact that the room was very small, and they were standing awfully close together.

No. Oh, no. He did *not* have time for this.

"You had a favor you wanted to ask," she reminded him, trying to redirect the conversation.

"Yeah. Favor." A drop of sweat was forming on her upper lip, and he fought down the urge to lick it off. "I'm curious about the pattern of cat adoption, if there's a period of time that a certain type of cat's adopted, at a given time of year. And if any one type of person—male, female, old or young—adopts any one specific type."

"And you expect me to do all that, off our computers, in my spare time?" She started to laugh.

"What, you can't do it?" His smile was a challenge, but she was smart enough not to fall for it.

"Better men than you have tried to talk me into things, Agent Patrick. And no, that oh-so-charming smile of yours isn't going to work."

The smile, if anything, grew wider. "I'll take that under advisement. Do you think you'd be able to do a quick search, see what you can turn up—just for your own shelter, of course."

"Of course." Her dry sarcasm was almost off the chart, and he thought that he might just have to take her back to the hotel with him. Nothing sexual—okay, almost nothing sexual—she just managed to hit all his buttons, in a good way. A very good way.

Mind out of the gutter, Patrick. "Also, if you could see what turns up by way of rituals that might use circles rather than the traditional pentacle or whatnot? Specifically, anything that might signify or require the use of cats, or touch on cats in any way?"

Lily eyed him the way she might a particularly large, possibly rabid dog. "Oh, sure. Why not? You don't have some eager-beaver researcher at the bureau who handles this sort of thing with a mega supercomputer?"

He let go of the charm for just a second. "And by the time I got through channels just to request the paper-work, it would be next Tuesday already. This is so low down on the pole it's barely visible."

It wasn't fun to admit things like that—you always wanted to think that your case was the hottest thing on the wire—but the truth was, with nobody except a few stray cats threatened, it was a wonder they were letting him stay out here past the initial once-over ruled out an incipient serial killer. Taxpayers' dollars for his hotel room, et cetera. So long as he could make the case that this might lead to a better understanding of the deviant psychology that led to serial killers, his boss would give him rope, but the easiest way to do that was to make it as cheap as possible for the bureau. And that meant not calling on resources until he could justify them on more than a fishing trip.

If he was wrong, he wasted a little of Lily's time and the taxpayers' already allocated dollars. If he was right…he had a possible monograph to write on the topic, which would go into his personnel file, help build his theory and bring his name a little more recognition, and ease the next step upward on the ladder. Plus, possibly, someday it would help identify and capture a killer before he graduated to animals, much less humans.

It was all good.

He smiled at her again, bringing forward just enough charm to balance his need, and put on his best don't-make-me-beg face. She might say the smile didn't work, but he never let go of a proven tool. "Please?"

"I like you better when you aren't trying to be so damn charming," she told him, and walked out of the meeting room.

He blinked, and then grinned. A real grin, not the one he'd just been using.

"You, Jon T., just got nailed dead to rights."

He definitely wanted to wrap her up and take her home. And very much in a sexual way, too.

Several hours later, Lily still had a warm glow when she thought about the dumbstruck expression on Agent Patrick's face as she left him in the meeting room. It was almost—almost—worth spending her afternoon here, instead of going home the way she had planned.

She tucked one foot underneath her on the chair and closed a file, tossing it down onto the thick pile on the floor and opening another from the pile on the desk. Although going home would have been more useful. The shelter kept detailed records on what cats were adopted by whom, and when, including chipping details and medical history, but the color markings were often pretty vague, and even once they started attaching photos…well, she'd just say that the volunteer with the camera was no Diane Arbus.

"I can't believe I let him talk me into this," she said, tossing that file and dropping it to join the others. Several hundred down, another pile to go.

"Yes, it seemed as though it took so much arm-twisting and coaxing." Ronnie was sorting through piles at the desk across the office, her back to Lily. "Because you'd otherwise be off doing all sorts of exciting things…laundry was on the schedule for today, wasn't it?"

"There's nothing wrong with having a routine. It's very soothing to know what you're going to be doing, when. Plus, I need clean socks."

Ronnie just laughed. If Lily trusted Petrosian, she *liked* Ronnie. The older woman never tried to mother her, or be buddies, or anything other than her boss, with the clear structure of that relationship giving them both a place to stand. But there was no mistaking the fact that Ronnie *cared*, and cared enough to do it on Lily's terms.

"Lil?"

Nancy stuck her head into the office, her strawberry-colored mop of hair looking like a Day-Glo dandelion about to go to seed. "I was just about to shut down for the night—just wanted to let you know that your Fibbie's back."

Lily rolled her eyes heavenward. "Since when did he become *my* Fibbie? Don't anyone answer that. What does he want?"

"Dinner."

All three women jumped slightly when the agent appeared in the door next to Nancy.

"Sorry. I get sort of used to walking in, it's a badge thing."

Arrogance, Lily thought, practically oozed out of his pores. A sort of "you'll accept my right to do this" attitude that was all the more annoying because damned if Ronnie and Nancy didn't do exactly that.

She also hadn't realized that it was dinnertime already. The afternoon had slipped by without her noticing. They really needed an office with a window.

"Are you inviting, or demanding?"

The words were hanging in the air, pregnant with challenge, before she realized she was the one talking.

His dark eyes turned to her, and she shivered. How had she forgotten how intense his attention could be? No wonder Nancy jumped to fetch her. Far more effective than the charm, that.

"Demanding an invite?" he parried.

Ronnie laughed. "If you don't take him, I will, and Mike might be a little annoyed by that."

Lily blushed, and Patrick pressed his advantage. "Come on, you've spent all day doing research for me, dinner's the least I can do while you tell me what you found out."

Nancy, still in the doorway just behind the agent, nodded emphatically, making Lily blush even more. "Girl, you need to spend more time with the two-legged sorts, I told you that a dozen times."

Trying to recover from the three-pronged attack, she

picked up another file, then tossed it onto her desk and gave in. "I agree…. Assuming your assumption was correct that I've done research—of any duration—for you at all."

He grinned again, supremely confident. She couldn't resist. She didn't even try.

This time she took him to Toro Rojo. It was cheap, cheesy and in no way could ever be considered a romantic place to dine. He took her arm as they walked from her car to the front door, and warmth spread from the point of contact, all the way to and down her spine. She would not shiver. She would not. She would—

"Are you cold?"

"No." She pulled open the door with a little more force than was needed, and stepped ahead of him to give her name to the waitstaff.

Behind her, she could hear him laugh.

"I don't suppose the police have made any break-through discoveries about the identity of the—" She stopped, not sure how you referred to the person they were hunting. "Killer" seemed overblown; as much as she valued feline life, it didn't seem right to put this person on the same level as a murderer of humans. And yet, anything else was too…soft.

"The unsub," he finished for her. "Which is profiler-speak for nothing fancier than unknown subject of an investigation, in case you were wondering. And no, they have nothing. And I don't expect them to; Detective Petrosian was quite clear about the fact that they don't have the manpower to follow up on a cruelty-to-animals case when there's no owner in the picture to make a fuss."

He obviously expected her to protest that sort of dismissal, but she had been doing this long enough to understand the way things worked. Limited time. Limited manpower. You had to make choices in the world.

"So it's just us, then."

"Pretty much, yeah."

They were shown to their table and handed menus. Lily already knew what she wanted, so waited until Patrick had scanned the listings and made his decision before she continued.

"So are you going to be able to get any tax-paid support from the subpar and slow-moving resources of the federal government?"

He mimed a blow to the heart, the look in his dark eyes amused. "Why do I need them when I have you, oh most wondrous of cat talkers?"

"Keep that up and you'll be eating dinner in your hotel room. Alone."

That seemed to quiet him, at least for the moment, and she wondered at the kind of man who could find humor even in this discussion. Her own disorientation this evening was a clear sign that she, at least, couldn't be that glib. Then again, she had never been glib, not in her entire life.

"Seriously, I don't know what you hoped I might find. I'm not a researcher, I'm a bank teller. I deal with figures in, figures out, and everything balances up neat and tidy on a good day."

"And on a bad day?"

"It balances up neat and tidy, only it takes longer."

"Sounds like my job, actually," he parried, and she shook her head. Maybe it was the seriousness of his job, the seriousness of him, that needed that release in frivolity?

"Less bloodshed in my job."

He acknowledged the hit. "Good point."

Lily could feel herself starting to relax. This had been a good choice; never mind that she had groceries back home that were going to waste while she ate out. This was…different. She was helping with something important.

Yeah, sure, she told herself. And he's a lot easier to look at than television. Unless George Clooney's on, anyway.

"But I'm betting," he said, "that those vaunted tallying-up skills served you pretty well this afternoon. Am I right? Despite your horrible skills with research, were you able to find anything of note, as you slaved over the files all afternoon?"

He was mocking her, she was pretty sure, and she would have bristled except for the fact that—to be fair—she had set herself up to be mocked.

"On our records? Not a lot. We've only computerized in the past couple of years. The rest was paper files, and I have the cuts to prove it.

"Seven of the cats adopted out in the past year specified a spotted pattern, and another eleven were tabbies who might have been spotted or striped, I don't know. I went back five years, and found another couple of hundred cats who might have matched. Not one hundred. Not three. *Five* hundred cats."

"I get the message. I'm buying. Any pattern?"

"Nothing. No particular time of year, no particular type of adopter—not even a gender pattern, which is weird, because usually women and men have different preferences."

"Really?" He considered that for a moment, and then waved the thought away. "Path for another hike. So that's a dead end. Sorry I made you go through all that."

He won points for the apology. "Don't know until you try, right? I did a little online research, though, too. I don't have—what does Nancy call it?—good Google-fu, yeah. But I found some interesting details about cat sacrifices. Did you know that very few magic rituals use animal sacrifice, traditionally?"

Patrick nodded. "Yeah. Animals were too valuable to sacrifice, especially in agrarian cultures. Which also increased the value of one that *was* sacrificed, because it would be without blemish, et cetera, et cetera." He rattled the facts off with ease. "Same with the calves sacrificed in the old Temple in Jerusalem."

She stared at him until he shifted in his seat. 'I know, it's weird stuff to know. My job, it pays to pick up whatever information you can. You never know when it might connect with something else, make random facts into a working hypothesis. I know how to put together a hot tub, sharpen an ax, tat lace—yes, really, and no it doesn't disturb my masculinity at all, thank you very much—and make paper in theory, anyway."

"Right." She was not going to laugh, even though his expression invited her to mock him. She was too aggravated to be amused. "Why did I even bother again?"

"Because you had a thought." He got serious once more. "An idea, a suspicion. That's good, run with it. I trust your brain. What I know and what there is to know are a portion and a whole, and the whole is far greater than the portion could ever aspire to."

She felt her lips finally twitch into a smile despite her annoyance. "What fortune cookie did you get that from?"

"After-dinner mints at Master Li's House of Chili in D.C.. Don't laugh, he makes a mean five-alarm vegetarian chili."

The trouble was, Lily was mostly sure that he was joking, but not *entirely* sure.

He let out a sigh and placed his hands flat down on the table, a gesture of surrender. "Honestly? Anything you think of, anything you see or wonder about… I needed your take on all this. Yeah, I'm the pro. But I never discount a talented amateur's abilities, especially if I can make use of them. You downplay your connection to the cats—fine. Whatever keeps you sleeping at night. But it exists, which means that there might also be a connection we can exploit with our unsub, and his fascination with or need for cats."

Lily was taken aback by his words, both the bluntness and the honesty. "I really, really don't like that thought. At all. About the connection between me and him, I mean."

"I didn't…" Patrick seemed to flounder for a moment. "I didn't mean it that way."

Maybe not, she thought but didn't say, maybe not. Or maybe he did, and was waiting to see what her reaction to that might be. He said himself, he'd use anything and anyone. Exactly what she had suspected about him. And yet, his saying it…somehow made it…less of a threat.

"I just meant that you have a better grasp than someone like me on what might be ticking inside a cat that he can hear. Not that—"

He stopped, looked at his hands, and she could practically see him throw that entire line of conversation out the window. "I've found that getting the point of view of someone outside the bureau, someone who hasn't been subjected to all the same meetings and memos and lectures, gives me a better place to start. We don't know everything—we just want to think that we do. The monsters are less scary if you can deconstruct them."

"Are they?" Lily wondered. She didn't think so. A monster you could understand was still a monster.

"Sometimes. For example, your basic Satanist isn't some kind of off-the-wall loon, but a magical theorist. He—or she—believes that there are certain actions and reactions in magic that can be manipulated. That magic is closer to science than religion. It's results-based, not faith oriented. It's all about sympathy…an object acting upon another, through some law of similarity or contagion. Like voudon, with their gris-gris bags and hex dolls."

Lily had no idea whatsoever what he was talking about. Her parents had been gently lapsed Protestants, which meant that her religious education hadn't ever really happened, and she had never gone through the kind of witchcraft-is-cool phase so many teenage girls seemed to. She'd never been particularly spiritual at all; the woo-woo never wooed her. But at least they weren't talking about her anymore.

"So why do crazies like this sort of magic theory?" she asked, honestly intrigued with the turn of the conversation.

Patrick considered her question, his gaze going sort of hazy, as though he was looking inside his brain. She watched him, fascinated, almost able to hear the gears turning.

"Order. Rationale of a sort that does not depend on the logic we consider, well, logical. If a miracle can occur because God wishes it to occur, because we implore God enough to make it so... Or, conversely and depending on the brand of crazy, if the universe may be influenced significantly by the sheer force of their will—"

"Or sacrifice," she said, bringing the conversation back out of theory and into the reality of their case.

Their case. Lily wasn't sure she liked the taste of that, any more than she liked being told that she was connected in any way, shape or form to the guy Petrosian was looking for. But it felt right. She was involved, from seeing the cats so tenderly, cruelly murdered, to hearing Patrick's thoughts. It felt...personal.

"Yeah. Or sacrifice. I've seen so many kinds, but cats are almost always the most popular."

Lily moved her silverware, adjusting it carefully on the napkin. Breathe, she told herself. Don't let anything through. Don't let the panic attack through. Because she could feel it rising up in her throat like a bad case of the giggles, only not funny at all.

Cats. Sacrifice. Personal.

The sand was soft and shifting underfoot, cool and granular. A cat's long, soft mmrow *following her as she was dragged away, her arm and shoulder making a furrow behind her.*

Breathe. Breathe, and be still.

Patrick didn't seem to notice her distress. "Cats, although traditionally it's black cats, would imply on the surface some kind of pseudosatanic thing. It all depends on if he's using some sort of religious-based ritual, or a purely magical one. Or one that he's making up, based on his own internal rationale." His gaze refocused on her. "That's the theory, anyway."

"Of course, there's another possibility," she said, finally breaking free of the too-vibrant images.

"Oh?" He looked up at her, his head cocked as though what she was about to say was the most important thing he had ever heard.

"This guy may just be crazy."

Patrick's entire face twitched, and before she could react, his entire body was swooping forward, his hand coming up to capture the curve of her jaw, and he had kissed her, swiftly but firmly, on the mouth.

His lips were warm, strong, and tasted ever so slightly of coffee. It wasn't an unpleasant kiss; nor was it a particularly passionate one. It said, clearly, "You delight me and I want to touch you," but didn't go any further over the line than that, and then he was back in position, his body as casually at ease as before.

And they looked at each other, her eyes widened with shock, his heavy lidded, watching her reaction.

"Why did you do that?" she asked, less shocked than bemused. Her lips practically tingled.

"Because I couldn't not." He swallowed, his Adam's apple jolting in his throat. Like his uncharming moments, she found that disturbingly appealing.

But she was solid, steady-as-she-goes Lily. She didn't jump into anything feet-first, not even after she'd measured the depth and tested the waters.

So she waited until he leaned forward again and touched those soft, coffee-scented lips to hers again.

Only then did she let her hands lift to touch the back of his head, stroking the surprisingly soft curls there, curving her fingers around the shape of his skull as she adjusted their angle for better contact.

He let her. She appreciated that. Agent Jon T. Patrick might be arrogant, aggressive and far too focused on the finish line, but he knew a thing or two about letting others take the lead.

Then his mouth opened, teeth capturing her bottom lip gently before his hands were around her neck, thumbs resting against her cheekbones, and Lily suddenly felt as though she were falling endlessly into a velvet-lined pit, the most fabulous room spins ever not brought on by alcohol.

They broke apart. "Oh." It was barely a breath, falling out of Lily's mouth as she tried to recover. She could feel a flush rising up her neck and around down to her breasts. Was that where "hot under the collar" came from?

"We got more than chemistry, Ms. Lily Malkin," he said, shaking his head almost imperceptibly. "We got alchemy."

Something about the words, the way he said them, or the sound of them, made Lily blink. The flush didn't recede, exactly, but the rest of her came back to room temperature.

"You're as dangerous as the people you chase, Agent Patrick," she told him.

"And you're not the kind of woman who would invite me back to her place to continue this discussion out of the range of innocent civilians, are you?"

No. As a profiler, he was right on target. She wasn't.

She very much wished she was, though.

Chapter 7

"Oh man, oh man, oh man." Lily replayed that kiss all the way home; as she brushed her teeth; as she slipped on her nightshirt and toed off her socks; as she crawled into bed and fluffed the pillow; as she flipped channels until, finally, still muttering under her breath, she fell asleep.

And then, she didn't dream of that kiss at all.

"My love." She brought the news to him as a gift, the proof of her devotion. "I have done as you asked of me."

"Have you now?"

His voice was lazy, oiled and smooth like his skin, and she paused in the doorway, suddenly uncertain.

"My love?" Her heart thumped irregularly, as though a dove were trapped within. Something was

wrong. Had she failed somehow? Had her efforts not been enough? She lived in terror of failing him, of seeing the light in his eyes fade, change from love to scorn, or worse, to indifference.

"Have you done all that I required?" he asked her.

"I have." And at great cost to herself; cost she could not allow herself to acknowledge. Pain she would not admit, even as it cut at her heart, crippled her ka, her inner soul. She could not doubt her heart now. He was worth it, worth all she had given up. All she had done, in his name. "There are none that might stand in your way now."

"There is still one," he disagreed.

"My love?" Even now she could not use his name, could not risk identifying him to a jealous ear, a lingering spy. She cupped the heavy bronze medallion that hung around her neck with one shaking hand. The comfort it normally bought her was absent, and in its place, an unease.

A sleek golden cat turned the corner, turned its head and looked at her, its large luminescent eyes watching her. She reached for it, and it disappeared.

Her lover rose from his chair, bronze skin glinting in the torchlight, muscles moving smoothly. She feasted herself on him, on his beauty, his strength, and the cat was forgotten.

In her distraction a shadow came from the wall behind her where nothing should have been, movement sudden and unexpected. She turned, confused. Pain, like a cobra's strike, bit into her side even as her lover came up to her.

She fell, still clutching the medallion, staring at his beloved face, even as blood and dust filled her mouth.

Why? The question filled her. Why, after all she had done?

"There is nothing more you may give me," he said *almost kindly, as the assassin took the medallion from her stiffening hands.* "Nothing, save your death. The body of the betrayer will earn me much acclaim with the pharaoh."

Love turned to realization, and then to rage, too late as he accepted the medallion from her killer's hands. I will never forgive you, she vowed. I will never forgive myself.

Her ka *shuddered, and slipped out of her body. It paused for a moment, touching her cooling skin with small white paws, then raised its head to the sky and cried for her shame.*

Not forever. Only until you learn to forgive.

Lily sat upright in bed, her heart racing, her skin coated with sweat. The old T-shirt she slept in, the sleeves and collar cut away, clung to her, and she pulled it off in disgust, preferring the cool night air to having the cloth touch her skin an instant longer. She wiped at the sweat, and a shudder wracked her body. "Oh, God."

Another nightmare. That was two in one week, which was two too many, even for her. They were getting worse, not better.

Had this one been about cats again? She didn't think so, but she couldn't remember. There were no details, just a sense of…anger. Betrayal. Sadness.

Lilly pulled up the blanket to cover herself. She lay on her back for a while, then rolled over, shoving a

pillow away as though it were to blame for the feeling
of suffocation, like something were pressing against
her face. The air smelled sour, sweet and warm; too
thick, too filled with odors she couldn't quite recognize, as though she had fallen asleep in a stranger's
kitchen.

Her mouth opened slightly, her lips pulling back
from her teeth as she took in short breaths, as though
sipping the air. She realized suddenly that she was
trying to taste the air the way cats did, and her laughter
conflicted with the business of breathing, making her
cough.

"Ugh."

Her entire mouth felt weird, icky, as if she had eaten
something nasty, or had had too much to drink.

She hadn't, had she? Lily reclaimed the pillow and
shoved it under her head, then gave up and rolled onto
her back again. She stared up at the ceiling, thinking
over the night.

No. She'd had two beers, well within even her limited abilities. Nothing she hadn't had before, foodwise,
and it had all tasted fine. She had gotten home at a reasonable hour…. Jon had followed her home in his
newly acquired rental car, against her protests, waiting
in his car until she had driven into her condo's garage,
gone inside and flicked the porch light at him.

Ridiculous. But she admitted to a faint glow at his
concern nonetheless. She had spent her entire adult
life looking out for herself. It was nice, even if just
for one night, to feel that kind of concern from someone else.

"Don't get too used to it, Lily Malkin," she said sternly. "Mr. FBI made it clear he had career plans. You don't get far with those sort of goals in Newfield."

"Field profilers don't get considered for management slots," he had said over taquitos and Dos Equis. "We're too valuable…so they use us until we're used up. And then we go write books about the experience, see if we can con some new kids into picking up the skills to replace us, start the cycle all over again. I'm not interested in that."

"You *want* a desk job?" It seemed impossible to imagine, an FBI agent bored with what he did.

"I want the ability to actually make a difference on more than a case-by-case basis. Make policy, make changes. And to do that, you need power."

He had grinned then, that surprisingly boyish expression that wiped the intensity from his face and lightened the mood, and they had moved on to another topic of conversation that had nothing to do with the case, his job or cats. The rest of the evening had touched on football, politics, their birth order—she was an only child, he was the youngest of four—and other topics that could have passed for first-date small talk.

And then, outside the restaurant, she had broken their unspoken truce, leaning in to touch her lips to his again.

Sparks. Sparks, and more. Lava.

She had pulled away immediately, and he had let her, not saying a word. But his dark eyes had been knowing. And amused.

"Gah," she said now, no more eloquent on the subject than she had been at the time. What was it about that man?

She was about to roll over yet again and try to get back to sleep, when the alarm clock went off. Already? She looked at the readout and realized that she must have fallen asleep for a few hours without realizing it—it was 6:00 a.m.

The temptation to lie in bed for another hour warred with routine. Routine won. Throwing off the blankets with no grace or dignity at all, Lily grabbed her sweatpants off the chair and staggered to the bathroom to become vaguely human.

Ten minutes later, she was outside her condo, dressed in black fleece sweatpants and a red-and-black hoodie, stretching out cranky muscles before she asked them to work. Her arms over her head, feeling the muscles pull in her back, she could practically feel everything from her heels to her ears align, like a cat stretching after a nap. She tilted her head to better take in the morning air, so much fresher and more interesting than the air inside the building.

She realized as she did so that she was pulling her lips back again, displaying the classic feline grimace as she tasted the air.

"Nancy was right. You need to hang out with people more, if you're picking up habits from the *cats.*"

Finishing her stretches, Lily pulled her hair into a ponytail and secured it with a scrunchie, made sure that her sneakers were tied and set off down the street. Three miles, down to the park and back, four times a week, and she had a chance at keeping her hips inside her size eights.

She wondered, as she started to catch the rhythm of her footfalls on the pavement, if Jon was one of those guys who liked his women sleek, or if he had a thing about ribs and hipbones showing.

"Lily Marie, you get your mind out of the gutter," she scolded herself, trying not to laugh as she crossed the street and headed into the park proper. Either she wasn't interested in the guy, or she needed to jump him, but she had to stop wavering between the two.

And if she was going to do the latter, she needed to do it soon. He had gotten all the information available off the scene, and all the facts out of her brain; there was no reason for him to stick around on the taxpayers' dime anymore. He'd be going home soon.

But he promised to find the guy. He promised.

The practical portion of her brain—the majority of it—warned the smaller voice: *Not everyone can keep their promises. Even when they want to.*

And he won't stop working on it, even when he goes home. He won't. He won't. The words worked their way into the slap-slap of shoes on pavement. *He won't. He won't forget.*

The one thing she was certain of, although she could never have said why, or what drove that confidence: *He'll catch the guy. He'll make sure he doesn't hurt anyone ever again.*

The trees were black. The leaves were silver and gray. He remembered, once, the leaves being colored. They had faded slowly, until he could not remember what that color had been. Three years ago? Less. No warning, just a click in his head, like magnets coming together. Sometimes he could almost remember who he had been, before the wake-up call came, and he awoke into this dream. Sometimes, but it was so very difficult, and so very long ago.

He tried not to think about it. It hurt when he did anything other than focus on the ritual, and what he needed to do.

He had been wandering since before the sun rose, searching. He needed to find beasts. Seven beasts, and he only had four. They needed to be right, but he had no more time to breed the perfect ones, and the shelter had said they had no more proper ones to adopt. He could leave his name and number, and they would call him when one came in. But the question smelled cold, and he had hung up without responding.

They would try to stop him. They did not understand.

He would find what he needed. He would hunt them, as they hunted, in the between-hours. In the between-places.

Among the trees would be good. They sometimes could be found living in between the houses and the park, where food was plentiful from picnics and mice. Three more. Four and three would be seven. Seven should be the number. Seven, minus the four he had…

Something tugged at his awareness. There. Over there.

His thoughts scattered. Distracted from his numbers, but why? What…

A flash. Like a bird flitting from branch to branch, only at street level.

A woman, waiting at the corner for the light to change.

Gold. She was hammered gold, gilded like a statue.

His brain caught up with his fancy, and he was able to focus better on her.

No, she wasn't gold. She was flesh and shadows, the same as all the rest. But he saw the glints in her, shimmering and shiny. Bright and sharp, moving quickly down the sidewalk, across the street from him. Into the trees.

Like the beasts.

It was Her.

No. His heart stuttered back down into a normal beat. It was just a woman, a normal woman. A mortal, human woman.

Beasts, he reminded himself. He was on a mission to find the beasts he needed. Not a woman. But he couldn't look away from her as she moved away from him, moving away. Golden, glowing like fire. He felt himself yearning toward it, as though it would warm him the way the gray sun no longer did. The way his dreams, filled with heat and wind, told him he had once been warm.

She was important. She could be… Her, come to this world? One of Her handmaidens, perhaps, lost the same way he was?

Yes. *Yes.* Something inside him thrilled to the realization.

He took a step toward the curb, intending to cross the street and follow her, when something yanked him back, as though strings were attached to his knees and elbows. The clarity of her warmth was suddenly clouded by apprehension, the appeal matched by an equal resistance. Important, but wrong. Dangerous.

No! The first warmth he had felt in so long, the first true connection to Her. He would not let it go.

Forcing himself forward, he followed the woman. Into the trees, down a path laid with dirt. She moved swiftly but with a steady pace; graceful, a predator on the hunt. Unable to do more than walk quickly without attracting attention, he was about to lose her, when suddenly she stopped.

What had stopped her? He drew to the side of the path, watching as she knelt. To tie her shoe? No.

A beast approached her. He jerked forward, instinctively ready to grab the beast, but it was not the right sort: red as clay, and useless to him. The revulsion he felt in the presence of the beasts overwhelmed him once the instinct fled, even with the amulet to protect him. He fought the urge to flee, to snatch the glowing woman away from the foul thing and destroy it before it could befoul her as well.

But the woman gestured, and the beast made obeisance as much as any beast ever could; tail erect and head forward, sniffing her proffered hand until it stroked its fur.

Something hurt inside, like a knife prying open a seal, and he stayed where he was, even as she rose from the beast and began moving again.

She confused him. She was beloved of the beasts, and therefore anathema to him. And yet, She was the most beloved of the beasts, wasn't She? So this woman was a link, a true link.

And yet, the woman was also part of the danger he had sensed. Women like that were not to be trusted. They were to be removed, offered up to the greater goal, before they could confuse people, tell lies….

And yet, he was drawn to her. Needed her. The confusion bothered him. Worried him. He had to know why she alone had color and warmth, the same warmth his dreams promised him, if he could do this one thing….

He hit his forehead with the heels of his hands, willing his brain to stop whirling. He had no room, no time for confusion. He knew what he had to do. A female had no place in his goals, what he must accomplish. Especially not a best-beloved of the beasts. Seven beasts, proper beasts, three yet to be found…

Yet, if he could find an answer in her…

Perhaps he would not need the beasts, after all.

But he waited too long to decide. She was gone.

No. His head ached, but he was calm once again. She was a mirage, a taunt. The gold he had seen was a phantasm, a delusion. He would continue with his plan.

Chapter 8

"Yes, sir."

Patrick paused in the middle of his note taking and twirled his pen, stretching his legs in front of him, wincing as his half-asleep leg twinged in protest. The narrow windowsill on the stairwell landing was not exactly suited to a tall man perching there for any length of time, but it was the only place in the warren of the police station where his cell phone could actually get reception. The bureau got pissy when agents were out of touch for very long; the fact that the entire country wasn't wired for perfect cell reception didn't seem to have sunk in to the powers that be in Washington.

"Yes, sir. I'm wrapping up my notes now. Yes, sir, I expect to be on a plane tomorrow morning. My report will be on your desk as soon as I'm in the office. Yes, sir. No, sir, I don't believe this was—"

A shadow fell over him, and he looked up.

Petrosian, looking like the Doom of Gloom in rumpled flesh.

"Hang up."

Patrick made a gesture to indicate the fact that he couldn't do that. Hanging up on your direct supervisor was bad form. Not that he hadn't done it a time or three. Or four. He needed more reason than a cranky cop to do it, though.

"Hang up," Petrosian repeated. "We got another."

"Change of plans," he said into the phone, already standing and reaching with his free hand for his coat. "Another incident. I'll check in later. Don't wait up, don't hold dinner."

His boss, used to him after seven years, merely grunted assent, and hung up, doubtless already dialing another field agent to ream out for some cause or another.

"What do we know?" he asked the detective, tucking the phone into his pocket and following him through the hallways. Already his brain was sorting through the known facts, clearing way for new information.

"Not a lot. Some guy had a bunch of cats snatched from his cattery—he's a breeder, down by Mazelle Park. Spotted cats," he added, as though Patrick was too slow to figure that bit out for himself. "Some kind of special breed. Thief took only males, not a surprise. Uniform got a pretty decent description of the guy off the security cameras, so we can distribute it. Our first real damn break in this damn case."

"How long ago?"

"The incident? Yesterday. We got news of it about three hours ago, more or less. The call went through animal welfare, and once they got a confirmation and checked it out they sent it on to us, and someone had to come find me."

"Yesterday? And then it took them three hours to find you?" Jesus, what was with this podunk police department? He should have been informed immediately! If they had a description of this guy on file already…

Patrick felt himself literally getting hot under the collar, and pulled it down a notch. Petrosian made a weary-looking shrug as he held the door to the parking garage open for the agent. "Whaddaya want me to say? Not everyone reads their memos."

The detective was right: there was no way everyone could have known to contact Petrosian just for a cat-napping. He knew as well as anyone how departments didn't talk to each other. "So we're checking this guy out? Or do we have—"

"That's where it gets interesting. We found the cats, yeah. Our boy's been busy."

That didn't sound good at all.

By the time they got to the site, halfway across town in the opposite direction from the first three locations, Patrick had managed to start up a new page in his log-book for this incident, listing what little Petrosian had been able to give him, factswise. He had only the existing police reports on the first two; it would be important to see firsthand how similar—or not—this scene was to the one he had checked out. His notes were his usual precise and factual work, without any of his own personal interpretation—those went on another sheet, to keep them separate and not confuse the issue. He also had a pencil sketch of the suspect to go with the sketch the artist had done from Lily's observations and extrapolations. All of which led up to…nothing. So far. The guy was careful, a planner. He—or she, don't make assumptions, he cautioned himself—was working toward something, a something only he—or she—knew about.

But things were turning. Patrick could feel it. To actually steal cats, in full view, suggested desperation, and desperation led to mistakes.

It also, he knew, often led to increased violence. His theories aside, they had to stop this guy before he—she—screw it, *he* escalated. Before any humans got caught up in this guy's fantasies.

"Oh great gobs of hell." Petrosian pulled the unmarked sedan to the curb and swore in disgust, making Patrick look up. In addition to the three patrol cars marking off the area, there were two vans. Even if they hadn't had the markings of the two local news stations on the side panels, the antenna rig on the roof of each gave the game away.

"The vultures have arrived," Patrick said. "Damn them. Can you keep them off the scene?"

"I'll do what I can," Petrosian said. "You go on around; I'll draw their fire up front."

Good man, Petrosian. He could see why Lily liked the cop. The fact that the guy was old enough to be Lily's dad, and looked like a particularly tired, overweight hound made Patrick inclined to like him even more.

The older cop stalked toward the flashing lights and cameras, waving his arms to catch their attention. "People! People, behind the tape, thank you very much. Geordie, come on, you know the damn drill, back behind the tape!"

While the detective corralled the news crews and started to feed them some line promising a full accounting of whatever dire disaster they were claiming this was—it had to be a slow news day, or these were the scrub teams sent out for filler—Patrick moved up the sidewalk toward the alley where two uniforms were talking to an older man with a grimy white apron tied over jeans and a sweatshirt.

"Yeah, I heard him down there, and I seen him in the mornings. I dunno, he looked like a guy, ya know? Don't bother me, go find the guy!"

The witness sounded as though he had watched too many episodes of *Law & Order,* Patrick thought as he came even with them. The agent wasn't much of a linguist, but the coarse accent seemed horribly out of place here in far more proper Newfield. Even Lily's West Coast lilt had been worn down over the years by the granite of New England into more of a drawl.

"Sir, if you would please answer the questions, that would be a great help." The cop was clearly out of patience. Patrick could relate.

"What do we have here?" He hated flashing his badge, but this wasn't his scene and Petrosian wasn't here to vouch for him.

The senior of the two cops answered him, after scanning the badge and deciding he had a right to be there asking questions. "Roger Hooperman. Owns the store next door."

"Not the owner of any of the stolen cats?" That guy was probably busy with insurance forms and client calls.

"Nope. I'm the guy as found 'em." Hooperman was clearly glad for a new, hopefully more appreciative audience. "Sick bastard, whoever done that. I got nothing against animals, ya know. They're fine, and a cat as is a mouser is a damn good thing to have, ya know? But they're just animals. I don't got nothing sentimental about them. But what that guy done, that's just wrong." Hooperman shook his head, the image of outraged citizenry.

The second officer gestured into the alleyway. "There's a door there, leads down to the basement. The door was open when Mr. Hooperman came out, and he—"

"I smelled 'em. Used to work in a butcher shop, I know the smell of meat."

"And you called the cops?" Patrick tried to keep his voice neutral, but his disbelief came through. Even the most upstanding of citizens didn't call out the cops for a whiff of spoiled meat.

"Nah, man, not until I saw it." Hooperman lost none of his bravado. "Saw what that guy'd done."

"And then you called the cops."

"Damn straight."

"Was that before or after you called the local television stations and informed them that you'd found evidence of a satanic cult in Newfield?"

The cops looked startled, but Hooperman simply

shrugged. "Hey, news is news." If he was even remotely embarrassed by his actions, he hid it like a pro.

Patrick had stopped being amazed by what people would do for publicity. "And your face and storefront in the news can only mean curious people coming by, which means business."

Hooperman kept his cool, even in the face of the agent's scorn. "Got it in one. But that guy, he's still scum. You'll find him."

That was the second time since arriving in Newfield that someone had said those words to him. He was used to being told to solve cases, find killers. But the words echoed with him oddly as he walked down the narrow stairwell, the smell of cat piss and bleach almost overwhelming the stink Hooperman had mentioned. Patrick didn't believe in fate, karma or predestination. But this case was almost designed for his skills, designed to bring him to this town, to this place, these players.

"And bring you to this specific basement? Get a grip, Jon T.," he told himself, then stopped, both his speech and his steps.

You had to know what you were looking for to smell it. But once you knew, there was no way to ignore it.

"Damn." He pushed open the door, already knowing what he would find.

The setup was almost exactly as the last one: a room filled with makeshift metal cages—fewer this time, and smaller—and another room with a black drape on the floor, seven limp bodies arranged nose to tail.

He knelt and inspected the bodies without touching

them. They were fresh—the time between the killings was definitely getting shorter. Not a good sign. But all the details were wrong, just as he'd said to Lily. This guy wasn't playing by the usual rules. He had some other game in mind. But what? He needed to get inside this guy's motivations, to figure out what had triggered the killing, what was driving him to such extremes, to breed his own victims and set up such careful scenes.

Patrick recognized Petrosian's tread on the stairs behind him, the walk heavy without sounding lumbering or awkward.

"The cuts are more jagged," the agent said without rising from his crouch over the grisly display. "He wasn't being as precise. Maybe rushed. Or nervous."

"Or the kitties were giving him trouble? Because that's been bothering me. How does he get them so calm?" Petrosian moved around to face Patrick, looking down at the bodies. "Tox came back. None of the cats so far have been drugged. When I try to clip my cats' claws, they put up a fight. But these…they just lay there and let him do it, one after the other?"

Patrick stared at the bodies. That was a good question. A damn good question. And, short of drugs, or restraints—neither of which were showing up at the scene or coming up on the toxicology screens, he could only come up with one answer. "Lily could do it, based on what you've said. Maybe we've got another cat talker on our hands."

"Jesus." Petrosian didn't sound happy. Good. Patrick wasn't happy either. He wanted to see Lily again, yeah, but not like this. Not over the bodies of more dead moggies. Not with her thinking about someone with her skill doing this. He selfishly wanted her relaxed, soft, not tense or worried.

But the job came first, last and always.

He pulled out his cell phone and dialed the number he'd already memorized.

"This is Lily. Leave a message."

Despite himself, he was amused. Short and to the point, just like the woman herself. Nothing in the voice even suggested the way she smelled, sun-warmed even on a cool evening, or the way she felt, sparks and shivers under his lips. Or the way she made blood rush from his brain to his groin in a manner definitely unbecoming to a federal agent on the case.

"It's Jon. Agent Patrick. Call me."

Nothing of what he really wanted to say. No time for that, not now.

The bar was wide but not very deep, and there were too many people crowded together. The news droned in the background, a woman with a microphone and a stylish wool coat, standing in a run-down part of town. Red lights flashed against the gray concrete walls, and the yellow stretch of tape kept people out of the alley between two buildings

The phone was in the back, near the bathrooms, and it was quieter there, nobody lingering to use the johns. The phone's receiver was cold in his hand, the plastic odd feeling and wrongly shaped. He hadn't wanted to call in the place he lived. He had gotten the number off the computer at home, written it down and walked with it in his hand until he came in here on a whim.

One ring. Two, and someone on the other end picked up before the ring was completed. When a woman answered, he closed his eyes and spoke clearly, calmly, with the proper enunciation. The language felt strange in his mouth, his brain wanting to use other words, but he forced his way through.

He had to be heard. They had to understand.

"You don't understand. I'm not dangerous. They should just leave me alone. I only want what's mine."

"Sir?" A clicking noise, and he was transferred, almost immediately. He could almost feel himself racing through the wires, up and down the building, until finally landing in the proper department, with the right person to hear him.

That was what it took; knowing how to make the right people hear you.

"Talk to me." A man's voice this time, commanding in a way that thrilled him with fear. He could almost see them scurrying around, waving their arms and trying to trace his call. It didn't matter. He would be gone soon. He would win this time.

"Tell your warriors to hold off. The Serpent hunting in the night does not wish to strike. It desires only to return to its home. To be safe and warm and dry, away from the talons of the hawk, the claws of the hunting cat. It will not strike unless cornered."

A cough, the sound of chairs pushing away from desks in the background. He had keen hearing, and he heard all, alert to every nuance, every dip and change.

"Are you telling us you are no danger? Are you the Night Serpent?"

"It is as good a name as any." He preferred talking to a woman; women understood things that needed to be done. Women understood that power ebbed and flowed, came and went, that it needed to be coaxed, cajoled before it would respond. They did not waste time naming things, but went to the heart of them. They had always been the heart of power.

Women. Woman. The woman he had seen. Maybe he had been wrong to dismiss her. She was golden, filled with life, where all others were gray and unreal. She had power there, inside. Golden shining power, sun and sand, not the drab of this world. Maybe the power he needed. If he could find her again, she would be able to tell him what to do, what he was doing wrong.

"The cat woman. She knows. She knows."

He had only meant to say it to himself. He didn't realize until the man repeated it, that the words had been said out loud.

"Knows what? Sir, if you'll talk to me, I can help you."

They had no idea who he was. He had wanted to reassure them, let them know that he would not bother them, so long as they left him be. But he knew now that it couldn't be. Just as before…

Before when?

In the place where he had been warm. Powerful. Before they had cast him down and thrown him away, sent him to this dreary place.

Everything was smaller here. Colder. Worn down.

He was confused again. But he knew where he had gone wrong.

"Sir, talk to me."

There was only way back to what had been. He needed power, yes. The woman *had* shown him, simply by her being. By the way the beasts responded to her. The beasts would bring him what he needed...but he needed beasts of the old world, not this cold new one, this suddenly unfamiliar one. He needed beasts who felt the taste of that golden shining in them. He needed to set that free, bathe in it, become it. Only then would he find his way home.

He hung up the phone carefully, the man still speaking on the other end, and walked through the crowd, out the front door and into the cool night air.

Yes. Oh, yes. He was on his way now.

Chapter 9

Lily came home from work to find a familiar unmarked police car sitting in front of her condo. "Damn it." All she wanted was to get through life without a fuss, without drama or trauma. Having cops staking out her home did not qualify under any of those headings, especially if the neighbors caught wind of it.

She probably should have called Jon when he left a message, but she'd not been sleeping well, and the thought of having to deal with him—or, worse, more of the case—pushed her over the line from exhausted to unable to deal. So she had left the message, undeleted, on her machine, and pretended it didn't exist.

Piper had come to be paid.

She pulled past them and into her driveway, leaving the garage door open so that they could join her.

"Gentlemen," she said. She was too tired for this; as much as the sight of her Fibbie, almost as rumpled as Aggie now, with his tie slightly askew, made her want to smile, she really just wanted to fall over on the sofa and cry herself to sleep. Except sleep wasn't such a good thing these days, because every time she closed her eyes she saw a dignified cat sitting there, tawny coat glimmering, green eyes glinting at her as though expecting her to do something brilliant, wonderful, heroic, and save him.

"I need coffee," Aggie said. "And so do you."

Lily tried to dig in her heels. "What happened?"

He shook his head at her. "Coffee first."

So she let them into her home, settled them at the table in the open space that served as a combination dining room/living room and went into the kitchen to brew up a pot of Hawaii's best. It was rare enough that she had company; she had to hunt through the cabinets for three mugs that would do.

"Milk? Sugar?"

Aggie took it fully doctored; Jon only wanted sugar. She fixed the mugs and brought them out, sitting across the table from Jon, next to Aggie. She didn't plan it that way, but having the table between her and him seemed like a good idea.

Until she looked at him and saw that intense gaze fixed on her. Suddenly she wanted Aggie to shut up and go away. And at the same time she was very glad that he was there with them.

Then that gaze flickered off, going from molten to

business cool. "Have you watched the news today?" Jon—Agent Patrick—asked.

"I read the paper this morning, but no. Why?" She turned to look at Aggie, struck by the look in his eyes. It was more than worry or exhaustion. There was… anger there.

He fiddled with his coffee, took a long sip. "Jesus, that's good. Better than the swill at the station."

"Aggie?" She trusted him to tell her the truth. But he merely looked away.

Patrick was the one who started talking. "There was another… We found more cats." The way he said it, she knew they were already dead. "We have a description of the guy who stole them. And we have a possible witness who may be able to identify him in person."

She turned to face him, warming her fingers on her coffee cup. Her hands were cold. Everything was cold. "Oh God, the poor cats. But it's good, right, that you have a witness?"

"It's good, yeah." He didn't sound convinced of that. "But the witness called the media, too. Bad luck for us, it's a slow day. They ran the story on the five-o'clock broadcast."

Lily drank her own coffee, hoping the warmth would spread through her, trying to understand why the publicity would be a bad thing. "He might see it and run?" she guessed. But that didn't explain why they were here, looking so nervous. "Jon? What did they say, on the news?"

He opened his mouth to say something, but couldn't get the words to come out.

"Lily." Petrosian took over again. "It wasn't what was on the news that was the problem. Exactly."

She turned to face Aggie again, feeling a cold curling unease in her belly that not even the warmest coffee could ward off. "What?"

"The guy? The killer, or someone who claimed to be him? He called the local station. The television station. After they ran the clip. He's crazy, or making a good show of it, but—"

Patrick interrupted Aggie's ramblings, finally managing to get to the point. "Lily, he mentioned you."

"What?" The cold abandoned her belly and went right up her spine, freezing her brain.

"Not by name," Aggie reassured her, putting his coffee down to reach over and pat her hand awkwardly. "But he definitely mentioned a cat lady. And who else could it be but you?"

"But…how? And why?"

Patrick slumped in his chair, for the first time since she had met him giving up entirely on the "agent in charge" arrogance. That scared her more than anything else. "I don't know. Maybe he adopted—or tried to adopt—a cat from your shelter and heard about you? Or, if he watches the news, which he seems to, maybe he's seen you on TV before, and somehow got you tangled up in whatever he's trying to do? Maybe, if he's a local boy.

"Christ. I don't even know that, maybe your coming here was what triggered him, or… The fact that he only started recently doesn't mean he just got here, he could have done this before our three-year mark, too. And if that's true, then the trigger could be anything."

He sighed, rubbing a hand over his face. "I haven't been able to get a fix on what he wants, or where he's coming from. I don't have anything yet."

He suddenly seemed to remember who he was talking to and straightened in his chair. "But I'm working on it," he promised her. "We know more than we did before. I have a call in to the bureau—he didn't make any direct threats against you, but the fact that you've been brought in even by implication raises the case's priority from animal to human threat."

Lily wasn't sure that made her feel much better. Not that she didn't trust him, it was just…the witness must be useless, otherwise they'd already be arresting the guy—the unsub was the term, right? They wouldn't be sitting here at her table drinking coffee and looking worried. If they didn't know who he was, or why he was doing this, or what had made him focus on her, how could they stop him? How could they even find him?

I can't help you, kitten, she whispered to the waiting cat of her dreams. *I'm not even sure how to help myself.*

"You shouldn't go back to the shelter," Aggie said.

"Excuse me?" That had the ability to shake her out of her thoughts.

The older man leaned on the table, his houndlike face full of earnest concern. "Lily, this guy, okay so maybe he hasn't hurt any humans yet. Yet. And what he said, it wasn't a threat. But I don't like him even knowing you exist. If he found out about you through the shelter, then that's where he's going to be looking. And no matter what J. Edgar here says, we can't spare someone to follow you around just on the off chance that this guy might actually be dangerous. You know that. So staying away from where he might look for you only makes sense."

Lily scowled into her coffee. It might make sense. But the thought of not being allowed to go to the shelter, not to be able to handle the new kittens so that they became used to humans; not to see the older cats as they came out of their shyness and started interacting, to be away from the soothing smells and sounds…

And then she had to laugh at herself. When did cats become comfort to her?

"Lily." Aggie was still talking. "And even if we manage to keep a lid on what he said, which I doubt, the media's gonna show up at the shelter soon too. Cats have been slaughtered, and Felidae No-Kill is the best game in town for publicity hounds. They'll want a sound bite, and they'll probably want it from you. And if somebody puts the pieces together, which they're smart enough to do…"

"What's to stop them from coming here?" she asked.

"This is private property. They can camp outside, but they can't harass you, or I get to come over and harass them in return." Aggie looked almost happy at that thought, and Lily felt herself smile a little in return. He so badly wanted—needed—to do *something*.

"You should take a leave of absence from work, as well," Patrick said, breaking into the moment.

"What?" Lily felt her hackles rise up. "I can't do that." Mr. FBI might be able to take time off on a whim, but she had bills to pay. And it wasn't as though there was anyone who could just step in and take over for her; they were shorthanded already. And—

"Lily, don't be an idiot," Jon said sharply.

"Excuse me?" Her gaze met his, ice cold to burning hot. As hard as he pushed her physical buttons he could nail the emotional ones too, apparently. She felt the urge to arch her back and hiss at him.

Aggie put his coffee down and pushed his chair away. "Children, play nice. I have to get back to the station. Patrick, you coming back with me?" The implication in his voice was that Agent Patrick should say yes, and leave Lily alone to deal with her own decisions. Jon, however, wasn't listening, still holding her gaze with his own.

"I'll be fine. I can call a cab. Go on."

Petrosian shrugged, abandoning them to their own fates. He wasn't fool enough to put his hand into a cat-spat, even before the claws actually showed up.

He reached over to pat Lily's hand again, not taking offense when she flinched. "I'll make sure patrol cars up their drive-bys. If anything's even the slightest bit hinky, or you just want them to stop by for some of this damn fine coffee, you let me know, okay?"

"All right. Thank you, Aggie. For everything." She stood up, intending to see him to the door.

"Just doin' my job, ma'am." He grinned at her; it was forced, but she appreciated the effort. "You stay safe, is all I ask. And don't hurt the Fibbic, okay?"

"I'll do my best," she said.

She came back and watched Jon, sitting at her dining-room table, turning the mug of coffee around in his hands. She didn't think he'd even taken a single sip yet. He was more worried than she was, she realized. He was worried about *her*.

The thought raised her internal temperature again, but this time not in anger.

Aggie worried, but he worried because he felt he'd brought all this on her. There was responsibility and guilt wrapped up in his concern. It didn't make the worry any less real, but there was a *reason* for it. This…

Agent Patrick had no reason to worry. He hadn't brought her into it; he hadn't brought this killer to her door. Potentially, she added. Potentially to her door. The news would do that, if it happened, and they had gotten the information from the guy himself, so it wasn't anything Patrick had done or not done….

It struck her suddenly. Jon was worried because there was a risk to her. And risk to her made him worry. It was a closed equation she wasn't used to: someone worried about her simply because they cared.

Something surged in her, thick and unfamiliar, and she tried, instinctively, to force it down. But it was warm, so warm, and part of her yearned for it, allowing it to slip through her body.

Be careful, a voice whispered to her. A thin, cold voice that stopped the warmth in its tracks. *No one is to be trusted.*

Confused and frustrated, she reached for the cold core of practicality that had always ruled her life. But it slid out of her grasp, suddenly distant and difficult to find. She felt the sting of tears, and blinked them away. As she did so, she became aware of a shadow falling over her eyes. Startled, she blinked again. And again. It was slight but clear: something was covering her eye the instant before her lid came down.

The more she focused on it, the more aware she was that her eyesight was strange, too. The colors seemed different: the blues and greens were deeper, while the deep brown tones of her furniture seemed almost gray.

"Jon?"

Her voice sounded strange, too. Oddly pitched, and filled with vibrato and echoes she couldn't recognize.

She must have sounded odd to him as well, because he reacted as though she had yelled, spilling coffee as he jumped out of his chair. The smell of the liquid, suddenly acrid and unpleasant, twitched in her nostrils and made her sneeze.

"Lily, what? Holy shit…" He reached out and touched her chin with his fingers, tipping her head up to look into her eyes.

"What?"

"Your eyes. They're all pupil. Like you OD'd on belladonna or something…."

She blinked again. His eyes were darker than she remembered, and his voice was weird, too. Everything felt strange, as if she was falling, her sense of balance completely gone. She felt the urge to lean against him, and fought it.

"Jon, what's going on? What's happening?" She started to shake.

Down on all fours, stretching. Lacking a tail, she could not mimic the temple cat's actions exactly, but her teacher knew the human was trying, and was patient with her, the way one might with a slow but beloved kitten.

"Miuuuuu. Miuuuu." *Thus, silly girl. Thus you bow before Herself, and receive Her regard. The cat was regal; lean, plush-furred, spotted tawny and black, like the desert itself. Great green eyes watched her, large ears twitching forward, as though to encourage her charge to learn more swiftly....*

Then she felt it, rising along her spine, from tail-that-wasn't to whiskers-that-weren't. A sense of connection, of power, of strength that was alien and yet entirely hers...

"Miauuuu?" she essayed, the sound rising from deep within her throat.

Those ears twitched sharply in approval, and she felt her mouth stretch in a purely human grin in response.

"Lily!"

He was shaking her, and she felt the urge to hiss, to strike at him with hands curved as though...

"Oh." She gasped, her world reeling. "Oh goddess…"

Lily felt her knees give way, and she collapsed into Jon's arms.

There were hands upon her head, ointment upon her brow. The soft touch of claws against her skin.

You are my daughter. I am your mother. We will always be tied to each other, forevermore. Not even your faithlessness will change that....

"Mother, forgive me…."

"Lily?"

The voice was familiar. And it sounded…right. Lily opened her eyes, feeling stickiness gumming her eyelids together briefly, before Patrick's face came into focus over her.

"It's so cold…."

He had a blanket wrapped around her before she

could finish. The intensity of his gaze warmed her almost as much as the fleece, but even as she thought that, a worm of unease crept back. His dark gaze was warm, but…disturbing at the same time. Too much: too focused. Too *wanting*. What did he want from her? Whatever it was, she couldn't do it. She could barely remember her own name right now.

Lily, a voice whispered to her. *Here, now, your name is Lily.*

"Are you all right? You scared the crap out of me, collapsing like that. Did you eat anything today?" He loomed in too close, his voice shaking.

"I'm fine, yes, and back off, will you?" She struggled to sit up, only to find her movement impeded by his hovering. "Come on, Agent Patrick, move. I—"

The sensation of *wrongness* hit her again. Only this time it wasn't wrong, but right, and when it left as suddenly as it swept in, Lily cried out at the loss, the bereftness of it.

Mother, forgive me….

"Lily. Lily, come back to me. Come on, open your eyes, look at me…."

She was in his arms. No, on his lap, cradled against his broad chest the way she might hold a kitten. His hands were warm, even through the fabric of her sweater, and the stroke of them up and down her arm, made her want to purr.

"I'm okay," she said, not moving.

"No. You're not. Lily, what's going on?"

"I don't know," she admitted. It was easier to talk with her face turned against his chest, her hair hiding

her from him—and him from her—like some kind of
privacy screen. "I keep…I've been having dreams. All
week. Dreams… I've always had nightmares, things I
didn't remember, but they're worse now. Cats, you
know? This one cat, sitting there, staring at me."

"That's…normal. I'm sorry." There was an odd tone
in his voice. Guilt? But why would he be guilty?

"No, it's okay." The irony of her reassuring him didn't
escape her. "I expected it. You can't see something like
that without it going somewhere, we both know that.
And I've…" She hesitated. "I've always dreamed of
cats." It was true; she was only now allowing herself to
remember the depth of it. How the dreams followed her
throughout college, becoming worse during times of
stress. Especially when she was in a relationship. When
a relationship was starting…or ending. But she wasn't
going to tell him that. It was just her insecurities taking
a classic form, echoing her waking fears. All of her
therapists had said so.

"It's not the dreams so much as… The cat I see is
alive and…waiting. Looking at me. Expecting me to
do something.

"And then this week I was so tired from dreaming,
from not sleeping, I…I started hallucinating."

It was easier to call it that. To pretend that it was all
just sleep deprivation playing tricks on her mind. Perfectly logical, and easily dealt with, via sleeping pills
and a few sessions with a new therapist.

Perfectly logical, and untrue. They weren't hallucinations. They were *real*.

That was impossible. So she had to be losing her

mind. Don't tell Jon that. Don't make him think of her as another crazy, someone to be studied and tracked and analyzed....

"Aw, baby."

If anyone else had called her that, Lily would have taken offense. But it came so easily out of his mouth, without any inflection that might have made it patronizing, or pitying, or insulting. She felt his arms tighten around her, and felt, suddenly as though she could melt into his body; seep into his bones and be safe and warm forever.

He cared for her. She cared for him. She could love him, if he let her.

The thought made her jolt away, as though someone had touched her with a live wire.

Don't trust him. Don't ever trust a man, not ever again.

"Hey." He let her move away, but kept one arm around her, keeping her on his lap. He was warm, so warm. What was she afraid of? Like cats...her own fear was the fearsome thing, not this attraction. This connection.

All it took was a turn of her torso, and they were face-to-face. Her hair came forward in a sheet, and he reached up to brush it back, tucking several of the thick curls behind her ear.

His hand was shaking. She liked that. Control over herself she knew about. Control of someone else...

"Your eyes...they're still dilated." His hand was still resting in her hair. She wondered if he realized that.

"Hrmmm." She could smell him, his arousal. Her mouth watered at the thought of what he might taste like. She already knew his mouth, the texture of his hair, the softness of his neck…. What other surprises might be hidden under that suit and tie?

It had been a while since she'd dated. Longer since then that she'd had sex. She thought that there might still be condoms in the drawer of her night table. They should still be good…. Did they expire? It hadn't been that long, had it?

Her thighs ached with the need to feel his weight between them, feel the heft and warmth of him there, inside her, a part of her. She wanted to feel the scrape of his hands against her skin, his fingers tangling in her hair, his mouth on her neck, her breasts…. She could feel her nipples harden at the thought, and the ache between her thighs turned into a liquid heat.

"What are you thinking?" he asked her, dropping his hand from her hair and bringing her attention back to the here and now.

Instead of answering, she slid her arms around his neck, brought him close and kissed him.

Jon had thought that he would have to be the aggressor, that he would be the one to make the first real move. And probably the second, too. He was okay with that; based on their first, totally unplanned kisses, Lily was clearly gun-shy: someone had done a number on her, probably, and she didn't want to jump into some fly-by-night thing. He liked that. It was frustrating, but he liked it. She wasn't old-fashioned, exactly, just… cautious. Like a cat, she would wait him out.

He was okay with that, too.

Not that he'd worked out any sort of plan in any kind of detail, only vague ideas that kept occurring to him without warning. He would talk to her, let her know he wasn't a bad guy for all that they got off on a bad start. Maybe coax a few more kisses from her, if the situation allowed. No pressure. Wrap up this case and then call her a few days later, when he was home in D.C. His life was crazed; he never knew where he'd be from week to week; federal agents, especially with his specialization, traveled a lot, and without much warning. But that was what cell phones were for, not to mention frequent-flier miles.

All that went out of his head the instant her lips touched his. Icy-hot, sweet-tasting, sliding like silk over his skin, her hands insistent, her hunger obvious. A man would have to have been a saint to resist, and he might have the name of a saint, but that was as far as it went.

"Lily…"

He tried, Lord knew, he tried. She clearly wasn't entirely in control of herself, between the sleep deprivation and the hallucinations and now this…. But it wasn't as though she had been unresponsive to him. He wasn't taking advantage—was he?

She pulled back as though sensing his hesitation, and smiled at him. Her eyes were normal; they were clear, and bright, and very much aware of what she was doing.

That was all the reassurance he needed.

"Lily." He whispered her name just before her mouth came down on his again, nipping the delicate flesh, sliding her tongue along the inside of his lips, tasting and suckling like…like a hummingbird, he thought. Or a cat, lapping cream…

"Get out of those clothes." She was standing, tugging at his shirt. "Too warm in here for clothing." She was smiling, tendrils of her hair, dampened by sweat and tears, were clinging to her neck like invitations to be followed. He reached for the buttons of his shirt, even as he was giving in to temptation and moving his mouth to that spot on her neck, doing some tasting of his own.

"You taste like…honey. Warm honey and whiskey. Ah, Lily." He was lost. He didn't even try to resist.

There was something deeply…sexy about turning a guy on. She had almost forgotten, maybe she had never known; the passion contained in a man who wanted, waiting only permission to take. The seduction was all about drawing out the process, letting him know that it was available but holding off on the go-ahead; knowing that they both knew where it would end, and therefore feeling free to play, to delay, to build the tension to where they were both sweating with the need.

His shirt unbuttoned, she let her fingers run from his shoulders down his chest to his belly, then back up again, close-trimmed nails barely scratching the skin. Dark hair started at his pectorals, covering his chest in a thick mat, then trailing to a narrow line down to his belly button. His body was firm, muscled but not bulky. Solid. He was solid in a way that made her—for the first time in her life—feel delicate.

Lily had no illusions about her body. She was lush. Hourglass-shaped. When she was in her twenties, she finally gave up. Exercise kept her muscles firm, but nothing short of starvation was ever going to give her a flat stomach or slender hips.

"C'mere" he said, his hand sliding down her back, cupping her rear and pulling her to where he sat on the sofa. The blanket he had wrapped around her fell to the floor unnoticed as she returned to his lap, this time for an entirely different purpose than comfort.

He slid his hands under her sweater, stroking the flesh upward, sliding his fingers over the strap of her bra up to her neck, and then down again. She raised her arms and he had her sweater off and tossed it to the floor.

"Fast reflexes," she practically purred.

"Government issue," he said, then his lips were caressing the valley between her breasts, and she *was* purring. His lips were warm, so warm, and greedy. His hands were flat against her back, his tongue soft and wet on her skin, and she felt as if he was drinking her up through her skin.

Her fingers threaded through his hair, suggesting, if not directing, his actions.

"Tell me what you want," he said, the whisper hot against her nipples. "Tell me. Talk dirty to me."

She had never done any such thing, had no idea where to begin.

"It's all right, Lily-kit. Just say what you want. What you want to do to me. I want to lick every inch of you, mouth to toes. Especially your belly. I bet your belly tastes so sweet…"

"I can't…. Hold me. Hold me down."

In the time it took for her to gasp her request, she was flat on her back on the floor, Jon's body looming over hers, her arms stretched over her head and pinned to the floor with one of his hands around her wrists.

"You want to test yourself against me, kitten?" He might call her kitten but he was the one purring, now. A big cat noise, smug and self-satisfied.

No. Yes. She had always been in control. Always been the one to initiate—and to leave. He would be the one to leave, in this relationship. Begin as you mean to go on....

"I won't force you," he promised, lowering his mouth to her breasts again. "But I won't let you go, either."

He was lying. She knew he was lying. But she could pretend, for this one night.

Then his mouth closed down hard on one nipple, and her back arched up, her legs closing around his and bringing his torso to hers. "Clothing. Off." She demanded. "Want to see what I've got."

He laughed, a low rumbling noise. "So much for letting me to be in control." But his laughter was pleased, inviting her to join in. "I need my legs free," he told her, and she released him immediately. He shucked his pants off with one hand, never letting her wrists go.

"Commando?" She was amused, her voice low and surprisingly seductive. She didn't recognize herself.

"I was out of underwear," he said, blushing just a little. "It's drying in my shower."

Lily felt something twist inside her, a few inches below her heart and above her gut. It hurt, but like a limb snapping back into place; a hurt followed by a sense of rightness, of something broken suddenly fixed.

Fuck me, she was going to say, had intended to say: trying to keep the encounter hard and fun and without any kind of commitment implied or asked for.

"Make love to me," she said instead, sitting up enough to whisper the demand in his ear, making sure that her tongue touched the outer tip of that ear.

"Oh, Lily, don't tempt me so…."

His mouth abandoned her breast and moved lower, sliding over her belly until she giggled because it tickled. His tongue dipped into her belly button, circled around it, then moved lower.

"Hang on a second, I've got this," he said when he reached the waistband of her pants. She waited, and then started to laugh as his teeth closed on the snap of her slacks. Her laughter stopped the moment he had them down on her hips, and his mouth went directly for the damp cotton of her panties.

"Jesus, Lily…I'm so going to make you come for me…"

Then her panties were shoved down her legs, and his mouth was on her. Both of his hands were on her thighs now, holding her open, but Lily felt no desire to move her arms from where he had pinned her. His tongue slid inside her, and lapped like he was the kitten and she was a deep, deep dish of cream.

"Oh…" Lily caught the endearment before it fell off her own tongue, biting her lip as Jon made her hips buck upward. She had asked him to make love to her and that was exactly what he was doing. But it wasn't enough. She needed more.

Her exercise routine might not have given her a flat

stomach, but there were muscles underneath the rounding, and she was able to sit up without using her legs, catching Jon unawares. A push back, and he was the one at her mercy, her legs straddling his hips as they sprawled on the floor, her hands on his shoulders, pressing him down.

"Wanna play rough, do you?" he asked, recovering quickly. His eyes were as hotly focused as ever, even as the muscles in his face were loose and soft, and she couldn't resist kissing the tip of his nose, watching with delight as his eyes almost crossed, trying to follow her.

"Want you," she told him. "In me. Now." She grinned, fierce to match his stare. "We can play…later."

Later. There would be a later. He took that promise and ran with it, fastening his mouth to hers in a deep sweet kiss, even as his hands brought her down onto his cock, sliding into her wet folds like coming home, like some impossible perfect fit. She wasn't warm, she was hot, and tight, and a little voice in his head warned him that they weren't using protection even as she shifted on him and he groaned into her mouth.

They fought for the lead, first one and then the other setting the pace. Sweat glistened and thoughts fled, until Lily arched her back and lifted her face, tears streaming.

"Lily?"

"Don't…keep going, keep…"

Her fingers gripped his shoulders, and she tucked her chin forward, hair falling around her face as she looked down into his eyes. It was almost a challenge, that wet stare, and he met it, keeping eye contact even as his own orgasm built.

She blinked first, her eyes closing, that odd shadow closing half a second before her outer lid, but then she was falling into a silky black spiral, totally caught up in her own sensations. She collapsed in his arms for a second time that night, his fingers tightening on her arms as he pulled out, reaching his own apex against the pale, sleek skin of her thigh. She swore, and he laughed, and followed her over into exhaustion.

He woke up, immediately aware he wasn't at home, or in the usual scratchy-sheeted hotel room. These sheets were soft, almost silky, as was the body snuggled next to him. They had made their way to the bed at some point during the evening, holding hands and stumbling against things in the dark.

He ran his finger along the lines of one creamy-skinned shoulder, listening to the sound of her breathing. Lily kept the thermostat in her condo higher than he was used to. Post-sex sweat always seemed, well, sweatier than when he worked out in the gym. Probably because you didn't usually end up cuddled with your workout partner.

The thought made Patrick snort with horrified laughter—his usual workout partner, Cal, was not exactly cuddling material, being six foot three and three feet wide, all of it muscle. Attractive to some, he supposed, but...

Yes, he definitely preferred them pocket-size and curvy. Call him old-fashioned.

His Venus rolled over to face the sound, opened one eye, then the other.

"Mornin'?" It sounded as though she was begging for a negative answer.

"Not quite yet," he reassured her. "But I should…"

"Yeah."

The dialogue sounded awkward. But he couldn't quite stop smiling, and Lily raised herself up so that she rested on one elbow, her dark curls falling over one bare shoulder like some not-quite soft-core-movie poster. Her skin was flushed across her chest and neck, and there was a dark purple hickey forming just below her jawline.

He didn't remember doing that, but the evidence was, well, evident.

"I have to go. Boss wants a status report, and I have to check the overnights, and…"

He didn't want to go anywhere. He wanted to stay, and not just because he was worried about that freak finding her. He wanted to stay in that bed, the sheets smelling of them, and feel her legs tangled in his, her hair tickling under his nose. He wanted to be able to roll over and have her in his arms, ready and warm and willing. Or even just sleeping: anticipation, when you knew what was waiting for you, was sugar-sweet.

She blinked lazily, and he was reminded again of the strangeness of the night before. But she seemed to have forgotten it somehow. Or dispensed with it as not important. Either way, he hesitated to bring it up again. Not here. Not now. Stress. She was under a lot of stress. Bad dreams and dizziness—she hadn't had dinner last night, either.

"I'll be fine. And I won't be offended by your early-morning departure. Go."

"I'll call you." He was still worried. That was a surprise, and an unwelcome one. Worry was personal. He couldn't afford that personal twitch, couldn't be distracted by it. Not now. Not yet. He hadn't thought about that when he had daydreamed his seduction of the delectable, desirable Lily. Idiot.

"Mmm." She smiled at him and he lost track of his thoughts again. "You'd better. You need coffee?"

"I'll get some on my way. Go back to sleep."

He kissed her on the tip of her nose, and she scrunched it under his touch, then sank down into the blankets and sighed, sliding back into sleep even as he picked up his clothes and headed for the bathroom. He should have already been focusing on the case, on what might be waiting for him, but all he could do was keep thinking that Lily Malkin was…

Was more than he had been expecting. Far, far more.

Chapter 10

Dale Mortman, agent in charge of the D.C. CID and various other governmental initials, was a very patient man. But even patience could reach an end, and his voice at the other end of the standard-issue police department phone carried that warning. "You realize what you're asking?"

Patrick crossed his legs more comfortably under the desk, stretched out in his borrowed chair and rolled his eyes to the heavens as though to ask for patience. "I'm not twelve. Yes, I know what I'm asking. Look, right now this is a mild curiosity that could become a localized media circus. Fine, not our problem, locals can handle it, yeah, I know. But his words are…worrying me."

The cat woman. She knows. The recording Petrosian

had gotten of the phone call replayed in his head on a seemingly endless loop.

What did Lily know? Did she even know that she knew? Or was it all part of this guy—the Night Serpent's—game, or psychosis, or whatever?

That was Patrick's job: to find out. It was what he was good at. All he had to do was step back and look at the pieces. And not think about how one of those pieces was probably just waking up right now, heading into the shower, standing under a stream of hot water, lathering up her breasts….

Yeah, definitely not thinking about that.

"We are not unaffected by the thought of a threat to a civilian…."

Patrick took another sip of his coffee and made a face. He should have accepted Lily's offer—this stuff was worse than swill. At least in the good old days you could count on one cop per shift knowing how to make a decent pot. Now, with the "pod" machines, it was all mechanized, and—in his opinion—crap.

"Save me the canned PR bullshit," he told his boss. "Just tell me I'm a good boy and to get on with my job."

Dale had a sigh you could hear from one end of the Beltway to the other, and no hesitation about letting loose with it.

"If you think you have a handle on this guy… Run with it. Whatever you need by way of support, CID will do their best to supply. Just try not to need anything expensive that I'll have to explain at a budget meeting, okay? And I need you back here by next Tuesday."

"Got it. Thanks."

It wasn't a home run—he'd *wanted* to get Lily some protection, above and beyond the little that the local cops could provide, but without an actual threat from a certified serial killer, he'd known better than to even ask. His personal involvement might be clouding his judgment, but it wasn't making him an idiot.

At least now he knew that his requests for information would get priority, without having to go the favor-for-a-friend route. Or getting Lily involved any further.

The bustle around him parted for a moment, and the smell of stale smoke and old coffee swirled down to him. Petrosian, scratchy-voiced, like a guy who had been chain-smoking all shift.

"You hear what they're calling him?"

Patrick wondered where Petrosian smoked, since the entire precinct was now officially and legally smoke free, all the way out to the parking lot. "The Night Serpent. Yeah." The morning news had picked up the story, lacking anything more bloodthirsty coming in overnight. He had heard a squib on the cab's radio, on his way. Inevitable, considering the guy's comments. More evocative than "sick bastard," he supposed. Sold more papers, got better ratings.

"It mean anything?" Petrosian pulled a chair from behind the other desk and sat down in it. "Give you a clue into his alleged mind?"

"Maybe." His brain went into "sift and filter" mode. "Serpents and cats are, historically and allegorically, enemies. They're also, however, both aligned with the devil in Christian mythology. Our unsub is killing cats in a ritualistic manner, and then displaying them in a circle, nose to tail. Similar to that of a snake, in both Celtic and Norse mythologies. I've got a search running to see if there's been anything entered into the system similar in the past twenty years." Lily hadn't found anything, but his search engine had access to more data. "Based on the witness's description, this guy's not old enough to have done anything noteworthy before then, or if he did, it would be under juvie seal."

"In other words, you got shit."

"I have…a couple of theories. None of which get us anywhere. That the tox report?"

Petrosian handed it to him. "Yeah. Same as the others—clean as a cat's innards can be. This guy is doing it all by hand. You ever get around to asking Lily about your idea, that he's another cat-whisperer type?"

The question was casual, but the glance sent along with it wasn't. Patrick suddenly felt like he was fourteen years old and caught trying to feel up Judy Clare after gym class. He shook his head. "No. She was still pretty shook up…. You think you could talk her into going to see a doctor?" He carefully didn't specify what sort of doctor; he honestly wasn't sure. She was exhibiting signs that in another person he would consider warnings of a breakdown, if not an actual psychotic break. And yet, having looked into her eyes, felt her in his arms—even against all evidence, he didn't believe that she was crazy.

He didn't know *what* to believe.

Petrosian slouched farther into his chair. "I'm not her daddy, Patrick. She's a grown woman, she does what she wants." And *with whom* was loudly unspoken.

The personal undercurrents thus navigated to their satisfaction, both men relaxed slightly and returned to the case.

He had not slept well since he saw the woman. That golden glow inside her haunted him, distracted him. And finally, finally, he understood the message that had been sent, in her appearance. A gift from Herself; one of her Handmaidens, yes, but innocent in this world. Born fresh, clean. Ready for him to write his message on.

He was smart. Had always been smart. Smarter than his teachers ever knew. Smart like…like the serpent coiled in the grass. The Night Serpent, they were calling him now. He liked that, yes. The serpent was wise. Don't show yourself. Don't waste energy attacking everything that moves. Let others flush out your target, and then strike once, effectively.

His knife to the beasts' throats; like a cobra's strike: swift and certain.

It was not cruelty, it was not bloodlust; it was not any of those things the reporters were claiming on television. It was need.

That last time he had felt it; as the blood dripped into the circle, he had felt the earth shift, the gates begin to open. He was almost there, the time was almost right, the cats were almost right…but something essential wasn't present. She wasn't appeased. Wasn't satisfied by his offerings, his sacrifice.

But he had another chance. One more before the window closed, his third chance was up, and he was trapped in this hell for another lifetime. She had given him that; had shown him the cat woman, the one who glimmered with gold, who brought the beasts to hand. She was the key to the lock. She would be able to tell him what he had been doing wrong.

And now he knew where she was. All he had to do was collect her.

Lily woke at nine that morning, sat up in panic before remembering that she was off today, and then fell back onto the bed, only to be reminded by the not-unpleasant aches that she had not spent the night alone. Or sleeping.

Oh God. She had actually…they had actually…

Not that she regretted it, she thought. She just wished it had been under less…weird circumstances. The night before was sort of fuzzy, after they told her about the phone call, and her inclusion in it, but she remembered getting dizzy, and Jon's arms around her, and…

And the memories that followed *that* made a flush rise up her cheeks. Aches in her thighs, oh yes. And also her shoulders, and her arms, and her stomach…

He was gone, long gone if the temperature of the pillow next to her was any indication. She had some memory of that as well, of waking and speaking and the faintest caress of his hand on her face before he left.

Getting out of bed, she ran through her normal routines before realizing, halfway through her shower, that she had nowhere to go and nothing to do today. She was supposed to work at the shelter this afternoon; they were gearing up for the year-end donation appeal, and she was supposed to do her share of envelope stuffing and stamping. But she had agreed to stay away from the shelter for a few days, she did remember that.

"I suppose I could get someone to bring over a box or two of letters," she told herself. Even Special Agent Jon T. Patrick couldn't object to that, and she'd love to see some overeager reporter try to stick a microphone in Ronnie's face. They'd end up tasting it all the way down their throat, if the shelter director was feeling particularly cranky. Or she would use the opportunity to get some free media attention for the shelter. Either way, goodness.

Amused despite the situation, Lily got out of the shower, grabbed the thick black towel off the rack and dried herself off. Clad in a soft robe, she padded to the kitchen to make herself some coffee and see what was up with the world.

The talking heads were still doing their shtick, but if the bastard who was killing cats was still newsworthy, it had been featured before she tuned in.

She would give this house arrest two days. Then she was supposed to be back on shift at the bank, and she would, by God be there.

The phone rang, and she jumped, then, shaking her head at the sudden attack of nerves, crossed the room and picked up the receiver.

"Yes?"

"Heya."

She suddenly felt like a teenager with her first crush, curling the phone cord around her fingers and leaning against the wall, the phone pressed to her ear.

"Hey yourself."

"I figured you'd be up by now. You okay?"

"I'm…okay, yeah."

What did you say to the man you'd met only days before? The man who had left your bed before dawn? The man you knew better than to get involved with, and still did?

"I'm not very good at this." She had always been brutally honest. No reason to stop now.

"I think you underestimate yourself," he said, and she flushed again.

"I mean…"

"I know what you mean. Don't worry, Lily. I think you're amazing, and brave, and a lot of other things I'm not going to say out loud with half a dozen cops sitting in the same room with me pretending that they're not listening in."

She was *definitely* blushing, now.

"I just wanted to check in, see… You okay?" he repeated.

She was puzzled—what did he think would be wrong?—when she remembered. Being cold. Not just dizzy, but dislocated. Hearing voices.

Mother, forgive me!

"Lily?"

"I'm here. I'm…okay."

No, she wasn't. She suddenly felt ill. Her stomach hurt, as if she'd been throwing up, and the muscles in her neck and shoulders hurt in a bad way, not the good of before, and her eyes were red and dry like they'd been sandblasted. Like she had the flu, or something.

"I'm okay," she said again. "Jon, I've got to go. I'll talk to you later, all right?"

She hung up the phone and made it to the bathroom just in time to dry heave into the toilet. She was shivering and weak kneed, but her head stayed clear, and her memories were her own.

Maybe she *was* coming down with the flu.

She called the shelter after that, planning to give some excuse, but none was needed. They had seen the news reports as well, and put two and two together and come up with five reasons why she should not come in that day, even before she announced her intention to take a few days off.

"Girl, that may be the most sensible thing I've ever heard you say, and you were *born* sensible," Ronnie cackled over the phone. "Stay home. Stay out of sight. And if anyone comes here looking for you, we'll sit on him until your gorgeous Fibbie comes to arrest him."

"He's not my Fibbie," Lily protested, but could feel herself flushing again as she said it. Maybe not hers, exactly, but she had laid a claim…and so had he. She touched the bruise on her neck and was suddenly almost thankful for the excuse not to have to explain it to anyone. Although if it weren't for this loon, she would never have met Jon, so there wouldn't be anything to explain….

She hung up the phone and reached for the cleaning supplies. Anything to keep from thinking. Not about this Night Serpent and whatever he was planning, not about Agent Patrick and his disturbing ability to get inside all of her defenses, and absolutely not about the weird dreams and weirder dizziness she had been feeling.

Although she hadn't had any dreams last night. And she felt fine this morning, until Jon's call. No weirdness with her eyes, no dizziness, no strange smells or sounds…

So maybe all you needed was a good romp between the sheets? It was a lowering thought, but the medicine had been sweet, so she really couldn't complain.

The day went faster than she expected; she finally got the deep cleaning of the kitchen done, and all of the laundry, and she was contemplating actually washing the floor, when the boxes arrived from the shelter. A hundred letters in one, a hundred envelopes in the other, with a huge roll of labels and stamps to go with it.

"You did ask," Nancy said half apologetically, handing the boxes over. Lily looked cautiously over the other woman's shoulder, but didn't see any news vans or stray reporters lurking.

"Thanks. You want some coffee, or…?"

"Nah, I gotta get back. And…Lil?"

"Yes?"

"Be careful, okay? Some woman came around the shelter this morning asking about you, and we've had a couple of phone calls. Reporters. Ronnie didn't want to say anything, didn't want you to worry, but…it's only fair you know, I thought. We didn't tell them anything, of course. Just that you were a volunteer and we didn't give out names, and certainly not addresses, but…"

"I'm careful," Lily assured her. "And the police are

doing regular drive-bys." An Officer Stephens was on the day shift, with his partner whose name she hadn't gotten, a dark-skinned, annoyed-looking woman. She hadn't met the night shift, but she knew they were out there. "If anyone tries to stick a camera in my window, I'll flash 'em."

Nancy laughed and left, reassured. Lily took the boxes back into the dining room and set them on the table. Some more coffee, and she should be able to get through this before it was time to make dinner.

She carefully did not let herself wonder if Jon would show up for that meal.

Chapter 11

Agent Patrick ducked into the darkened room, barely the size of a supply closet, and shut the door behind him. "What've we got?"

The room was filled with monitors; on two of them, tapes were running, the familiar black-and-white flicker of security tapes, the time and date running at the bottom right hand of the screen.

"Security-cam footage. Came in this afternoon." Petrosian tapped one of the technicians on the shoulder. "Run it again."

The tape flickered, blurred in rewind, and then started again from the beginning. Two views, one on each screen.

"These are from our local zoo," Petrosian said. "Not going to compete with the big'uns, but it has a few decent exhibits. Out in Dover, about ten-minute drive north of here. Our guy has a car."

"You sure it's him?"

The first tape showed a sweep of the exterior, one side of a low-slung building gray and black in the predawn light. "The monkey house," Petrosian identified it. "If that is our guy, he did not do his homework."

A shadow flitted across the tapes. Tall, fast-moving and agile. No way to identify it, even with well-placed house lights. The camera clearly caught him jimmying the window, however.

"Silent alarm," one of the techs said. "Alerts the owners and the security company without freaking out the critters."

"Or letting the intruder know he's been twigged." Scaring someone away before they even got in was better security, but if an intruder was determined, he wouldn't be scared off by anything short of a shotgun being loaded behind his ear.

The second tape started rolling. This was inside a long open space filled with dead trees and what looked like—Patrick squinted—yes, old tire swings. What looked like a shallow pond lay at the far end of the space.

"Tiger enclosure. Damn, he's got balls. No way I'd go anywhere near there, not without a stun gun and backup." The second tech shook his head, either in shock or admiration.

At night, the cats were kept in a separate enclosure, but the intruder didn't seem to realize that, looking into the wooden structures as though expecting to find a cat hidden there.

"This guy may have done some research, but yeah, he's not all that clued in, otherwise he wouldn't be wasting his time there. And what does he think he's going to do when he finds them, anyway?"

"He's not a pro," Petrosian said. "Like a junkie tossing a house for whatever he can pawn fast, he's going by gut and instinct. Here's where it gets interesting."

The intruder lifted his head, as though hearing a noise, then turned and headed for a small door at the end of the enclosure. The tape stuttered, and then jump-cut to another location, this one an indoor hallway lit by fluorescent bulbs, with a handful of doors off to the left-hand side. The intruder walked quickly along, stopping at the second door as though pulled by a magnet.

"That's where the younger cats are kept," Petrosian told Patrick.

The guy knew. Not because he'd looked at plans beforehand, or read a sign on the door; he *knew*. Just the way Patrick knew the guy knew: not brain-knowing, but gut-knowing. Spooky-knowing.

The intruder had just placed his hand on the doorknob when the door at the end of the hallway burst open, the lights flashed on, and two—no, three security guards came into the hall.

Patrick noted absently that they had pretty good form, for rental cops. They didn't do anything wrong. It wasn't the fault of their training, what happened next.

"Stop where you are!" the lead guard shouted, going low so his companions would have a clear shot over his head if the intruder decided to get cute.

The unsub turned, his hand falling away from the

doorknob, raising his hands as though to indicate surrender. The camera wasn't advanced enough to zoom
in on his face, but Patrick was pretty sure it creased up
as though he'd tasted something sour, and then he
started yelling. It was gibberish, nonsense words, but
in a pattern that sounded as if he was saying something
with meaning. Patrick frowned. It sounded…like the
words that Lily had said last night. Or not the exact
words, but in the same language.

Connection. But what kind, and what did it mean?
And was Lily keeping something from him? He hoped
not. He really, really hoped not, and not only because
it would make him seven different kinds of fool. "Do
we have any idea what he's saying?"

"Not a clue. Was hoping your boys would be able to
do something about that."

Patrick nodded; he had been about to request a copy
of the tapes for exactly that reason. "Give me a copy,
and an audio strip-out. I'll see what they come back
with."

"Already on digital. Give me an e-mail address and
I can zip 'em over posthaste."

Some days Patrick really loved technology.

"Hang on," Petrosian warned. "There's more."

The unsub's left hand lowered, still over his shoulder
and not looking as if it was reaching for anything, but
suddenly there was a small object in his hand, about the
size and width of a CD. He shook it at the guards as
though expecting something to happen. When it didn't,
he let out a roar and rushed them, knocking the first one
over and colliding with two and three. There was a

strange spray of sparks where their bodies met, and then the guards fell to the floor, gasping and grabbing at their clothing, trying to put out the flames that had somehow started in the fabric.

The intruder threw his head back and yowled something, waving the object at the ceiling, and then ran out the door.

The tape ended.

"What the hell?" Patrick asked, not expecting an answer.

"Some kind of flamethrower, we guess. Butane torch, like they use in kitchens?"

Patrick had used a kitchen torch before, in a miserable attempt to make crème brûlée. They didn't look anything like that, nor did they throw sparks without visible flames, even when they malfunctioned.

"Anyway, the guards are okay. But before the guy ran, he opened half a dozen cages. Hell, he stopped to do it, even with the alarms wailing. Freaked-out critters everywhere. Zoo staff is trying to round them up, and keep the predators from eating the other displays."

"Nice." Patrick's tone indicated he thought that it was anything but.

"That guy's nuts," the tech who had earlier commented on his cojones said, this time far less admiringly. Nobody in the room disagreed.

A few hours later, Patrick wandered out of the building to get some fresh air and clear his head. Something about what he'd seen was bothering him, but he couldn't quite place what. Other than the fact that the unsub might have been speaking the same unknown language that Lily—a potential target of obsession of the killer—had muttered in during her dizzy spell. A dizzy spell that also included physical symptoms that were weird at best, and worrisome at most.

All the pieces were important, Patrick was sure of it. Lily's connection to cats, the Night Serpent's need to kill them, the shared language, the physical symptoms…

He just had no damn idea what any one of them meant, much less how they fit together.

"Hey." Petrosian, cigarette dangling from his lips, unlit.

"Those things are gonna kill you," Patrick said, indicating it with a jerk of his chin.

"Only if I'm lucky," Petrosian replied, the inevitable cop response. "Besides, bastards won't even let me light up anymore."

He was going to make a wiseass comeback, but his phone vibrated, demanding his attention. "Patrick."

He shifted his cell phone to the other ear to hear better. "Uh-huh. Great. What've you got for me?" The worst part of the job was waiting for other people to do their job. The best part was when they came through, setting you on the next stage of investigation. That was when the blood surged, the brain leaped into overdrive, the neurons all fired and the case got solved.

"It was what?"

The voice of the FBI linguist came through the phone lines, clear, sarcastic and heavily put upon. "Ancient Egyptian, New Kingdom, around 1500 B.C. Do you know how long it took us to figure that out and find someone who could translate? This ain't Stargate. We don't have that kind of brainpower just sitting around twiddling their thumbs."

"But you guys are brilliant and figure it out anyway."

"No, we know enough to call the Smithsonian. And even they aren't sure they've got it right." The linguist rustled paper for effect, then read off the translation for the agent.

"Jesus. You're sure?"

"Hell, no, we're not sure. But that's out best guess. It make any sense to you?"

Yes. Yes, it did. And it made his blood run cold.

The Way Must be Opened. Her Blood will Turn the Key.

"Pack something. Basics, jeans and sweaters. Toiletries."

"What?" Lily stepped back to let Jon in, surprised to see two uniformed officers come in right on his heels. One of them was Stephens, of her daytime drive-by patrol. She knew him vaguely from previous cat-related cases. She gave him a small wave, and he shuffled his feet, clearly awkward with actually being in her home. The other was a man she didn't know, who was carefully not looking at her.

"You can't stay here. He hurt people last night, Lily. Whatever he was before, he's escalated. And he's got you in his brain. I want you somewhere else, now."

"You want?" Lily stood in front of him, her hands on her hips. The solid build she had admired— caressed—the night before was now a barrier, a challenge to her. "What about what I want?" Her eyes widened, and she felt her fingers flex in sudden agitation. How dare he just drop this on her, as if it was all his decision and she had no say in anything at all. When did she become his property, just because they'd slept together?

"Lily, please." There were two cops with him. Would they side with her, or him? Jon—Agent Patrick—would rather they were federal agents, men he could boss around rather than play nicely with.

She tried to rein in her anger. He probably had his reasons, she was sure he had his reasons. Pure logic said that if she was at real risk, he could protect her better somewhere else, somewhere he could control everything, someplace secret. Wasn't that the point of safe houses, in every TV show she'd ever seen?

Logic, though, seemed to have gone out the door the same time he came in and started ordering her around all the wrong way, and she couldn't seem to stop herself from reacting badly.

She was angry. No, she was furious. She was also, she discovered, more than a little turned on by the stubborn set of his jaw, and the way his eyes had gone flat not in anger, but determination. Lily was taken aback by that realization. She didn't like men who were bossy, any more than she liked ones who were overly ambitious. But this was…it was the whole FBI-man thing. Power. Not ambition, which had made her uneasy, but a man aware of his own abilities and consequence, and not unwilling to use them.

She reacted to it, yeah, okay. Male-in-Authority

kink, check. But getting told what to do and don't ask questions? Her spine stiffened like a steel rod in reaction against it. She was an adult, damn it. She had her own power, in her own right, and she would not let him ride roughshod over it. And if that made her unreasonable so be it. She was tired of *men* always deciding her fate.

"No." She shook her head, glaring at him. "This is my home. I'm as safe here as I will be anywhere, and a lot more comfortable. You have no idea that he's actually going to threaten me, you said so yourself. He thinks I know something, something that he needs. That doesn't sound like intent to commit violence. And even if he does come here, I have my security system, I have you, and now I've got two cops of my very own." She assumed that they were here to protect her, and not just carry her suitcase to the car, anyway.

"Damn it, Lily, it will be easier to protect you in a safe house." He ran a hand through his hair and stared at something over her shoulder.

"You don't own me," she said. "And you don't get to order me around." His gaze swung back to her and she was struck again by the intensity of his stare. Burning, focused and more than a little unnerving. The man who had made love to her was gone, and the man who tracked killers for a living was back.

"It's important for you to maintain control, isn't it?" he asked, obviously trying to be reasonable.

"Don't try to analyze me," she snapped. "I pay someone to do that. And years of therapy have told me that yes, I need control. I need to be the only one who makes decisions for me. If you have a problem with that—"

He grabbed her arm and tugged her off to the side, away from the overtly eavesdropping cops. "I'm not going caveman on you," he said. "I'm just trying to do my job. Lily. It's only for a little while. Just to be safe."

She stared at him, then back at the cops. There was something he wasn't telling her, and that cooled her anger even as determination solidified. "I can't do this. I can't... Post guards at my doors and windows if you want. But I'm not going anywhere."

She didn't know why she was being so stubborn. But it felt right. This was her home, a place she had worked hard to afford, to make into a refuge, a place where she felt comfortable in a world that she never quite felt in sync with.

Now he wanted to take her away from it, in the name of "safety." Without telling her why. Even she knew that if there was no safety here, there wasn't safety anywhere. No matter how safe a safe house might be. The Night Serpent wanted her, he would find her. It was that simple.

The phone rang, and she broke away from him to answer it.

"Who is this?" She looked at Jon, who had followed her into the kitchen.

"You know." The voice was flat, but somehow wired, as though it were about to explode. It made her skin crawl just hearing it.

"I don't know."

"Yes. You do. He's there, so you know what's happening. You can fix it, I know you can. She told me. She showed me. You're the key. You're the messenger. You have to tell me what I'm doing wrong. How do I convince Her to open the door? You *know!*"

Seeing her agitation, Jon took the phone from her. "This is Special Agent Patrick. Who am I speaking with?"

There was silence. "The Night Serpent. But you knew that already. Let me talk to the woman. I don't want to talk to you."

The smart thing to do would be to keep him on the phone, keep him talking. But there was no way to track him—with all the fuss over federal phone tapping recently, he hadn't wanted to open that can of worms to hook her phone up, hadn't thought the guy would contact her like this. Lily was right; he had been so focused on the physical risk, he had overlooked the more passive threat, the indirect approach....

The Way Must be Opened. Her Blood will Turn the Key.

"The lady doesn't want to talk to you. What makes you think she'd talk to a cat killer like you, anyway?"

The Serpent took a deep breath, as though the accusation had shocked him. "We do things...that must be done. There is always a price. She understood. She showed me the way, through Her beasts. But I can't open the door all the way. Let me talk to the woman, she's here to show me how!"

The Serpent's voice was rising, almost a yowl, and Patrick made the instinctive decision to hang up before the guy got even more worked up.

The moment the receiver was back in the cradle, he

punched in *57. Somewhere in the phone company's system, the caller's number, and Lily's number, were being recorded. Normally it took two or three calls to get the cops to do anything. Patrick suspected that he would be able to get a warrant for that number on just the one call.

"He knows my number."

"You're listed."

"I never thought… How did he learn my name?"

He wanted to take her in his arms, reassure her that nothing was wrong, everything was going to be okay. "Media, probably. Someone didn't see the harm in giving him the name of the cat lady the cops turn to. This guy, he looks normal. Sounds normal, if a little tightly wound. And you're a local celebrity…."

"Am not."

"You've been on TV, however unwillingly. To some people—" He broke off what he was saying and opened his cell phone, speed-dialing somewhere.

"It's Agent Patrick. The unsub just called the home of one of my consultants, made vaguely threatening comments. I've instituted a trace-back through the phone company. Yeah." He gave her phone number to whoever was on the other end of the line. "Yeah, thanks. I figured. No, I have officers here with me now, I'll arrange for them to…yeah. All right. Thanks."

"You'll arrange for them to do what?"

He didn't answer her, instead going back out to the foyer where the two uniforms were still standing, awkward without anything to do. He spoke to them softly, and she could see their entire demeanor change, going from useless to directed with the speed of a few words. He might have been an outsider, cops versus fed, but he was Authority.

Stephens looked over at her, and she shrugged, a sort of "you think I get any say in this?" motion. He gave a twisted smile in response that, weirdly, reassured her immensely. He wouldn't do anything that she didn't agree to.

"Lily, this is Officer Dunkirk—" that was the shorter one "—and this is—"

"Karl Stephens. We've met."

Stephens smiled at her again. "Ma'am."

She nodded her head politely at them both. "You're going to be my guard dogs, is that it?"

"Ma'am. We're good at barking. And completely yard trained."

Stephens clearly had the right attitude about all of this.

"All right, I'll keep them. But only if it stays low key. I don't want any of my neighbors upset, or the condo board screaming about loitering strangers and 'bad elements' hanging around the building."

Stephens didn't seem to mind being called a bad element, either. "If anyone asks, ma'am, we'll tell them we're part of the mayor's initiative to get more patrols actually out on the street, meeting locals and getting our faces known."

"Great. You mean I'll have to vote for him next election?"

The laughter didn't quite overcome the irritation she was feeling, though. When Jon turned to her as though to continue their discussion, she felt the urge again to hiss at him, warning him away. It was all…too fast. Too much. He came in here as though he had the right to reorder her life, tell her where to go and what to do. Arrange for cops to guard her, as though she were some sort of possession…

A small part of her mind knew that her reaction was overblown, that he wasn't thinking that—probably, that she was reacting to things that weren't in the picture. And Aggie had arranged for the cops in the first place—Aggie had been the one to suggest her staying home, playing it safe. But she felt as though it was *Jon* who was steamrolling over her, refusing to accept her ability to make decisions, to control her own life.

And yet she reacted positively when he went all alpha male on her. She admired his competence, his aggression. She found it appealing, sexy.

And she…feared him for it at the same time.

It didn't make any sense. But it was real, and Lily had learned that while facing your fears was good, denying that they were real was the worst thing she could possibly do.

She needed space to figure this out. Space she wasn't going to get with Alpha Male Special Agent Jon T. Patrick trying to protect her.

"I've already allowed enough changes, against a threat you aren't even sure exists. No more." She stared at him, daring him to override her. "I stay here. They can stay. You have to go."

It was cold, standing in the shadow of the old tree, but for once he did not mind it. The cold was nothing compared to the anticipation inside. So close. So very, very close…and so easy to find her, after all! To hear her voice…

It was a small, narrow building, two stories, crowded on either side by identical structures. A one-car garage shared a driveway with the building next door. The symmetry of the structures pleased him.

Lights were on in the lower level of the house, and people moved in front of the windows. One figure, slender and short, then another, taller and bulkier. A man. The Night Serpent scowled. Who was that man with her?

A sound; the front door opening, shadows under the lights. The man was leaving. Good. And two more, behind him—were they guards? Attendants? There, they were leaving as well. The man drove away, the others walked down the street, the slow pace of trained fighters. Guards, but not belonging to the man? No matter. They were no longer in the house. They had left her to him.

And yet, the thought that she was now left alone disturbed him. She too should have attendants about her, attendants and guards to protect her, protect that brightness within her. It was wrong, as wrong as everything clse in this world. The way he had seen her before, that was right. That was correct. She should be striding free, not locked away in that narrow house. There was so much inside her, so much glinting gold, this world could not, *would* not reward, any more than it rewarded his own superiority.

But he knew her value. He would reward her once

he got what he needed from her. But first, the woman must tell him what he needed to know.

He needed to talk to her again. Now that the man and the guards were out of the way.

He stepped out of the shelter of the tree, and then stopped. One of the guards was back, a rucksack over his shoulder. He went up the stairs, and she let him in without hesitation.

"Damn." The Night Serpent glared, but the door remained closed. After a while, a light went on upstairs, while one remained on in the first level.

They were in for the night.

He hesitated, wanting to stay, watch over the house in hopes of a chance to speak with the woman alone. But the beasts needed feeding and watering; it would not be good for them to become angry before he could ask them to intercede for him. No, it would not do at all.

Chapter 12

Lily was fuming. She had thought it was all settled. She had been a good girl, allowed Stephens and Dunkirk to babysit her all weekend without complaint, alternating shifts sleeping on her sofa. She had taken her leave from the shelter. She had even rescheduled her hairstylist appointment, leaving her with a mass of unruly curls that she had resorted to stuffing under a baseball cap rather than fight with Jon about going out in public spaces. But this was… This was one step beyond too much.

"I don't need an escort," she snarled.

"Fine." Cool, oh so cool, Agent Patrick was. Like nothing could scratch his surface.

She glared at him. He ignored her, pulling the car out of the parking lot. It was his rental, an economy compact, and handled like crap. She missed her own car. She missed driving herself. She had been fuming about it all day, even as she was smilingly pleasant to the customers.

"You are the most high-handed, overbearing, impossible, *insane* human being—"

"I told you—you're not going anywhere alone."

"I didn't need a driver. I don't need a guard. Bad enough you and Aggie have the boys wandering around my house…."

"*The boys,* is it?" She thought she heard jealousy in his voice, but decided that she was probably imagining things. "Lily, we don't have patrols assigned to your home on a whim."

"No, just a theory," she muttered, and was almost immediately ashamed of herself. It was a theory she agreed with, even if she didn't like the results.

He ignored her, and went on. "That bastard is still on the loose. He knows where you live, your name, he probably knows where you work by now, if he didn't before—you really want to give him a clear chance at you? Would you rather have a patrol car drive you everywhere?"

"I want to go to the shelter."

It was a ninety-degree turn in the conversation, but it made perfect sense to Lily. She had been away for over a week now, thanks to Patrick and Aggie's insistence, and she missed her cats. Ronnie had been updating her by e-mail on who was adopted, and what new cats had come in, but it wasn't the same. They needed her there. More, she needed to be there.

"Lily, you know why…."

"Yes. I know why. And yes, I want to stay out of this guy's sights more than you can believe. That's the only reason you've won chauffeur's rights. But I can't…"

She paused, and then decided to fight dirty.

"You don't understand. I was seven the first time it hit. This total, unrelenting, impossible-to-describe feeling." Even now, talking about it, she felt cold, even with the heat on in the car. "It wasn't fear, or discomfort, or the usual sort of phobic terror. Just…every inch of my body felt uneasy. Something was wrong, and something was coming at me, and I had no way to deal with it because I didn't even know what it was. I couldn't explain it to my parents. But I knew what triggered it."

Patrick made a sound that she took to mean "go on."

"Cats. They would walk into a room and stop and…*look* at me. That old saying, 'A cat may look at a king'? It doesn't mean what you think it means. It's not about a cat's rights…it's about their abilities. Their…. A cat looks at a king, and he doesn't see a member of royalty. He sees a human, in all its vain ego and uselessness."

She paused, feeling her mouth dry up in a way it hadn't for years. She swallowed anyway, and went on.

"A cat looks at you that way, and they see all the way through you. At first I thought that they were… that they didn't like me. But they kept coming to me after they looked at me like that. They would rub against me, and demand to be picked up and carried, and I *couldn't*. I couldn't hold them, touch them. After a while I couldn't even be near them. I couldn't bear to have them look at me. I used to cry the moment one of them came into the room. I wasn't allergic, I was *traumatized*."

"And now you work with them…?" He clearly didn't understand how that leap had happened, or why.

"I guess there's only so long you can let something like that rule your life. It took me a lot of therapy, a lot of talking myself up to it. I'm still not…entirely comfortable with cats outside the shelter, but when I'm here working with the kittens, or even the older cats, I can stand to have them look at me. It's okay. *I'm* okay."

She paused again.

"I need that right now. I need a sense of being okay. All right?"

There was a long silence from the driver's side, and even without looking she knew that she had him. What else could he do but give in?

"Okay. I'm going to regret this, but…okay." He turned the car into a strip-mall parking lot to turn around. The shelter was on the other side of town. "An hour, and you stay inside, and away from any visitors, and I'm with you at all times. All right?"

She smiled, just a little. "All right. Thank you."

The familiar facade of the shelter made a tightness she didn't even know was in her chest ease slightly. She walked through the door, Patrick a disapproving shadow on her heels, intending to go directly to the main office to say hello and let them know that she was there. But the moment she entered the lobby, the tightness in her chest came back like a metal fist squeezing tight, and she would have fallen to her knees if he hadn't been there to catch her.

"I'm making a habit of this," he said in her ear, the humor not masking his worry.

"Something's wrong. Something's…" She started to hyperventilate, each breath coming faster and faster until she felt as though she could never catch up with the air leaving her lungs. Weight crushed her rib cage, and sweat poured down her neck and the sides of her face. It was never like this, not even at its worst. This was…gods, the *anger* she felt! The outrage, and the snarling fear…

"Lily?" His voice was edging on panicked, and the fact of that gave her something to focus on. "Hey, anyone in there? I need some help!"

There was the rush of feet on the linoleum tile, and familiar hands on her. She should have been comforted, but instead she wanted to throw up.

Too much. Get them away from me. They'll see. They'll know. The guilt is all over me and I cannot bear it….

There was a howling in her ears, like a thousand sirens going off in a thunderstorm.

"Oh my God, what's going on?"

Lily came back to herself enough to realize, as some of the hands released her into a chair, that the howling came not from sirens but living throats. It was the full-bodied scream of an enraged cat. More than one, more than a dozen. It sounded as though every adult in the shelter was screaming at her.

Mother, I am sorry!

And then it stopped.

When Jon was able to focus again, he discovered that Lily had passed out in the chair.

"Damn it!" But even as he crouched over her and tried to remember what the protocol was for someone who had passed out, her eyes opened.

"Jesus."

He fell back onto his heels, staring. Her eyes—her lovely hazel eyes—had been completely swallowed up by pupil, until there was nothing left but inky blackness, looking back at him.

"Come on, Lily. Stay with me. How do you feel?" he said, touching her shoulder.

"I'm okay." She shook her head gently, as though testing her equilibrium. "I'm okay."

He would have argued that point, but his cell phone rang. Never taking his gaze off her, he answered. "Patrick. What? Are you sure? Where? I'll be right there."

He shut the phone with one hand, slipping it into his pocket while still keeping the other hand on Lily's shoulder.

"What is it?" Her voice was almost back to normal, but he didn't trust it. Not after the little scene he had just witnessed. And not the way her eyes still looked, all spooked and strange.

"Nothing. Just…you need to go…sit with the cats a little. They sounded as freaked as you looked."

"Jon. What?"

He looked into her weirdly black eyes, and was swallowed up by them.

"Jon?" Her voice dropped to a whisper, almost a purr. Soft. Seductive. "Tell me."

Sheer force of will brought him out of her eyes, allowing him to step back, literally and emotionally. *What the hell?*

But she was right; she deserved the truth. Even if he was going to have to sit on her afterward.

"That was Petrosian. Someone turned our unsub in, gave us a name. They want me down at the station, to go in after him."

"Let's go!" She struggled to get out of the chair, and he pushed her back down, gently. "Not you. Go get some cat therapy or have a cup of coffee or something."

"Patrick!" Her tone was outraged, and he couldn't help but smile. She was just adorable when she was pissed off, even more so than when she was trying to be a seductress. Seduction came naturally, in her every movement. He buried that thought, and tried to keep a stern face.

"Lily, you just had a major panic attack and collapsed. You're not going into a…" He looked at her, and lost track of his thoughts. Her eyes weren't back to normal yet, despite how she sounded and was acting. It was starting to really freak him out, all the more so because she seemed totally unaware of it.

"There might be cats there, Jon. Or… Whatever. You're going to need me. You do need me, otherwise you wouldn't have kept me around this long."

Damn it. Patrick wanted to send her home, if she wouldn't stay here. But she was right, if not for the reasons she thought. He stood and reached to give her a hand. "You'll stay in the car until the scene is cleared. And if you get dizzy, or anything—*anything*—gets weird, you tell me immediately. And the moment we're done, you're making an appointment with a doctor, because *something* is wrong. Deal?"

She grinned, triumphant. "Deal."

Chapter 13

He was restless, tired of waiting. Too many days of waiting, outside her home, outside her job. They never left her alone, and he did not want to approach her in front of others. She would hear him; they would not.

Now. Now, now now! His impatience practically danced on his shoulder.

Not yet.

But she's there. She's here. Right here.

And so is the man. And so are all those beasts. I will not go near that place; it stinks of Her. Now is not the right time. Not without proper preparation.

But she's never alone! Impatience wailed.

The voice was right; he could feel himself quiver with the need to reach her, talk to her. The cat woman. Time was short. Too short. He needed to know, *now*.

No more waiting. Everything was in place; all he needed was the woman.

If he could not go to her, then she would have to come to him.

They had gone directly from the shelter to the police station to meet with Petrosian, arguing all the while about what Lily called his overprotective machismo bullshit, and he called pragmatic protection of a material witness.

Lily didn't mince words. "I'm not a witness, material or otherwise. And you're a bully."

Jon smiled. "You're right."

"And you snore."

He nodded his head once. "Guilty as charged."

She glared at him, and he placed his hand low on her back, escorting her through the visitors' parking lot toward the building. "Lily, be honest with me. How many times in the past week have you been dizzy? How often have your pupils dilated like that? You swear you haven't hit your head or taken any sort of pharmaceutical, and I'm trusting you."

"Gee. Thanks."

"But I'm not going to let you do anything that might worsen whatever it is that's causing this."

"*Stress* is causing this, Agent Patrick. I told you. It started after I saw the kittens. It will end as soon as you nail this bastard. So let's go let you nail him."

It amused him; that they were already squabbling like a couple. But he had felt her muscles tense when he touched her, and he knew that no matter how light her tone might be, there was something she wasn't telling him. Something more than could be explained by the circumstances. And something *definitely* happened back there in the shelter. Not only her spell, but the reaction of the cats. When they calmed down, she calmed down. Or was it the other way around?

He'd get it out of her. Later. When he wasn't on the clock. For now, he had to think of the case, and only the case. Everything, everyone else, had to wait. Starting now. He took his worry about her condition and their chemistry, and everything even remotely Lily-shaped except for the potential of a connection between her and the Serpent, and put it into a box and closed the lid firmly.

"Jon, if you would just—"

"Lily, I told you—"

"Hey! Somebody grab that bastard!" A man's shout, annoyed but not really worried.

Patrick turned in the direction of the shout, only to feel something slug him in the chest, knocking the air out of him. He bent over, catching a glimpse out of the corner of his eye of a shadow looming over him.

"Grab him!" the voice yelled again. "Grab the son of a bitch!"

Patrick was more than willing to, as soon as he could stand up again. Then he heard another voice yelling, "Get off of me!"

Lily sounded more pissed off than scared, but instinct took over even as he was realizing that, and he had his gun out of its holster and was turning to aim at the figure clad in black jeans and hoodie. In work mode

Patrick's well-trained brain took in the instant basics: solid build, white, five-eight or so, shaking as if he had a bad case of the d.t.'s, but with a chokehold on Lily, his other hand snaking around to reach for the purse dangling from her left shoulder.

"Lily, down!" he yelled, unable to get a clear shot while she was struggling with their assailant. Damn it, damn it, damn it!

Instead of going down, she threw her head back, knocking hard against the man's face. The guy dropped her, and looked up to see a federal agent's gun aiming at him.

Kill him, something shouted in Patrick's brain. *He threatened her! Shoot him!* But a cooler, better-trained control remained, and his finger stayed on the safety, not the trigger.

The guy snarled, frustration contorting his pale, drawn-looking face into something barely human, and rushed him: a crazy movement, a desperate movement. At the last moment possible, Patrick flipped his grip so that the butt of the gun came into contact with the guy's head. Two blows were what it took to drop him, and Patrick made a mental note to give Lily half the credit for the collar.

Only then did he hear the sound of feet running on the pavement toward them, and shouting. Unmistakable, the sound of cops on the move.

"I got him, I got him, Jesus, the guy just freaked on us!"

Only then did Patrick notice that the man's hands were cuffed in front of him. That was what had hurt so much, when the guy nailed him.

"You should have gone peacefully into booking," he told the body at his feet, even as he holstered his gun and turned to check on Lily.

"We're making a bad habit of this sort of—Lily!"

She was still on her knees, blood flowing down the side of her face. "Lily?" He went to her, using his sleeve to blot the blood away.

"Bastard hit me!" She sounded so outraged, he almost laughed.

"He hit me, too," he said, feeling the blow all over again.

"Yeah, but…that's your job! Nobody hits me! How dare he! How dare he raise a hand to me!"

"Lily?" He hesitated. Anger was a normal-enough reaction to being mugged, but…her voice sounded… different. Strange. Thinner, more nasal. Had the guy broken her nose? Was she having a reaction to her earlier weirdness in the station? Jesus, he should have insisted that she go directly to the hospital, do not pass go, do not… He placed his hands gently on either side of her face, trying to get a better look at where the blood was coming from. The frission of pleasure that came from touching her was muted by the warm drip of blood. Scalp wound probably. But… "Lily, look at me."

She drew away, as though affronted. "Who are you? Where is My Lord? How dare you touch me?"

"What?" He gaped at her, and then looked over his shoulder. "Hey, someone, get a paramedic here, stat!" Two dozen cops and not one of them useful.

"Take this idiot inside and book him," he heard a

gruff voice say, and then the scuffle of their assailant being taken away.

"Moron." It wasn't clear if the cop was talking about the criminal or the cop who hadn't been able to control him. "Sorry about that. I swear, it was like he saw you guys and totally flipped out. Ambulance is already on the way. Check both of you out, make sure everything's okay."

"I'm fine," Patrick said. The guy had hit him hard with the metal bracelets, but nothing was broken or otherwise in need of taping up. He'd cracked enough ribs in his time to know what that felt like. "Lily…she got knocked in the head." All right, technically she had knocked her head into the prep. Not a useful distinction right now.

There was a siren and the heavy crunch of the ambulance; the EMTs wasted no time when the call came in from the police station.

"Oh God. God. What's…?" She was looking at her hands, flexing them, fingertips into her palms, shaking her head back and forth. "My fingers feel funny. They itch. And burn."

"Ma'am?" A paramedic squatted next to her, reaching out with a cautious hand to get Lily's attention.

"What's happening to me? Where am I? How dare he lay hands on me?"

The paramedic looked up at Patrick, who shrugged, feeling unutterably helpless. "The guy rushed us, grabbed her. She gave him a serious head butt…"

"That'll knock some confusion into ya, yeah. What's her name?"

"Lily. Lily Malkin."

"Ms. Malkin? We need to get that bleeding stopped, is that okay? We're going to take you to the hospital and patch you up, make sure everything's working okay. You good with that?"

"Jon?"

Her voice was soft, thin, and it hurt worse than the mugger's fist. But the box's lid held tight. He couldn't, wouldn't, give in. The clock was ticking, and the Serpent was still out there, waiting. Threatening.

"You go with him, Lily-kit. I'll go get this guy, and it'll all be over."

Lily didn't remember much about the trip to the hospital. A lot of questions, and fuzzy-outlined men in faded white uniforms, and sirens that made her skull want to shatter until she started to cry, and they made the driver turn it off.

Then they were there, and she was being unloaded into the E.R. It was surprisingly, blessedly quiet. Lily was stripped of her jeans and sweater, the items going wherever her coat had already disappeared to, and wrapped in a flimsy paper robe that barely wrapped around, but came down her knees.

It bothered her that she couldn't stop her fingers from curling and uncurling. A nervous twitch, and if the doctors saw it, they'd sedate her, try to keep her. Lily didn't mind doctors, but she didn't want to be here. Not now. Now with her brain all fuzzy and noisy, like a radio station picking up two different signals and only one speaker.

"Hush." The static gave her the finger, and continued. "Ms. Malkin?"

"Yes." She looked up to greet the doctor. He had a clipboard and an air of competence that she found reassuring, even if he did seem barely twenty.

"All right, let's take a look at you, shall we?" He stepped closer, and removed a light pen from his coat pocket. "Look up, please?"

Lily hesitated, and then looked up.

"Well…" He paused. "How's your vision?"

"Okay. The light's sort of weird, but no blurriness or blind spots." The paramedics had asked her the same thing.

"And you haven't…"

"Taken any drugs or alcohol, no." Telling him that her eyes had been doing that on and off all week probably wouldn't help her get out of there, so she didn't. And she hid her fingers in the flimsy paper cloth of her exam gown.

The doctor went ahead and checked her vitals, finding nothing particularly off kilter. Her reflexes were, in his words, fabulous, she didn't have a headache, and he didn't notice the way her fingers kept flexing. She didn't tell them about the ache in her fingertips, either.

"All right, let me go check up on your X-rays. I'll be right back."

She sat on the edge of the cot and waited, her legs swinging annoyingly in the air. Who designed these exam rooms, anyway, the Jolly Green Giant? God, while she waited here, who knew what was happening out there? What had Jon found?

A nurse walked by, and she reached out to grab at her sleeve. "Where's a phone?"

"Excuse me?"

Lily mimed picking up a receiver and dialing. "A phone?"

"There's one down the hallway…oh, no, it's broken." The nurse frowned. "You don't have a cell phone?"

"Never needed one," Lily said, cranky. Why did everyone assume everyone else felt the need to be in touch at all times? All she wanted was to make a simple phone call. And her purse was off somewhere with the rest of her belongings, she realized. The cops had taken it as evidence, or something. "Never mind. I don't have any change on me anyway."

"I'll tell you what. Let me get a chair, and we can let you use the phone at the desk. Okay?"

Lily tried to smile at the woman who was, after all, trying to help. They grabbed a wheelchair from the hallway and the nurse—Georgia, according to her name tag—pushed her to the nurses' station, where a quick conversation with the woman behind the desk got a heavy sigh and access to a phone.

Lily closed her eyes and tried to remember Jon's number. She usually had an excellent memory for numbers, but…there it was.

"This is Special Agent Jon T. Patrick. Leave your name, number and a brief message, and I will return your call as soon as I am able."

Lily put down the phone and thanked the nurses numbly. There were a lot of reasons why his phone wasn't picking up. He might be in a warehouse, or a basement. Somewhere a signal didn't get through. That happened, didn't it? Even to FBI-issue cell phones? No reason to assume anything was wrong.

"You okay, hon?" Georgia wasn't that much older than her, if at all, but her concern had a definite maternal feel to it, and suddenly Lily wanted to cry. Her own mother had died when she was a child, and while her father had loved her, he wasn't exactly the sort to use nicknames or endearments.

"Yeah. I just…" Just what? Was upset because her Fibbie wasn't answering his phone? That he was more concerned with the stats of his case than her well-being? He had shoved her off to the paramedics fast enough, not even letting a mugging slow him down.

Lily was angry but she wasn't sure why. At Jon, Special Agent Patrick, for thinking of the case before her? Or herself, for letting it matter? She had no claim on him, and he had no obligation to her.

"We need to get you back to the cubicle," Georgia said, turning the chair around and pushing Lily back to her cubicle. "Doctor will be here soon, not good to have him thinking you slipped out on him. Gives them complexes when that happens. Fragile egos, these doctors."

"Ah, there you are. Georgia, what have I told you about kidnapping our patients?"

Georgia helped Lily out of the chair and back onto the cot, not giving the doctor the benefit of a response. "You hang in there, hon."

"Thank you."

"So." The doctor consulted his clipboard, and then looked directly at her, as though he had already memorized everything he needed to say. "Your X-rays show nothing wrong. Your heart rate is elevated slightly, but nothing that is out of place for what you've been through. You have, as expected, a concussion. The pupil enlargement is worrying, but without anything setting off alarms…. I'm willing to release you so long as there is someone to drive you home and stay with you for the next twenty-four hours."

There was a dry cough from just outside the cubicle's heavy white curtains, where Officer Stephens was unapologetically, part-of-the-job-ma'am eavesdropping.

"I have a police escort," Lily said dryly. "I think I'm okay."

After the doctor ascertained that yes, Officer Stephens was there for the sole purpose of making sure she didn't fall down and go boom again, and would stay with her until a family member could arrive, he agreed to release her into the gentle care of Newfield's finest.

They brought her her clothing and drew the curtains for privacy. She managed to get re-dressed without too much difficulty, but her sweater snagged on a finger-nail and the threads dragged out, making her swear un-happily and without much enthusiasm. She had never been very good at cursing.

Lily finally got her shoes on and laced them up, then pushed the curtain aside to interrupt Stephens and the doctor still talking.

"I'll be right back." She was moving slow, but her feet were steady under her, the walls weren't doing the woobly thing again, and everything smelled and sounded normal. She made it to the phone at the nurses' station and looked at the woman behind the counter with the best pitiful expression she could manage.

It must have been pretty effective, because the desk-bound nurse just waved a hand at the phone as though to say "have at it."

She could recall the number easily now. But the result was the same: it went directly to voice mail.

She should have gone back to Stephens's custody, had him drive her home, taken the pills they were going to give her and settled in on her sofa with a blanket wrapped around her, surfing the TV. Maybe she'd order food and invite the boys in. It would be the least she could do.

Come to me.

Maybe she would have him stop on the way home and pick up a few movie rentals. Something to keep her mind off whatever was going on with Jon. Keep her from worrying about whatever was happening to her, which couldn't be anything because the doctors didn't find anything. Something to de-stress by. A romantic comedy maybe, or a Marx Brothers movie.

Come to me.

Lily shook her head, trying to dislodge the odd whisper she kept hearing. She just wanted to go home, that was all. Go home, and have Agent Patrick call her and say he'd gotten the guy, that he would never hurt another cat again, never call her house or break into another cattery. And then Agent Patrick would return to Washington, and she could get her life back under control.

Without conscious volition, Lily moved away from the nurses' desk, across the lobby to where a large picture window would have let in sunlight during the day. The hospital was built into part of a hill, so they were raised above ground level slightly, even though the E.R. was technically on the first floor.

She looked into the sky, noting that the moon was almost finished waning. The end of the week would be the new moon, when the sky would be lit only by the distant stars.

Come to me. I need you.

She looked down, as though searching for the source of the whisper. A half-moon driveway, with an ambulance waiting outside, and beyond that a parking lot, cast into shadows by the streetlights.

A smaller, more distinct shadow moved by the ambulance, catching her attention. A man, half hidden, looking up into the window.

Looking at *her.*

I need you. Come home.

She couldn't see his face at that distance. And yet, she knew it. Lean and regal, black hair oiled back off the high forehead, a hawk's nose and black eyes that saw everything and valued far less.

It looked nothing like the face in the drawing they had shown her. But she knew him. The Night Serpent.

And then she remembered. Everything.

Chapter 14

"Ms. Malkin?"

Lily turned to see Officer Stephens standing there, her coat and purse over his arm. "They just need you to sign some paperwork. I'll go get the car, okay?"

"Yes. Thank you."

She looked back, but the figure was gone. Had it even been there? She was operating on autopilot, her body moving and her mouth talking while her mind was somewhere else entirely. All the nightmares, the shadowed hallucinations, the voices, the strange unease and desires she felt...

All real. And impossible.

You are not who you are.

Impossible.

You are the Superior of the Guardians of the Children of Bastet.

Impossible.

And yet the memories flooded her, the solid pain each one brought proof that impossible did not mean unreal.

…Dancing in the gardens under Her approving eye…

…grooming a sleek spotted cat, its head resting trustingly on her bare forearm, the rumble of its purr a blessing from Herself…

…the appearance of a man in the temple, seeking wisdom and guidance…

…hushed conversations, avoiding the attentions of the beasts she had once catered to, guilt-stricken as she did what her lover asked of her, never asking why he asked, why she gave….

…the heat of her lover's gaze as he touched her…the heat of his gaze as he repudiated her, betrayed her, murdered her….

That thought stilled her.

Murdered. She had been murdered, the blood pooling on the cool stone floor, her body left for the temple beasts to discover.

Lily shuddered, feeling the information break over her, drowning her, even as her body left the hospital, got into the car, was driven away.

Murdered?

You betrayed them first. You gave Her secrets to an outsider. For what?

For love. The memory of a face again. Dark, intense eyes burning with need. Ambition.

For love unrequited. The need was not for you, but power. He used you for his own ambition. And you died for it. Died unjustified, cast off by the Mother and forbidden peace by all the gods...

Eight lives passed behind her eyes, all lived so much as this current one had been, with hesitation and uncertainty, alone and afraid... Each life a cycle of the same choices, the same failures, century after century. Never able to trust, to make the leap, to break the cycle. Always ending in failure.

Until this life. Until the day she moved to Newfield. The day she stepped inside the cat shelter, determined to overcome her fear. That had made the difference, she was certain of it.

There is something I'm supposed to do. Something important. But I don't know how. Or when.

Another dream-memory, recent this time. A lean, elegant tawny cat, its pelt covered with black spots, sitting in a classic temple pose. Pale olive-green eyes staring at her, the pupil growing larger and larger until she was about to fall into them.

"The Night Serpent." She spoke out loud without realizing it.

Stephens took his eyes off the road and looked at her. "Yeah?"

"He said...that I knew. That I could tell him... what?"

Her escort turned his attention back to the road. "Ms. Malkin, you can't think too hard about what crazy folk say. Leave that to people like Agent Patrick. He specializes in crazy."

Lily absorbed that. Yes. He did. And did that explain his fascination for her? Was she crazy, too? Was that why the Night Serpent found her, because they were both crazy together? Had they met before, in previous lives? The connection Jon had spoken about. Cat-scratch crazy.

It didn't make any sense, otherwise, all of it. Her life was quiet, contained. And now, suddenly, she was stalked, mugged, escorted by cops, having fabulous sex with a guy she'd only known a week....

And convinced that she'd lived another life before this one. A number of lives, actually. Eight, to be precise.

This was her ninth.

She was out of lives.

And she had no idea, still, what she was supposed to do.

Come home.

The Night Serpent knew.

"Hey."

"What?" She practically jumped out of her seat, held in place only by the seat belt.

Stephens was looking at her oddly. "We're here."

They had pulled onto her street without her even noticing. She struggled to control the things in her head, shoving them away so that she had time and room to think.

The cop saw her struggle, but misunderstood the cause. "The doc said he gave you a prescription for something for stress, help you relax. I forgot to ask if you wanted to drop it off at the drugstore to be filled—should we go back?"

Lily touched her shoulder bag almost reflexively, reassuring herself that the slip of paper was still in there. "No. I don't think so." It was tempting: take a pill, make everything go away. No more stress, no more hallucinations, no more weird freaky feelings or eyesight problems or feeling as if she was about to slide out of her own skin… Except it would still all be there. She just wouldn't care so much.

She had the feeling that it was important to care. It was important to remember.

"You sure? No offense, Ms. Malkin, but you look like you could use something, and I'm thinking you're not much for a knockback of whiskey."

She almost smiled at that. No, she wasn't much of a drinker, other than the occasional glass of wine or beer with dinner. She didn't think she even had any alcohol in the house, except for some cooking sherry.

But she said the only thing that he might understand. "I'd rather keep my head clear."

Stephens pulled into her driveway, hesitated, then turned to her without turning off the engine. "About five years ago. My partner and I were involved in a shooting downtown. Totally justified, I did everything by the book, but for a while I had the shakes pretty bad. Took time off, went on some meds the doctor suggested when things got too bad. I was scared it would screw with me, make me not able to do my job? But…it helped me do my job, on the bad days. I wasn't trying to second-guess what was a real doubt, and what was a stress-memory."

That hit home, quivering like an arrow thunking into flesh. She had never talked about that with her therapist, had never thought to ask. "How do you tell the difference? Between real and…stress?"

He shrugged. "You have to trust yourself. And accept that mistakes are gonna happen, but if they do, you're gonna take responsibility for them too."

"Yeah." Lily leaned her head back against the seat and closed her eyes, willing the quivering to go away. "That's always the trick, isn't it?" She shook her head, smiled and reached over to unhook her seat belt. "I'll think about it. That's all I can promise."

Stephens turned off the engine and got out of the car in time to help her out of her own seat. "And if all else fails," he said only half jokingly, "there's always whiskey."

She shook her head as he escorted her to the door.

"Thank you for the ride home. But you're off duty. You don't really have to…"

"Ms. Malkin. Even if I were willing to leave you alone after getting mugged in *our* parking lot, Detective Petrosian would have my—" he started to say one thing, and then switched midthought "—badge in a minute if I didn't make sure you were okay until Agent Patrick got here."

Her eyes narrowed, and the itch in her fingers came back with a vengeance. Even as she knew her anger was probably unwarranted, she let it come, relishing in the outrage. "Has this all been worked out then? That the helpless female has a keeper at all times?"

Stephens might not have been married, but he knew when he'd overstepped. He also knew his job. And nobody would ever fault his bravery.

"No, ma'am. But you have a concussion. If you want

to call a friend to stay with you instead, that's fine. But I will wait until they arrive."

Lily stared at him, his crew cut and square jaw making him look like a grown-up Cub Scout. She could call half a dozen people; she had people—not many, but Ronnie and Aggie—who would drop everything if they heard she had been injured and needed help. But if she did that, asked for help, they would assume she was worse off than she actually was, and they would never leave her be, after. Stephens, at least, knew the limits of the job.

And if Agent Patrick did show up? After abandoning her to the E.R., turning off his phone, ignoring her for hours? Too much. Too much to handle right now. They'd deal with that if and when it happened.

"Did you get anything to eat at the hospital? All I've got are leftovers, but we should be able to put together something reasonably healthy." She hung her coat in the closet and went into the kitchen. If he was going to play nanny, he could hang up his own coat.

"There's…brown rice and sesame chicken. Some salad. Half a parm—"

The radio at Stephens's hip squawked, and he tabbed it on, listening to whatever was being reported. Lily felt herself tense, the hand on the refrigerator door tightening until the knuckles turned white. Her fingertips tingled again, and she felt a faint burn, as though the skin was splitting under her nails.

Stephens came into the kitchen, and she forced herself to go back to inspecting the contents of the fridge. "What happened?" It wasn't Jon. It wasn't. She would not allow it to be….

"Shooting." Lily's gut tightened with cold fear until he continued, "Down by the Bridges." A series of inter-locked pedestrian walkways over the river, by the park. Not the best neighborhood. "Somebody took potshots at a patrol car." He shook his head, resigned but not worried. "Every now and again, the gene pool gets cleaned out."

"Idiots," she said in agreement, feeling her chest begin to expand and contract again. "So, you want—"

The doorbell rang.

"You expecting someone?" she asked Stephens. Maybe it was Dunkirk or one of the other cops on drive-by duty, stopping by for coffee. They didn't, as a rule, but you never knew....

He shook his head again, and motioned her to stand closer to the refrigerator. Stephens went to the door, right hand by his hip, near where his gun was hol-stered. He approached the door sideways, looking out the side window. The tension released, and he went to open the door.

"Agent Patrick."

"People who turn off their cell phones and don't call don't get any dinner," Lily sang out, suddenly feeling reckless. He was alive. He was safe. He was an utter bastard for abandoning her like that, casting her...

Casting her aside in order to focus on his job.

"You have no more use to me. They will never trust you again, once it is discovered what you did. But the man who brings the betrayer to justice, he will be rewarded beyond measure...."

Her lover's face, shadowed and cruel. She reached

for him, tried to touch him, to bring him back to her. Then there was a hot blow to her side, and a cold red haze crept over her eyes....

"No."

"Lily?" Jon was at her side, and she stared blankly at him. The man she had seen outside the hospital had looked nothing like the man suspected of being the Night Serpent. But his eyes, his face...

He looked an awful lot like one Jon T. Patrick.

Laughter—more than slightly hysterical—bubbled up inside her. Never say she didn't have a type....

"Lily?" Jon looked over his shoulder at Stephens, who was reaching for his coat, the very picture of a man getting the hell out of the way. Petrosian was behind him, closing the front door against the night chill.

"You didn't get him." She wasn't looking at him. What was wrong?

"No. But we found his lair."

"More dead cats?" Her voice sounded...flat. Monotone.

"No cats at all. No real ones, anyway. There was... Lily, are you all right?"

"Yes. I'm fine. The doctor said so."

Ow. Patrick winced. He had meant to get back to her, to meet her at the hospital, but the things they had discovered at the site had to be dealt with right away. Lily wanted the guy caught; she understood that had to be priority. Didn't she?

He sucked at relationships. He always had. And when had this suddenly become a relationship? What had happened to some fun sex with a lovely and willing woman?

And who the hell was he trying to kid? He would have laughed, except it would have gone down completely wrong, and possibly gotten him killed with a kitchen knife.

The words the cop had said in the parking lot came back to him. "It was like he saw you and flipped." The guy was a meth-head, fried and finished. Maybe he looked like an old teacher who'd flunked the guy, or Lily like an old girlfriend who dumped him. There was no way there was a connection between some random junkie and this case.

There was no way the Serpent had somehow lured them to the police station, set that guy on them, to harm Lily, to separate them. That was... Crazy.

"Sir?" Stephens beckoned to him and, with a worried look at Lily, who was busy pulling cartons out of the fridge, he went back to speak with the two cops. A quick update on what the doctor had said, and Lily's comments on the trip back to the house, caught Patrick up.

Something was wrong. Something was...crazy. Right now, he wasn't discounting anything, and he wasn't taking any more chances.

"Thanks. And thank you," he said to Stephens. "Go home and get some rest. We'll take over for tonight."

By the time he got back to the kitchen, Lily had a platter piled with an assortment of leftovers, and was placing it in the microwave.

"I assume you didn't have dinner."

"Or lunch," he said in agreement. "And I'm an ass."

"Yes. You are."

Her voice was still flat. He wanted to protect her, keep her safe. He also wanted to tell her what they had found, get her take on it. He wanted that lovely brain that went with the lovely body. But he didn't know where to begin, with this monosyllabic, quiet-voiced woman who was so clearly pissed at him. Somehow, he didn't think that running down to the quick-mart for flowers was going to do the trick.

The detective, having seen Stephens out the door, came back into the kitchen. "Hey, Aggie," she said in greeting, still in that monotone voice.

"Lily. You scared the hell out of me, girl."

Petrosian got a smile for that, and Patrick felt an unexpected pang of jealousy hit him. Jealousy, and anger—why did the older man get a smile, and he got the freeze-out? He had apologized….

Maybe flowers were the way to go. Not lilies, though.

The microwave went off, and the moment was lost. The next few minutes were an almost comfortable fuss of getting glasses, platter and plates to the table. But once everyone settled themselves with the food, he felt the awkward silence return.

It was a marked contrast to their first meal together, when he had actively pursued, and she had been cautiously amused. Now he felt as though he were walking on a minefield, and she…

He had no idea what she was right now.

"The doctor gave you a clean bill of health, Stephens

said." Her eyes looked normal, the few times she'd let him catch her gaze. She was twitchy, though: her fingers closed over her fork as though she wasn't quite sure how to hold it, and her head kept cocking to the side, as though she was listening for something.

"Yes. Physically, I'm fine. What did you find?" The question was directed to Petrosian.

The cop looked over at Patrick, and then shrugged. "Weird. I'm not any kind of expert on crazy, but this seemed pretty textbook. Empty—he'd skedaddled, probably just before we got there. But all his stuff was there. He was building some kind of archway, all draped in black. A couple of stuffed cats, the taxidermy kind of stuffed, the ones that are meant to look cute but are just creepy? Like he was using them as placeholders or something, moving them around until he was satisfied it looked right. And there was a statue, a cat statue, made of—get this—foam, and spray painted black, too. A bunch of symbols on the wall, chalked outlines, like he hadn't gotten around to filling them in yet."

"Symbols? You mean something satanic?"

"Not quite," Patrick said. "Hieroglyphics. Egyptian."

Her eyes flickered to him, and then back to Petrosian, but in that instant Patrick saw something in them, something that set him on edge, set off all of his alarms, both professional and personal.

Fear. No—terror.

Chapter 15

Lily excused herself to go use the bathroom. Once there, she rested her forehead against the closed door and let herself give in to the shudders.

Egyptian. Of course.

She couldn't deny it any longer. Whatever was happening, whatever had brought the Night Serpent to her town, and into her life…she was the cause. Or the catalyst. Or somehow responsible in a way she couldn't avoid.

She had to tell them.

"Oh sure, right," she said, hearing the near hysteria edging back into her voice. "This guy? He's here because of me. Only, not the me I was. Or something that's trying to get through, using me. I don't know what. But I have memories, and he thinks because of that I know something he needs.

"How does he know? What, do I look like I have the answers?

"Oh, and Agent Patrick? I don't trust you worth a damn, either. Except I don't have any choice but to trust you."

Hysteria. Definitely.

She splashed water on her face, dried it roughly to bring some color to her skin and stared at herself in the mirror.

Black hair. Hazel eyes. Skin more golden than pale. She had always thought that she looked like her father's side of the family, a mixture of Italian and Spanish. The snub nose and rounded chin were from her mother.

She didn't know what an Egyptian might look like. Mummies were all she knew about that country. Mummies, and pyramids, and things blowing up on the news, and…

Bast. Bastet. The cat-headed goddess.

She knew more about the goddess than she should. If she would only let herself completely remember.

But if she did, if she let the memories come back over her—where would Lily go?

That was the thought that terrified her.

Where would Lily go if she was someone else, as well?

By the time she came back, the guys had cleared the table, and the coffee machine had been started. Jon. It should have been nice, having someone feel so comfortable in her home. It wasn't.

Nothing felt nice right now.

The guys were sitting in the living room, photos spread out over the coffee table in front of them. The television was on, turned to the 11:00 p.m. news, the sound turned low. A reporter was standing in front of the Newfield Zoo. A follow-up to the break-in. Lily hoped that nobody got hurt—Jon hadn't told her. Jon—Agent Patrick—hadn't told her shit. She liked the sound of the swearword. Shit. She felt like saying it out loud, but didn't.

"We sent e-files to the office," Patrick was saying. "There are specialists they can work with to see if there's anything we're missing. But right now I'm building a case that this guy is fixated on ancient Egypt specifically for the cats."

"They were considered holy back then," Lily said, sitting down on the sofa next to her lover. She was still angry with him. But she wanted to be near him, too. "Killing a cat was considered murder, and families went into mourning when a pet died. They shaved their eyebrows."

"Really?" Petrosian raised his own shaggy brows.

"So he's killing them in front of a statue of a cat-headed goddess…and this one—" Jon pointed to one of the photos showing a close-up of a statue of a man with the head of a jackal "—that's Osiris, god of the underworld. He judged the dead, decided if—"

"That was Anubis," she corrected him.

"What?"

"Anubis. He weighed the soul against a feather. It had to balance before a soul could move on to its reward."

Jon looked at the photo, then back at her. "What happened if it didn't balance?"

Lily stared at the photos, but couldn't bring herself to answer.

Ma'at. The word came to her, a match lit in the darkness. Truth. Harmony. *Justice.*

But justice for whom? Was that what the Night Serpent was saying, that she should know? Was the Night Serpent there for her? To bring her to justice for a sin committed lifetimes ago?

Or was she the one who had to bring *him* into harmony? Impossible to know. Impossible, period. One thing she did know: he was looking for her. And that couldn't be good.

"All right." Lily came back to the conversation that had continued while she zoned. "So he's gone from killing cats to killing cats in a ritual manner, to killing and building an arch, and you think that he's invoking, or trying to reach, an Egyptian god or gods?"

"Short version—he's a nut."

Jon grimaced at Petrosian's summation, echoing Lily's comment days ago. "But he's a nut with a plan. And one that involves Lily somehow. Or he wants it to, or thinks it needs to. Whatever he's doing isn't working, and because of her connection with cats in the media's eyes, he's focusing on her as having the solution."

"He thinks I know what he's doing wrong." It wasn't a question, but Jon treated it that way.

"Probably. He seems to have a fixation on cats, so you're an authority figure in his eyes. 'She knows' he said—he thinks that you know what this goddess wants.

It makes sense—your skills with cats, and a female cat-headed god...."

Lily, frustrated, shook her head hard enough that her hair came out of her barrette. He was so close, but there was no way he could make the leap to the truth. Not without her telling him, and she couldn't. Not without coming across as a total crazy herself.

"Except that it sounds like he's claiming that she—Bast—is giving him information, that she told him to find me. That doesn't make any sense. She's associated with cats in a positive way, and he's killing them."

"I don't think he sees it that way," Jon said. "He was taking good care of them before they died. Food, shelter. None of them were abused or injured. And they trusted him enough to rest quietly while he cut their throats, without any kind of drugs or restraints."

Lily shivered, suddenly cold despite the heat coming up through the vents. That connection thing again that Jon had mentioned. They must think that this guy, the Night Serpent, was a cat talker, too. Connected to Bast, somehow. That was why the cats hadn't fought him, but laid down to die.

A connection. Another connection between them. The cats should be fighting him, not giving way. What had he done?

She stood and went into the kitchen to check on the coffee. It was ready, so she loaded up a tray with mugs, sugar, milk and the coffeepot, and—balancing it all carefully—went back into the living room. Petrosian stood and took it from her, obviously worried she was going to pass out again and drop his coffee on the floor.

Jon had gotten up and was pacing, thinking out loud and waving his hand as though lecturing. "He's not harming the cats, in his eyes. He's sacrificing them. Sending them on to…this cat-headed goddess—Bast? He wants something from her, her and this other god, Anubis or Osiris or whatever. But it's not working. He's starting to get desperate. And that's when we've got him. The moment he stops thinking and starts reacting."

"Patrick. No." Petrosian saw where that was heading.

"What?" Lily put her coffee down and stared at Jon. "What are you thinking?"

"You aren't gonna like it," Petrosian warned her. He clearly didn't, anyway.

Agent Patrick stopped in front of Lily, crouching in front of her. His dark eyes were shadowed; he hadn't been sleeping much, either. Not all of that was her fault. They had slept, after. For a little while.

"There weren't any cats at his last hiding spot," he said as though trying to convince her of something. "No cages, even. Just the setup, more elaborate than before. Larger. Like it was a taunt." His eyes met her, and she read the knowledge in them: they both knew that the call-in had been fake, that they had been meant to find that lair. Meant to have the knowledge. But only Lily knew why.

"He may still have his breeding queens, but the way his sacrifices have sped up, he thinks that he's running out of time. Or he's got a deadline of some kind," Patrick went on. "If so, he's screwed. The Serpent believes that he needs the cats to be of a certain age, and a specific color and pattern. He tried to steal some that fit the requirements, he's tried to adopt some, and he's been blocked at every end. That run at the zoo— he might have been crazy enough to try for a leopard or something, before the rent-a-cops showed up."

"If it was him," Petrosian objected. "We don't know that for certain."

"It was him," Lily said, not liking the cold feeling of certainty in her gut. "If he really thinks that he's reaching Bast, or touched by her, or whatever crazies believe, maybe he also believed that he could get his hands on a leopard or something without getting turned into dinner?"

"Or he wanted you to do it," Jon said, putting into words exactly what she didn't want to hear.

"Are you crazy?" Lily shook her head, denying it. "I'm just, okay, yeah, the cat lady." She hated the title even more now. "Those things? The great cats? They weigh more than I do, and have claws like dinner knifes, and—"

"They're cats," Petrosian said, reluctantly agreeing with Patrick. "Like that one you dealt with in the apartment complex."

"And I had half a dozen cops with guns backing me up. Anyway, an ocelot is *not* a tiger."

"And a house cat isn't an ocelot. But you did it. If this guy knows that… Maybe he didn't want you to do it, just to show him how. That could have been what he meant. He's stronger than you are, being a guy…." Agent Patrick was back in control, thinking out loud.

Lily felt ill. "They got them all back though, right? The cats?"

"What? Oh, yeah, all safe and sound, and they only lost a few antelope in the process." He tried for a reassuring smile. She didn't buy it, but appreciated the effort.

"Whatever he's been trying, it's not enough," she said. "You think that he went after a big cat, maybe thinking more would be more effective? He's afraid that he's not doing the right thing…."

"Or the sacrifice wasn't the right kind. Oh God, I hope he hasn't made that jump."

"Jump? What jump? Jump to what?" Lily wasn't quite sure she was following his thoughts, and she wasn't sure she wanted to, either, not with the look on his face.

"He thinks this guy's going to go after the cat lady next," Aggie said bluntly, his hound dog face looking even more mournful than usual. "Not just a person of interest—a part of his whacked out plan. Cat-headed goddess. Cat-talking woman. Guy said it himself; he thinks you know what he's supposed to be doing. Maybe if you can't explain it to him, you get to graduate to *being* the sacrifice."

She had been following him, then. She'd been afraid of that.

"To the Night Serpent, to his internal logic, it would make sense," Patrick said in his cool FBI-guy voice, as if it was all theory and happening to someone else.

It made sense to Lily, too. But for reasons other than Jon's crazy-person-thinks-like-that logic. If he knew what she…had been, then how much more useful a sacrifice she would be than cats, degraded over centuries from their temple origins.

He had already killed her at least once. What was one more?

"Either way, his fascination with you might be to our benefit." Patrick was still talking. "Especially if he's starting to speed up and panic."

"You want to use her as bait." Aggie was working up a good pissed-off.

"You used her already," Patrick retorted, not denying the accusation. "You brought her into this, not me. You're the one who got her into the media's eye!" The FBI voice was gone, stripped down to…fear?

"Hey!" Lily's shout cut into whatever Aggie was going to respond. "I'm here. I'm not a chunk of meat to be fought over by two chest-thumping male apes. Okay?"

"She's already bait," Jon said more quietly, almost under control again. "The media made sure of that. Or have you forgotten why your men are patrolling the area?"

Petrosian glared, but had no comeback.

"Your food's getting cold, Aggie," Lily said quietly. "Eat."

He picked up his fork, and then pointed it at her. "You don't have to agree to his schemes, Lily. I'm not going to carry around guilt for bringing him in if you do anything stupid."

"I'm not going to agree to anything stupid," she told him. "But he's right. The Night Serpent wants to talk to me. If we can use that to catch him… I have a responsibility to do it." It was her way out; she could do what she needed to do, and not have to risk telling them anything. She didn't have to risk Jon looking at her, not with sexual interest, but professional curiosity: one of the crazy people. Something to use.

Or, if he was going to use her, let it be on her terms. This time she would get something out of it, for herself. No more being a tool to be discarded the moment the job was done.

Not that she really believed she had lived previous lives. That was…insane. But something was happening. And she had a responsibility because of it. Or despite it. She could stop any more cats from being killed if they caught this guy. And if Jon's theory was right, maybe stop any people from ever getting killed.

Including herself. Again.

"Not without backup," Aggie was saying, having accepted that she was serious. "I'll have the department—"

"And I'll be able to call an official backup for this. Plus, we can use the media…" Jon started to say.

She held up a hand to stop their words. "I don't care. You figure something out. I'll do it. For now, I've had a really long day, the painkillers are wearing off, and I'm going to bed. Aggie, I'll see you tomorrow. Jon, either lock up before or after yourself, your call. Good night."

She woke up three times to darkness, her breath gasping, and cold sweat pooling between her shoulder blades and the backs of her knees.

The third time there was a warm presence next to her, solid and reassuring, even as he hogged most of the blankets. She had heard him in the living room, talking on his cell to someone back in D.C., when exhaustion finally claimed her. Apparently even Fibbie endurance had its limits. She curled on her side, facing her lover, and reached out to touch the shadowed skin of his shoulder.

Shadows. So many shadows, inside and out. Her mind was not letting her rest, unable to let go of the questions there were no answers for. As usual, she did not remember her nightmares, but the shadows remained, along with the image of a cat watching her. Asking the impossible of her. She woke each time asking the same things, over and over again.

Who was the Night Serpent? A deranged man playing out some sick fantasy of power that made sense only to himself? Or was he…

She skirted around the thought, but was unable to avoid it entirely.

Or was he the reincarnation of an ancient Egyptian, a man of high status, who used and cast aside people on his quest for more and more power? A murderer, without conscience or guilt?

Or…her mind skittered further from the thought, until she held it down firmly and faced it. The fact that the man in her visions, the man she saw outside the hospital, looked nothing at all like the man suspected of being the Night Serpent. And everything like one Special Agent Jon T. Patrick. A man of passion and conviction…and self-admitted ambition. A man who, though regretful, would use his lover to achieve his goal.

She let her hand rest on his shoulder, fingers curling

into his neck until her claws cut gently into the flesh, and he stirred in sleepy protest.

Could she trust him? Even if she was wrong, and he was an innocent bystander…could she trust him?

Only as she was drifting off to sleep did she suddenly realize that, although the room had been cast in darkness, she had been able to see perfectly in the faint moonlight.

Cat's eyes.

Finally, she thought, too tired and worn-down to be alarmed. Something *useful.*

Chapter 16

"The moon's almost gone," she said, looking up into the early-morning sky. The sun was still below the horizon, and the sliver of moon still held on to the pale blue expanse. Jon came behind her, wrapping his arms around her and looking out the window over her shoulder.

"The full moon is traditionally a time of higher activity for abnormal behaviors," he said, his voice muffled by the tangle of her hair.

"Not this time," she said. "The dark of the moon is what he's waiting for."

Jon's arms tightened around her slightly. "How do you know?"

"I don't know. Maybe you're right, and there is a connection between us. I…" She wanted to tell him.

She truly did. But the resemblance between him and the man in her visions was too close, too unnerving. He was fond of her, he maybe even had real feelings for her. But the woman in her not-memories had thought her lover was true, too, and had been wrong.

Lily wasn't brave enough to risk it. She only had so much courage, and what she was about to do was using every drop of it.

"I just feel that we don't have a lot of time," she said finally.

"We don't. It's been a week since his last scene. He's been escalating, building up steam, and a week is about as long as he can do without erupting now. Especially since he's refocusing on you. If he's running to pattern, he's working himself up to something, something major. Are you sure you're ready for this?"

"No. But I'm going to do it anyway."

They hadn't come up with a plan so much as a plan had come up and slapped them in the face. The day after agreeing to let her play bait, Aggie came over for dinner, and they had a brainstorming session. The TV was playing in the other room, and Lily's attention was caught by the tail end of a follow-up to the break-in at the zoo.

"The break-in was, according to officials, a professional job, and not the work, as was previously suggested, of teenagers, similar to the rash of break-ins last summer. Last night a privately owned animal park was also hit and several animals were stolen. Officials speculate that they were taken by black marketers, to be sold to so-called big-game hunters to become 'easy' trophies. From the Newfield Zoo, this is Alissa Kent, for Channel 3 News."

"Thank you, Alissa. Terrible news, just terrible. And now for the weather…"

"I never knew we had that many animal parks in town. I—" Lily stopped, looking suddenly at Jon. He had the same expression she was probably wearing: dawning, horrified suspicion. Jumping. Escalating. The killer was escalating.

Petrosian was already dialing by the time Jon reached for his cell phone.

"What do you mean you don't know what was taken? Get the damn report and check!"

"It was him. He took their cats. At least one, probably more."

"We don't know for certain…." Petrosian began, then held up a finger as whomever he had been yelling at came back with the report. "Shit. Yeah. All right, yeah. Thanks. You do that."

He closed the phone and looked at them, his heavy eyes mournful. "They had a breeding pair of cheetahs. The male's missing."

A day later, Lily had found herself in the overly warm studio of the local news show, being interviewed by a perky reporter trying for her best serious face while clearly thinking that this was nothing more than a publicity puff piece. The segment had aired this morning. They had been waiting ever since.

"Anyone want another donut?" The feds had shown up at the crack of dawn, bearing cases of electronics and serious expressions. Aggie had arrived an hour later bearing a box from Dunkin' Donuts. So far, all Lily had been able to stomach was a strawberry-filled donut and three cups of coffee. A bowl of vegetable soup sat in front of her, cooling, but she hadn't done more than poke the spoon at it.

The phone rang.

Lily froze, looking at the machine as though she had never seen it before. It was him. She knew it, the way she had known him outside the hospital. It was him, and she had no idea what to do. She wanted to run, hide, pretend that she had never come to this town, never walked into the shelter....

"Lily-kit, it's okay. We're here."

"We" in this case was Patrick, Aggie, a very young-looking woman named Abigail who was handling the tech and an older Asian man they called Abraham, although she wasn't sure if that was his first name, last name or nickname. The FBI had come through, although she got the feeling that Abraham at least thought it was all a waste of time.

"Lily. Showtime."

She nodded, picked up the phone. "Hello?"

"You know."

The reporter was wearing a dark pink sweater that made her complexion look sallow. They should have put her in something with more blue. "Do you think that the person who stole the cheetah intends to keep it as a pet, the way the ocelot you rescued last year was?"

"Oh, I hope not." Lily had done her best wide-eyed expression at the camera. "Big cats aren't the same at all as these little fellows," and she had cuddled a small spotted cat on her lap. Jon had told her to pick a tabby,

but she knew what would push the Night Serpent's buttons. The temple cats were spotted, but not tabbies. She had specifically requested a Mau, an Egyptian breed. They had to bring one in from a breeder in New Hampshire. Had there been one closer... Had there been one closer, they would all be dead now. "No more than, oh, a fighter jet is the same as a Cessna two-seater. One's fun and dangerous if you're not careful—the other...well, I've never flown a fighter jet, but I can imagine there are a lot more ways you can kill yourself faster than in a little passenger plane."

Jon and Abraham had put together a script for her to follow when the Night Serpent called. But it didn't feel right in her mouth.

She could hear him breathing on the other end of the line. The sounds in the room around her hushed the moment she picked up the phone, faded into nothingness. "I know a lot of things," she said, instead of what the script in front of her suggested. "What do you need from me?"

"The key. I need to know how to turn the key. Everything is ready, but it has to be tonight. It's my last chance. You know how to make everything go right."

Selfish, she thought. *Always selfish. Why hadn't she seen that before?* Then: *Tonight. The new moon. She had been right.*

"Why should I help you? What's in it for me?"

There was silence, as though he had never considered the question before. She was off-script in oh so many ways, but the men in the room couldn't interrupt her, not without giving the game away. *She* was in

control here. She was the one calling the shots, directing the action.

"She says…" The Night Serpent's voice faded out,
then came back more strongly. He had a nice voice, if
a little too…narrow for her taste. His vowels were thin,
not rounded. Odd, the things you noticed.

"What does She say?" Lily put capitals into the
word, the same way he had.

"She says you know. You know. You have to tell me!
I can't stay here any longer. Tonight, it's my last chance.
The last chance there will ever be. I have to get it right."

"I'll trade you," she said, finally going back on-
script, to the palpable relief of the others in the room.
"I'll tell you what I know…and you give me back what
you took. *Unharmed.*"

There was a silence. "I need…"

"You won't," she said as persuasively as she could.
He was not going to kill another beast. Not one more.
"Not once I tell you what I know."

Another silence, the weight of his decision hanging
over them.

"All right."

"Where are you? I'll need to show you… You have
to have everything just right." It was a risk, but based
on his use of a specific pattern and the elaborate prep-
arations of his last hiding spot, Jon thought that he
would respond well to the suggestion of a ceremony or
set-dressing that needed to be done.

The Serpent gave her directions. She didn't know the
area, somewhere out of town proper, but Abraham
nodded as though it made perfect sense to him.

"Be there. An hour."

And then he hung up.

"Wasn't he supposed to say 'and come alone'?" Lily wondered, as much to break the grip the tension had on her as to actually wonder.

"He's too focused on himself, his own needs," Jon said as Abigail gave Abraham a thumbs-up, indicating whatever they were doing with the tech had worked.

"Selfish," Lily said, this time out loud. "He's always been selfish."

Her lover gave her an odd look, but continued, "Anyway, they only really say that on television shows. Real criminals know that only an idiot goes in alone, without backup."

"Ms. Malkin?" Abraham approached them. "If we're to be there on time, we need to get moving. You will drive your car. We will follow at a distance. Try to keep us in your rearview mirror at all times, but don't be too concerned if we disappear—we will have you on display at all times."

"Display?"

"We put a tracker in the vest and on your car," Jon said. "Just in case we get separated by traffic."

"Oh." She thought a moment. "You'll take it out again, after."

"We have to account for every bug and bite at the end of every mission," Abraham assured her with a perfectly straight face. He might have been kidding. She didn't think that he was.

The technician packed up her stuff, and Abraham and Jon went into a huddle off in the corner.

Aggie, who had been watching silently, came up and put a heavy hand on her shoulder. His other hand reached into his pocket and came out with what looked like a small cell phone.

"Take this."

She did, turning it over in her hands.

"If anything goes wrong, or even feels like it's going to go wrong, you just press this button here, the green one, and you'll have half a dozen very cranky cops attached to your hip, k? Don't you wait on those federal nitwits."

He didn't like this; his feelings were clear on his face and in his voice. But he was going to put on a good, confident show for her. She couldn't do anything less for him.

"I got it, Aggie. Let's do this thing." She tried to put a swagger into her voice that she wasn't feeling at all, and gave a twisted grin in return before the agents came back with a tangle of wires and microphones to attach to her, and Aggie stepped into the background.

Abraham had told her to park at the far end of the lot, away from the other cars and most of the lights. She pulled into a slot and turned off the engine, and an SUV with tinted windows came up beside her.

Five minutes later she had been surrounded by half a dozen federal agents, having her jacket taken off and the electronics that had been attached to her double- and triple-checked, and adjusting the fit of the bulletproof vest under her jacket. They didn't think he would shoot her, they assured her; it was standard operating proce-dure, sending anyone into a potentially dangerous situation. Plus, they still weren't sure what he had used on the guards.

"I really don't like this thing," she said, tugging at the confining weight of the vest.

"Leave it alone," Jon said as he elbowed aside the last tech and adjusted her shirt with almost impersonal hands, letting his fingers linger a bit longer than might be normal at her waist. His touch was loving, but his voice was, barely, all business. "Just forget it's there, go in and get him talking. All we need is for you to engage him, get him to tell us where he has the cat. We can't risk it getting loose once we have him."

Lily nodded. It could have been worse. A tiger, for example. But any big cat was dangerous, if injured, or hungry or frightened. And in the hands of a half-mad, untrained psychopath? It was a disaster waiting to happen. And she was walking right into the den, so to speak.

He couldn't fiddle any longer, and sighed, stepping away. "It would be simpler to just go in there and take him out. I could have gotten a sniper in position…"

"He's not worth a sniper," Lily said, echoing Abraham's decision. "And you need him alive."

She wasn't just talking about the bureau. Jon needed this guy, too. He needed to talk to him, study him. Add that information to how he worked. And, not incidentally, justify his decision to go through all of this to catch him. The feds didn't need to be involved in all this, the state and city police had made that very clear. But Special Agent Patrick had put his fingerprints all over

the case, and now he had his own people running
the show.

His reputation was on the line.

She had never been important to anyone before.

*Yes, you have. And been discarded once you were no
longer useful.*

It was different now. Jon Patrick was ambitious, but
not a user. He would not abandon her. She had to
believe that, or she'd never be able to walk in there.

"Piece of cake, right?" She gave him what she hoped
was a reassuring smile, picked up her purse, and walked
away from him and into the restaurant.

A well-dressed and very handsome young man met
her the moment she walked in the door. "Good afternoon. Do you have a reservation?"

"I'm…supposed to meet someone at the bar."

"Of course. This way, please."

It was a nice place. Out of the way, but pretty, and
the air smelled of—she sniffed the air, lifting her chin
slightly as she did so—it smelled of steak, and fresh
herbs, and the tang of wine and spirits.

She suddenly, badly, wanted a drink.

"Can I help you?" the bartender asked. He was also
very handsome, if not so well dressed.

"Ginger ale, please?"

The one thing she wasn't going to have was alcohol.
Not until they had this guy, and she was home, and she
decided right then and there that as soon as this was all
done and settled, she was going to go down to the shelter
and adopt a kitten. A gray one. Or maybe one of the
tigers.

She felt the cool plastic of the receiver hidden in her collar. They could hear her, and she could hear Jon if he flipped a toggle or some high-tech variation. The weight of the vest was like a tether to the earth, convincing her that this wasn't all simply some strange hallucination.

She reached into her pocket and felt the cell phone Aggie had given her.

She left it in her pocket. She wouldn't need it. Everything was going to be fine.

Her ginger ale came and she paid for it, idly twirling the straw to make the ice sink and then rise up again. Was she supposed to ask if there was a reservation under her name? Or maybe Serpent, table for two?

Or would it be more accurate to say it was a table for four?

"Lily Malkin."

She turned at the voice, and was greeted by a pleasantly bland young man with an open, friendly expression on his face. She started to open her mouth to say that yes, she was Lily, when the gentle blue eyes shaded dark, narrowed, his entire face becoming harder, more predatory.

The man from the shadows.

The man who had haunted her un-dreams.

Her lover.

Her killer.

"Lily." Jon's voice in her ear. "Lily, is it him? Give us some info!"

The man in front of her raised his hand, drawing her attention away from the facial overlay. Something dangled from his fingers, a dull clay-red and ugly and—

Lily swayed, trapped by the amulet in his hand. Her gaze narrowed, and her vision grayed to black.

"Lily!" Jon's voice in her ear, unheard. "Lily, talk to me!"

Chapter 17

Lily opened her eyes to a gray haze and aching muscles. She lay very still and tried to remember. Walking into the restaurant, ordering a drink. A man, approaching her. And then…nothing.

As her vision cleared, she realized that she was lying on her back, staring up at a featureless gray ceiling. No, not quite featureless. It had a texture to it that was almost familiar….

Concrete. The ceiling was made of concrete?

She turned her head to the right, and noted that the wall was made of concrete as well. No windows. No lights, except one dim lightbulb hung high up on the ceiling.

The room was, in fact, almost pitch-black. But she could see. Not quite as clear as day, but well enough.

"Your pupils are dilated again," she said. "You're using whatever light is available, like a cat...." Like a cat. Her eyes, dilating. Her fingers, flexing as though she was kneading, displaying claws. Her ears, hearing things she could not possibly hear. *I'm losing my mind....*

She almost convinced herself that she imagined the noise that followed her vocalizing. Her body froze in place, apprehension crawling all over her skin. There was another, similar noise, and Lily moved her head slowly, slowly on the cold—concrete again—floor, forcing herself to look to the left.

One look, and she sprang backward, sliding to her right—or she tried to, until the cold metal cuff around her wrist reached the end of the chain that was bolted to the floor, halting her progress.

What the hell?

The black-rimmed eyes of the great cat lying next to her watched her curiously, as though wondering what strange thing the hairless kitten would do next.

She was chained to the floor. She was—her brain starting to kick in slowly—stripped down to her underwear and bra, and chained to the floor of a windowless room. Made of concrete. *Cold* concrete. Next to a very large, very-much-not-a-moggy feline.

It blinked, the pale green eyes alert, but the pose unthreatening. A long, narrow tail flicked once, thumping down on the floor, but otherwise the cat didn't move from its side-sprawled pose next to her.

Literally—even after her attempted bolt, there was barely a foot between the two of them. The cat was grayed out in the non-light, but she could see well enough to tell that it was not quite as long, paw to ears, as she was tall, with lean muscle and a sleek build to go with that lazy tail. A surprisingly small, almost triangular head. Huge paws, with claws that would glint under a desert sun.

And it, unlike herself, was not chained or tied to anything.

"Oh God." Lily forced herself to start breathing again, and slowly blinked her eyes at it, the way she would a cat in the shelter she was trying to reassure. She had no idea if the gesture would work with a great cat.

It made that noise again. Not a purr, or a meow, or a roar. More like a chirp, like you would expect to hear from something the size of a groundhog, not a big cat. Almost as though…it was saying hello.

It seemed rude not to respond.

"Kurr, kurr," she ventured, hoping she wasn't actually saying, "Hello, come eat me while I'm chained up here and you're not."

It chirruped at her again, still watching with deceptive laziness, its eyes closing and opening slowly the same way hers had. A cheetah, her memory told her. The great hunting cat of the desert. The royal cat of the pharaohs.

The cheetah from the zoo. They had been right. Fat lot of good it did them now.

"You deserve better than this, swift one," she told it.

A grinding noise drew both their attention: a door was opening in the far wall. Light from outside came in, making Lily squint in pain.

"You brought others with you," he said in accusation. "You were wearing police gear. A wire."

The Night Serpent; backlit, she couldn't see his face. A haze surrounded him, making it difficult to focus. She didn't need to. She had known his face once better than she knew her own. Dark, handsome. Like Jon. But nothing like him.

"You didn't say to come alone." A joke, she wasn't sure how she managed it.

The foot that hit her ribs was a shock, and the cat growled but didn't move.

"You can eat him if you want," she said to the cat, refusing to let the man see her in pain. She didn't know where these wisecracks were coming from; it wasn't like her to mouth off. But it wasn't like her to be stalked by a lunatic, to become an FBI-approved piece of bait, to be drugged and stripped and chained to a *floor,* either. She was, she discovered, royally *pissed.* She glared up at her captor. "Or was that what he was supposed to do to me? Eat me?" How hungry did a cheetah have to be to make human flesh smell good?

He shrugged, less indifferent than refusing responsibility. "If the beast harms you, it is Her will."

A voice came out of her throat, her jaws moving, but not her words. "She cast me off long ago. Your doing."

A blade, a dark shadow, a searing cold pain in her side… Nothing compared to the pain of Her eyes turning away, refusing her….

Lily forced the memory down. She could not afford this, not now. Whatever was happening, she had to keep her mind clear. No confusion, no dizziness, no anything other than logical, rational thinking.

He came forward, allowing her night vision to see

him more clearly, but the haze remained. It wasn't a trick of the light, but rather her vision. The flesh was ordinary: a man of regular build, shaggy blond hair and mild features. Underneath, or over: the man she remembered in her nightmares. The face she saw outside the hospital, then again in the restaurant. The man from her past, her very first past. Had he been there in the others, too? The times between, where nothing had gone right, dooming her to repeat, over and over again…

"She cast us both off," he said. "Promised us everything, and delivered nothing. The power you gave me, it should have taken me to the next level, given me the abilities I craved, the abilities *you* have."

"You deserved nothing!"

His leg swung out again, crashing into her ribs. "All I needed was to turn the key in the lock you provided. All power and glory would have been mine then, with Her power at my disposal. But the key would not turn!"

The pain allowed the memories to sweep back over her, filling the spaces in her brain. "And they found you," she gasped, glaring at him. "Found what you had done. And you were judged…and found wanting."

"They stripped me of my status. Cast me out, cast me from power."

"They didn't kill you. A mercy you didn't show to me."

It was insane. Lily knew it, even as the words came out of her mouth. Talking to this man as if they were entirely different people.

She was Lily Malkin, damn it. She was an American.

She lived in the twenty-first century. She was a bank teller, for God's sake! She was not an ancient Egyptian priestess of some cat-headed god she didn't even believe in. And he was not an Egyptian high-caste noble with a thirst for power that overrode all other considerations and morals. It was impossible.

She would not accept it. She would *not*.

"You will tell me what I need to do. This time the key will turn, and I will be able to call forth the powers of the underworld. Be as one with the gods."

Real or unreal, both bank teller and priestess spoke with one unified voice: "You're insane."

He smiled at her. "Yes. Of course I am."

Lily blinked. *Oh.*

He spoke a word that resonated of command, and the cat rose to its feet slowly, almost as though moving against its will. "You see, it would love to attack me. It would love to rend me apart. And yet it cannot. I spent the years since awakening attaining the charm that protects me from claws and teeth." He touched his chest, and she saw a thin silver chain around his neck, dropping down below the collar of his shirt. The same thing he had used to—distract? Hypnotize? *Control* her, back in the bar. "She hungers for worship, in this cold world…but Her beasts do not trust me."

"Imagine that," Lily said dryly. He bent and tugged on the chain at her wrist. It came free from the floor with a flicker of sparks, and Lily tensed, wondering if she could rush him, knock him over….

Her ribs twinged where he had kicked her, and she relaxed her muscles. Even if she could take him by surprise, all he had to do was release the control he had over the cheetah, and she'd have about as much chance as a wounded gazelle of escaping. And where would she go, half-naked and shoeless? She didn't even know where they were, or how long…

Jon. How long had she been missing? Why hadn't he found her yet? Damn it, what use was backup if they didn't back you up?

Lily eyed the chain that now rested in his grip. "I have no idea what the key is, or how to turn it. She lied to you. She will not give you anything." The gods did not share, willingly or otherwise.

"She never lies. You know how to make Her lock turn. You just don't remember that you know. Yet. Get up." He yanked on the chain, and she had no choice but to obey.

They made an odd little parade: the cheetah walking ahead of them, tail slung low, ears flicking first forward then back as it led the way along the narrow hallway, then the Night Serpent, looking like a refugee from the suburbs in his khakis and button-down shirt, leading a half-naked woman by the arm—by means of a foot-long metal chain.

She was cold. Wherever they were, there wasn't much by way of heating. The floor was smooth and cool under the soles of her feet, and goose bumps were rising on her arms and legs.

Jon. Agent Patrick. Where the hell are you?

There was no answer. Fine. She was on her own. She always had been, really.

Inside, in some deep shadowy recess of her soul, something stirred and stretched, restless.

* * *

"Damn it, what do you mean you can't get a signal?"

Jon was ready to rip some hair out. His own, another's, he didn't much care. The moment Lily had walked into that damn restaurant the entire plan had gone to hell and it kept getting worse.

"Tell me again how a woman disappears from a restaurant with only thee exits, all of which were *supposed* to be watched by trained officers? Tell me again how the newest equipment we have can't track the woman who disappeared from that supposedly secured and observed location? And tell me—"

"Sir, if you would calm down…"

"Don't sir me. Just get me a signal."

He stalked off, leaving the small bustle behind as he stood under a tree, looking up at the sparse brown leaves without seeing them.

Nobody had taken this seriously enough. Not even him. Oh, he had taken the Night Serpent seriously enough—another data point for his charts, another example to build his theories around…another step up the agency ladder. Another career milestone.

But not as a threat. He hadn't considered the man enough of a threat. Not a deadly one. Not one he, in his ego, couldn't counter, just by being smarter, better prepared. His ego had put Lily in this situation. His arrogance had put her directly in the worst possible situation.

He turned away from the others and slammed his hand into the side of the tree. The pain didn't help.

Where are you, Lily? Help me find you….

* * *

They walked up a flight of stairs, and the floor changed from concrete to rough carpeting, like you might find in a low-end office building. A fire door swung open under the Serpent's hand, and Lily walked through into another room. This one was larger, with a skylight that let in faint sunlight.

Morning. She had been in that room overnight. The good guys weren't coming.

There was an arch against the far wall, made out of what looked like foam plastic, spray painted black, just like his last one. It was probably twice as tall as she was, and wide enough that she could have walked through it with her arms outstretched—assuming that she was then willing to walk into the wall it was leaning against. Directly in front of the arch was a large step, maybe five feet long, and draped in a black cloth.

Lily felt her gorge rise. It was the storefront all over again, only on a larger scale. And instead of seven house cats, he had one big cat to sacrifice. And he would make her watch, she had no doubt about that. And then she would follow, if—when—that didn't work. Would his…whatever he had that kept the cat obedient, would it have worked on more than one? She didn't think so. It was almost a shame he didn't take the pair, then.

"Beast. Sit. There."

The cat walked to the step and dropped his haunches, curling his paws under him and watching the man with an unblinking gaze.

"And you. Must I rechain you, or will you behave?"

"What am I going to do, make a break for it?" She looked down at herself, then back at him.

"Good. You have nothing to gain from fighting me. And you would lose. Again."

Lily sank against the wall, as far from the arch as she could get, drew her knees up and wrapped her arms around them. She was alone. She had no wires. No bulletproof vest. No cell phone with panic button. No… She made a noise that could have been a cry or a snort of laughter. No pants.

The Night Serpent was drawing a circle on the floor with red chalk. There were sigils along the circle. Seven of them. Something in Lily's memory—no, not her memory, that *other* memory—stirred, recognizing it, but she refused to allow it to rise into awareness. It didn't matter. None of it mattered. And even if it mattered, what could she do? The spark that had allowed her to talk back to the Night Serpent had gone as quickly as it appeared, leaving her cold and empty.

She had failed. Whatever madness the madman wanted, he would get.

The circle completed around the steps, he stood on one of the sigils—*Ren,* her other-memory told her. *Name.*

Sekhem. Energy of the dead.

Ab. Mother's heart.

Akh. The immortal aspect.

Ba. Personality.

Ka. Life force.

Sheut. Soul-shadow.

The seven sigils. The seven cats. The seven parts of

the human soul. *Sekhu. The physical remains. The Serpent himself.*

What was he doing?

Another memory crawled upward. Doors. Great heavy sliding doors, sealed with the touch of the Protectress, the fierce Lady of Flame, the goddess Bast. *Bastet. Lady Mother.*

The seven parts of the human soul. The parts of death. The doors to the underworld. Turn a key. Open a door. The words he had spoken rattled around in her head, fluttered delicate wings in her brain.

He wanted to open the doors to the underworld, to travel the paths of the dead. He was looking to reclaim the life that those shortsighted, hidebound fools had taken from him. A way to go back and exact revenge.

Impossible. She raised her gaze to the ceiling, as though expecting something to appear. Wasn't it?

He did not think so. He thought it was possible. The prickling of her skin told her that she—some part of her—thought it was, too.

The cat stirred, restless, clearly not wanting to remain passive. The Serpent—she could think of him no other way now, clearly seeing in his movements the relentless, almost hypnotic movements of a cobra—touched his amulet, and the cat stilled. The light glinted on his knife. Another life, another glorious, innocent life, sacrificed to his ego. His hunger.

"I'm sorry, beautiful one," she said to the cat, barely a whisper, but she saw the ears flicker toward her, and knew that it was listening. "You really do deserve better than this."

You cannot allow this.

You cannot allow this.

You cannot...

I know! she shot back, furious.

The voice, startled, left her alone.

The Serpent raised his knife, as though showing it to others in the room, and started to chant. A part of Lily recognized the words, but she let them wash over her, becoming background noise. It wasn't important. What was important was...

What? What was she supposed to do?

Stop him!

It wasn't rational. It wasn't smart. It was pretty much doomed to failure. And yet, without warning, a hundred and thirty pounds of incensed female slammed into a hundred ninety pounds of muscled male.

Surprise was in her favor. Entirely focused on the ceremony, his arrogance allowed him to ignore her once she agreed to stay still.

But that surprise fled, and once he recovered from the stagger, a powerful backhand across her jaw sent Lily halfway across the room.

"Bitch! I would have rewarded you, made you as powerful as you once were, but again you defy me!"

Instinct made her reach out when she saw his hand coming at her. Her fingers closed around something even as she was moving backward.

It was a toss-up who was more surprised: Lily or the Serpent, when she looked down at her hand and—despite vision dizzy from another probable concussion—saw the chain from around his neck wrapped in her fingers.

The amulet, freed, had slid off the chain and landed on the floor between them with a hard clunk. It laid there, a seven-sided disk made of bronze about the size of her palm, with a triangle-shaped hole cut in the middle. There were small red stones set in it, and some sort of writing between the stones.

The Serpent lunged for it at the same moment Lily shoved herself across the floor, trying to get to it first. The amulet was the secret. If he didn't have it, he couldn't control the great cat. Or the smaller ones. His power—his danger—lay in possessing the amulet.

He reached it first.

Desperate, Lily scooted backward, and, instead of trying to attack him again, flung open the door behind her.

"Go!" she screamed, loud and harsh enough to make the Serpent pause, his hand just over the amulet, for an instant.

In that instant, the cheetah leaped off the step and disappeared out the door.

"No!" he cried, scooping up the amulet and racing after it. Lily rolled over onto her side, ignoring the crackling of her ribs, and closed her eyes. *All right. All right.*

In that instant, she could *feel* the great cat moving through the halls, heading unerringly for an open window at the end. Muscles flexing for the first time in days, blood streaming, eyes alert. The human was behind, but far enough that the nasty-smelling metal could not affect it. They were on the first floor, and the air between the cat's whiskers was testing the distance, the width of a half-open window, the environment outside the window even as its muscles were bunching to leap, land and escape.

Gone.

The rush of power hummed in her veins, and Lily smiled.

She kept smiling even as the Serpent slammed back into the room, grabbing her by the arm and hauling her painfully to her feet. She kept smiling even when he slapped her hard across the face with the hand holding the amulet, the metal cutting her cheek open.

She kept smiling even as he hauled her across the room and shoved her down to her knees on the step.

"She thought to trick me. She thought to cheat me again! But not this time. No, not this time. She outwitted herself. I know what the key is. The true key. The reason I failed last time, more fool me. It is not the beasts whose blood binds the way, but Hers. And you are Her, here and now. *You* are the key." He fumbled for the knife with his free hand.

It is time, my daughter. You are almost done. Come home now to me.

The priestess smiled, and opened her eyes. Everything was brighter, sharper, the colors muted but the details clear, intense. When he raised the knife over her head, the itch in her fingertips became a burn. When the knife came down, she blocked it with her arm, her claws raking along his skin. The smell of blood rising from the scratches she left behind made her smile into a teeth-baring grin, her lips pulled back to better taste it in the air.

She twisted under his next blow, her spine moving,

more supple than anything human could manage. All hesitation, all distance was gone, and she lived in the moment, felt herself caught up in the greater pattern. She was *connected.* She landed a blow to his face, claws scoring him under his nose, up the side of his face.

"Bitch." The Serpent spat at her, a gob of saliva landing on her forearm. She could swear she heard it sizzle, even as he yanked her by the hair, bringing her face onto the floor. She felt the knife hiss against her skin, down the line of her spine, and she smelled the familiar tang of her own blood as it came to the surface. His hand scraped along the cut, pulling the wound open until she screamed from the pain, his hand dipping *into* the wound. Pain moved into agony, and she convulsed, arms and legs flailing as though in a fit.

Just as she thought she might—*must*—pass out from the intensity, he dropped her, moving across the room. He was muttering something under his breath, getting louder as he strode to the makeshift archway. The words swam in her ears: she thought she should understand them, but they refused to make sense. His intent, however, was unmistakable.

No! the voice—her voice—cried. *It must not be allowed!*

She rolled onto her side, stretching out as though she could reach him by force of will alone. Her fingers, the small, sharp claws curling out from under the tips, flexed, and then fell to her sides as her strength failed her.

I am not enough. Not then. Not now.

He was shouting now, flicking his fingers onto the

archway—no, through the archway. The words were not in English, but she understood every one.

"If you will not accept the key, then let the lock be broken! If you will not accept the key, then let the lock be broken." Again, his voice shaking with the force of his words. "If you will not accept the key, then let the lock be broken! With this once-sanctified blood, let the lock be broken, and the gates be opened!" He flicked his fingers again, scattering blood—her blood—into the space under the archway. "Open the secrets of the underworld to me! I will walk forever, and know death never again! Never again, do you hear!"

"You fool," she whispered. "You horrible fool."

He flicked blood again, a third time. And the archway shimmered, a terrible, awe-ful blackness taking form...

Chapter 18

The archway might only have been foam. The wall behind it might have been solid as stone could get. But that was in *this* world, and the Night Serpent's actions had broken the Gate between *this* world and *that* one. Sprawled prone across the step and bleeding heavily, Lily could only turn her head and watch as the black swirled and emerged from the archway, the wall-that-had-been now an abyss of flickering black sparks rising from a darker black pit.

She was Lily. She was herself. But the priestess's memories stayed with her, surging through her, telling her what to do.

She slid backward, her body screaming protest, until she was off the step, half hidden behind it. The Serpent stood in front of the archway, his arms spread as though welcoming a bride, or a long-lost friend.

Fool, she thought, the back of her neck hackling. *Fool.* It was as much a hiss as a thought. The muscles in her legs and arms twitched to be away, to leap and race down the hallway, away from what was coming, but she could barely move beyond where she had landed. Her spine twitched, as though a tail had just swished in agitation behind her.

This is... Bad. So very very bad. The priestess's memories were telling her that, but Lily knew it for truth on her own. Whatever was on the other side of that Gate, she did not want to be around for its arrival.

The sparks grew, coming closer, and her nose scrunched at the horrible smell that reached it: dank and dry at the same time musty and sharp. Underlying it all, bitterness. It was familiar, the way too many things recently had been familiar.

"Goddess, no, Mother, protect me!" she whispered, her eyes going wide and dark as the room filled with an ominous light. *Things* were visible now through the archway: large, misshapen *things,* moving with a heavy shuffle that did not hide the sense of menace rising from them.

The Serpent shuddered, his entire body quivering under the force of their approach, but he held steady. No one could ever have said that he was not brave. But he had never been privy to the workings of the temple, to the doings outside of the public eye. He was not a priest, despite the amulet he held. The amulet that would do nothing to protect him against what was coming.

I cannot allow this, Lily thought. *I cannot allow this to happen.* She owed him nothing; she would have been pleased to let the walkers of the underworld teach him what it meant to truly walk the Paths of the Dead. But it would not end there. The woman-she-had-been knew that, knew that the way she knew everything else. The Gate was locked for a reason. Locked, and left closed for all these ages…

Dizziness assaulted her, the blood loss and stress conspiring to make her head swim. Visions assaulted her: the long deserts of home, the cool marble, the sun and shimmer of light on the river followed in an endless stream of other lives. The cold of a forest where no light broke through. A wooden house filled with the emptiness of loneliness and age. A long gilded hallway, empty but for the ghosts of couples dancing. More, until the last, of standing at the doorway of the shelter. Terrified, determined and holding tight against the wave of uncertain emotion. She had thought it was internal, her own failures battering against her.

Now, in this instant, she knew it for what it had been: the welcome of the hundred-plus souls within, their small sparks recognizing what had been so deeply hidden within her.

All this, filtering through her like water into limestone, leaving behind the grit and coming out cleansed and whole. Complete.

She was the priestess. The priestess was Lily.

Eight times she had failed. Not from any flaw within her, save the one she allowed others to place there. Doubt. She had not trusted herself.

The first figure stepped across the sill of the arch. Another followed, hard on its heels.

Lady of Fire, Guardian of the Hearth, allow me to serve...

The words of the morning prayer rose to Lily's lips, even as she forced her body up into some sort of crouching position. The pain faded, and she felt her body begin to...

Change.

"Naaaaaaaah!" The sound was torn from her throat in a long scream: a mad, wild sound. Ignoring the pain of her ripped and bleeding body, she threw herself forward, stretching into the air, her arms forward, legs back, head tucked as she went past the Serpent, past the misshapen figure, to the archway itself. Her paws flexed, huge curved claws extending to swipe hard across the face of the archway, knocking several of the shambling figures a few steps back into the swirling abyss.

Another swipe, and the misshapen things retreated farther. They moaned, hungry for the light and life held in front of them, and Lily snarled, a harsh-edged, angry warning. She had no desire to destroy them—it was not their fault the door had opened—but she would not allow them to leave the underworld, either. Dead was dead, and must not move among the living again. The worst zombie movie ever barely touched on the horrors that would follow, not only for the living but also for the dead whose *ka,* spirit, would be disturbed, unable to find peace while their bodies walked....

Go sleep, she told them, her voice a harsh snarl.

Return to your crypts and fade into the shadows so your souls may be reborn without burdens, without pain. Sleep, sleep forevermore.

The words failed to halt them, and the figures started to shuffle forward again, drawn inexorably toward the light and warmth of the living world.

She raised a paw to stop them, part of her dimly aware that her hand was glowing with a faint blue light. Or was it just the way her skin looked against the red-black light coming from the Gate?

Stop, she snarled. *Go back. I command you.* Her body lurched forward, the adrenaline that supported her initial lunge having long since drained away. One of the figures lurched as though a mirror image. Its face was misshapen, eye sockets torn, nose ripped and decaying. It looked at her, not with hatred, but pleading.

Stop, she said again, this time more softly. *This place is not for you.*

The blue light met the red-black, and a darker green appeared, pulsing like a heart, in and out, fast at first then slowing until it stilled. The nearest figure tried to fight her off, grabbing at her arm as though to tear it off, but the green barred it from her.

Close, she told the Gate. *Seal.* Her voice came through firm and in command, the wind blowing from a faraway land. *The Lady of Flame commands it.*

"No!" A hand grabbed at her, pulling her backward, knocking her off her feet. The green light pulsed once again, spreading to cover the entire surface of the archway, sealing it once again.

"No!"

If she had thought the Night Serpent insane before, he was maddened now, his jaw hanging open, bubbles of froth flowing over the corner of his narrow lips. His eyes had gone shallow, flicking back and forth like the movement of the creature whose name he had claimed, quicksilver and dangerous. He hissed, his jaw dropping even wider, and lunged as though to sink his fangs into her flesh.

She reacted to him not as woman to man, but cat to snake, hissing and lashing out with teeth and claws, slashing at his face and forearms, looking to drop him into the dust and rend his poisonous flesh. She struck hard, but her claws were not enough to finish the job, and he knocked her aside once again, looming over her.

The blue glow around her seemed to hesitate, then condensed into a darker glow, closer to her skin. Lily closed her eyes, then, despite the blood still seeping from the gaping wound in her back, somehow found the strength to spring at him again, her teeth trying to find his jugular and rip it out.

He fought her off, a heavy backhand landing across her face. "Bitch. Traitorous bitch! I would have—"

"Killed me. Again." She spat blood, struggling as he tried to wrap his hands around her own neck. A squirm, her spine twisting until she landed on all fours, inches away. But the wall was to her back, and he was between her and the only door.

She was going to die. Again.

"You wanted power, but always someone else's, taken from them. Fool!" She laughed, bitterly amused despite the blood dripping from her mouth and the feel of teeth loosened in her mouth. "You always…were…a fool. And me, for trusting you. But not this time. Not this time… I stopped you. *I. Stopped. You.*"

She might die. She probably would die. It was all right: she had done what she came back to do. Finally.

Distantly, she heard a commotion outside, far away, but getting closer, coming toward them. The Serpent reared back, readying for a final blow.

Lily should have ducked, should have tried to run. All she could do was stare up into his eyes: dark burning pits of desert fire, wrapped around with the sound of sand blowing and the low muttering growl of a crocodile on the sun-warmed mud of the Nile. She felt herself start to sway in rhythm to his own lithe movements, even as she told herself to blink, to look away.

A hissing cough broke into the sounds in her head, and vision flashed away from her. When it returned, her line of sight was lower to the ground, moving rapidly as things came into focus and then faded again. The look of things was wrong: too flat, too gray and blue. The sun was not bright or warm enough for comfort, and the air tasted of harsh metal, not the warm comfort of blood and flesh.

Cat, she thought, barely holding on to any sense of herself under the onslaught, and felt its agreement. *Beautiful one. Run.* Agreement again, but not the way she intended. It wasn't running away. It was coming toward her. And it wasn't, it proudly informed her, coming alone.

Her mate was with him.

Lily barely had time to process that before the door

from the hallway crashed open. The Serpent went down to one knee, turning and with one arm crushing Lily to him, the other hand grabbing his knife off the floor. Her vision returned to her with a snap, hard enough to make her dizzy—or was that the blood loss? She wasn't sure anymore. Everything was becoming fuzzy, grayed out around the edges.

Then the shining tip of the Serpent's knife nicked the delicate skin under her chin, sliding to rest directly over her pulse, and her concentration returned with a hard crunch.

Suddenly, she wasn't ready to die.

"Stop!"

The voice was painfully, wonderfully familiar. Lily didn't have to look up to know who it was; she did it merely to satisfy the desire to see him again. Jon: his gun held in both hands, his body turned sideways like some hero on a television show. Beautiful man. He was dressed in black and gray, a windbreaker over a bullet-proof vest like the one they had given her, and the cheetah was a molten golden and black statue at his side.

Her gaze flicked from the green-eyed stare of the cat up to the stark cold lines of the gun, and stayed there. Her bloody claws flexed, and she knew that Jon saw them. She *meant* for him to see them. But the gun never wavered.

He saw me. He saw me, and understood, and came, the cat told her. *Good mate.*

Very, she told it back.

"I'll kill her," the Serpent said, his voice cold and

cool, as though he had never lost his temper in his entire life. In all his lives. "I will kill her and you will have lost."

"You think that you can beat a bullet, be my guest," Jon said in a voice just as cold and cool. Lily felt the knife dig in a little more, and raised her eyes from the gun to look into her mate's face.

He wasn't bluffing.

She had been right about Jon T. Patrick, and she had been completely wrong. Agent Patrick was dedicated to his job, and the demanding mistress named Justice. She respected that about him. She might even love that about him. He was also a man who had been able to take a leap of faith, no matter how improbable: to see the glimmer of a cheetah's body in the grass, and know what it meant. To follow it. To trust it.

But her body hurt too much to follow that thought any further. Held upright only by the Serpent's grip on her throat, every cell of her body was screamingly aware of what it had been through. If he let go, even for an instant, she would collapse in on herself, and possibly never come back. Her fingers itched horribly, and she risked a look down to see the claws slowly retract back into her fingertips, leaving behind blood-smeared tips over unbroken skin. Whatever gifts she had been given, they were leaving her.

It was all right. She had done what she needed to do. The Gate was closed. Jon could shoot this bastard and it would all be over. Nine lives, game over. No replay this time, not for either of them.

She wasn't ready to die, but who ever was? She only hoped that Anubis' judgment would be gentle this time.

Lily's gaze dropped again, resting on the blunt lines of the cheetah's muzzle. Green eyes stared into hers, the lids closing once, slowly. A sleepy wink, the sort one cat gave another to indicate that all was well, he wasn't a threat, there was peace between them.

"Thank you," she said to the cat. For coming back. For not killing her in that storeroom, despite what must have been overwhelming instinct. For being a reminder of the beauty she had once known.

Sister-two-foot. This is not over yet.

Mrrraaai she told it, and felt the cat's amusement at her kitten-acceptance.

The Serpent jabbed her with the knife, stopping the conversation and drawing blood from her throat to match the red clotting in the rims of her nostrils and down the line of her back.

There was blood inside her throat, too, and her ribs made breathing difficult. She was aware of all this now, merely mortal again. She was dying. But that was all right. The Gate waited, and there would be peace on the other side. She hoped.

She braced herself for one last lunge, willing her fingers to work, even without the gift of claws. If she could distract him, Jon could finish the job. The Serpent must not escape. His punishment must be final this time.

Before she could do anything, a noise vibrated up through the soles of her feet, up into her bones, a strange guttural humming. She felt it, and saw the great cat's long tail twitch once, a hard *thwack* against the air. Those were the only warnings, and they happened so quickly the Serpent didn't have a chance to react before that long line of lean muscle was airborne.

But the cat wasn't aiming for the Serpent. A jaw that might have clamped down on him and done damage, claws that might have shredded skin from bones, none of those made contact. Instead, that jaw closed firmly but gently on Lily's shoulder, while the cat's own shoulder knocked into her with a solid thunk.

All three went sprawling to the floor. The cheetah twisted in midair, a seemingly impossible move, to land *under* Lily rather than on top of her, forcing her to land on her side rather than her injured back.

It still hurt like hell, but she managed not to pass out. The Serpent was down on his knees in front of her, and she wanted oh so badly to kick him between the legs, hard. If she could just move her leg. Or even her arm. She'd be willing to hit him, too. All of her rage came back and spilled over, fueled by the rumbling breath of the cat beneath her. Selfish, stupid...he had opened the Gate, all for his own selfish desires and wants, like a spoiled five-year-old. Did he not understand that the dead needed to stay dead? That allowing the Gate to open...

Disease. At the very least. Imbalance.

The Serpent looked across at her, and she shivered. His eyes were no longer blue and kind, or even black and intense; now they were flat and inhuman looking. Not even a serpent's eyes, but dull as a river stone. A trickle of blood came from his left nostril, matching the one at the corner of his mouth. She tasted her own blood pooling in her mouth, and felt no sympathy.

"I...I would have..." he rasped, staring at her as if she still held some kind of answer. She had no answers to give him, and he seemed to realize that, because he started to get to his feet, the knife still clutched in his hand.

"Stay down!" Jon commanded. Who was he talking to? Lily could hear more noises from the hallway—someone else was coming? Help, or did the Serpent have allies? She struggled to back away, get to her own feet and out of his reach, only to have the heavy, meat-sweet breath of the cheetah hit her cheek. He had stretched just enough so that the heavy triangular head rested against her cheek, as though it were trying to scent-mark her, and the weight pressed her down to the ground.

Down. Stay down. Do as the mate says.

Not words now, but a sense of insistence, of concern, of worry that the small one would not be wise, would get hurt.

All right, she thought. *All right.* She didn't have the strength to do anything else anyway.

"Down, I said!" Jon sounded pissed off. "Robert Bergman, you are under arrest for the kidnapping and unlawful imprisonment of Lily Malkin, among other bad moves. Lie on the floor with your hands over your head. Now!"

Instead, the Serpent closed his fist tighter around his knife and swung at Lily, aiming directly for her heart. A name from this time, this place, had no power over him. Whatever Jon had discovered could not be used to stop him.

The cat screamed, a sound that should not come

from a cheetah's throat, and Lily felt it as though it came from her own mouth, even as there was a harsh heavy noise, the sound of gunfire and an acrid smell like blood-warmed dust in her nose.

The Night Serpent hovered over her; a boogeyman slithered out from under the bed in the dark of night, the knife no longer glinting but covered in gore and blood. A matching blossom of red bloomed on the front of his shirt, and his throat was torn away, making his head loll to the side. The entire room crashed into silence that hung for one, two, three breaths….

Then he fell, the cheetah's bloody muzzle shoving Lily out of the way just before he would have landed on top of her. The room exploded into noise and action, men in dark blue and gray everywhere, filling every available space.

The Serpent lay on the floor next to her, his face slack, his pale blue eyes open and sightless. A lock of pale blond hair fell over his forehead, making him look absurdly young.

Is done, the cat said in satisfaction. *Judgment.*

Lily turned away, rested her face on the dense plush fur of the cat, and felt one hard, bitter tear fall from her eye.

She had no idea whom she was crying for.

"Ma'am? Ma'am? Ms. Malkin?" Abraham, the guy who had come up from D.C. to oversee the operation. He was in her face, and she batted at him, trying to make him go away.

"Don' like you."

He looked taken aback, then grinned. The grin looked strange on him, like he didn't do it very often. "Very few people do, Ms. Malkin."

They had given her something for the pain. It didn't make the pain go away, but she didn't give a damn about it anymore.

"You got him." She would not give him the benefit of a name. Not the one he'd worn here, not the one he'd had in their days together, not even the one that the media had given him. He would be nameless to her, forevermore. It was right. It was just.

"More like to say the cat did," Abraham said. "Damn cat—we can't figure what killed the guy, the bullet or the bite. That guy won't be hurting anyone again, though, not anymore."

"No. Not anymore," she agreed peaceably. Abraham had no idea. No idea at all.

Then the EMTs returned and bundled her into an ambulance, securing her in her stretcher so that she wouldn't bump or slide on the way to the hospital. It was a little like beings trapped on a roller coaster, she thought. There was a burst of conversation, someone arguing, and then they closed the doors and the ambulance pulled away, hands and voices still fussing around her. Even through the fussing, with her eyes closed, Lily knew that Jon was there, beside her in the narrow, crowded space.

"That was," he said, his voice still cool, "possibly the stupidest thing anyone has ever done. Ever."

Lily opened her eyes and looked at him, then raised one hand—a human hand, with human nails, not claws and pads—and touched the side of his face. It took too much effort, and exhausted her, just that one movement. The skin of his cheek was dry, prickly with beard growth. It was the most wonderful thing she had ever felt.

"Which part?" she asked.

He caught her hand with his own, holding her touch against his face. "Yes," he said, and his voice was warm all of a sudden. "Yes."

She smiled, feeling the texture of his skin and the weight of his gaze on her. Unblinking. Unflinching. He had seen. He might not know what he had seen, but he had seen. And he was here. He was still here. He hadn't thrown her away, hadn't walked away.

She had broken the cycle.

"I'm a heroine," she said to him, drowsy from the painkillers. "You gotta tell me. What does the T stand for?"

This time, he laughed. "Tiberius," he admitted. "My mom was a *Star Trek* fan, but my dad wouldn't let her name me James because he had an Uncle James he didn't like. I hate it."

"Jon Tiberius. Goddess, that's awful," she said dreamily. Then an EMT shoved Jon aside and leaned over her to adjust the flow of liquids into her veins. She closed her eyes and let the darkness take her.

It was all right. Jon T. would be there when she woke up.

Chapter 19

The air was cold, an arctic front swooping down and reclaiming the season. Lily stood on the tiny balcony of her condo and looked up at the sky. There were no clouds, and the stars were still and clear.

For the first time ever, the stars looked *right*.

The sliding door opened and closed behind her, and Jon came up behind her. He paused just before actually making contact, waiting for her to lean into him. When she did, he wrapped his arms around her, careful to avoid the bandages under her sweater, covering the cuts and scratches on her shoulders and arms. They were all from the Serpent's knife; the cat's claws never touched her, even as he was knocking her to the ground.

The cheetah had taken the brunt of the Serpent's knife in its side, even as it knocked her clear, allowing Jon an open shot at the man. One of the agents, risking his own life, had bundled the injured cat into the back of his car and driven it to the hospital himself, yelling at the emergency-room staff until someone got on the phone with the zoo, getting instructions over the line on how to sedate the cat and sew it up.

Lily had heard the story after, when it was funny, not terrifying. She suspected that the agent and the E.R. crew would all dine out on that story for months to come.

As though he knew what she was thinking, Jon told her, "The cat's gotten a clean bill of health, and will be picked up by his facility tomorrow morning."

She nodded. She knew that already, from the cat's humming contentment she could feel even now in her bones, even across town. She knew that connection would fade the way the rest of it, the memories and the scars, were already fading. But that awareness wouldn't go away, not unless she wanted it to.

She very much didn't want it to. Not now. Not that she knew what it was. What *she* was.

"I still can't believe he found you," she said. Cheetahs had been used as hunting animals back then, and even now, but they were sight hunters, not smell. The ability to find Jon, and bring him back, across an unfamiliar, probably terrifying city…

"It was a miracle," she said finally, not willing to

push it further. Not willing to say the word the cat had bandied about so carelessly. Not yet.

"It was something," Jon agreed. He still wasn't sure what, hadn't been able to say the words, but his training was to follow the evidence, and build theories on what he knew for a fact. And he knew for a fact that a cat had helped him save his lover.

And she knew that he knew for a fact that his lover had eyes that reflected light like that cat's. That cats adored her, spoke to her. That when they made love, sometimes he felt the prick of claws, gentle, on his skin.

"There's going to be holy hell to pay when I go back to D.C. Boss isn't going to be happy to have his fair-haired boy wandering away from home."

The shooting, in full sight of half a dozen Fibbies and local cops, was ruled—what phrase had they used?—righteous—and Special Agent Jon T. Patrick was, if not a hero, then a guy who done good.

She leaned her head back against his shoulder and looked up at the sky again. "Done good" had such a lovely sound to it. So did the idea of him transferring here. It wasn't D.C. He wasn't going to climb the ladder quite so fast. But if he was okay with it, she was more than okay with it. Anyway, that was why they put "federal" in FBI; he would travel, and then come home.

Home.

She closed her eyes, and breathed out a prayer. In the distance, she could feel the whisper of cats' thoughts as they moved through the night, intent on their small, secretive ways. They dreamed of tasty mice and grand schemes, of warm hearths and gentle hands. And deep inside them all, the soft and fierce presence of the goddess rested.

In Lily's heart, as well.

"Making a wish?" he asked, only half joking.

"Should I?" She used to wish for all sorts of things: a best friend, a lover, an end to her phobias and her nightmares. A place where she felt that she belonged.

"Nobody's ever going to believe any of this, you know," he said, going back to the discussion they had started over dinner. "The cat finding me, the way I found you… They're creating reasons that work for them, that make sense."

"What makes sense to you?" It was the first time she'd had the courage to ask him directly.

He chuckled, low in his throat like a purr. "Nothing. None of it makes any sense. But I have this theory I'm working on…."

"Of course you do."

His arms tightened around her, and he looked up at the sky as well, reciting, "Star light, star bright, I've got every damn thing I want tonight."

She giggled, the way he had intended her to.

"It's over?" he asked, solemn again. "Your spells, the attacks…?"

"It's over," she agreed, settling against him, feeling totally, completely secure in him, in herself. In them. And, quietly, she thought to herself, *Or maybe it's just begun.*

She thought that maybe it *was* time to go to the shelter, bring someone home.

And somewhere in the non-distance of time, she felt a vaguely feline, powerful purr of approval.

* * * * *

*Mills & Boon® Intrigue brings you
a sneak preview of...*

Delores Fossen's Branded by the Sheriff

*When a family feud led to brutal murders in this
Texas town, it was up to the Sheriff Beck Tanner to
protect single mother Faith Matthews and her baby
from the killer. But Beck didn't expect to feel such
fierce protectiveness over mother and child,
especially when saving their lives meant facing
off with his own family...*

Don't miss the thrilling second story in the new
TEXAS PATERNITY: BOOTS AND BOOTIES
*mini-series, available next month from
Mills & Boon® Intrigue.*

Branded by the Sheriff
by
Delores Fossen

LaMesa Springs, Texas

A killer was in the house.

Sheriff Beck Tanner drew his weapon and eased out of his SUV. He hadn't planned on a showdown tonight, but he was ready for it.

Beck stopped at the edge of the yard that was more dirt than grass. He listened for a moment.

The light in the back of the small Craftsman-style house indicated someone was there, but he didn't want that someone sneaking out and ambushing him. After all, Darin Matthews had already claimed two victims, his own mother and sister. Since this was Darin's family home, Beck figured sooner or later the man would come back.

Apparently he had.

Around him, the January wind whipped through the bare tree branches. That was the only sound Beck could hear. The house was at the end of the sparsely populated County Line Road, barely in the city limits and a full half mile away from any neighboring house.

There was a hint of smoke in the air, and thanks to

a hunter's moon, Beck spotted the source: the rough stone chimney anchored against the left side of the house. Wispy gray coils of smoke rose into the air, the wind scattering them almost as quickly as they appeared.

He inched closer to the house and kept his gun ready.

His boots crunched on the icy gravel of the driveway. No garage. No car. Just a light stabbing through the darkness. Since the place was supposed to be vacant, he'd noticed the light during a routine patrol of the neighborhood. Beck had also glanced inside the filmy bedroom window and spotted discarded clothes on the bed.

The bedroom wasn't the source of the light though. It was coming from the adjacent bathroom and gave him just enough illumination to see.

Staying in the shadows, Beck hurried through the yard and went to the back of the house. He tried to keep his footsteps light on the wooden porch, but each rickety board creaked under his weight. He knew the knob would open because the lock was broken. He'd discovered that two months earlier when he checked out the place after the murder of the home's owner.

Beck eased open the door just a fraction and heard the water running in the bathroom. "A killer in the shower," he said to himself. All in all, not a bad place for an arrest.

He made his way through the kitchen and into the living room. All the furniture was draped in white sheets, giving the place an eerie feel.

Beck had that same eerie feeling in the pit of his stomach.

He'd been sheriff of LaMesa Springs for eight years,

since he'd turned twenty-four, and he'd been the deputy for the two years before that. But because his town wasn't a hotbed for serious crime, this would be the first time he'd have to take down a killer.

The thought had no sooner formed in his head when the water in the bathroom stopped. He had to make his move now.

Beck gripped his pistol, keeping it aimed.

He nudged the ajar bathroom door with the toe of his boot, and sticky, warm steam and dull, milky light spilled over him.

Since the bathroom was small, he could take in the room in one glance. Outdated avocado tile—some cracked and chipped. A claw-footed tub encased by an opaque shower curtain. There was one frosted glass window to his right that was too small to use to escape.

Beck latched on to the curtain and gave it a hard jerk to the left. The metal hooks rattled, and the sheet of yellowed vinyl slithered around the circular bar that supported it.

"Sheriff Beck Tanner," he identified himself.

But his name died on his lips when he saw the person standing in the tub. It certainly wasn't Darin Matthews.

It was a wet, naked woman.

A scream bubbled up from her throat. Beck cursed. He didn't know which one of them was more surprised.

Well, she wasn't armed. That was the first thing he noticed after the "naked" part. There wasn't a gun anywhere in sight. Just her.

Suddenly, that seemed more than enough.

Water slid off her face, her entire body, and her midnight-black hair clung to her neck and shoulders.

Because he considered himself a gentleman, Beck tried not to notice her small, firm breasts and the triangular patch of hair at the juncture of her thighs.

But because he was a man, and because she was there right in front of him, he noticed despite his efforts to stop himself.

"Beckett Tanner," she spat out like profanity. She swept her left hand over various parts to cover herself while she groped for the white towel dangling over the nearby sink. "What the devil are you doing here?"

Did he know her? Because she obviously knew him.

Beck examined her face and picked through all that wet hair and water to see her features.

Oh, hell.

She was obviously older than the last time he'd seen her, which was…when? Just a little more than ten years ago when she was eighteen. Since then, her body and face had filled out, but those copper brown eyes were the same.

The last time he'd seen those eyes, she'd been silently hurtling insults at him. She was still doing that now.

"Faith Matthews," Beck grumbled. "What the devil are *you* doing here?"

She draped the towel in front of her and stepped from the tub. "I own the place."

Yeah. She did. Thanks to her mother's and sister's murders. Since her mother had legally disowned Faith's brother, the house had passed to Faith by default.

"The DA said you wanted to keep moving back quiet," Beck commented. "But he also said you wouldn't arrive in town until early next month."

Beck figured he'd need every minute of that month,

too, so he could prepare his family for Faith's return. It was going to hit his sister-in-law particularly hard. That, in turn, meant it'd hit him hard.

What someone did to his family, they did to him.

And Faith Matthews had done a real number on the Tanners.

© Delores Fossen 2009

0110_I0ZED

2 FREE BOOKS
AND A SURPRISE GIFT

We would like to take this opportunity to thank you for reading this Mills & Boon® book by offering you the chance to take TWO more specially selected books from the Intrigue series absolutely FREE! We're also making this offer to introduce you to the benefits of the Mills & Boon® Book Club™—

- **FREE home delivery**
- **FREE gifts and competitions**
- **FREE monthly Newsletter**
- **Exclusive Mills & Boon Book Club offers**
- **Books available before they're in the shops**

Accepting these FREE books and gift places you under no obligation to buy, you may cancel at any time, even after receiving your free books. Simply complete your details below and return the entire page to the address below. You don't even need a stamp!

YES Please send me 2 free Intrigue books and a surprise gift. I understand that unless you hear from me, I will receive 5 superb new stories every month, including two 2-in-1 books priced at £4.99 each and a single book priced at £3.19, postage and packing free. I am under no obligation to purchase any books and may cancel my subscription at any time. The free books and gift will be mine to keep in any case.

Ms/Mrs/Miss/Mr _____ Initials _____

Surname _____
Address _____
_____
_____ Postcode _____

Send this whole page to: Mills & Boon Book Club, Free Book Offer, FREEPOST NAT 10298, Richmond, TW9 1BR